PROGRAM FOR A PUPPET

Every computer function described in the story
has either happened, or is happening today.

RJP
October 1979

PROGRAM FOR A PUPPET

BY

ROLAND PERRY

CROWN PUBLISHERS, INC. NEW YORK

To my parents,

TREVOR and LILLIAN

With special acknowledgment to

JACK GROSSMAN

JAMES CARDINAL

AUBREY DAVIS

PETER MILLER

and all those who put themselves in jeopardy

First American edition published 1980
by Crown Publishers, Inc.
Copyright © 1979 by Roland Perry
All rights reserved. No part of this book
may be reproduced or utilized in any form or by any means,
electronic or mechanical, including photocopying, recording,
or by any information storage and retrieval system,
without permission in writing from the publisher.
Inquiries should be addressed to Crown Publishers, Inc.,
One Park Avenue, New York, New York 10016
Printed in the United States of America
Published simultaneously in Canada by
General Publishing Company Limited
Library of Congress Cataloging in Publication Data
Perry, Roland, 1946—
Program for a puppet.
I. Title.
PZ4.P46474Pr   1980   [PR9619.3.P376]   823   79-23840
ISBN: 0-517-541017
10 9 8 7 6 5 4 3 2 1

PART 1

THE COMPUTER CONNECTION

"This computer . . . is the greatest expansion of the human mind since writing."

1

It was drizzling in the early morning of a July day in Paris as a black Maserati pulled up opposite a hotel at number 31 Boulevard Duval in the city's Latin Quarter.

A tall, attractive woman with short auburn hair alighted from the car and waved to the driver as she turned to cross the boulevard. Just as she stepped off the road onto the sidewalk, the car swung over toward her. There was a dull "whack" as the car mounted the sidewalk and hit her. The woman was knocked unconscious and thrown about four yards against a brick wall. The driver had stopped the car about ten yards farther along. He looked in the side mirror at the crumpled body and calmly steered the car back over the woman, changed gear and drove away with a squeal of tires.

In less than thirty seconds, lights went on in apartments and hotels on both sides of the street as people moved to the motionless figure. First on the scene was an elderly man who shone a flashlight at the woman. At first sight the woman seemed undamaged, her long black evening dress intact. But seconds later, when a woman tried to move her, blood had begun to seep around the body. . . .

Edwin Graham was stunned. A voice on the other end of the line was telling him his girl friend had been killed in a hit-and-run accident in Paris. He tried to speak but the meaningless words got in the way.

After a long silence Graham replaced the receiver. He ran both hands through his black hair from the temples to the back of his head and stared out through the glass of the press office in the

3

ballroom of the Washington Hotel. A look of anguish covered his rugged features as his serious dark blue eyes narrowed on the convention going on to elect a candidate for the presidency of the United States. For a moment the thousands of party faithfuls waving banners and chanting the names of the winning candidates appeared to be out of focus, dancing a silent ghostly pantomime.

He sank into a chair. For a few minutes he sat in front of the typewriter, his face buried in his hands, and wept. As fellow journalists gathered around him his brain began to telegraph uncoordinated messages. Stand up. Shuffle papers. Sit down. Collect things. Try to dial London. He found the number he wanted and minutes later in a conversation he would never recall, the shocking news was confirmed by a close relative of the dead girl.

Fifteen hours later, during a flight from Washington to London, Graham was able to think more rationally. Yet he could not stop his brain from going over the depressing realization of what was lost. With Jane Ryder he could have made it, had it all. Since he had left his native Australia a decade ago she was the first with whom he had had the confidence to take on a more permanent relationship.

It had taken a long time to find the right chemistry. There had been many affairs in Graham's free-wheeling, hard-living existence as a journalist. But he was the first to admit they were superficial. Never as good as the deeper, warmer, more meaningful real thing. Dead. . . . He shook his head and fought more tears by gritting his teeth. Read a book—impossible.

What had made it worse was his guilt. He had left her to grab the opportunity to cover a U.S. presidential election for a London publisher. At thirty-five, it was the big break he felt he had to take to enhance his career. Ultimately the move was to be for both of them. But the vivacious, attractive, tempestuous Jane had said no. She didn't like the idea of giving up her job as a reporter on a London daily to live out of a suitcase the length and breadth of the States. For a start, she did not have his love for the place. And after a year of living together Jane wanted marriage and children. At twenty-nine the timing for her was now. Not in the promise of another year.

Graham had argued that the time would go quickly. He

would be able to take trips back from Washington to see her and they could go on that holiday to Greece together. There had been arguments and no compromises.

The finality was unbearable.

The Australian tried hard to think about the circumstances leading up to her death. Before he had left for Washington he had suggested she go after a big writing assignment herself. Something to challenge her journalistic skills. He had thrown her a few casual suggestions.

One of them had been about a computer scientist in Paris who had recently delivered a lecture on the "uncontrolled flow of strategic equipment from the West to the Soviet Union." He had read of the lecture and filed the idea away. It was the kind of story he might follow up himself, if he had more time. Yet the Australian thought he had bigger fish to fry. An American presidential election.

Due partly to bitterness, frustration and ambition, Jane had managed to get six months' leave from her job to chase the story. She had convinced her book-publisher grandfather, Sir Alfred Ryder, that it would make a successful fact-novel. He had given it his indulgent blessing with a handsome advance. It was partly an attempt to appease her. Sir Alfred had given Graham the contact with a newspaper publisher which led to the Australian's American assignment.

After her initial research, Jane decided her story would center on advanced Western computers being smuggled into the Soviet Union against American and NATO regulations. She was not a computer specialist writer, she needed good contacts.

Although Jane had tried to interview the scientist who had given the controversial lecture in Paris, he had refused to speak to her when she telephoned him from London.

That was all Graham knew when he touched down in London at 6:00 A.M. on July 25. He felt uneasy about the whole affair because of his knowledge of computers, which stretched back sixteen years.

After a brilliant college record in computer sciences, and a lot of soul-searching, he had made the switch to journalism. First, because of his background, as a science correspondent, then a political writer. Always in the background, as a hobby, almost, he kept a keen interest in computers. He loved the logic of systems analysis—the design of computer networks. Networks that controlled air traffic, hospitals, rocket systems, nuclear reactors. Networks for everything. Yet Graham cared as much for how the metal beasts affected society and what they meant for mankind.

He often went on complex part-time courses, some of them run by universities, others by private organizations—the leading computer corporations.

He became aware of the power wielded by the corporations in business and politics. Over the years the Australian learned of the interrelationship. And his instincts and knowledge told him that if Jane Ryder had been right about computer smuggling, she could have run into trouble.

His fears intensified when he returned to his apartment in King's Road, Chelsea, where he and Jane had lived together for six months before he went to the States. Jane's relatives had asked him to sort out her belongings. It was a depressing task. Her books, records, guitar and many objets d'art were agonizing reminders of the tragedy.

As he was going through her filing cabinet, he came across his own name in the index. Graham had no idea the file existed. In it was a sealed package marked clearly in Jane's handwriting: *Ed. Open in the event of my death.*

He stared at the package, and turned it over a few times. Then he took a deep breath and tore off the top. A small note accompanied about sixty pages of unedited material—background material to her computer smuggling operation. "If you are reading this, Ed darling, then something has happened to me. Follow it through. For once in your wavering life follow through. I love you always, Jane."

A cruel, slightly bitter joke? His failure to follow through with her? Had he not many times explained the reasons . . . why he had to take the American assignment?

Perhaps Jane meant his failure to make it as an actor? Or because he had not gone on with his career as a scientist . . .?

His thoughts gave him the answers.

The Australian began to read the notes, which took him well into the night until jet lag caught up with him. He got to bed around 2:00 A.M., and was glad of a sound sleep.

6

The next day Jane was to be cremated.

Graham could not help thinking about her investigation as he drove his battered old red Alfa Romeo saloon in the funeral procession to a small crematorium just north of London. Questions that had been swimming around in his subconscious during the night were percolating forward. Why had she left the background material for him to find? And why "in the event" of her death? Did she fear for her life? Had she been threatened?

In the church these thoughts were temporarily blotted out by sadness and emotion as the minister delivered the address. Graham could not help staring at the knotted pine coffin and thinking how unreal everything seemed. A thousand thoughts, all incoherent, rushed through his mind. He thought of the laughing, dynamic personality that had been Jane. He had loved her deeply, passionately. Then the irrational feelings of guilt returned and his eyes welled with tears. He felt weak at the knees and was sure he was going to break down like several of her family around him.

The minister had finished. He walked across to the front of the coffin and pushed an invisible button. The coffin was lowered on a conveyor belt. At that moment it really struck Graham. He had been thinking about the past. In seconds, Jane would be ashes. The shock of seeing the coffin slide away transformed all his emotions into anger. Anger, that he had left her, anger at her impatience, anger at her death and the person or persons responsible. Was it murder? he wondered almost aloud. He made up his mind there and then. He had to know the truth.

Outside in the afternoon sun, he spoke briefly with a few of Jane's close friends and relatives. In the solemn crowd he spotted Sir Alfred Ryder. If anyone knew anything it would be Sir Alfred. Graham edged his way through the crowd toward the tall, slightly stooped figure and was struck by the deterioration in his appearance. The last time Graham had seen him, he had been alert and bustling. Now he looked every bit his seventy-five years. The loss of his favorite grandchild had taken its toll, and Graham realized then that the older man's feelings of guilt were probably stronger than his because he had financed her abortive mission into investigative journalism.

7

Graham shook hands and gripped Sir Alfred's forearm as he did so. They had met through journalism eight years ago. A strong bond had been built between them in that time, and the publisher had introduced the Australian to Jane.

"Sir Alfred, I was wondering if we could have a talk before I return to Washington?"

As Graham entered the reading room of Sir Alfred's Pall Mall club and looked for him, the dignity and hallowed atmosphere reminded the Australian of the publisher's considerable influence. He had built a publishing empire over the last forty years which had spread its tentacles into twenty-five countries. He also had other financial and property interests around the world, and especially in France, which he regarded as his second home.

Sir Alfred rose from his armchair and greeted the Australian. They discussed the latter's American assignment and the battle for the presidency before Graham got quickly to the point of the meeting.

"I'm not convinced Jane's death was an accident."

All the anguish of the last few days returned to the publisher's face. "I've had my doubts too," he sighed. "The French police are doing everything they can."

"What evidence have they got? Do they know what kind of car killed her?"

"Not yet."

"But in a collision," Graham began in an exasperated tone, "there must have been some damage to the car. A dented fender that has to be repaired in some garage, somewhere in Paris."

"The French police will let me know the minute they have a lead. I've been on to the commissaire of police himself."

"Did you know much about Jane's investigation?" Graham asked.

"I read some of her notes."

"I've a feeling she was on to something very big indeed. The Soviet attempts to build their own super range of computers to compete with the best the Americans were producing; did she tell you about that?"

"Yes. She was under the impression they couldn't match American technology." Sir Alfred frowned. "That was something I never really understood," he said. "Why were the Russians behind? I thought they were highly advanced in science, space, technology and so on."

"Stalin's fault really. He set the Soviet Union back a decade in computer development when he claimed it 'alienated man from his labor.' When the Soviets woke up at the end of the 1950s, they were way behind the Americans. The combination of tremendous computer development in the military and free enterprise, and spinoff and cross-pollination between them, pushed the Americans miles ahead."

"So you think the Russians may be smuggling in computers to keep pace with the West?"

"That was Jane's theory. It could be right. Computers form the backbone of all scientific development. And that includes the military. You must have computers to fire weapons with precision and accuracy."

"Haven't the Russians' missiles become more accurate lately?"

"Yes, and it fits Jane's theory. If the smuggling is going on, then the Russians will be getting the technology they so desperately want. Eventually they would have to reach parity with the U.S. in the precision use of all weapons. Then just watch the Russians begin to throw their weight around."

Sir Alfred was suddenly agitated. "You think she may have been murdered?"

Graham stared at Sir Alfred. "I wouldn't discount it," he said, lighting a cigarette. "You say you've contacted the French police. I'd like to talk with them before I head back to the States."

"I think that could be arranged." As an afterthought Sir Alfred added, "Was there anything in Jane's notes that gave you any clues to why she may have been killed?"

"No. But she did send me a letter a few weeks ago saying a public relations representative from a New York-based corporation approached her soon after she began her investigation. They didn't like her probing one little bit. They wanted to buy her off it, and offer a PR writing exercise for big money instead."

"And?"

"She told them what they could do with their money. . . ."

"Which corporation was it?"

"Lasercomp."

• • •

9

Clifford I. Brogan, Sr., a wiry eighty-one-year-old megalomaniac, had bullied, cajoled and preached Lasercomp into existence, starting from nothing as a door-to-door salesman in America's Midwest more than six decades ago.

He had pushed the corporation on the way to being the most secret, ruthless and ambitious of organizations and as big in financial terms as many medium-sized nations. It generated enough income to buy and sell a couple of Canadas, and had more political muscle than even bigger countries.

Brogan had made Lasercomp a nation unto itself with people and property, territory and assets, to be protected and expanded in a never-ending march to greater production, higher revenue and profit.

For most of the time Brogan's zeal had been the driving force behind an enterprise selling products ranging from foodstuffs to business equipment. The corporation was his religion, his god, his way of life.

Over the last two decades the other figure to have a major influence on Lasercomp was his ambitious son, fifty-seven-year-old Brogan Junior.

Where the father was volatile, crude in his business tactics and unpredictable, the son was urbane, subtle in his ways, cultured and conventional. He was a modern manager, Harvard educated, and trained in the unemotional decision-making necessary for survival in tomorrow's business world.

When the son first entered the corporation he was completely overshadowed by his father to the extent that he developed a speech impediment in the older man's presence.

In an attempt to make his own way in the corporation, Brogan Junior eventually showed even greater vision than his father. Instead of putting his faith in the corporation, and many products, he put it in the development of just one product: the computer.

Brogan Junior poached the best computer brains from other companies. If he couldn't buy them, he literally stole and patented their designs and ideas.

He finally won some funds from his father to test the new metal beasts in the marketplace. And when in the first two years computers dragged in more revenue than all the corporation's other products combined, the old man agreed to concentrate resources on one product.

It marked the end of the one-man rule at Lasercomp.

Father and son, with their opposite but complementary styles, worked together to make the corporation one of the world's biggest computer manufacturers. But that wasn't enough for the Brogans. They wanted to be number one.

The chance came with the advent of laser technology. Brogan Junior suggested harnessing the new power to computers. He wanted to combine the coming era of even smaller silicon chips—where billions of pieces of information could be stored electronically on minute chips—with lasers so that information could be stored by powerful light concentration. The Old Man gave his blessing to expensive research and optimistically changed the corporation's name to Lasercomp to imbue its shareholders and the market pundits with confidence. More and more money was poured into laser development and it soon became one of the biggest gambles in American capitalism's history.

The promising laser beam proved a difficult wild horse to tame and train, not just in computers but in most areas of science. Lasercomp's machines carried laser technology but initially proved to be no better than others on the market. The Brogans, however, were confident that a breakthrough was around the corner.

Secretly and meticulously, using the developing laser technology and their own best scientific brains, they began to plan a master program to make Lasercomp the most powerful corporate force on earth.

The master program was the result of calculations that took into account literally billions of different factors affecting the market for computers and everything the corporation did. Lasercomp's scientists took the approach that if something existed, it could be quantified. Factors ranging from the financial position of a rival to Lasercomp's influence over a head of government were given a value and became part of the program, which could be continually updated. After a decade of developing a laser computer and the master program, Lasercomp finally came up with a computer that was a giant step ahead of the rest.

The Brogans called it the Cheetah.

Cheetah was a super computer that soon began to knock out all competition. It gave the master program credibility and the Brogans' ambitions took on a new dimension. Suddenly they were having visions of the future they never dared contemplate before. They began to look beyond the time when Lasercomp would be the world's number-one corporation, and to think in terms of a corporate dynasty, indestructible because of its hold on society, and indispensable because of its computer superiority.

Absolute power became the secret long-term aim and obsession. Nothing was going to be allowed to stop the advance. Even opposition from the American presidency—the biggest single threat to Lasercomp's plans—was being catered for. From its beginning, the Brogans had had built into the master program a plan to have their own man as President. They secretly selected him and called the ten-year plan the PPP—Program for a Potential President.

2

The night before Graham was due to fly to Paris, Sir Alfred phoned him at his apartment to confirm an appointment. But it wasn't the French police as planned.

"The investigation has been transferred to a special unit of French intelligence known as NAP 1," Sir Alfred said with a note of concern.

"What's that?"

"It was set up in the mid-1970s to counter terrorism."

"Why are they involved?"

"I'd better let NAP 1's chief tell you. He happens to be a personal contact of mine I first met in 1941 when he was over here with the French Resistance and I was in Army Intelligence. His name is Colonel Claude Guichard. Would you be able to meet him at noon tomorrow?"

Graham reached for a diary. "I think so. Where?"

"First floor, 93 Avenue Kleber. Oddly enough, the building was once occupied by the Gestapo for the Paris sector. Could you ring me as soon as you've spoken to him?"

"Of course."

"Good night and good luck tomorrow."

The Australian put the phone down slowly and stared at it for several seconds. What the hell had Jane stumbled onto? he wondered.

Graham arrived in Paris at 8:30 A.M. He spent two hours reading Jane's notes once more, just in case they became relevant to his meeting with French Intelligence. Minutes before noon he arrived at the imposing, typically French baroque building on

Avenue Kleber. When Graham's arrival was announced over the desk intercom Colonel Guichard asked for five minutes before Graham was sent to his office.

The colonel felt he was one of the busiest men in France. Often he looked more than his sixty years. With his unsmiling, drawn features he had a permanent look of harassment about him. If it was not a minister of state hounding him, it might be the President of France making his life hell. His worries had made him bald and thin as a greyhound.

Yet he had always loved his work, first with the French Resistance, then during the troubled 1950s in the Algerian conflict, and latterly as a counterforce to French and foreign terrorists and assassins. The last two weeks, however, had been an exceptionally bitter time for him. News had come to him that hiding out in France was one of the world's most wanted men, a terrorist-assassin named Alexandro Emanuel Rodriguez. The colonel desperately wanted to see the man captured. Guichard had a personal score to settle.

Five years ago, his NAP 1 team had had the assassin cornered, but he had escaped, machine-gunning to death three NAP 1 men and one civilian hostage. Two of the NAP 1 team had been Claude Guichard's dearest friends.

Guichard was thorough in his dealings with the media. He had files on every French political journalist and many foreigners. Graham was one of them because of his writing about the French nuclear industry.

The colonel spent a few minutes skimming the limited computer printout dossier on Graham, which mainly contained articles written by the Australian. There were two photographs of him, both taken three years ago at an antinuclear rally in Paris. They showed him balancing precariously on scaffolding, preparing to photograph French police scuffling with students. Finally, he was satisfied and put the file in his desk drawer and buzzed his secretary to escort Graham from the receptionist to his office. The two men shook hands as they greeted each other, and Guichard felt his knuckles pressed close under the strength of the Australian's grip. He looked hard at Graham for several seconds. The Australian would win no beauty prizes, Guichard thought, yet there was an immediate substance about the man which commanded respect. This was perhaps accentuated by Graham's trim and well-dressed appearance. The visitor was about medium height. His thick but not unruly, curly black hair, which failed to completely cover large ears, was swept back with no parting. The cheekbones were wide and flat, and seemingly disproportionate to a thin, bumped nose, which on second inspection was slightly crooked. The determinedly set jaw and upper lip, and the finely drawn slightly cruel mouth added to a face which showed more than a hint of aggression.

What bothered the Colonel, however, were the penetrating dark blue eyes. Those eyes mirrored a tenaciously inquiring mind, the last thing Guichard wanted around at that moment.

He was in no mood for any meddling in this affair, even if there was only the slightest chance that a recent hit-and-run killing had a connection with Rodriguez. He planned to make that quite clear to this visitor, albeit politely because of the man's connection with Sir Alfred Ryder, one of the few Englishmen he knew and respected.

Graham quickly realized from the colonel's brisk manner that he was not going to have much time there.

"Sir Alfred tells me you are here to investigate the death of his granddaughter."

The Australian nodded expectantly.

"That is not possible, monsieur," he said abruptly. "And if I tell you why, not a word is to be repeated outside this room, except, of course, to Sir Alfred."

"Whatever you say."

"Your friend was last seen in the company of a man who may be connected with an assassin. A very dangerous man. Alex Rodriguez. You will no doubt have heard of him."

Graham nodded.

"We have little to go on," Guichard added, sighing, "but a few days before Jane Ryder's death, we learned that Rodriguez had been seen in a Normandy seaside resort with a man. He fitted the description of the fellow who was last seen with her."

"Which was?"

"The man is either German or Czech, about fifty. He has a scar below the left earlobe, and a slight limp. He dresses well."

"And that's all?"

"As I said, not much to go on."

"Who gave the information?"

"An informant."

"Could I speak to him?"

The colonel's eyes narrowed on Graham. "It's out of the question. We want to catch these men. More than you can imagine. Besides . . ." He paused. The colonel was finding Graham's eyes more disturbing as information was revealed. The Australian had an unconscious habit of swelling the irises noticeably whenever he was probing for facts. His gaze pierced searchingly into Guichard. The colonel felt obliged to put him off. . . . "Believe me, monsieur, you will end up like your friend if you investigate further. These men, if they are involved, are professional killers. They do not hesitate to destroy anyone who stands in their way. Leave the work of finding them to us."

The bluntness of the words sent a chill through Graham. "Okay. But do you know why Jane was murdered?"

"I did not say she was murdered. We have no proof of this."

"But it is likely . . ."

"It is only a possibility." The colonel shrugged.

"You know she was investigating—"

"Of course," Guichard butted in. "Sir Alfred told us what she was doing here. Nevertheless, there is not as yet a shred of evidence to connect her death with a theory about computers being smuggled into Russia."

"I was under the impression that Rodriguez was never completely absolved of a strong Kremlin/KGB connection."

"Rodriguez has become a mercenary. He is now up to the highest bidder. He has become rich. It seems to suit his life-style much better than working for the Soviet export of revolutionary terror."

"Then why has he resurfaced in France?"

Guichard stroked his bald pate. "He may be on assignment."

"In Europe?"

"It's possible, but who, where, what, how? We do not know. I am doing all I can to find out." The colonel's voice trailed off. He felt he had said enough. Looking at his watch, he said, "If you have no further questions . . ."

"Just one more. I believe Jane was trying to see an American scientist, Dr. Donald Gordon, here in Paris. Do you know where I might find the man?"

"Oui. We had him questioned by American authorities the day after she died. We believe he is back in his home near Washington."

"Jane never actually saw him then?"

"No. But they did speak over the phone. Gordon spoke to her about the computer smuggling."

"Was there just the one conversation?"

"Yes, but she tried to speak with him again."

"Oh?"

"It was after Gordon had left Paris. She left a message at his hotel asking him if he had told anyone to contact her."

"Had he?"

"He said definitely not."

"Then it could have been the man she was last seen with?"

Guichard nodded.

"How did he get her Paris address?"

The colonel took a deep breath. "We went through Gordon's hotel room thoroughly the day after Jane Ryder was killed. It was bugged."

"Bugged? Do you know anything else about Gordon?"

"He was once with a computer company, but has since retired. He still does the odd invitation lecture. That's why he was in Paris."

"You don't know which computer company he used to work for?"

"I think it was one of the big ones. IBM, Univac, or Lasercomp."

"Thank you for your time," Graham said.

"Monsieur," Guichard said firmly, "I must impress upon you once more not to continue your inquiries in France."

"Don't worry, Colonel," Graham said ruefully, "I'm leaving Paris this afternoon."

Graham had to give himself time to think before he called Sir Alfred. He taxied to the Champs Élysées, and drank a cup of coffee at one of the sidewalk cafés near the Arc de Triomphe. He had no intention of probing further into Jane's death. Yet the ramifications of her investigation were beginning to intrigue him.

As he sat in the warm afternoon sun watching the Parisians and tourists pass by, several questions nagged him. Were computers really being smuggled thousands of miles deep into Soviet territory? If so, why? Was Lasercomp involved? And Rodriguez. What was his connection?

The Australian called for the check from a waiter scurrying to and fro beneath the sun-drenched canopy. Graham had made a decision. The American assignment would have to wait at least another week while he looked into the smuggling. Since he knew this would not be tolerated by the English newspaper publisher for whom he was working, Graham realized he would have to resign the assignment or be fired.

What did Jane say in that note? he thought, as he stubbed out his cigarette. "For once in your wavering life follow through." Easier said than done.

To do it he would have to dump the American writing which he had considered the biggest break in his career.

On returning to London, Graham immediately booked a flight for Vienna.

Jane's notes indicated that she had planned to go there because she believed Austria could be the main East-West link for the computer smuggling. Graham decided to make a quick, cautious probe there. He didn't have much to go on. Just a few names and telephone numbers. He wanted more. Again he decided to ask for Sir Alfred's help.

The publisher was at first in two minds about Graham's following up Jane's assignment. On the one hand, he was obsessed with finding the truth behind her death; on the other, he didn't want to see Graham risk his life.

When he saw the Australian's determination to investigate further, he reluctantly agreed to the request for contacts. But they were to be contacts that would possibly protect as well as assist the journalist. The publisher once more turned to his connections in Intelligence, this time closer to home at MI-6.

Most of the old-boy network Sir Alfred had known since the Second World War were now retired or had passed on. His one contact at Intelligence now was Commander Kendall Gould, the son of a close friend who had served with him in Intelligence during the war.

It always amazed Sir Alfred to see Gould. Dressed in his

customary plain dark suit with tight-fitting vest, he looked almost a perfect replica of his father, now dead five years. They were the same medium height and weight. There was that same high intelligent forehead, deep-set gray eyes, and full beard with reddish hue on the tip.

As they strolled in the midday sun through Green Park, a stone's throw from Buckingham Palace, the old man found it a little disturbing to look at the Intelligence man. It brought back too many memories of the father. They had been close friends.

Sir Alfred kept his eyes on the green in front of them. Occasionally he looked up to watch a game of lunchtime cricket some boys were playing nearby.

"Why is your man going to Vienna?" Gould asked, although he had been informed of the circumstances surrounding Jane Ryder's death.

"Jane's notes indicate there may be some sort of base for the smuggling in Austria."

"Any proof?"

"No."

There was a short silence before Gould said, "Coincidentally, we are watching Vienna very closely at the moment. There has been a disturbing build-up of KGB operatives there in recent years. They come and go at short intervals for all sorts of minor reasons. We'd like to know what's going on."

He paused and added, "There are of course several East-West link-ups there to do with scientific research and so on. All convenient KGB covers."

"Graham wants contacts there."

"Hmmm . . . could be a little delicate. We are having trouble planting our people. We don't want them exposed. . . ."

The publisher gave an understanding nod. It was what he was half hoping he would hear.

Gould looked up at Sir Alfred. "Tell me about him."

"What do you want to know?"

"Oh . . . his background, education . . . interests . . ."

Sir Alfred glanced briefly at the commander. "You may be able to help?"

"I can't answer that right now."

"He was educated as a computer scientist, specializing in communications networks."

"A bit of a whiz?"

"Yes."

"Why the switch to journalism?"

"He is intellectual but not academic. . . . Likes to apply his mind pragmatically. He joined a newspaper as a science correspondent, specializing in writing about computers."

"A daily?"

"Yes, one of Australia's best. A far-sighted editor wanted an expert to interpret computers . . . the technology . . . the sociological aspects . . . everything. . . ."

"I see," Gould mused, stroking his beard. "Would you like to sit down for a while?"

The publisher nodded and they moved to a park bench facing the palace.

There were many Londoners and tourists out taking advantage of the fine weather.

"What made him start writing about politics?" Gould asked, lighting his pipe.

"He's naturally an ambitious, competitive type," the publisher said. "He told me that to get on at the paper, it was important to write about politics. He worked hard, built contacts and advanced rapidly."

"I've read his political articles here. He's very good. Shows a deal of insight. But why did he leave Australia?"

The publisher cleared his throat.

"He was apparently a trifle wild in his twenties. He had an affair with a married reporter on the paper. From what I can gather, his prudent editor sent Graham packing here. He was to have a roving commission as a foreign correspondent in Europe and Africa. When the assignment was over, Graham stayed. Everything here suited his style."

"What does his father do?"

"He's a neurosurgeon. Reputedly one of the world's best. You know of his mother . . ."

Gould smiled. "One of my favorite actresses. She returned to Australia when the film industry began to boom there, didn't she?"

Sir Alfred nodded. "She's sixty now, but still plays the odd theater or TV part."

"Graham has quite a lot to live up to."

"Indeed. Two brilliant, successful parents who wanted him to follow their respective careers. . . ."

"How did that affect him?"

"You'd have to ask him. Jane once told me he said it put him under pressure. An only child. Always in the spotlight with the mother or father. He apparently wanted to impress both parents. Not let them down."

"He tried acting?"

"His mother had him on the stage and in front of a camera from age five."

"How long did he keep it up?"

"Oh, he only stopped getting bit parts in films and TV series a few years ago. The money was always good and easy. When there was a lull in his freelance writing assignments he always managed to pick up some work to tide him over."

"Was he good?"

"Yes, as a character actor. Usually he was cast as a villain. . . . But he never really had his heart in it . . . couldn't stand waiting for bigger parts. He likes things to happen yesterday." The publisher stole another look at the Intelligence man. "Journalism suits him better. I would doubt that patience has ever been one of his virtues. . . ."

"Why did he choose computer science to study?"

"His father apparently had the greater influence over him. He urged Ed to study sciences at school in preparation for a medical career. Just before entering college he followed his instincts and went his own way. He had an aptitude for mathematics and logic."

"Tell me, is he a disciplined man?"

"Under authority, I should say absolutely not. He went freelance as a journalist because even a newspaper, a relatively unbureaucratic institution, stifled him."

Gould did not appear to be put off. Sir Alfred was becoming slightly apprehensive about having approached the Intelligence man in the first place.

After a thoughtful pause, Sir Alfred asked, "Then you are interested in helping him?"

"I would have to meet him first, of course. And frankly

there isn't enough time to prepare anything. . . . It could be a little too risky. But I would like to meet him when he comes back from Vienna."

Sir Alfred was relieved. "I'll arrange it."

"Does he play chess?"

"Yes, brilliantly . . . why?"

"I suspected he would. All that aptitude for computers. Takes logic."

"I warn you, on his day, he would even have beaten your father. He can think up to twenty-five moves ahead."

"And when it's not his day?"

"His method breaks down. Tends to be too aggressive. . . . He rushes things. . . ."

Oil sheiks in their flowing white robes stood out among the heads of state, businessmen and diplomats from many nations who had answered the invitation to attend the unveiling of a "super computer." It was Lasercomp's biggest machine in the Cheetah series. The location was the corporation's headquarters at Black Flats, high on a hilltop in a former apple grove, near New York City. The six hundred or so guests were wending their way from the high pillared entrance hall up a rich carpeted stairway, through an oak-paneled corridor, into the reception room. One wall was almost completely glassed to catch the sunlight and display an exquisite Japanese garden.

Most people attending knew of Cheetah. It had been on the market for the last ten months. But this was the first time the corporation had considered it opportune for a lavish function to announce it officially. Alan Huntsman, Lasercomp's corpulent and cherub-faced chief PR man, had won the internal battle to show it off now rather than later. As perhaps the organization's shrewdest tactician, he had argued that the corporation should demonstrate its development of superior technology before a decision in a six-year-old court case between it and the U.S. Government, expected in a few months' time. In this legal battle, the biggest and most expensive in America's history, the government's legal arm, the Justice Department, had charged the corporation with a long list of illegal activities which had been designed to give Lasercomp complete control of the American computer market. A win for the government would be a tremendous blow to the corporation's secret long-term master program. It could mean being split up into smaller separate corporations.

Guests stood in small groups as they arrived, rather than sitting on the inviting chairs and sofas, upholstered in shades of brown. A portrait of George Washington stared unsmilingly across the room. The buzz of conversation heightened perceptibly with the arrival of important guests, most of whom made their way to the center of the room to pay their respects to Clifford Brogan, Sr. Immaculately dressed in a navy mohair suit, the old man appeared in an easygoing, avuncular mood. He was showing a rare deference to people outside Lasercomp—a mood reserved for heads of states and others of similar standing.

He greeted the newly nominated candidate for the American presidency, Senator Ronald MacGregor, and his running mate, former Nevada Governor Paul Mineva.

"Congratulations to you both," Brogan Senior said, his large wrinkled features cracking into a smile as he wrung their hands. "I'm betting you two give the White House one helluva shake-up."

"More than that," MacGregor rejoined, "we'll break in there after November fourth."

"Well, I wish you luck. We need a change down there."

"Thank you, sir," Mineva said, as he flashed a toothy grin and swept a wisp of graying fair hair from his forehead. "It's going to be a rough run home and we need every little break we can get."

As he spoke, an announcement from PR man Huntsman that the unveiling was about to take place moved the milling guests toward the four doors that led to an adjoining auditorium—a vast imposing hall glowing from ceiling to walls with diffused light. At the edge of a raised area at the rear end of the auditorium a curtain created by holographic patterns representing computer circuitry screened the Cheetah from view.

Brogan Senior, in a vigorous shuffling action, led the corporation's senior management to seats on the raised area. As a digital clock high in the auditorium registered 2:30 P.M., Alan Huntsman waddled over to a microphone.

"Ladies and gentlemen, our senior vice-president, Clifford I. Brogan, Jr."

Tall, with a healthy head of silver hair that contrasted with his suntanned, outstandingly handsome features, Brogan Junior looked cool, even serene. When polite applause had died, he looked up confidently and nodded to the audience. "Thank you for coming to what we here at Lasercomp consider to be a historic day, the unveiling of a super computer—the Cheetah." He paused to clear his throat. "It will revolutionize man's very existence in the organizational environment. It is, we believe, the greatest expansion of the human mind since writing. . . ." He was reveling in the moment as he looked out over the sea of attentive faces. "What, you may ask, gives us at Lasercomp the confidence to make such grandiose pronouncements? Well, why don't we let Cheetah itself tell you why it's a 'revolutionary' super computer?" With a sweeping gesture, he pushed a button on a lectern. The holographic patterns seemed to dissolve back into the machine itself, exposing the flashing lights and revolving disks of a bright red computer system, surrounded by television display units. On the wall at the back, a large screen began to display words that also boomed from the Cheetah's sound unit in a chilling staccato monotone: *"Hello and welcome. I am Cheetah. Like my namesake, I am the fastest and most powerful of my species. Let me tell you about my special new features. . . ."*

The machine drummed on and emphasized its speed, "infinite" memory capacity and the ability to perform more functions simultaneously than any previous computer. All through the monologue there was a return to a central theme: Cheetah represented progress. It promised to be of great benefit to mankind as it *"fought its way on the short and tortuous route to the twenty-first century. . . ."*

This benefit would be progress in the so-called social areas—education, resources, food allocation, pollution, medicine. The words had been carefully selected to help lobby support in the corporation's legal battle with the federal government's Justice Department.

While the computer spoke, thirty Teletype machines placed around the auditorium printed the speech as the words were heard, until 2:45 P.M., when it finished with: *"I am Cheetah . . . I am the future now. . . ."*

As Lasercomp personnel darted around distributing the speech to the guests, Brogan Junior beaming with pleasure, got up once more and nodded to the cluster of media people to his right.

"I would now like to invite members of the press and other

media to ask Cheetah some questions," he said. "Take note of those cards you've been issued, please. They have a simple code."

The press studied their cards as he added, "Start with one of the words on the card: What, Can, Will, etcetera, and continue with one of the alternative phrases listed. Let me start the ball rolling."

He stepped up to the computer's control panel, flicked a switch marked *Control*, and said, "Cheetah. What will be the value of computers Lasercomp will sell outside America in three years from now?" He then turned the knob marked *Voice*.

"*Thank you, I understand,*" the machine replied. "*The answer to your question is, ten billion dollars. Repeat. Ten billion dollars.*"

There was a ripple of excitement from the audience. One by one the press edged its way up to the machine.

Questions were restricted to those that would elicit responses that had been carefully prepared. This time the propaganda was to show how important, economically, a prosperous and intact Lasercomp was to the American nation. It was all part of the lobbying campaign for the court battle.

It was hardly a penetrating press conference. Even if it had been thrown open, very little would have been revealed about Lasercomp's seemingly impregnable domain. Probing, inquisitive journalists would not have been invited. They were anathema to the corporation.

Graham arrived at Vienna's Schwechat airport at midday on August 3. The weather was warm, and the sky a cloudless blue as he took a taxi to an inconspicuous little hotel on Graben Street, opposite OESC, the Vienna States Savings Bank. He took a creaking elevator to the second floor, where the manager, a tall, handsome, middle-aged woman, Frau Schiller, greeted him cheerfully and showed him to his room. When he had unpacked, he walked a few hundred yards to a café, the Hermit, on Naglerstrasse.

The sun had lured many people to the sidewalk chairs and tables under a canopy. Inside the café, middle-aged Viennese read papers and magazines strewn on tables, sipping coffee and eating pastries. Outside, young students chatted loudly about Austrian politics. Graham, casually dressed in a light blue open-necked shirt, light slacks and sneakers, sat at the only available seat outside at the same table as three female students.

A white-coated waiter addressed Graham with the customary "Herr Baron." The Australian ordered coffee and sandwiches in faulty German, much to the amusement of the girls, and settled down to work out his strategy for the next few days.

Graham had little to go on. Jane had not been to Vienna herself, and while she had left transcripts of telephone conversations, there were no specific comments except on a mysterious international computer-using organization called IOSWOP—an acronym for International Organization for Solutions to World Problems. There was a list of several people to see, mostly connected with computer companies. Graham considered one as top of the list, a trucking contractor called Joachim Kruntz.

In thirteen years of journalism Graham had had some tough, sometimes dangerous experiences, ranging from covering murders on Melbourne's notorious waterfront to war on several African fronts. But there were always rules. Keep your mouth shut. Keep your head down. If you worked within the rules and kept your wits about you the risks were few.

In this investigation there were no given parameters of caution. No rules. It put Graham on edge. If he proceeded on the assumption that Jane had been murdered, he would have to follow those rules.

He walked back to his hotel and decided to call the trucking contractor. He found Kruntz's number in Jane's notes, lit a cigarette, and dialed. The telephone at the other end rang several times. Just as Graham was about to put the receiver down, a man answered.

"Ja?"

"Mr. Kruntz?"

"Ja?"

"You speak English?"

"Yes. Who is this?" His voice was deep.

"My name is Graham. I'm a friend of Jane Ryder."

The Australian forced himself to keep his voice steady when he mentioned her name.

"Who?"

"Jane Ryder. She rang you earlier this year about . . ."

"I remember," the man said; "she was an English journalist."

"That's right," Graham said, pleased he had got that far.

"What do you want?" the man asked bluntly.

"Some information." Graham was thinking quickly. He had no idea if Kruntz knew of Jane's death. He thought that if he mentioned it, and the man did not know, it might frighten him off.

"Who are you? Another journalist?"

Graham bit his lip. "Yes—I was wondering if we could meet."

"What information do you want?"

"It's about your work," Graham said. He was feeling in the dark. Kruntz fell silent. The Australian thought he might lose him. "I'm willing to pay for information."

"I don't know if I want to speak to the press again," said Kruntz. "They are of no value to me."

"I'll make it worth your while."

There was another pause.

"Do you know the district of Heurige?"

"Not well."

"Do you know the district of Jeurige?"

"Yes."

"I meet you there tonight."

"Fine."

"Go to Klosterneuberg. As you enter the village square there is an abbey on the left. Go to the closest wine cellar to it. In the basement is a seventeenth-century map of the area. Sit near it at ten."

"How will I know you?"

"Don't worry. I will recognize you. No tourists normally go there."

Graham walked to a nearby garage, picked up the Mercedes coupé he had reserved from London, and dined alone at the Budavar, a Hungarian restaurant opposite his hotel. Just after 9:00 P.M. he drove to Klosterneuberg village, north of Vienna in the rustic wine valley district. He parked the car in the village square and, finding he was half an hour early, decided to wander around. He found an old house converted into an art gallery and spent about twenty minutes there admiring the local art.

Right at ten o'clock he made his way to the abbey with its dignified spire, and entered the thick oak door of the nearest wine cellar. He moved downstairs toward a steady hum of conversation from a mixture of locals of all ages. They were sitting at wooden trestle tables enjoying the locally grown wines. He spotted the map Kruntz had mentioned, found a seat near it, and ordered white wine from a sturdy waitress dressed in a mock-peasant costume.

Twenty minutes later, a brawny, square-shouldered man well over six feet entered and sat down two tables away from Graham. Fingering thick stubble on his lantern jaw, the man glanced around and ordered wine. When the waitress brought it to him, he looked around at Graham, picked up his glass, and moved to a seat opposite him.

The Australian looked up. "Mr. Kruntz?" he asked.

The big man nodded. "I suppose you want the same information as the girl?" he said cautiously.

"Basically, yes."

The big man took some wine. "How do I know you are not here for another reason?" he asked, his dark, deep-set eyes narrowing.

"I don't know what you mean," Graham said, producing his identification and press cards.

Kruntz looked at them and handed them back. He didn't appear completely satisfied. "Can you get information published easily?"

"My contacts are good."

"Where?"

"Mainly in Britain. But elsewhere, if I want."

The big man took more wine and considered Graham. "Your friend promised publicity for certain information," he said skeptically, "but she did not even send me evidence of it."

"She would have preferred to have seen you personally. That's why I'm here—on her behalf."

"I want money, before I tell you anything," Kruntz said.

Graham casually slid his right hand underneath his coat and pulled out an envelope which exposed a wad of money. "You'll get paid when I get the information."

"What do you want to know?"

"First, why you wanted publicity."

"I thought some newspaper reports about certain things could force my debtors to pay up."

Graham was confused. "You'd better explain that."

Kruntz's eyes flashed feeling for the first time. "As long as the source is not revealed," he said nervously.

Graham gave him a reassuring nod. "Who has not been paying you?"

"Znorel Electronics."

"An Austrian company?"

"No, German. Stuttgart-based."

"You have a trucking contract with it from Vienna?"

"I did have," Kruntz said bitterly, "but they would not pay. So I stopped working for them."

"What goods were you trucking?"

"Foodstuffs, chemicals, farm machinery, and other things."

Graham decided to take a chance. "Jane Ryder said you have trucked computers."

The big man hesitated. "I may have," he grunted. "Not any more."

"For this Stuttgart company, Znorel?"

Kruntz did not reply immediately. He leaned back in his chair and cracked each knuckle in his hands. Then smiling slyly, he said, "You are interested in computers?"

"Yes."

"You will write something about them?"

"Possibly."

Kruntz looked annoyed. "Computers gave me the biggest trouble."

"In what way?"

"Well, sometimes we did not get paid at all. It was usually because of the Russians."

"These computers were shipped from Vienna to the Soviet Union?"

"Ja."

"And the Russians would not pay?"

"They pay in cars."

"They don't use foreign exchange?"

Kruntz curled his lip. "They say they have none."

"Cars for computers . . . a sort of barter arrangement?"

"*Ja*," he said disgustedly. "This is the problem. A buyer has to be found for the cars, so people like myself can be paid."

"Who finds the buyer?"

"Znorel."

"Is it difficult?"

"*Ja*. Russian cars are bad. Buyers complain. This happened with Nigeria which received a hundred thousand cars. About ten percent were not good. The Nigerians were not happy. I don't think they have paid for any of the cars yet."

"Where did you pick up these computers?"

"Znorel leases a warehouse just south of Vienna at Stölenburg."

"When did you make deliveries?"

"Usually at night."

"Where did you deliver the machines?"

"The Czech border."

"Would you know when the next shipment is?"

"No."

"Could you find out?"

"Perhaps."

Two men a few tables away got up to leave. Kruntz watched them and seemed edgy. "I have said enough. I want payment now."

"Just a few more questions," Graham said.

Kruntz looked around. "No!"

Graham nodded reluctantly and pulled out the envelope containing the money. "If you could just find out when that next trucking consignment is . . ." he said, handing it to him.

Kruntz quickly pocketed it. "Call me tomorrow morning." He finished his wine in one swig, stood up and walked out.

Graham took his time finishing his wine, paid the bill and walked out to the Mercedes.

He considered the meeting a useful start, if Kruntz was telling the truth. Graham felt he was a shifty type who would sell his own mother for a dollar. Whoever employed such a person, the Australian thought apprehensively, was unlikely to be any better.

Clifford Brogan, Sr., was in a foul mood as his private jet roared on its way from New York to Washington. Despite the huge PR efforts and legal moves behind the scenes, all was not running smoothly for the corporation in its court battle with the Justice

Department. In recent months, inexplicably to the Old Man, the corporation's position was beginning to look shaky as the end of the case drew near.

Brogan Junior, seated on a velvet couch in the main section of the flying penthouse's lounge, was reading newspaper accounts of the case. Standing a few feet away and looking a little anxious over a Teletype print-out carrying the latest stock prices, was Henry Strasburg, the trim, balding fifty-five-year-old former attorney general of the United States, and, for the last ten years, Lasercomp's chief legal counsel. He was the man in charge of fifteen hundred attorneys fighting Lasercomp's legal battles.

The pipe-smoking Strasburg had an air of superiority about him—from his fine-cut suit to his manicured nails. He was the classic example of how lawyers had come to penetrate the higher echelons of the corporation over the last decade. They had become an indispensable part of the Lasercomp defense against the state and other corporations as it expanded and gained more power.

If anyone could get Lasercomp off the hook in the increasingly difficult situation with the Justice Department, it was Strasburg. He knew a lot of important judges who sat in the most influential federal courts in the land. He had recommended many of them for appointment when he was attorney general. One such judge was Peter K. Shaw, currently presiding in the Justice Department case. Strasburg and he sponsored the same charitable cause and belonged to the same clubs in New York and Washington.

The gloomy silence was broken by a snarl from Brogan Senior.

"What did the stock do?"

"Down ten," the lawyer replied. "That's twenty points we've lost this week."

"What about the other blue chips?"

"They're down a bit too."

Brogan looked up at the lawyer and stared at him for a moment through his thick-lensed spectacles which somewhat hideously distorted the shape of his eyes. "Henry, I want to know what's going wrong with the case," he said with quiet menace. "After six years, I find it hard to believe we may be in trouble. . . ."

Reverently Strasburg sat down opposite the Old Man. "C.B., I wouldn't worry about what the press is saying. You know a lot of journalists would like to see us carved up," he said, trying

3 1

to sound confidently reassuring. "Besides, just because a little bit of pep is coming into the prosection's case now, remember we've been on top for most of the time. . . ."

"But I thought you had Sagittarius," the Old Man said sardonically. "What was it you said? 'Don't worry, Sagittarius's computer bank has every piece of documentation connected with the case . . . it has optical scanners which can read information into our law team's office. . . .'"

Strasburg wanted to say something but the Old Man went on rapidly, his anger rising: "'Don't worry, the computer can instantly compare a day's trial testimony with everything in Sagittarius . . . it can pinpoint discrepancies between testimony and submitted evidence . . . don't worry, it can tell our lawyers how to win!'" The Old Man gesticulated wildly and yelled, "Well, I *am* worrying and you had better start doing something about it!"

"Look, C.B.," Brogan Junior said, coming to Strasburg's aid, "there is nothing wrong with Sagittarius. It's a successful part of the master program . . . the prosecution will cause it only temporary problems."

"Maybe, but they're still problems! No one can tell me why we have them!" Brogan paused, frowned, and then added introspectively, "I think it's because of that ungrateful bastard running the prosecution. He must have gathered detailed information in those years with us and just waited for the chance to stab us in the back!"

"But he was a computer engineer with us. Not a lawyer," Brogan Junior said defensively.

"So what goddamn difference does that make? He had big ears and eyes, didn't he? I told you both to stop him from being allowed onto the prosecution team! I told you he spelled trouble!"

"C.B.," Strasburg said, pleased for the support from Brogan Junior, "I feel the press is largely to blame. They're whipping up hysterical opinion against us by billing the case as man versus machine. Some journalists want us to lose to prove the computer is fallible. Others want us beaten because we're big."

Brogan Senior sat seething as his son added, "We have a few months to go yet. Henry will make the case a sure thing."

"He'd better!" the Old Man said fiercely, "or I'll start taking action. I'll get people that can handle goddamn upstart governments or anything else!" He struggled out of his seat belt and stood up, keeping his balance as the plane banked slightly. "We've been slipping in the courts since you two have taken over the legal department," he said, waving his hands wildly at both of them. "Why? Because you're too damned weak! You won't show muscle or money. Every man can be had by either. This pathetic situation never arose years ago. We'd tell companies that if they tried to take us to court we'd put 'em out of business in a month. And we did! Now every fifth-rate little shit organization thinks it can milk us." He clenched his teeth, his rasping voice dropping to a hiss. "And governments . . . I've had presidents eating out of my hand . . . because without us they knew the system would collapse. We would keep reminding them . . ."

The Old Man slid back into his couch, breathing heavily as the other two looked on silently, Strasburg frightened to say another word, and Brogan Junior knowing it was best to stay cool when the tyrant rose in his father. The Old Man deliberately turned off his hearing aid. The ranting was over.

Graham started early on his second day in Vienna with a four-mile run around the city's narrow winding streets. He liked strenuous exercise at least once a day. It had become a habit, especially when he was on assignment, living out of a suitcase. By 7:30 A.M. he had showered, dressed casually and taken a breakfast of orange juice, eggs and bacon in his room, in preparation for a full day.

He began by making several calls.

One was to Joachim Kruntz, who told him that the next Znorel trucking assignment would leave at about one A.M. the next day from a warehouse at the village of Stölenburg.

Another call to a local journalist Graham knew heightened his interest in contacting IOSWOP. The journalist said that like some other obscure organizations in Vienna, it was probably a front for something, although he didn't know what. He added that there were always Russians coming and going. One in particular was the IOSWOP's chairman, a Professor Letovsky, who was possibly worth an interview. Graham knew of him. He was a leading trade ambassador for the Kremlin.

Graham decided to give it a try. He phoned IOSWOP and was put through to its PR man, a German named Hart. Graham was quizzed for several minutes and had to bluff his way by claiming to be writing articles for several papers and magazines in England, Europe, America and Australia which would be about Vienna's several prestigious international organizations, like OPEC and IOSWOP. Finally convinced, Hart invited Graham to visit IOSWOP's office at the Opernring in the heart of Vienna. A special IOSWOP bus would take him to Stölenburg at 11:30 A.M.

Graham arrived with his usual gear for an interview—a 35-mm. Minolta, a tape recorder, and an 8-mm. movie camera. He liked to record an important interview in as many ways as possible, and had a good working knowledge of all kinds of cameras and tape equipment.

He found the IOSWOP office, and was greeted unsmilingly by a tall, leggy girl who asked him to wait with several other men and women. He had time to unload his gear and smoke a cigarette before the girl ushered them out to a Volkswagen bus.

Two guards rode in the front seat with the driver, and Graham noticed they were wearing hip holsters.

The bus rattled on its way for about twenty miles to the Stölenburg village and palace, which dated back to 1388.

Once a summer residence of successive Hapsburg emperors, the sleepy surroundings were conducive to much wine in the warmth of the afternoon or the cool of the evening, and the Empress Maria Theresa blamed many of her sixteen children on this. It fell into disrepair after 1917. In 1970 the Austrian Government offered to renovate the palace for IOSWOP in an effort to persuade another institution to make its home in Vienna. Shortly thereafter, IOSWOP was in the palace's red court.

Originally the brainchild of heads of the American and Soviet foreign ministries in the 1960s, IOSWOP was hailed as contributing to scientific détente. Scientists of nations East and West could work together to find solutions to the world's most pressing problems of pollution, energy conservation, medicine, food supply and population control, using advanced computer techniques.

A clock struck noon just as the bus pulled up to iron gates at the front of the palace, a mighty gray and yellow edifice. Ten huge pillars supported the portico entrance, and on a balcony above, two guards watched as the occupants of the bus filed out.

Another two guards swung the gates open as German shepherd dogs barked a fierce disapproval.

Graham was greeted by a squat, heavy-featured man with a pockmarked face.

After a limp handshake and a gutteral, "I'm Hans Hart," the grubbily dressed PR man proceeded to show Graham around the palace, stressing that no photographs were to be taken. They walked up a marble stairway to the second floor, where there was an excellent view of the palace grounds, of about twenty acres, which were as plush and smooth as a green pool table. The grounds were dotted with small "pleasure pavilions." One had a tennis court, another a swimming pool. About a dozen people dozed under canopies. Several German shepherds were chained to a barbed-wire-protected high wall, beyond which a thick forest unrolled to the horizon.

Motioning for silence, Hart led Graham into a library. All its shelves were stark and bare. Every piece of information was apparently on microfilm. About twenty people sat at desks watching miniature TV display units.

At 12:45 they returned to Hart's office, where he gave out PR material, including photographs and brochures, and some papers on the organization's research into world problems.

After a few minutes they were informed that Letovsky would see the Australian. They were ushered into the professor's office. Its green silk and gold-paneled walls and ceiling were typical of the restoration, befitting the heads of state to which it once catered. A huge, glittering candelabrum hung from the center of the ceiling.

Letovsky, a heavily built Russian with black bushy eyebrows and alert brown eyes, unhurriedly eased himself up to shake hands with Graham. Hart spoke rapidly about the reason for the Australian's visit while Letovsky nodded slightly and stood close, as if he were a prizefighter sizing up an opponent. Apparently satisfied that the stranger was worth a minute or two of his precious time, the Russian motioned them to sit down as he moved back behind his leather-topped desk.

With his eyes on Graham, he said in near-perfect English, "I didn't realize we would be news on such a wide sphere, Mr. Graham. But if an article can attract fresh funds, then we are always interested in speaking to the Western press." He offered Graham a cigarette and lit one himself.

The Australian pulled out a tape recorder, saying, "You won't mind if I . . ."

Letovsky waved an indifferent hand. "Use a tape if you wish." He regarded himself as experienced in handling the Western press.

Graham nodded a thank-you. "I've often read about you making trips to the West with Soviet trade delegations," he said. "You split your time between that and your work here, I suppose?"

"More or less, yes," Letovsky said. He stacked folders on his desk impatiently. "What would you like to know about IOSWOP?"

Graham switched on his tape. "First, who is financing you? I see in your hand-out material that you have about thirty million dollars' worth of computer equipment here. That takes some funding."

"Of course," Letovsky said, brushing a bit of ash from his floral Dior tie. "Academies and institutions in the Soviet Union and the United States are our biggest supporters. But there are many others from many countries that want membership with us. There are several on the waiting list. It would not, you will understand, be prudent for me to name the smaller contributing nations at this time."

"Where are all the scientists from?"

"Mainly the institutions that support us."

"In proportion to their financial support?"

"Yes."

The next question had to be as offhand as possible.

"I see that the Brogan Foundation, which is entirely financed by Lasercomp, is down as a contributor. Is it the biggest, Professor?"

"One of the biggest."

Graham nodded. "And," he began, as he frowned and scratched his head, "one of the things I noticed was the rather strong contingent of guards around the palace, and even armed guards on the bus that brought me here. Why is that necessary?"

Letovsky leaned forward and flicked ash into a tray. "We have top-secret assignments here," he said.

"Like what?"

"Well, for example, right now we have two clients, both governments, looking for nuclear-power-plant locations. We work out progress on computer to calculate the best location in a country to avoid pollution."

Graham nodded as if he accepted the reply. "That leads me to the next question. Could you explain how IOSWOP functions?"

The question seemed to have relaxed Letovsky. "We work at solving world problems, like the one I mentioned. To solve these important problems, our people need information to work on. Our computer people have devised an excellent system based on three big computers and two smaller 'minis.' It allows information to flow from important sources anywhere in the world. If we have a problem, and the data needed to solve it are in some far-off academy, say in Warsaw, our man here can request the data via a terminal connected to a satellite, which in turn is connected to a computer in Warsaw. The data can be bounced to us here."

"Who is linked into this system?"

"All major academies funding us."

"I see," Graham said thoughtfully.

The professor plowed on. "The real beauty of our operation is that we transcend national boundaries," he said haughtily, "but of course, we only suggest solutions. If an institution such as the United Nations likes what we suggest, then pressure might be brought to bear on the problem in a practical way."

Graham decided to move on to the topic that would be sure to arouse Letovsky's suspicions.

"I'd like to change the subject, if I may," he said. "It is rare that a Western journalist has such an opportunity."

"Well, I'm afraid we have not much time, Mr. Graham," Letovsky said. "But please . . ."

"Thank you. At a recent Soviet Party Congress it was announced that the Soviet Union would produce a major new series of computers in a long-term plan. But at your last Congress, there was no mention of its progress. Has it been dropped?"

There was an almost imperceptible flicker of uncertainty from the professor. But it was there. Leaning back in his chair, he said coldly, "I am not involved in this area, but it was endorsed by the Party. As far as I know, the plan went ahead."

"Then it is continuing?"

"Yes."

"You are manufacturing all your own equipment?"

"Of course."

"How many computers are involved?"

Letovsky paused. Until now he had been arrogantly self-assured. Suddenly his manner changed. He shifted in his seat. "I have no idea," he said slowly. "I said before, Mr. Graham, I am not involved in the planning."

Letovsky was on the defensive now, so Graham decided it would be prudent to stop. The Australian closed his notebook and switched off the tape. "Thank you very much, Professor," he said evenly; "that about covers the questions I had."

"May I ask you something, Mr. Graham?" Letovsky said. "Why are you so interested in Soviet computer production?"

"Anything new the Soviet Union produces makes news in the West," Graham replied nonchalantly.

"I would expect that you will submit your writings to us before they go to press," Hart said.

"I have a policy, gentlemen," Graham replied firmly as he stood up. "I always refer back to source if there is any doubt."

"I would like to see it, please," Letovsky said firmly, "in any event."

Graham stood his ground. "I cannot guarantee that, Professor. If you want public relations, write it yourself."

Letovsky looked annoyed, but said nothing. Hart, in a real dither, opened the door.

Graham turned to the professor. "Thank you for the interview," he said. "You've been most helpful."

Letovsky had not got up to shake hands.

George Lionel Revel, chief prosecuting lawyer for the U.S. Justice Department, was unexpectedly alerted to the strain in the normally confident tone of his opposite number in the Lasercomp defense.

Perhaps no one else in the packed New York courthouse sensed the change in David L. Cartwright, the usually superconfident gentleman for the defense in his elegant lightweight suit of conservative gray. Suddenly he seemed to be feeling the heat. For the last thirty minutes he had droned on about the virtues of Lasercomp's importance to America's economic health through employment, and income from massive sales abroad, and the "great" technology it must be allowed to bring the nation and the world. Now he conferred earnestly at the prosecution lawyers' table before he turned to the judge once more. "Your Honor," he said, blinking several times, "throughout this case the government has seemed to want to sacrifice ingenuity, ability and progress—the very qualities that made this nation great. It seems to have a formula for mediocrity, incompetence and failure, which will ultimately reduce our great nation to the level of a banana republic. The defense firmly believes that this lawsuit is part of a socialist conspiracy by certain members of the present administration in Washington to destroy free enterprise in this country"—he paused as several people in the packed public gallery voiced their disapproval. He spoke louder—"by attacking corporations that have been successful!"

There were more groans from the public gallery. Judge Peter K. Shaw called for order.

"Yes, a conspiracy. And I submit to Your Honor that it stems from the White House itself!"

Revel, his large gray eyes and sharp features alert, was on his feet, bumping the table in his haste to be heard.

"Objection, Your Honor," he yelled. "Apart from being absurd, this is totally irrelevant to the case."

"Objection sustained," the judge said. "All reference to a conspiracy shall be stricken from the record. The defense will kindly refrain from red herrings and irrelevancies."

The damage had been done, and the defense's outburst would be sure to bring into the open the festering conflict between the President of the United States, Everett Rickard, and Lasercomp. "Conspiracy" may have been misleadingly emotive, but the defense had highlighted a point. Everett Rickard had been the first President to attempt to bring justice to the marketplace, dominated by the major corporations. He was telling the multinationals to come to heel, and they were not liking it.

Lasercomp had always been his prime target. With the election close and incidents like this, the battle was being drawn into the open. A victory for Rickard would boost his stakes on polling day. A win for Lasercomp would be a major blow for Rickard and leave the corporation all but invincible.

For George Revel, it too was an important battle, on a personal level. Revel had come from a lower-middle-class Jewish family in the Bronx. His father, a refugee from Hitler's Germany, was a poetic dreamer who barely managed to support his family as a tailor, but instilled in his son a burning desire for knowledge and a deep respect for intellect. His mother, like her husband a refugee from Nazi tyranny, was a shrewish, domineering woman who constantly nagged her husband for his failure to rise in the world. From her, Revel acquired a lifelong drive to excel. Graduating from America's number-one public high school, the Bronx High School of Science, at seventeen, his outstanding academic record earned him a scholarship to the Massachusetts Institute of Technology. At twenty-one he had already earned his master's degree in engineering and was working on a doctorate. Then the reaction set in. He had come to loathe the cloistered world of the academic.

Abandoning his original plan to finish his doctorate and to teach at MIT or Harvard, he was lured into the intriguing world of computers by Lasercomp, which scoured the campuses for talent. At first he enjoyed the challenge of being at the creative forefront of one of man's greatest inventions. He was quickly acknowledged for his ability and shot up the Lasercomp ladder until his superiors were forced to give him managerial responsibility and steer him into the marketing side. Then things began to sour. When he got the sniff of the Lasercomp modus operandi, it sickened him. The forces behind the façade were not what he expected, or wanted to be associated with. After nine years he eased his way out. Disillusioned, and now past thirty, Revel left his wife and two young daughters to travel to Europe, Asia and Australia for eighteen months. He began to search for a new career.

It was law—the only other professional area that had always fascinated him. After three years at Harvard, where he topped every examination and was an editor of the *Law Review*, he again tried the business world and corporate law.

At thirty-five, his first legal job was with a medium-sized New York law firm. Revel soon found himself defending a company that was polluting the river and countryside of Virginia. He won the case, and every one like it that followed.

Soon he was the number-one choice for the defense in the big money cases. And, as before at Lasercomp, he began to hate his work. He cried out for a chance to excel at something socially redeeming in law. He left the firm.

Simultaneously, President Rickard appropriated more funds to the Justice Department for its fight against Lasercomp. More money meant more people on the undermanned prosecution team. George Revel applied for one of those jobs. The Justice Department was very pleased to have such a wealth of experience to add to its team. Not only was he outstanding in court, but he could offer an unparalleled knowledge of the defendant. Lasercomp, in a predictable move, objected strongly to the presiding judge, but failed to block Revel's move onto the case. Within eighteen months he became chief prosecuting lawyer and changed the face of the trial. After the years of legal charade, in which the eventual result seemed only a formality, there was suddenly a feeling in American legal circles that Lasercomp could be in trouble. The possibility of its being beaten in the case and fragmented was now conceivable.

For this reason, the mention of the President of the U.S. being involved in a conspiracy reminded George Revel that it was Everett Rickard who had given him the chance to stretch his talents to the full.

Professor Letovsky was concerned about his interview with Graham. Five hours after it, he called Hans Hart to his office. "I want a complete check on that journalist's background, employers, the lot."

"What's wrong, Professor?"

"Three days ago he met a trucking contractor, Joachim Kruntz. This man used to make Znorel-Lasercomp consignment runs to the border. The journalist has paid him for information."

Hart blanched as Letovsky added, "I hope you did not disclose anything before he met me."

Hart shook his head as he thought quickly through the questions Graham had asked him.

"No. No, I'm sure."

"We must stop him writing anything. He may be dangerous to our operations. You must find out where he is staying and insist we see anything he intends to publish."

. . .

By seven that evening, Graham had completed telephoning through a 1,200-word article from his hotel to Sir Alfred's company, Ryder Publications, in London. From there it would end up in a London daily paper the next day, and within twenty-four hours would be on network wires to press outlets around the world. Sir Alfred had hesitantly agreed to see that Graham's article would be published. The Australian thought it might provoke a reaction from someone.

With the story on its way, Graham decided to try to follow the late-night smuggling consignment. There was just a chance that he could obtain some vital information.

He had several hours before the consignment was supposed to leave for the border, so he planned to hear *La Traviata*, at the Staatsoper, and dine out after it. Before leaving, he booked his return flight to London for 6:00 P.M. the next day.

At 11:30 P.M. Graham left a Rumanian restaurant and walked the short distance back to his hotel. He changed into his black tracksuit and running shoes and packed a valise with a change of clothes, his passport, tape recorder and all the notes on the assignment. Almost as an afterthought he decided to take his movie camera. He took a couple of minutes to study a map of the route to Stölenburg village and the location of the warehouse of the Stuttgart-based company, Znorel Electronics before he left the room.

Graham emerged from the hotel at midnight and moved into the deserted streets to his Mercedes. After speeding through Vienna's suburbs into the countryside and past the Stölenburg Palace, he found the warehouse, and pulled onto the side of the road about half a mile away from the entrance. It was a moonlit night and he could make out the warehouse easily across the flat countryside.

He decided not to go any closer until there was some activity.

About an hour later, Graham heard the roar of trucks and the sound of voices. A few minutes later, he could make out several vehicles moving off from the warehouse like a giant, squat centipede. The convoy was followed by a station wagon.

When all the vehicles were well on their way along the main road running northwest toward the border, Graham drove carefully, lights off, about four hundred yards behind.

He followed in a slow crawl for the next three hours, until he heard the trucks clatter across a bridge. He pulled off the road, got out of the car, and climbed onto the roof. Above the trees of a thick wooded area he could see an oblong building where the trucks had gone. Graham wanted the safety of the Mercedes but he certainly would be spotted if he took it any closer. He had to go on foot if he wanted to see what was going on inside that building. He turned the Mercedes round to face the way he had come and drove it across the road, under some overhanging trees, close to a dry creek bed.

Hurriedly camouflaging the car, Graham collected his camera and made his way stealthily across the creek bed in the direction of the warehouse.

After about two hundred yards, he suddenly reached a seven-foot wire-mesh fence. He could see and hear several men. They were sitting on crates and passing around flasks of drink. Graham made his way along the fence until the men were out of sight. He gripped the top of the fence and hoisted himself over it. Crouching low, he crept to the wall of the warehouse. Then he edged along the wall to the back of the building. He found a door. Graham tried the bolt. It wouldn't give. Moving along another ten yards, he found another door. This time the bolt slid back easily and noiselessly. He inched the door open. Crates piled ten feet high surounded the door. Graham moved inside, leaving the door ajar. Above the line of crates he could make out a ramp which ran at sixty degrees almost to the roof. It was connected to another ramp with sides about three feet high which ran the full length of the building. It was very near the roof. If only he could get up there. It would be a perfect vantage point to film whatever was going on below under high-powered quartz lighting.

On the other hand, he would be a sitting duck if anyone with a weapon spotted him. He eased between the crates and could see several trucks at the other end of the building. Creeping over to the sloping ramp, Graham lay flat against it. Using his strength he hauled himself up using the foothold slats. At the top it was easier going along the roof ramp. He kept his body low as he crept along it to avoid throwing a shadow. About halfway along he had a close look at his light meter. It was showing a poor reading. He rolled on his back and opened the camera aperture to its widest.

4 3

Graham straightened carefully and then swung over the side of the ramp, one leg hard against it to avoid toppling over. He zoomed in on crates being hoisted by an overhead crane from trucks belonging to Znorel and lowered to ground level, where they were unpacked and inspected and repacked for other trucks. Graham held the zoom on this operation and captured clear shots of computers, all unmarked. After thirty seconds the strain on his back was too much. He eased himself back and lay flat on his back for three minutes.

Then he swung his body out again, but this time too far. He slipped and grabbed desperately for the side of the ramp as the camera fell to the ground, nearly hitting one of the workmen directly below. Graham just managed to clamber back as a group of men shouted and pointed at the struggling figure. In the confusion, a crane driver lowered a crane too close to the side of one of the trucks. It smashed against it. Several men yelled and ran for cover as the crate swayed and bashed the truck's side. In the panic, Graham's only instinct was to run. He raced along the roof ramp to the one that sloped to the ground and slithered down to the crates. He had some difficulty finding the door as men converged from every direction. He slipped out and sprinted the fifty yards across the compound to the fence, hauled himself to the top and leaped clear, but twisted his ankle as he hit the ground. He felt the painful tear of a ligament as he stumbled on his way through the wood. The compound was now bathed in brilliant light. He heard the station wagon start up as he reached the creek bed. He limped along in a panic and had trouble making out his crude camouflage of the Mercedes. Just as he was yards from it, the station wagon crossed the bridge and skidded to a halt. Graham flung himself flat as two men jumped out of the car and ran along the road. Graham's heart sank as the car headlights went on. He could see his own shadow on the wall of the creek.

Two voices bellowed instructions to one of the men who had stopped about twenty yards from Graham. The man yelled angrily to the other to turn out the lights. The lights were doused. Graham felt he had to do something. He picked up a rock and hurled it high and hard on to the other side of the road. The man turned and ran in the direction of the noise. Graham scrambled to the car, got in and shoved the key in the ignition as the lights on the station wagon went on once more. The Mercedes sprang to life. He put his foot flat on the accelerator, and the car snapped its way out of the camouflage and off along the road. The station wagon gave chase.

Graham drove recklessly as the other car seemed to be gaining on him. But with a straight flat stretch of about five miles, the Mercedes, flat out, pulled away. After ten minutes the station wagon driver gave up. Graham kept up speed until he reached the outskirts of Vienna a little over an hour later.

Finding an unmade track, he pulled off the road, stopped the car and slumped over the wheel.

Seated at his desk, in the Oval Office, the President looked through black-rimmed spectacles at his formidable schedule for the day. With the election looming, he was under tremendous pressure, and it was beginning to show in his appearance. His craggy features had weary fatty bags under the bloodshot blue eyes, and a pasty skin had become apparent over the last few months. The pressure, too, had manifested itself in his manner and temper. This was not helped by the tedious lobbying that had to be done if he were to remain in the White House for another term. He felt more comfortable with the minute-by-minute, day-to-day decision-making, especially in foreign affairs. Yet he seemed to be giving more of his precious seconds to worrying about media coverage, and pressure groups. The bid for political power was a new experience for Rickard. He had won office by fate and chance, not by the nation's vote.

Rickard had been selected as a compromise choice by the previous President to be his vice-presidential running mate. Both right and left of the party found the selection acceptable. Rickard's middle-of-the-road views were so indistinct that no one saw him as a threat. A few months after the inauguration, the President died suddenly of a cerebral hemorrhage, and Rickard, the son of a poor Ohio tool and die maker, was in the Oval Office. Nothing in his small-town background, or bland, uneventful career—Ohio State University law graduate, assistant district attorney, Ohio State Legislature, state attorney general, and seven years in the Senate—gave a hint of the way Rickard was to develop as President. He quickly found a strength of character few knew he possessed. He was impelled by the office's awesome tradition and became determined to reach a high standard and a prominent role in history.

In his forty months as President, Rickard had run headlong into conflict with Lasercomp by beefing up the Justice Department. Now he was preparing to confront them on an even more significant issue: the illegal flow of strategic computers to the Soviet Union.

The latter was the first item in today's long agenda—a meeting with the Secretary of State, Edward Grove, and the assistant Under Secretary, Gregor Haussermann. As the two men entered the room just at 7:45 A.M., the President did not bother with even the briefest greeting, but said to Haussermann; "What have you come up with?" The assistant Under Secretary, a thin, bearded man with a nervous disposition characterized by large furtive gray eyes, and an occasional stammer, handed him a thin folder, and then, at Rickard's request, left the room.

A week earlier Rickard had asked for a report on the illegal eastward flow of technology, particularly computer equipment and classified data related to offensive and defensive military systems. He flicked through the twenty-odd pages while Grove sat quietly, watching him frown and hearing the occasional mumbled expletive. By the time he had finished, he looked fit to explode. "Goddammit!" he exclaimed vehemently. "This tells me next to nothing!"

Turning to Grove, he said, "Ted, I want to know two things fast. Who is supplying those machines, and what they are being used for." He leaned forward in his chair, elbows on the desk, and whacked the report with the back of his hand.

"Surely someone in our twenty-two Intelligence agencies can tell the Commander in Chief a little more than that!"

"Everett," Grove began, "we know there is a build-up of computers and satellite systems inside the Soviet Union. Our electronic surveillance has picked this up. But we need people on the ground to get a definitive picture. That takes time."

Rickard sighed. "We haven't got time! If the Soviets get the best equipment, their military systems become better. Eventually better than ours. Every computer that improves their firepower is a nail in the free world's coffin!"

He paused. Suddenly his manner changed from frustrated anger to decisiveness.

"Let's put a team together. I want a secret group of experts—in Soviet weaponry, foreign affairs, computers and intelligence—sworn in within seven days. They're to investigate everything from what's going on in Russia to our major computer corporations, especially Lasercomp. . . ."

Grove was a little surprised. "You don't think—"

"Yes, I do," Rickard interrupted intently, "Let's cover every possibility. Lasercomp has just produced the most advanced computer ever. It has built that machine so that it can be converted to direct military use; the control of guided missiles, lasers, you name it. The damn thing gives us an incredible first strike lead on the Russians. In any conflict right now, we win every time."

Grove sat silently for a moment, then, with a puzzled frown, said, "There is a great deal of expertise needed to convert Cheetah for military use. Only a handful of top Lasercomp scientists can effect it. You're not suggesting Lasercomp would deliberately build the Soviet Union's firepower?"

"I'm not suggesting anything. I'm just looking at history. Modern history. Brogan Senior moved into munitions when he smelled Hiltler's rise in the thirties."

"There's no law against opportunism."

"Even if it supplied the Nazis after we were involved in 1941?"

"Are you sure about that?"

"Have a look through our own State Department records. Lasercomp was among a select little number doing deals with Hitler. It waited like a jackal to see who would win. If it had been their darling Adolf, they would have been first in the door to back the German war machine."

"That is a long time ago, Everett."

"So? Lasercomp's management hasn't changed. Nor has its mentality. If it can act that way in war, how far will it go in peacetime? Remember Lasercomp earns more than sixty percent of its revenue outside America. Its main allegiance is not this country any more."

Grove shook his head. "That's disturbing . . . I'll start getting that team together now."

"Right. And the first name in it will be George Revel, if he's willing."

"Revel in Justice?"

Rickard nodded. "He's wrapping up the court case right now. He has a tremendous knowledge of Lasercomp. And he has a taste for blood . . ."

Rickard had an enormous respect for Revel and his handling of the Lasercomp case. The President knew Revel had taken a special interest in the flow of computers into the Soviet Union, not so much because they could be used for increasing Soviet military strength, but because of rumors that they were being used as a method of controlling society—especially dissidents and minority groups such as Jews, Ukrainians and Lithuanians, fighting for greater human rights. It had also been an area of special significance for Rickard. Perhaps his only uncompromising political attitude before he became President was on Soviet oppression in Eastern Europe. Opposition to it was popular in Ohio, with its vast numbers of Eastern Europeans and large Catholic population. His mother was of Irish-Polish stock, and her family were all immigrants. She never lost contact with relatives in Poland, and Rickard's one-quarter Polish blood gave him a personal interest in Soviet domination. It had been driven home to him when he served in the U.S. Army in Germany during the early Soviet and Allied occupation.

Graham's report in a London paper had put pressure on Professor Letovsky. One phone call set his nerves on edge. It came crackling over the line from Moscow. But the message was clear enough. KGB intelligence in London had already passed on details of the newspaper article. Explanations were needed. Letovsky did his best to heap the blame on Kruntz. This, however, was not enough. The professor had to give an assurance that the journalist who caused the flurry would be handled in a "suitable" way. Something drastic had to be done, especially after Letovsky learned an intruder had nearly been caught filming computer warehouse activities on the Czech border. The professor was certain it was Graham. They had his camera. It was being checked for ownership.

Letovsky requested that Anatoli Bromovitch, deputy chief

of KGB's Department Four, the functions of which included assassinations outside the U.S.S.R., be immediately dispatched to Vienna.

At 2:00 P.M. Letovsky found Bromovitch among the tourists in the gardens of Schönbrunn Palace, sitting on a bench throwing parts of his sandwiches to the pigeons. It was an uncomfortable meeting for both. They were opposites in appearance, manner and attitude.

Letovsky was a leading member of the Soviet elite, mainly because he had married the foreign minister's daughter. He regarded himself as an international sophisticate. The professor enjoyed dealing with powerful Westerners and secretly admired the trappings of Western life-style.

Bromovitch, a short, slightly plump man who always wore ill-fitting gray suits, hated Western "decadence."

Just one factor linked them: a dedication to Soviet world dominance.

Letovsky sat on the bench next to Bromovitch, but refused to look at him. He hated that benign face and especially those deceptively pleasant light blue eyes. They were inhuman scanners that held your gaze and never left you as they searched for a hint of weakness or deceit.

"How was your flight?" Letovsky asked quietly.

"Terrible," Bromovitch grumbled. "I hate Aeroflot. No lunch. Not even vodka."

"I am sorry. You have been briefed?"

"No. Is it *Mokroye Delo?*" Bromovitch was referring to the KGB term for blood being spilled.

"It is."

"Where?"

"That is up to you."

"You have no preference how?"

"Of course not. As long as it is neat."

Letovsky was relieved to be washing his hands of a sordid problem. Building sophisticated computer networks was his business. Never murder.

After his narrow escape, badly shaken and sore, Graham slept in his hired car just outside Vienna rather than return to his hotel, which he feared could be checked. The previous night's harrowing experience had left him with one aim: to get out of Vienna quickly.

His flight was scheduled for 6:00 P.M. and he had left himself enough time to collect his gear from the hotel and drive to the airport. At 3:00 P.M. he telephoned his hotel from a public booth, ten minutes away.

"Ah, Mr. Graham," said Frau Schiller, the manageress, relieved to hear the Australian's voice. "You did not stay in your room last night and you did not return this morning. I nearly called the police!"

Graham tried to sound at ease. "I'm very sorry, Frau Schiller," he said. "I stayed the night with friends outside Vienna. I shall be in to the hotel to pay you and collect my luggage in an hour. Have there been any messages?"

"No, but it was strange, Mr. Graham. Three men came in, not half an hour ago. They said they were friends of yours, but would not leave a message."

Graham froze. "Is that all?"

"They wanted to know if you had checked out. I told them you would be flying back to London on the six o'clock flight. Was that correct?"

"Yes, of course, Frau Schiller. Thank you."

"I hope I have not spoiled things," she said softly.

"Why?" Graham asked sharply.

"These men said they would probably meet you at the airport. They told me not to bother telling you. They wanted to surprise you." There was a long pause. "Mr. Graham, are you there?"

"Ah, yes, Frau Schiller," Graham replied slowly as he gathered his wits. "If they call again, please don't tell them I've been in touch or that I'm coming back to collect my things. I want to surprise them also."

"They are your friends then?"

"I think so. Could you describe them?"

"The man who did all the talking was a short gentleman. Very, how do you say, polite?"

"Austrian?"

"Oh, no, Mr. Graham," she said with indignation. "He was Russian."

"How could you tell?"

"His accent."

"And the other two; what were they like?"

"They did not speak. They could have been Russian, Austrian or German. One was probably a little higher than yourself. I remember him well because he had a very ugly bald head. The other . . . I cannot remember him at all."

"Thank you so much, Frau Schiller," Graham said, trying to sound cheerful. "I'll be in shortly. Goodbye."

He put the receiver down. Hell! he thought. Three men including a Russian wanted him. Was it because of the article, or last night's escapade? And what to do now? They wanted to "surprise" him at the airport. He had several hours. No need to panic, he told himself. Just then, there was a rattle of the telephone booth door. He jerked around. An angry little old Austrian woman waiting impatiently was gesticulating at him. Graham breathed a sigh of relief.

He forced a smile, and quickly looked up the number for Austrian rail information. The next train out of the country didn't leave until eight. Graham decided it was his safest bet, even if it meant having to stay in Vienna another five hours. It might be easy to trace the Mercedes, and he didn't feel in any state for a long drive. He had strapped his twisted ankle, but it was still swollen and tender.

The welcoming party would be at the airport until six, leaving only two hours before his train left. This, he hoped, would not be enough to trace his escape.

He was certainly not going back to his hotel because he was sure it would be watched. There was nothing essential there, and his suitcase and clothes could always be retrieved some other time. Graham drove to a little coffee shop he remembered from his other visit to Vienna. He lingered an hour over two cups of steaming coffee, alert to every customer that came and went.

He next drove to the Richard Lidmer art gallery across town. It was practically deserted, as good a place as any to keep out of sight.

After speaking with Frau Schiller, Bromovitch and two other KGB agents had waited two hours for Graham outside his hotel. When he did not show up, they had sped to Schwechat airport. They sat quietly for half an hour in the entrance lounge with a clear view of the cars and taxis depositing travelers. Then the chubby Bromovitch rolled across on one elbow to whisper something in the ear of his companion, known as "the Skull." Ugly protruding bones seemed to be pushing out of his skin above the ears and through the top of his completely shaven head.

The Skull moved to the information counter and asked the girl to page Edwin Graham.

The call came over the intercom: "Would Mr. Graham, traveling to London on Flight 809, please come to the information counter . . . Mr. Edwin Graham."

As the message was repeated, the three agents moved in different directions so that they stood about twenty yards from the counter. No one turned up. After ten minutes, the Skull asked for a repeat call. Within thirty seconds, a smartly dressed dark-haired man of medium height, accompanied by an attractive woman of about thirty-five, strolled confidently to the counter.

"You ask for Gramanni?" he asked the girl quizzically. He sounded Italian. The girl nodded toward the Skull. Bromovitch waddled up to the counter and looked hard at the man. He roughly fitted the professor's description of the Australian.

"You are Mr. Graham?" he said with some difficulty in English.

The man swung around, bemused. "Gramanni, I am Gramanni," he said, using his hands freely.

Bromovitch gave a very long, cold stare, which embarrassed the other man, who nodded to the girl at the counter and moved off with his companion, turning twice to look back at the Russian.

Confused, but not wanting to be fooled, Bromovitch acted quickly. He beckoned the Skull and the other agent and ordered them to stay close to the couple, who had moved into the dining room. When they had settled down at a table, the agents did the same nearby. On finishing his coffee, the man calling himself Gramanni stood up and marched to a toilet on the other side of the airport lounge. The agents moved off after him. The man had just finished at the urinal when the agents walked in. As he was washing his hands, he looked up inquiringly at the three who had surrounded him. Before he could react, he was hauled and pushed into a cubical. The Skull had him in a strong headlock, his bicep hard against the man's throat. The other agent had a glove roughly over the man's mouth to stifle cries for help. The man's eyes bulged with fear as Bromovitch tore at his inside coat pockets, grabbing all his documents. The Russian fingered through them, causing bits of paper and business cards to fall to the floor. Passport, driver's license, personal photos and company identification were all marked clearly: Silvio D. Gramanni, Managing Director, Gramanni & Co., Milano.

Bromovitch gathered the papers and shoved them brusquely back into the man's coat pockets, warning him to keep quiet about what had happened. The Skull released his grip from the man's throat and he took in several quick gulps of air. His attackers left him disheveled and sitting on the toilet bowl.

Back in the lounge, Bromovitch had the Skull page Graham once more. It was 5:29 P.M. The three circled the lounge watching people filing through customs and into the waiting area that led to the planes and the London flight. But Graham did not appear to be with them. Bromovitch decided they should wait another twenty minutes.

At six Graham left the art gallery and drove to Johannesgasse in the city center. He locked his gear in the trunk, caught a trolley car to the thirteenth-century St. Stephen's Church, and headed for the roof restaurant Haus Haus, which gave a fine view of the church. After spending an hour and a half over a light meal, he returned to his car and drove to the train station. It took him time to find a parking space, and when he got to the ticket booth it was too late to buy a first-class ticket to Paris.

He settled for the second-class couchette. It wasn't private, but it would have to do for the eighteen-hour trip.

Looking cautiously around at the faces of people scurrying for the train, the Australian moved briskly onto the platform and stepped on the train at the nearest doorway. As he began to wend his way down the narrow passageway past other passengers to his couchette, he kept looking down at the people on the platform. Graham's skin prickled as he noticed a tall man wearing a light gray overcoat and hat. He seemed to be paying careful attention to people running for the train. The Australian looked away and kept moving. He found his couchette, threw his valise on the bottom bunk and slumped back into it. Several people were moving past, checking the numbers of the couchettes. Graham was relieved that it appeared no one was going to join him.

Just as the train began to pull out of the station a man moved past the open door of the couchette and fleetingly locked eyes with Graham as he did so. It was the man who moments earlier had been checking the passengers from the platform.

The Australian stayed in his couchette for an hour before wandering down to the dining car. Many people were seated taking meals. Several men and women sat on stools at a bar with a large mirror behind it. The Australian immediately noticed that one man at the bar with his back to him had an unusually bony bald head, similar to the description given to him by Frau Schiller at the hotel in Vienna. The man had a hat and a light overcoat over his knee. He was the only person there not making conversation.

Graham kept an eye on the bar as he sat down at a table next to a middle-aged couple and a young woman. He was facing the bar and could see the reflection of the bald man's face.

The Australian looked around and noticed someone at an opposite table looking at him. It was the man he had seen on the platform and had later exchanged glances with from the couchette.

Graham was nervous. His first instincts were to leave the dining car. But before he had made up his mind to go, a waiter was asking him for his order. He asked for a sandwich and a beer. His English drew glances from several people, including the man opposite. The waiter had stood in a line between the man at the bar and Graham. After the waiter had taken the order and moved away, the man at the bar went out of the dining car.

Half an hour later Graham had almost finished his meal when the couple next to him left the table, leaving him with the girl. The Australian wanted to stay in the dining car as long as possible. He felt a little more secure there with so many people about. The man opposite him had almost finished his meal and was drinking coffee.

"Going to Paris?" Graham asked the girl sitting in front of him, mustering as much charm as possible.

"Oui," she replied, surprised at being spoken to.

"You are French?"

"Yes." The girl smiled faintly. Graham was relieved. She didn't appear to mind making conversation.

"Have you been on holiday in Vienna?"

"Holiday and business."

"You are a model?" Graham said, keeping up the small talk by asking the obvious. The girl was tall, beautifully dressed and groomed, with a lavish amount of make-up which accentuated the hollow, angular structure of her face.

She nodded. The conversation continued with the girl opening up a little to Graham about her rich Austrian boyfriend in Vienna who had put her up for the past week at the opulent Hotel Sasher and shown her the sights.

The dining car crowd began to thin out. Still the man opposite the Australian lingered, ordering a second cup of coffee and a cognac. Graham decided to stay there as long as he could. He ordered an expensive wine and two glasses, and pretended to turn more of his attention to the girl.

As midnight approached the bar began to close down and the man opposite moved off. Graham walked the girl to her couchette, trying to keep the conversation going at her door while lightning flashed from a violent storm that had hit Austria and promised to be with the train most of the night journey to France. He began to think it would be safer to stay the night with her, but it became obvious that she was not prepared to let him in.

"Will you be staying in Paris?" she asked, sliding the couchette door across.

"Possibly."

She fumbled for a card in her handbag. "If you do, please phone me," she said, handing him a card. They shook hands.

As Graham moved off, he heard the click of the couchette door lock behind him.

Two carriages away the Skull waited.

After Graham had failed to turn up at the airport, Bromovitch had left his other man there in case the Australian should try to get on any later flight. Then he drove back to the city with the Skull and ordered him to check the trains. Bromovitch went back to the hotel where Graham had been staying.

The Skull had arrived twenty minutes before the Paris train

was due to leave and had waited for Graham on the platform. He had not seen the Australian get on, but caught the train just in case he had missed him.

After arranging a couchette with the porter, the Skull had sidled down to the dining car, and had sat with his back to the diners, watching them in the mirror.

When Graham came in, the Skull was alerted. He fitted the description better than the Italian at the airport. His suspicions were confirmed when he overheard Graham speaking in English to the waiter.

The Skull left the dining car and made his way to the porter's cabin.

"Good evening," he said in German to the porter, who was writing down the numbers of the passports he had collected in the first hour of the journey. "I was wondering if you could tell me the couchette number of a friend. We have missed each other."

"His name?"

"Edwin Graham. He is Australian."

The porter spent some time sifting through passports until he came to one with a dark blue cover and Kangaroo and Emu emblem. "Number ninety," he said.

Graham felt a real sensation of fear as he made his way along the carriages to his couchette. If anything happened there was no place to run and hide. He felt claustrophobic.

The Australian entered his couchette cautiously and was pleased to find it still empty. He drew the blinds, switched on the light, and then sat back on his bunk to calm himself. The second-class shared couchettes could not be locked. If someone on the train was after him he could force his way in. He had to do something.

Pulling all the spare blankets and pillows off other bunks, Graham arranged them on the bottom left bunk to make them look like someone sleeping. He switched off the light, hoisted himself onto the top bunk and slid around into the luggage rack above the door. Making do with a remaining pillow and blanket, he made himself as comfortable as possible in the tight space.

From his elevated position Graham could see through a window along the length of the carriage corridor. He was determined to keep vigil until dawn.

At 2:30 A.M. the train began to slow down for the first stop of the journey. At the stop Graham could hear doors slamming and he strained hard to see anyone getting into his carriage. Few people seemed to have embarked.

Minutes later he noticed a man standing at the end of the corridor. He didn't move for five minutes. Then he walked slowly up to the couchette next to Graham's. The Australian froze. It was too late to run.

The man seemed to stand there for an eternity. After about twenty minutes he took a pace forward. Graham could feel his heart pound as he watched the man move up to his couchette. He desperately wanted something to defend himself with. His hand touched the bronze buckle of his belt. He unbuckled it. He could see the figure standing there, rigidly, a foot away from the door.

Graham tugged at the belt. It was tight within his trouser loops. Because of his awkward position it couldn't come out easily. The man began to slide the door across. It was the tall overcoated figure of the Skull. He trained a gun on what looked like a body on the bottom bunk just as Graham freed his belt completely. The man stepped right into the couchette and pulled back the covering on the bunk. Before he could act on the deception Graham had looped the belt through the buckle to form a large noose. In one swift movement he leaned out from the luggage rack and dropped the noose around the intruder's head and neck, whipping it tight. The Skull fell back against the half-open door and pulled against the force of the belt. His gun fell to the floor. Graham was lurched half out of the luggage rack, but hung onto the belt with all his strength. The Skull jerked his body in every direction as he clawed at the belt. Graham was hauled from the rack. He landed on his feet and still gripped the belt as he slipped behind the Skull and brought a knee up into the base of the man's spine. The man's torso snapped upward, almost knocking Graham over. But it was almost a reflex action, as the Australian had not let up the pressure on the belt.

Thirty seconds later, he felt the Skull go limp as a rag doll. Graham gripped tighter and tighter, until he could feel sweat on his brow and pain in his forearms. He let the body slump to the floor. Contorted and grotesque, it twitched as if reluctant to expire. Graham fell back on the left bunk, his breathing shallow and quick. His whole body was shaking. It must have been five minutes before he began to open and close his hands to flex the strained arm muscles. He got to his feet and caught the smell of the body. He dry-retched as he shut the door, drew the couchette blinds and switched on the light.

"Oh, Christ!" he breathed, as he looked down at the KGB agent. His only movement now was a large red and frothing tongue that gave a few involuntary flicks.

Graham switched off the light. He tried to think calmly. His first rational thought was the storm outside. At least it was unlikely that anyone had heard their struggle. But what should he do now? He switched on the light once more and looked around the couchette. He had to clean it up. The train began to rumble on its way again. Graham pulled the belt away from the man's neck. He started with shock as a trickle of blood bubbled beneath the Adam's apple.

Looking around, he grabbed a towel from his suitcase and applied a crude tourniquet around the neck to stop the flow of blood which had begun to move in little rivulets down to the chest. He struggled to lift the body. With some effort, he propped it on the ladder to the top bunk, and then maneuvered it up so that the torso lay on the bunk and the legs dangled over the side.

He tried the window. Rain swept in as he opened it a maximum of two feet. He pushed the legs so that the feet stuck out. Keeping his shoulders under the man's body, he gradually slid it out of the window. It fell like a sack of potatoes. Graham threw the gun and the towel after it, then took his gear to the washroom three doors away. He washed himself and cleaned his belt, on which tiny spots of blood had congealed.

Graham returned to his couchette exhausted and still sweating. He resumed his uncomfortable vigil from the luggage rack.

Outside the storm had subsided. The steady beat of the wheels could be heard for the first time on the journey as the train sped on its way.

Just before dawn Graham was disturbed again, but this time it was the porter returning passports for the coming routine inspection at the German–Belgian border.

"Did your friend see you?" the porter asked as he handed the Australian his passport. Graham was shocked.

"No," he said, almost too quickly, as he tried to act surprised. The porter shrugged and left.

At the border an old Belgian couple joined his couchette for the journey to France. Graham sat quietly on a top bunk as daylight broke and worried through every possibility. How long before the body on the track was discovered? The porter must have been asked where Graham's couchette was. . . . Would that Russian still be after him?

At Paris's Gare du Nord he taxied straight to Charles de Gaulle airport and waited two hours for a standby flight to London, arriving at Heathrow midafternoon.

Although fatigued, the Australian decided to waste no time in going underground. He rented a furnished apartment with a lock-up garage he knew at Strand-on-the-Green overlooking the Thames, and loaded his Alfa with files, clothes and other effects he would need for an indefinite stay. After informing his kindly old Cockney porter that he would be gone for some time, he drove to the apartment, which was in a quiet suburban area.

It would be a strange new life. For how long, Graham had no idea. But for the moment he was on the run.

3

Brogan Senior punched a button on the control panel in the war room at Lasercomp's Black Flats New York HQ. Seated at a semicircular conference table, he, Brogan Junior, Huntsman and Strasburg watched as Graham's article on computer smuggling appeared on the screen at the back of the room—a clinically functional miniature of the U.S. Defense Department's auditorium for waging war.

"**Soviets smuggle in Western Computers.** By a special correspondent." The 1,200-word article said the Soviet Union was smuggling in advanced strategic computers in violation of strict American and NATO regulations. Without drawing a direct link, it discussed the activities of IOSWOP and made reference to the preponderance of Soviet scientists at the palace. The article went on to discuss the kind of computers the Soviets might require from the West, without direct reference to any manufacturer. However, it did mention the major computer corporations selling nonstrategic machines to the Soviet Union.

"As you can see," Huntsman said, "we are listed along with six others."

Brogan punched another button.

Next up on the screen appeared a head-and-shoulders shot of Graham.

Huntsman gave a scant synopsis on him gained in the last few hours from Australia, England and Austria.

As the lights went up, Strasburg frowned. "You say this guy was once a computer industry writer," he said. "Is that how he has gotten so much information?"

"Partly," Huntsman said. "We believe he is following up

6 0

the investigation of another journalist who was apparently very interested in our Soviet operations. She tried to contact Donald Gordon in Paris."

"Let's call Cheznoir in on this," Brogan Senior said. "He's standing by."

He pressed a button on a television channel selector and the head and shoulders of Jean Marie Cheznoir, Lasercomp's director for Europe and Asia, came on a large set below the screen. He was Lasercomp's senior executive in Soviet marketing.

"Jean," Brogan said, turning to the set, "I thought you'd like to be in on our discussion about this article from Vienna."

Cheznoir's large gray-green eyes, which had that bloodshot, continually-dipped-in-whisky look, flashed concern. "*Merci.* The situation is serious from our point of view. My information is that our Soviet clients have decided to act alone on this."

"You gave them the go-ahead?" Brogan asked angrily.

"No. I 'ad no choice in the matter!" Cheznoir said, gesticulating freely. "They consider it very serious."

"It could have been even worse! If they go around . . . doing crazy things without asking us if it's okay. What's the current status?"

"They are trying to contact the journalist. He may have left Vienna." The discussion had honed an edge of tension around the table. Everyone sensed the Old Man was just managing to control his temper. "Okay, Jean. Just get this message to our Soviet buyers," he said, pointing aggressively at the screen; "they don't make any moves—none at all—without consulting us. Otherwise, no computers. None! We call the shots, and they better believe it!"

Cheznoir blanched noticeably at this outburst. "I'll tell them . . . but, er, if Graham manages to avoid them . . . and he has more bombs for us . . . what do we do?"

"We shall contact him," the Old Man said less vehemently, "and if he does not cooperate . . . then . . ." He hesitated. Everything said in the room was recorded for later minutes dictation by secretaries. They were speaking about murder. There could be no direct reference to it. "Uh, we would look a little further on down the road, as we've done before. Just don't worry about it. No one will be allowed to obstruct our plans."

"And Dr. Gordon?" Cheznoir asked.

"Gordon is a slightly different problem. He had an agreement with us not to mention anything about our plans. It has stood since the day he left Lasercomp. He seems to be violating that agreement. We shall speak to him soon."

"Jean, how is your press reacting to the article?" Brogan Junior asked, deflecting the topic slightly.

"Ah!" The Frenchman gesticulated. "We are under great pressure. We would like to put out a statement on our official position on selling to the Soviet Union."

"Okay." Brogan Junior nodded approvingly. "Go ahead, but say nothing except that we have no immediate plans for expansion of markets in the Soviet Union or any other communist country. Get in something about us complying with COCOM,* the American National Security Council and the American State Department."

"Thank you," Cheznoir said. "I'll do it today."

"Right," the Old Man said. "And get back to us soon."

Cheznoir's image faded, and Brogan Junior tapped out a numerical code on the keyboard of his control panel. It called up the latest report on the PPP.

PPP: PROGRAM FOR A POTENTIAL PRESIDENT. 1009, FACTOR 31, DEFEAT OF INCUMBENT. SUGGESTION 1.

INCREASE DEFAMATION ACTIVITIES BY AUGUST 11. MAIN REASON: POPULARITY AT YEAR HIGH. METHOD: INFORMATION TO ALL MEDIA, AND SOVIET GOVERNMENT. MAIN AREA OF INCUMBENT'S VULNERABILITY: SOVIET FOREIGN POLICY.

"What do you think, Alan?" Brogan Junior asked.

Huntsman took a deep breath. "We have a good chance coming up soon. All the networks want to hold a debate between MacGregor and Mineva on one team, and Rickard and the Vice President on the other. We may be able to get some embarrassing questions thrown at Rickard."

"Fine," the Old Man said. "I want a list of similar suggestions between now and the eleventh. We must really turn the screws on Rickard from now on."

Huntsman first decided to carry out Brogan Senior's instructions where it would have the best effect, and that happened to be with the Federal Broadcasting System's Douglas Philpott, America's top-rated television commentator.

Huntsman had once been his mentor at FBS and had been

---

*Coordinating Committee Machinery of the NATO Alliance.

influential in boosting Philpott's career ever since he had moved from a Texas radio station to the big time as a news reporter at FBS. Huntsman was then the network's top producer/director and a friend of a Texas oil magnate who had been a patron of Philpott's since his days as a star football player at Texas University. Hillier had employed the young Philpott at one of his radio stations.

Because of his debt of gratitude to Huntsman, Philpott never hesitated in giving Lasercomp publicity. Lasercomp's computers could always be used for political telecasts or sporting events. Occasionally there would be a TV commercial where his male-model looks and smooth commentary would be used to extol the "many fine virtues" of the corporation and its machines in research into cancer, education or pollution. All seemingly harmless, worthwhile stuff which never interfered with his political commentaries, but for which he received substantial payments. In the last two years they became fatter and more frequent. Philpott had become very much under the corporation's thumb.

Huntsman knew exactly where he would find him any morning—in the basement gymnasium of FBS's Washington studios. The blond Philpott, with his straight-arrow, all-American-boy good looks, spent a lot of his leisure hours pounding away at the weights, chasing away the devils of paunchy middle age from his six-foot-two-inch frame. Apart from the vanity, he firmly believed that his ratings were dependent on his looking as trim as possible.

Huntsman wanted to speak to him about the big Rickard versus MacGregor TV debate. For the first fifteen minutes they chatted about the good old days when they had worked together, until Huntsman broached the subject of the debate.

"So it has leaked already," Philpott said nonchalantly, as he picked up two heavy dumbbells and began biceps curls in front of a wall mirror.

"Yeah. It's around town. I hear you are chairing it."

"Right," Philpott said, as he grimaced his way through the exercise.

Then he lay on his back on an inclined bench and rested before pushing weights vertically.

Huntsman waited until he had finished this before he said, "We hope you are going to make it tough on Rickard."

Philpott stopped preening in front of a mirror, and turned

6 3

to Huntsman. "That will be pretty difficult, Alan. There will be three interviewers, and I'm only chairing the goddamn debate."

Huntsman moved close to him and looked around at others training nearby. They were out of earshot.

"You know what I mean, Doug," he said softly.

"Yes," Philpott said sullenly.

"Good," Huntsman said with a grin. "I'm going to have a sauna. I'll be in touch."

Philpott dumped a barbell down hard and moved across to a pile of boxing gloves. He pulled a tight-fitting pair on and started a two-fisted attack on a heavy punching bag suspended from the middle of the ceiling. Sweat flew everywhere as he furiously belted the bag so that it stayed at forty-five degrees under the weight of his onslaught.

On his mind was the sudden realization that he was not really his own man any more. Philpott belonged to Lasercomp, not only because he was on its payroll, but because of a letter, a few scribbled pages from FBS President Cary Bilby to him. It had fallen into Huntsman's hands and Philpott knew that if it ever resurfaced it would destroy both his and Bilby's careers.

It was a love letter.

Fear kept Graham in his hotel hideout for the first two days back in London. His mind continually ran feverishly over the possible retaliatory actions of the KGB, who he was convinced would attempt to track him down.

He managed only three or four hours' fitful sleep a night as he repeatedly woke in a cold sweat after having a vivid nightmare of the struggle with the Skull on the train. The dual horror of the nearness to his own death and the fact that he had taken another human life tormented him.

To preserve his sanity, the Australian forced himself to venture out of the apartment on the third day. He drove to a nearby shopping center, bought papers and a stock of food to last himself several weeks. He found himself perpetually checking the rear-view mirror and watching the faces of people driving past.

The outing turned out to have a settling effect, and later in the day he began to think rationally for the first time since his narrow escape.

After weighing up the options carefully he decided to tell

absolutely no one about the train murder. If, as he thought, the man on the train had been a KGB agent, it would hardly be announced in the daily news. There would be little logic in announcing his culpability for the moment, or perhaps at any time. Murder or not, he was sure to be hunted.

Graham could only adjust as well as possible to his situation.

As the days drifted by and nothing happened, his confidence slowly returned and he began to think that the only way out of his cornered position was to cautiously attempt to go on with the investigation in the hope that he could expose something that would move the heat off him and on to his adversaries. It was a slim hope, but the only one left.

The Australian decided to focus his investigation on any connection with the smuggling in England. He first turned his attention to a small, London-based company, Computer Increments, of Upper St. Martin's Lane. Jane had noted that it had been blacklisted by companies with which it once did business. She suspected this was because it might be somehow mixed up in the smuggling.

Graham met Sir Alfred at his Cambridgeshire estate ten days after escaping from Vienna. The old publisher liked to spend his weekends there, usually alone, and the Australian thought the isolated, large two-story mansion was safe enough for a visit late one night. He hired a car under an assumed name and drove there, being careful to take an obscure route along back country roads.

Over a port in the huge drawing room, Graham outlined his findings in Vienna without mentioning the murder on the train. He explained his being in hiding by saying the investigation was definitely extremely dangerous, especially since the Russian gentleman and his two friends had asked for him at his hotel in Vienna.

This greatly worried Sir Alfred. But he could see from the Australian's determination that there would be no stopping him. He resigned himself to assisting him.

"Where do you go from here?" he asked.

"I've found a possible way into Computer Increments," Graham said, "but I'll need your help."

"Which is?"

"I'm going to pretend I'm from a London paper interviewing secretaries for a Secretary of the Year award. This is given each year to secretaries from small to large companies."

"I can fix that. But be discreet and careful," Sir Alfred said. He paused to light a cigar. "Tell me, why a secretary?"

"How much does your secretary know about you, your work and your private life?"

"Too much." Sir Alfred laughed ruefully.

"It's a long shot," Graham said, lighting a cigarette, "but it's worth a try."

George Revel was still reeling from the events of the past week as he sat back and loosened his tie aboard a Brussels-bound 747 from Washington. Time to have a vodka martini and read the newspapers' flattering accounts of the Justice Department's comeback in the legal wrangle with Lasercomp. Six days earlier he had received a phone call from Secretary of State Edward Grove, who wanted to arrange a rendezvous at the U.S. attorney general's New York office.

Grove outlined to him President Rickard's team—called PICS, for Probe Into Computer Smuggling—set up to examine the flow of computers into the U.S.S.R. His role would be to head corporate investigations, especially in Europe. He would file a report on the accounts and business activities of American corporations which might be involved in the smuggling of computers into communist countries.

Revel was given twenty-four hours to think it over. From his point of view, the timing was perfect, because the Justice Department versus Lasercomp battle was over. There was, of course, always the problem of behind-the-scenes maneuvering by Lasercomp to delay the judge's decision and influence his judgment in some way. This had happened several times. Yet this might not be a major problem. Revel's subordinates could handle most things, and if any emergency arose, he could go back to the case.

Revel was excited by the PICS assignment. Anything to do with curtailing the illegal power of Lasercomp interested him greatly. He accepted the appointment, and was ordered to appear in Washington three days later to meet the rest of the PICS team, and to be briefed on his assignment.

At this meeting he learned of his official cover for his inves-

tigation. European Economic Community government prose-
cutors, who wanted to put more stringent legal controls on
multinationals, had issued a long-standing invitation to U.S. Justice Department officials and lawers to come and help them.
George Revel would accept the invitation and visit Brussels, Paris,
Stuttgart, Milan and London, and would have a couple of days'
"rest" in Vienna. In all these places except Vienna he would have
special EEC authority to examine the accounts and files of any
multinational.

Brussels would be his first call. It was to be fairly routine
with some publicity given to his visit, to promote the idea that a
highly esteemed U.S. Justice Department official had come to help
EEC in their legal fight against the big multinational corporations.

Revel would be in London in less than two weeks. There,
among other things, he hoped to arrange a meeting with the journalist who had written an article on computer smuggling.

"Oh, and there was a call from a Mr. Huntsman of Lasercomp," the private secretary to Sir Alfred said, sending a chill
through Graham as he made his daily call to Ryder Publications.

He had arranged for an answering service to pass all calls to
his apartment on to Ryder. "He's staying at the Savoy. He wants
you to contact him."

"A Lasercomp reaction!" Graham thought nervously, as he
strode away from the telephone booth near Kew Bridge, a few
hundred yards from his apartment. His first feelings were to avoid
any contact with the corporation, the possible enemy. Then he
had a second thought. Why not meet this Huntsman and at least
find out what the corporation wanted? Hadn't they got in touch
with Jane? Suddenly he remembered. A man by the same name
had met her a few weeks after she had begun the investigation. He
had wanted to buy her off. An attempt at a subtle bribe. Big money
for a PR book about Lasercomp. She had refused . . .

Graham turned and walked back to the telephone booth. He
looked up the Savoy's number, called the hotel, and asked for
Huntsman.

"Yes?" a rasping voice said.

"Ed Graham here."

"Ed Graham," the voice repeated, implying familiarity.
"I'm on a flying visit to London. Name's Alan Huntsman, Vice-

President, Communications, at Lasercomp HQ, New York. Really would love to meet you . . ."

"I'm very busy at the moment . . ."

"I have a little proposition. I think you might like it . . . could we meet for lunch or dinner, maybe?"

"What's the proposition?"

"It's a little difficult to explain over the phone. How about meeting me at the Savoy for dinner? I've only got a couple of days in London. . . ."

Graham shoved another coin in the box. "Tonight is about the only—"

"Fine by me. See you at, say, nine, hotel lobby . . ."

"Okay, Mr. Huntsman."

The Australian walked slowly away from the telephone, this time deep in thought. A vague tactic was beginning to form in the back of his mind. He would keep the appointment. There would be no way anyone could trace him if he arrived by taxi. The only trouble was leaving the hotel. . . .

Graham arrived at the Savoy three hours earlier than the appointment time and familiarized himself with the hotel and its surroundings. It took him only twenty minutes to find an exit which would allow him to slip away unnoticed. It went through the hotel kitchen on the ground floor. This led to a deserted back alley and apartments which ran down to the Thames embankment. He had only one seven-foot-high wall to scale into the apartment block nearest the hotel.

Huntsman's brief on his trip to London was simple. Locate Graham, make an offer and return to New York with the response. To achieve this the chunky, ruddy-faced PR man decided on a familiar drinks-softening-up-and-lavish-meal-routine in order to evaluate the Australian.

After a few drinks in the hotel bar and another hour in the dining room Huntsman found it was not quite working out the way it usually did. He was doing most of the talking about himself and the corporation.

He tried money talk. It was tough going. He learned that the Australian was never short of work. A couple of major assignments he had recently written had brought him in some "good" money. That was all the PR man was told. Neither would Graham be drawn when Huntsman turned the conversation to his interest in the computer industry. Toward the end of their dinner he even found himself on the defensive and trying hard not to show it, as Graham began to ask questions about Lasercomp's court battle with the U.S. Government.

Huntsman managed to stave off queries by inviting Graham to his room for a nightcap and a look at the direct telecast from Washington of the debate between Rickard and Cosgrove, and MacGregor and Mineva. The show began at seven Washington time, midnight in London. When he switched on the set, Douglas Philpott was introducing the two teams and the three interviewers. Huntsman fixed his guest a very large cognac and an even bigger one for himself and they both sank back into red velvet chairs facing the television.

Huntsman had taken off his coat to reveal a hefty paunch. Loosening his necktie, he said casually, "I believe you're writing a book."

Graham nodded.

"How far have you gotten?" Huntsman wheezed. His asthma was playing up.

"I'm well into the research."

"It's about the computer industry?"

"Yes. But predominantly about Lasercomp."

Huntsman kept his eyes on the debate, which had begun in earnest. This guy, he thought, would pull no punches. He geared himself for some blunt responses.

"Have you a publisher?" he wheezed.

"Yes."

"Who?"

"Ryder."

"We could help you in the U.S."

"Ryder will handle it okay," Graham said. He paused to look at the debate, then turned to Huntsman. "You didn't look me up to foster my publishing interests. What's on your mind?"

Huntsman's expression tightened. "We are concerned that you get the right information," he said, having to squeeze out the words. His asthma always gave him hell when he was under pressure.

"What do you mean?"

"Sometimes writers can be misinformed," Huntsman said,

6 9

swirling his brandy. He added hesitantly, "We would like to have a look . . ."

Graham shook his head. "No way," he said adamantly, and focused on the debate. Rickard was making a point forcefully.

The debate almost got out of hand as Ronald MacGregor, his features knit in concentration, thrashed a reply back at the President and the two running mates joined in. Douglas Philpott adroitly called for a commercial break while the verbal punches flew.

Huntsman stood up and poured himself more brandy. "You're a good journalist, Mr. Graham," he said, trying hard not to sound condescending. "You're obviously interested in Lasercomp's internal affairs." He sat down and added pompously, "We understand that. We are damned big and successful." Taking a sip of his drink, Huntsman added, "I want to put a little proposition to you."

"Fire away," Graham said casually.

"We are looking for a top-line writer to put a big story on Lasercomp together."

So that was it, Graham thought. They were going to try to buy him off, the same thing attempted with Jane Ryder.

"PR?" he asked.

"Not exactly. Would you be interested?"

Graham shrugged. "Keep talking."

"We'd give you every assistance. And you would be paid well."

"How much?"

"Two hundred and fifty thousand," Huntsman replied, without batting an eye. "Travel and expenses on top."

Graham was amazed at the figure. They must really be worried about his investigation.

"With all Lasercomp files open to me?" he asked.

"Those that are relevant."

"No one would interfere with what I wrote?"

"We would have to have a look, of course, for the sake of accuracy."

Graham appeared to be contemplating the offer. He had to stall for time.

The debate was a verbal free-for-all once more. Mineva seemed to have lost his cool. So had the Vice-President Adrian Cosgrove.

After Douglas Philpott had reined them in, Graham looked at his watch.

"I'll give your offer some thought," he said. "It's very tempting. I'll get back to you soon." He stood up. "I have an early start tomorrow. Thanks for the evening."

Huntsman got up from his chair to shake hands. "Have you an after-hours number I can catch you on?" the PR man said as he opened the door for Graham.

"Unfortunately not," the Australian replied apologetically. "But you can always leave a message with Ryder Publications."

"When do you think you can give us an answer?"

"I'll ring you within a week," the Australian said, backing down the corridor. "Good night, Mr. Huntsman."

Graham moved to the elevator and pressed the call button. He waited five seconds or so and then made for the stairs. When he reached the ground floor he hurried to the kitchen and passed four of the staff who were cleaning up dishes.

They looked surprised as he ran out of the back door and into the alley.

The Australian slowed to a walk, went round a corner and along a straight stretch of about thirty yards. There was practically no light, but he remembered that if he kept about two yards from the right wall he would not bump into anything. There was a loud clatter of a trash can lid near the end of the alley. Graham stopped and listened. Above the pounding of his heart he could hear the sound of scurrying feet. Small animal feet. Then the reassuring howl of a cat. Graham walked on, slowly this time, until he could make out the wall in front of him that led to a block of flats.

He stood there listening for about thirty seconds and then gripped the top of it.

Hoisting himself to the top he heard something behind him. He looked back along the alley. In the light thrown from the kitchen he could see the figures of two men. They moved toward him. Graham jumped to the ground and sprinted round the back of the building and down a winding narrow street to the Thames embankment and the underground.

He didn't bother to buy a ticket but hurried through and down three flights of stairs. He had to wait three minutes for the next train. No one else came onto the platform. Once on the train, he felt safe.

On a tortuous route underneath the streets of London on the last trains of the night that took him near his hotel, the Australian wondered if the two figures in the alley intended harm, or if they were simply a tail. Maybe they had just been the kitchen staff. But why had they not called out? And why had they moved after him? He concluded they must have been following him.

That would have to be the last time he could come into the open and take such a risk.

Graham was haunted by the specter of the shadowy figures in the alley all through the night. He awoke to the sun streaming through an open window on his second-story bedroom and lay on his bed looking at the fine view along the Thames and Strand-on-the-Green, with its quaint terrace houses fronting the river.

A cup of steaming black percolated coffee and the peace—interrupted only by a small boat which chugged slowly toward Kew Bridge—helped Graham sort his thoughts since last night's meeting with Huntsman.

Lasercomp had pushed in front of him a very large carrot, and maybe the men in the alley had been the stick, he thought, running his hand over his bristly chin. Well, he would play the donkey . . .

At 8:30 A.M. he pulled on a tracksuit, jogged to the telephone booth at Kew Bridge and rang Huntsman.

"I've thought about your offer," Graham said evenly. "I'd like to work for you."

"That's fantastic," Huntsman wheezed with genuine pleasure. "But you'll be working *with* us, Ed, not for us . . . I have a contract. . . ."

"I'll be in the States in about two weeks to wrap up my presidential assignment."

"You're going to stop, er . . . writing your book on computers too?"

"Yes. I'll be in touch when I arrive in New York."

"Great, Ed. I'll have a contract ready. See you then. Take care . . ."

"Yeah, you too," Graham said, and replaced the receiver.

He imagined the shifty-eyed Huntsman shuffling his way to the nearest telex to inform HQ: "Carrot and stick successful. Stop. Donkey works for us. Stop. Mission accomplished. Stop. Return soonest." Within three weeks someone would ask about the donkey. Telephone calls would be made to Ryder Publications. The Australian figured he had twenty days at the most before the corporation started hunting for him.

There was not a day to waste. Later that morning he rang Computer Increments.

"Is that the managing director's secretary? My name is Walker. I'm from the *Evening Standard*."

"Oh, yes. A representative rang yesterday about the Secretary of the Year Competition," the girl said with a soft French accent, "but I really don't think—"

"I would like a quick interview with you," Graham broke in. "It will only take about twenty minutes of your time."

"I don't think my boss would like the publicity."

"That only comes if you win the award for this week. I have to interview several girls. If you do win, then you can ask him if it's okay. We won't publish if he doesn't agree."

"I don't know . . ."

"Don't forget Secretary of the Week is worth fifty pounds. Secretary of the Year, five hundred."

"Why have you chosen me?"

"Someone from your company has recommended you."

The girl laughed. "That's a surprise. Who?"

"We are sworn to secrecy," Graham said cheerfully. "Can we meet for a drink after work?"

"I suppose there is no harm in that. What was your name again?"

Françoise le Gras was not classically attractive. Her bust was small for her height and her legs could have been a shade slimmer. On the plus side were her long black hair, almond-shaped hazel eyes, which gave her a slightly Oriental appearance, generous lips, and well-rounded curves. Most importantly, she had an unmistakably sensual presence which radiated a rare warmth. It touched Graham the instant they met at a West End bar for drinks.

Fortunately for him, there was a quick and easy rapport between them. The drink after work extended to a two-hour discussion and then dinner. The Australian turned on the charm and soon had Françoise talking.

She had a French father and English mother and had lived most of her life in Paris. The past year she had lived in London, partly for a change and partly to escape the memory of a broken affair.

Her job with Computer Increments would run out in six months, after which she intended to work as a stewardess for British Airways.

After dinner and a little dancing, it looked as if the wine and the atmosphere might open Françoise up.

"Really," she giggled, "you have the wrong girl. I would never want to be involved in any award for this company."

"Why not?"

"Well," she said, with a typical French pout of indifference, "I don't like my boss . . ." She broke off and looked quizzically at Graham for a few moments. "You journalists are nosy, aren't you?"

Graham fondled his nose. "There's no need to get personal," he said, with a look of mock hurt.

Françoise hesitated, not sure whether she had used the colloquialism correctly. Then she laughed, reached across the dining table and touched Graham's arm affectionately. "You know what I mean."

The Australian laughed. He decided not to push any further tonight. Pleased that he had at least made contact, he reflected on that touch on the arm. It went further than skin deep. Graham knew it would be some time before he would allow himself another emotional involvement. Thoughts of Jane Ryder were too near. Yet his physical needs were strong and this was the first chance in some time for that familiar stirring in his blood.

Graham was hoping for a successful encounter, if he used his experience and tact wisely.

Four nights later on their third date, the Australian was in a dilemma. Over dinner at a quiet little French restaurant it was clear that the timing was right for trying to bed her and he wondered whether he should tell her the truth before or after.

Preferring to gain her confidence completely, he had not asked her anything more about the company, but she had become curious about his work and his life. The deceit was beginning to make him feel uncomfortable. And despite trying to keep an objective head about his reason for meeting her, the Australian had become increasingly attracted to her warm, demure charm.

As Françoise was driving him back to his apartment, she stole a glance at Graham. "That is a long way back to Strand-on-the-Green. Are you sure you know the way?"

"I know the way," Graham said, running his hand across the back of her shoulders and neck. "Just keep your eyes on the road."

Back in his room he switched on a bedside lamp and some late-night radio music. He opened the balcony to a warm, clear, early autumn night. While she looked out over the still Thames, he poured them both a cognac.

Walking over to Françoise he silently admired her curves, accentuated by tight-fitting slacks and knee-length boots. His desire had reached a tantalizing peak.

He handed her the drink and she caressed the bottom of the glass with her fine long-fingered hands. He moved close and kissed her. She draped one thin arm around his neck and responded willingly.

Graham pulled away gently, cleared his throat and sipped his drink. He looked into her eyes.

"Look, ah, there are a few things," he began with a sigh, looking away from her and then back. "I want to make love to you now very much. . . ."

"So do I." She smiled widely. "Can we finish our drinks?"

He nodded, threw his head back and laughed.

"Is there a problem?" she asked, frowning slightly.

"Yes, well, no . . . you see . . . I've not told you everything. The truth, I mean really . . ."

Françoise pulled away and put her drink down. She moved to her handbag on the bed and took some Gauloises filters from it. She lit one and gave the Australian one.

"I am not so naïve," she said softly. "This is not your home. You were worried about being followed here. You are probably married with children. Your name is not Ed Walker . . ."

"That's not what I mean . . . how did you know my name wasn't Walker?"

"You've been careful not to let me see you sign your name on the three occasions we've been at a restaurant . . ."

"You have it wrong."

"Oh?" she said inquisitively. The romance seemed to have faded.

"Partly wrong. I have no wife or children. Not even a girl friend. My name is Graham." He looked hard at her. "I am a journalist, but I don't make a living out of interviewing secretaries. I have an assignment, part of which is investigating the company you work for . . . ."

"About what?"

"Smuggling."

Françoise's expression was a mixture of surprise and disdain.

"So this . . ." she said, moving to the balcony, "and the dating—all a softening-up process?"

"No," Graham said, annoyed with himself. "I really do want . . . ."

She went to pick up her handbag. Graham held her gently. "Don't run off. Stay. Have another drink. Talk it out . . . ."

Françoise looked annoyed but said nothing.

"Don't you see? Why would I tell you all this at this moment?"

Françoise stood staring at him for several seconds. "You say your name is Graham," she said, puzzled.

The Australian nodded.

"Now I remember." Her expression opened. "Your photo is filed in our office." She sat on the bed. "You're Edwin Graham. You wrote that article about smuggling in Vienna."

"Correct."

"Yes," she said reflectively, "it caused quite a stir. You're not very popular with my boss."

Graham sat next to her. "Maybe you believe me now . . . ."

"I am not sure . . . perhaps you should tell me exactly what you are doing."

"And then you'll give me information?"

"I don't know until I hear your story."

Graham's eyes searched her expression. "But if you run to your boss . . . ."

She smiled triumphantly. "I suppose you would say the boots are on the other legs."

"The boot is on the other foot . . . ."

She laughed. "Pardon."

"Yes. You're right. I must trust you. . . ."

Graham was apprehensive. It was difficult to gauge her intentions. He would be gambling on her attraction to him.

"Okay," he said slowly, as he leaned forward to kiss her, "I'll tell you all in the morning. . . ."

"Oh, no, no, no, no, no," she said, pushing him gently away. "Now . . ."

Graham sighed and leaned back on the bed. He lit another cigarette and looked at her.

"You win . . ."

For the next twenty minutes he carefully outlined the salient points of the investigation without telling her anything that her company or Lasercomp would not already know he knew. Françoise sat, fascinated, occasionally asking him a question. Graham felt by her response that she was with him. But he was not sure.

At the end he said, "Now, can you tell me anything?"

She smiled mysteriously. "Maybe in the morning . . ."

They both laughed. Graham moved close and kissed her. Françoise slowly responded.

She looked at him with mock circumspection as they began to undress.

"You're really a spy, aren't you?"

"No. I am a journalist."

"I've never made love to a spy . . . nor someone with such a hairy chest . . ."

They pulled back the bedclothes and lay beside each other, touching and kissing.

"Have you been in love?" Françoise asked.

"Yes, once."

"Tell me about her."

"She was the one . . . the one that was killed . . . I just told you about . . ."

"Oh, I am sorry. Tell me about your first . . ."

"I'm more interested in the next . . ."

First light squeezed through the half-open curtains and fell across Graham and Françoise.

Half an hour ago they had made love for the fourth time so vigorously that the bed was now a good foot clear of the wall it had been hard up against before they started.

Her hand rested on his thickly matted chest which rose and fell to the gentle tempo of a light snore. She had time to reflect as she snuggled close to him.

At first she had been stunned by the fact that he had met her under false pretenses. But his eventual honesty and protestations during the night that his affections for her were genuine overcame her initial misgivings. Françoise was a great believer in the theory that a person could not deceive another about their feelings in bed. Certainly not repeatedly. She was also influenced by his telling her about his love and lingering emotion for Jane Ryder. That challenged her and warned her to be patient if the relationship was to develop. Françoise wanted to believe in him. He attracted her greatly.

When Graham awoke, he wandered into the kitchen, put on coffee and returned a few minutes later with two cups. She sat up in the bed and admired the magnificent morning view. Turning to him she said, "I want to help you. But you must promise not to involve me."

Graham sipped his coffee. "You have my word. Don't worry."

"Do you have a robe?"

The Australian took one from a clothes closet. She put it on and wandered out to the balcony. He followed her.

"Do you always come out here like that?" She laughed.

"Only the birds can see me," he said, opening his arms to the trees. "I like to give them something to chirp at."

"Exhibitionist."

"You look at birds, don't you? They never wear clothes . . ." She went to kick him. Seconds later her expression changed as she said, "Apart from anything else, I want to give you information because Computer Increments' operations are, I think, crooked."

"In what way?"

"They are heavily involved in some sort of smuggling chain—a link in a chain of middlemen moving computers into the Soviet Union."

"Can you get me any written evidence of this?"

"Anything to do with contraband is under lock and key. Difficult to get hold of. Sometimes I see material. But everyone there is very careful and secretive. Only occasionally there is a slip-up."

"For instance?"

"A Russian from the Soviet trade mission here in London arrives unannounced on the doorstep every so often. It causes much embarrassment. He usually rings the office from a phone booth."

"Name?"

"It starts with Z. I can easily find it for you."

"Please."

Graham walked into the bedroom, pulled a pair of jeans from a rack in a closet and hauled them on. "Your news is giving me goose pimples. Is there a file on this Russian?"

"Yes. It's hardly seen by anyone except my boss. He never lets anyone near it."

"You mentioned links. What other companies is Computer Increments involved with?"

"Several."

"The big ones . . ."

"The biggest is Lasercomp. The head of its Soviet marketing operations, a Frenchman I hate to say, named Cheznoir, and a German named Herman Znorel, met my boss a few weeks ago just after the Russian visited the office for the last time."

"This is the sort of information I want. Cheznoir and Znorel, fantastic!"

"The whole office was jumping. My boss, a typically cool upper-class type of Englishman, was extremely nervous. They were both very important to him."

"Any idea what the meeting was about?"

"Again, it was all kept very quiet. But my boss planned to visit the Soviet Union. I had to go to the Soviet Embassy for a visa. An itinerary was mapped out."

"When is he going?"

"He's not. He has been very ill with a serious blood virus for the last week. It looks as if it's off indefinitely. He has dictated letters of apology over the phone from the hospital."

"To whom?"

"Znorel in Stuttgart and Znorel's Soviet director in Moscow."

"Hmmm. That's bad luck. He might have brought back

some important information you could have been on the lookout for. . . ."

"Could I have some more coffee?"

Graham hastened to oblige. "Anything, dear lady, anything . . ."

He returned with the percolator, and a tape recorder. Switching the tape on, he said, "I think we better get all this down. . . . What's your boss's name?"

"Harold Clarence Radford. . . ."

Brogan Senior was annoyed at the slow progress being made in the efforts to smear Rickard. On the morning of Sunday, September 7, the Old Man stepped off his private jet after a brief visit to the Soviet Union and was immediately chauffeur-driven straight to Hitchcock Presbyterian Church in Scarsdale, New York. There he knew he would find Huntsman and most of Lasercomp's senior management. They were all aware of the Brogans' strong family religious tradition going back long before his grandfather, John Clifford Brogan, and his family of five had been driven by poverty from Scotland to Ireland and finally to the U.S. in 1840.

In the eighty-five-minute drive the Old Man briefed himself fully on the PPP via a small terminal in the back of the Rolls, and had time to view a cassette replay of the Rickard-MacGregor debate.

Outside the church, after a string of deferential nods from Lasercomp people, Brogan Senior spotted the PR man and pulled him aside.

"I watched the replay of the Rickard-MacGregor interview this morning. It wasn't good enough, Alan."

"To my mind, MacGregor and Mineva acquitted themselves well," Huntsman said defensively.

"No, they did not!" the Old Man said vehemently. "Philpott should have called the shots as chairman. Instead, he let Rickard get right on top! I thought you said Philpott was with us. You spoke to him last week, didn't you?"

"Yes, but, C.B., it was an open debate. He had to handle three interviewers. Rickard is skilled at handling open debates. No one could control him."

"All right. It was difficult for Philpott. But his failure to embarrass Rickard highlights a weakness in our efforts to get him out of office."

The Old Man nodded to an executive making sure he was seen moving into the church. "We must step up our efforts. A lot more has to be done. By tomorrow night you'll have PPP directives involving certain media personnel. You will not have to rely simply on Philpott. You have to go right to the top. To the network presidents. To people such as Cary Bilby."

Huntsman's flesh crawled. The old bastard was going to push all the way.

Brogan sighed. "I don't want you telling me there is no way of getting to him. We've got to have him on our side to crush Rickard." The tone of his voice hinted that he knew there was a way. "Once we have an important network president convinced our cause is right, the TV programming might come out a little differently."

"I know we need the media, but—"

"No buts, man!" the Old Man said, glowering as they moved into the church. "What the hell do you think we hired you for?" he sneered. "Your good looks?" He fumbled for his wallet in an inside coat pocket. "You're supposed to know all the skeletons. Dig them up and earn that goddamn three hundred thousand dollars I pay you!"

The Old Man placed two fifty-dollar bills on a plate and found a seat in a front aisle.

FBS President Cary Bilby did not know how to take what had just been said to him by Huntsman. His former colleague had just attempted to blackmail him over an issue he believed had been buried twenty years ago. It concerned a love letter Bilby had written. The problem was that the recipient happened to be a man, Douglas Philpott. Bilby was bisexual. He had kept his homosexual experience discreet, but the appearance of the golden-haired young Philpott changed all that. For the first time he hadn't cared what others thought.

The TV superstar was ambitious about reaching the top, and prepared to do anything to get there. After a cautious first few months, the two became more adventurous and were seen together at the racetrack, on vacation in Paris and Honolulu, and at private parties. It lasted about a year before the odd rumor began to fly around Washington media circles. Philpott, frightened that it could end rather than enhance his career, was soon involved in a mild flirtation with a Washington female gossip columnist. Bilby had reluctantly agreed to split. But Philpott's callousness in dropping the affair so quickly had hurt him. Bilby wrote several rambling, impassioned letters.

Philpott was enjoying his return to a straight path and after six months threw the gossip columnist out of his apartment and planned to replace her with a film starlet. His face and name were getting any woman he wanted. When he asked the columnist to leave, she produced one of Bilby's epistles that she had taken from Philpott's private files and photocopied.

In desperation, Philpott had turned to Huntsman. With priestlike sobriety and inner relish, he went into action. Through his many connections, he persuaded the girl with a mixture of bribery, cajolery and veiled threat to surrender the letter for a handsome payoff and a better job. At the same time, he warned Cary Bilby to be more discreet and urged him to cover his wavering sexual tracks by getting married.

Bilby took the advice, and within six months was walking down the aisle with an attractive young New York socialite. The incident was forgotten and both Bilby and Philpott believed Huntsman had destroyed the only evidence of the affair. They had seen him burn the letter in question. Now he was revealing he still had written evidence.

"What has that corporation done to you, Alan?" Bilby asked, his fine, sensitive features quivering with emotion.

Huntsman ran a finger round a sticky collar. "Cary, I was hoping to avoid the letter business," he said with an anguished look, "but we really want Rickard out. It's best for the nation."

"I cannot do it," Bilby almost whispered.

Huntsman shook his head. Fumbling in an inside coat pocket, he pulled out a folded paper and tossed it on the desk. Bilby looked at it in disbelief. It was a photostat.

The FBS president's eyes widened as he unfolded it. "You never said you copied it," he said incredulously.

"Well, I did . . . and there is one other."

Bilby lowered his head. The words in his own handwriting leaped up at him. "My Dearest Doug, I have been so lost these last weeks without you. I love you and it hurts so deeply that . . ."

Bilby put the letter down. He buried his face in trembling hands.

Huntsman seemed affected. "I don't really think we are asking that much," he said pleadingly. "All we want is for you to consider a program of ideas over the next seven weeks before the election."

"But my board members are not fools," Bilby protested. "They will sniff any change in our approach."

"Not if you follow our suggestions. Rickard is not so popular. His policies are getting a lot of criticism. MacGregor and Mineva look like a good, sound presidential package. Besides, there may be bonuses, for yourself and the network, when they get into office. What about that West Coast radio license FBS hasn't been able to get?"

Bilby shook his head grimly. "No, Alan, I don't think I can do it."

Huntsman sighed. "Think of your career. When do you retire? Five years, is it? And your wife. How will she feel? And your daughter, Cary. You told me she was just about to be introduced into society. Oh, and your son, a West Point graduate in six months . . ."

Bilby had had enough. He stood up. "Get out of here!" he yelled in a shrill voice.

Huntsman's forehead creased as he stood up and backed toward the door. "Sure, Cary," he said, holding up both his hands as if to calm him, "but remember you have forty-eight hours. We'll be having a word with Philpott. He has a career to think about too."

Huntsman left Bilby to ponder his dilemma. But even in the emotion of the moment, Bilby knew which of the two evil choices he would make.

"Commander Gould wants to meet you," Sir Alfred told Graham when the Australian made his daily call to the publishing house. "I have a feeling it's for more than just a chat."

"Meaning?"

"Apparently you both have broadly the same aims. He has expressed an interest in your cooperating with him ever since I approached him about helping you in Vienna. Incidentally, I have briefed him on Vienna and everything you've told me."

"Thanks, Sir Alfred. The timing may be just right. What

does he want me to do, feed a pelican at a place of his choice?"

"No." Sir Alfred laughed. "I think he'll want you to visit him at his office. . . ."

The prospects of MI-6 "cooperating" set Graham thinking again about the direction the investigation was heading. He had to face the fact that all roads, it seemed, were leading into the Soviet Union. Somehow he had to find out what was going on there. But how?

The Australian lay on his bed for hours staring at the peaceful Thames view or slowly jogging along the water's edge before the how, when and where of a daring plan emerged. He would make every effort to see if he could risk going in himself.

He obviously could not go as Graham. He would have to obtain a false passport and the necessary papers. Perhaps the planned meeting with MI-6 was fortuitous. . . .

Second, and on his mind since Françoise mentioned it, was the aborted visit of her boss to the Soviet Union. She had passed on the details of the itinerary to the Australian. The temptation to take Harold Radford's place was nagging him.

The night before he was to meet MI-6, Françoise and Graham were at his apartment going through some files she had managed to smuggle out of the office for the night, when he asked, "You haven't sent those letters off saying your boss wasn't going to Moscow, I hope."

"No, but I'll have to do it tomorrow or they will be suspicious at the office."

"Right, Do it. Go through the normal procedure. Someone else in the office will check it and sign on his behalf?"

"Yes, Mr. Larsen, the deputy managing director . . ."

"Okay, do that, but make sure you don't send them off."

Françoise nodded. "What are you planning to do?"

The Australian smiled ruefully and stood up from the couch they were sitting on. He walked a few paces and stood near the door.

"I want you to tell me about your boss."

Françoise was puzzled.

"How he walks first . . ."

"But why?"

"Darling, we've been together a week now. Do you trust me?"

"Of course . . ."

"Then just help me. How does he walk? Is he aggressive?" Graham lumbered across the room. "Or lightfooted?" He floated back to the door.

"More like the second one," Françoise said, bemused, "but not quite as light."

"Toes in or out?"

"Out."

"Head up, I suppose, stiff back, very British?"

"Yes, yes, nose in the air, that's right!" She laughed. "You have it, excellent! . . . but please tell me why."

"I'm going to impersonate Radford."

"How?"

"I'll tell you. . . ." He practiced the walk again. "Always like to get the walk right when I'm acting. Helps me feel the character . . . now the voice . . . very upper crust, of course . . ."

"Of course."

"How deep . . . like this?"

"No, deeper."

"Oh, I see, like this, is it? Jolly good show."

"How did you know he said that?"

"I didn't. An educated guess, you might say." Graham returned to the couch. "End of act one."

"You're not planning to go to . . ."

"I'm looking into it."

"Oh, no, you're crazy, I will not let you . . ."

"It's only early days yet. I'll see when I've assembled as much as I can. That's where you can help me even more. I want you to write down everything, I mean everything, about Radford. The type of clothes he wears, his interests, his background, where he went to school . . . and if you can get me a photo . . ."

Late in the evening of Monday, September 8, the Brogans met in the Black Flats war room to discuss intensified PPP strategy with the presidential election drawing closer.

The screen and the television monitors were running through all the important factors of the PPP.

The Old Man had not had a chance to speak privately to his son about his recent visit to Moscow, where he had taken the opportunity to act on the PPP's suggestion that Rickard's Soviet foreign policy should be attacked.

As the relevant item came up, the Old Man broke the silence.

"The KGB bought the whole idea of embarrassing Rickard," he said ebulliently. "I've convinced them that with our man as President, they'll be able to expand. There will be no one to stop the flow of Cheetahs to them."

Brogan Junior had to bow to his father's expertise in handling the Soviets, whether it was KGB chief Andropolov, Premier Brechinov or anyone else in the Kremlin.

"What are they planning to do?"

"Andropolov plans to put pressure on the Politburo to step up the Soviet arms race and forget about previous arms limitation agreements. He says he will personally set up action against dissidents, which is sure to upset Rickard."

"Do you think Andropolov has that much power?"

"Yes, and we've helped him get it. The Soviet administration thinks it's his great influence with us that has kept the Cheetahs rolling in to the Soviet Union. They see what that has begun to do to their own central control from Moscow, and in increasing the nation's firepower."

"What about Brechinov? He was never slow to put rivals in their place."

"True, but he's old, quite ill and out of touch," the Old Man said, shrugging. "He and his supporters don't realize exactly what modern computer technology means to the Kremlin's power."

"And Andropolov and his young cohorts do?"

The Old Man nodded. "I had the feeling they may well have control already. It's only a matter of time before Andropolov is number one."

"So Rickard will soon be feeling the pinch from abroad as well as at home."

"That's the idea. Huntsman assures me we've gotten FBS and Cary Bilby by the balls," he sneered. "Literally."

"We must keep Andropolov informed on Rickard. They must know some of his foreign policies in advance. We'll have to step up our access to classified information."

The Old Man pressed the button to allow the PPP to flow on. "That gives us the all-clear on the PPP's suggestion about eliminating our man's rival." He deftly keyed in number 55 on the panel in front of him. Up on the screen appeared:

FACTOR 55. ELIMINATION OF RIVAL. MUST BE NOT LESS THAN 35 DAYS BEFORE ELECTION.

"What do you think?" the Old Man asked. "Do you want to have another look at the consequences?"

"We've considered them often enough." Brogan Junior shrugged. "As the PPP suggests, it's really only a matter of timing now."

On his arrival at the Whitehall building of Her Majesty's Defence Department at 10:00 A.M. on Tuesday, September 9, Graham was given a thorough search before being escorted by a security guard to the department's third floor, along a maze of corridors. The guard stopped at the commander's office and knocked. On the directive, "Enter," he opened the door for Graham, and left.

"Mr. Graham, please take a seat," Gould said, shaking hands firmly. He sat down at a plain wooden desk pushed against the left wall of the office. On the other wall was a library of books and folders, and a large combination-locked steel file cabinet. Above the desk on the wall were pages of Soviet newspapers, several maps of the Soviet Union pinpointing naval, army and air force bases, and other military data. A notice board had pinned on it several messages on scraps of different toilet paper, apparently from all over the Soviet Union. One in clear handwriting caught Graham's eye. It read: "I picked this up in Tashkent. Much better than the Kiev rubbish I sent you last time which I wouldn't bother wiping my nose with. This stuff made a fairly clean sweep of everything. But I think you'll find it's still a bit like sandpaper, compared with good old Whitehall white. See you. Yours shittily, Steven."

The commander started with some polite talk about his father's long friendship with Sir Alfred. Then he turned to Graham's investigation.

"I don't mind telling you we are vitally interested in your area of investigation," he said, his gray eyes fixing on the Australian. "We and the Americans are most concerned with the recent Soviet military build-up. They're breaking all previous arms agreements. What's more worrying still is the apparent growth in the sophistication of the hardware controlling their military missile forces. We're getting some information out about this. But nothing really definitive."

He turned to the toilet paper with the message from Steven. "You noticed that note," Gould added, now showing the flicker of emotion. "Unfortunately that was the last communication we ever had from him. He's dead. He was one of our best agents gathering intelligence in the same area you are. We know he was tortured for weeks in a mental hospital. He died in Moscow last week. The KGB is paranoid about any intelligence concerning computers leaking to the West."

Graham felt his nerves tingle with fear.

"I was thinking of going there. . . ."

"Sir Alfred didn't tell me."

"I've only just decided to see if it's possible."

"It would be extremely dangerous." Gould paused and added, "Especially since the incident on the train. . . ."

Graham was stunned. He didn't know how to interpret the allusion or how to reply.

"When the Austrian police learned that a man had been strangled and apparently dumped from a Paris-bound train," Gould continued, "they soon found him to be a member of the Soviet Embassy in Vienna. The matter was taken over by Austrian authorities. We were alerted about you. The Austrians are satisfied the matter can rest with us, but the Russians are far from pleased. . . . Of course, we've been protecting you."

Graham looked hard at the commander.

"This doesn't alter my aim to get into the Soviet Union."

"How do you plan to get in?"

"I thought you might be able to help here. I'll need a false passport."

Gould stroked his beard thoughtfully and scrutinized the Australian.

"And once you're in?"

"I have contacts in Kiev and Leningrad and a chance of access to how the computers are used in Moscow. . . ."

"Can you tell me more about your Moscow contact?"

"It's a little rough at the moment. I've found a most helpful contact inside Computer Increments. . . ."

"Ah yes. Sir Alfred told me about that. A bit of luck . . ."

"I'm building up as much knowledge as I can about its operations and the managing director, Radford. He had planned a visit to Moscow until struck by illness two weeks ago. I may just be able to impersonate him."

Gould pulled a pipe and tobacco from a desk drawer, and some matches from his vest pocket.

"The Moscow connection doesn't know he's not coming?"

"No. All communication between London and Moscow is done by letter. Everything was set up for the visit. All Radford had to do was to confirm by letter that he was coming. My contact has stopped the letters saying he wasn't coming. I have dictated letters of confirmation. They're ready for mailing."

The commander filled the pipe and lit it.

"You know, once you're in, you'll have no protection."

"I'm aware of that. . . . Is there any way you could help me?"

"I'll look into it. How long before you would want to go?"

"There's an Intourist tour of Kiev, Leningrad and Moscow which would allow me to impersonate Radford and gather other information. It leaves England from Gatwick a week from Saturday."

"Going as a tourist would be the only way. You would be too conspicuous otherwise. . . ." Gould stood up and moved to a window at the end of the room. He stood with his back to Graham and looked out over dull rustic tiles of the floor below. He watched a pigeon float down and land before he turned and said, "We may be able to help you with false identification but there is so little time. We must find someone whose identity and passport details you could use quickly."

"I've already prepared for it. I have a passport-size photo of an old school friend in Australia, a Dr. Ross Boulter. He is an anthropologist. I have not seen him for more than ten years but we still correspond. He took his family to New Guinea to undergo a massive study there. He's compiling a volume called 'Earliest Man Today.'"

"How much do you know about his work?"

"We still write. I have been interested in his progress. From time to time he sends me voluminous notes on the study."

"Could he be traced?"

"Not in the time frame I'm thinking of. He spends most of his time in primitive regions. It takes three months for a letter to reach him."

"It sounds reasonable. All you would need for a passport would be immigration stamps into and out of New Guinea, and from there to London. . . ."

Graham nodded. Gould's interest sounded hopeful.

"Best if you leave us the photo and details, and all the documentation on Radford. Visa and so on. Could your contact get copies?"

"Possibly."

"See what you can do. I can't make promises right now. But we'll see." Gould moved to a filing cabinet, took a folder from it and handed it to Graham. "You might like to have a look through this to see what you may be up against."

The Australian turned over the folder. It was headed *The KGB Today—Recent Operations and General Tactics.*

When their meeting was over Gould took the elevator to MI-6's operations communications center to send a coded telex to his superior, who was out of the country. It would ask if there was any chance of using Graham.

Since meeting the Australian the commander had a much rounder, deeper perspective of the man. He couldn't remember meeting anyone with more self-possession. There was a simmering self-confidence about him, as if he was always holding something back. Gould put this down to Graham's family background, high intelligence and wide experience. Yet all this had to be seen, perhaps, in another perspective. The Australian had had many years' experience as an actor. In front of a camera performances could be turned on. Graham may have done that for him just now. A performance to get help. Perhaps under the pressure the strain would crack the façade. . . .

The commander thought of Graham's just detectable reaction to the true story of poor dead Steven. But it didn't necessarily put Gould off. On the contrary. It demonstrated that the Australian was no fool. He was aware of what he might be walking into. Only a fool would be oblivious of the dangers.

Yes, caution was one of the man's characteristics, especially apparent, Gould thought, in the methodical planning of his investigation. What was it Sir Alfred had said? He was a brilliant chessplayer with the ability to think many moves ahead. . . . He had a logical mind.

Gould pondered Sir Alfred's remarks about the Australian's lack of discipline. Yet that was under authority. What would count in the Soviet Union was the man's level of *self*-discipline. Graham gave the impression that this was definitely one of his strengths.

What worried the commander most was the publisher's comments on the man's aggressive tendencies. Tendencies that sometimes led him to rush things. Was it a counteraction to his methodical, meticulous planning? Or was it a complement to it—an innate ability to time his dynamism?

Gould put the question out of his mind for the moment. Using Graham now depended on the commander's superior, and whether the agent over there would be in place.

At a casino in the Honfleur seaside resort in Normandy, a dinner-suited, tall, middle-aged man with trim brown hair and short mustache let his chips ride on black 13 for the third successive spin of the roulette wheel. His regular features, marred by a faint but long scar running from below the left earlobe to his neck, remained impassive as he watched the whizzing ball with cold, gray eyes.

Just as the spin neared completion, the man was distracted by a tap on the elbow. It was a young German courier, who an hour earlier had arrived from Stuttgart. They moved away from the table. The middle-aged man had a slight limp, a legacy of a mild dose of polio as a small child.

The two men spoke rapidly in German for a few seconds as a noise went up from the table. The ball had jumped into black 13. The courier slipped the winner an envelope and left.

Collecting his mound of chips and changing them for cash, the middle-aged man moved into an adjoining bar. He sat down on a stool, ordered a beer and opened the envelope. There was a typewritten message in German, which read: "Herr Director, Research done. Script prepared. Interview set up. Ready for shooting. Await your direction. Crew."

He left the casino and drove the hundred miles to a hotel in Le Havre.

The next day he took a train to Paris. He thought about his current year-long assignment which was to culminate soon, and resolved it would be his last. His would be fifty-four next birthday and the money from this contract would net him around two million dollars. His business was murder by contract, and for the Director, business had always been good.

Too frail by the end of the Second World War to fight for Hitler's Germany, he fled to Brazil with his parents. His father, a colonel in the Waffen SS, wanted to sever all evidence of his past. He bullied his son into finding a career. The young man chose photography, but soon found that an early passion for firearms, sparked during his years in the Hitler Youth, had reemerged when he left home and traveled around the turbulent American subcontinent.

Later he drifted into the life of a mercenary soldier and guerrilla, while never completely discarding photography and film. Occasionally it brought him income from capturing action on civil war fronts, and earned him the title Director.

During this time he met an Argentinian Marxist, José Boliva Rodriguez, who was helping to finance revolutionary wars. Rodriguez had not let his ideology stop him from becoming a multimillionaire through big property deals in Brazil, Argentina and Venezuela. Money was a useful weapon to fight capitalism. The Director carried out two lucrative contract hits for him, and made a lasting impression on his teenaged son, Alexandro Emanuel, who admired the German's fearless dedication to fighting, and his great knowledge of arms. The encounter between the Rodriguezes, with their ideological verve, and the Director, who was strictly a mercenary, was disrupted when the Director moved to greener pastures in Africa. There he gained an underworld reputation as an efficient contract killer.

Despite the split, the Director never lost contact with José Rodriguez, who continued to finance revolutions and educate his son. The Director urged the father to give the young Rodriguez a taste of Europe. His son spent the next decade there, a high-spirited and sophisticated period, especially in Paris.

Then the father thought it was time for the real thing. Young Rodriguez was packed off to Patrice Lumumba University in Moscow for four years. Only once did he return to Paris: in 1968 during the weeks of the near-revolution.

The influence of the Director on the young Rodriguez eventually had its decisive impact. The German had worked on two occasions for the KGB in Eastern Europe and he urged his contacts in Moscow to recruit and train the Argentinian student. The Soviet secret police were grateful to the Director. They found Rodriguez excellent material, suitable for exporting Soviet-style revolution. Yet not even they could hold him completely. Soon he went out on his own as a terrorist assassin, heavily subsidized by his father—as long as it was for a Marxist-Leninist cause.

The young Rodriguez again met the Director in London, at a time when the former was losing his ideological zeal, and yearning for the easier life he had experienced in Paris. The Director urged him to take advantage of the several revolutionary causes wanting to use him, and to charge high fees for his services. And he did. The reasons behind his killing assignments soon became confused between ideology and money. He was pleased if they coincided, and this led him into a partnership with the Director. He had moved to France, returning to Africa and going twice to Eastern Europe for a "hit" to maintain a lavish life-style. The two men had a lot in common: the love of arms, the spilling of blood, photography, film, Paris and a life-style fit for a king.

Using the guise of a film crew, the two men began working together. They carried out two successful contracts in Europe and North Africa and decided to use the front once more for an elaborately planned major hit. A very wealthy client was prepared to pay them a small fortune for their efforts.

On arrival at his apartment at 4 rue Brunel in the sleazy Pigalle area of Paris, the Director began to make final preparations for this latest assignment. He hauled a heavy aluminum-padded case from a cupboard, unlocked it and removed an Ariflex 16-mm. B.L. camera. He detached the side to reveal the gate mechanism and unscrewed a metal plate backing the film path. This uncovered a secret chamber in which the barrel and frame of a highly modified Walther P.38, 9-mm. revolver had been cunningly concealed.

The Director, with loving care, removed each gun piece from a false bottom in the metal case, and cleaned them. This included a tripod, scope mount, scope, silencer attachment and other equipment which allowed the gun to be used as a handgun or a high-powered close-range rifle. Once at his destination he would transfer this doubtful contribution to ballistic science in component form to a small Grundig tape recorder, a Pentax camera and the tripod's hollow legs, which all fitted neatly into the Director's metallic briefcase.

Satisfied that everything was in order, he packed the camera weapon away and them thumbed through two sets of forged documents. One, a *carnet*, would allow the Director to move his equipment in and out of any country. The other set confirmed that he was a representative of a small reputable documentary film group based in Munich. Finally he poured himself a strong Pernod and water.

After months of careful preparation, the Director was going to do some shooting. This time in North America.

"I think we could be of mutual benefit," Gould told Graham. He had asked the Australian to meet him again in his office, the morning after their first meeting. "The situation is this. We have had enormous trouble getting data out over just what the Soviets are doing with computers in their military set-up. Steven was our number-one expert in this field in Moscow before the KGB tracked him down. All other relevant operatives who are specialists in this field at this time, even inside the Soviet Union, we suspect, are actually known to the KGB. I'm not being melodramatic when I say that any of our people would be dead at the first false move. We simple cannot risk them. You happen to have the expertise, especially in computerized military systems, that we want. If we assist you all we possibly can, would you agree to helping us get that intelligence out of the Soviet Union?"

Graham was a little stunned. It was more than he expected. He lit a cigarette. Gould took out his pipe.

"I'm willing to cooperate, if I agree to your plan," the Australian said cautiously. "What I'd like to know now is how much of this 'intelligence' I would be able to publish."

"We could come to some arrangement when you returned. It may be useful for us to have some of it public."

Graham nodded. "Okay. What have you in mind?"

"We want to put you through a crash program. It means you will have to be closeted away for about three or four days commencing next Sunday. We have an operations center near Oxford. I shall be in charge. You're going to hate the sight of me. We will have to go over your covers as Boulter and Radford until you know them in your sleep."

"You said we . . ."

"There is a third person. He will be involved in your Radford impersonation in Moscow. Call him Radford three. Radford three will be on the flight the real Radford would have taken, because otherwise the KGB will become suspicious of the empty seat on the plane. You would be picked up immediately you tried the impersonation. Radford three will arrive in Moscow and check in at the Hotel Berlin. Then he'll disappear. At the same time you will pick up a taxi near the Berlin and carry out your impersonation."

"How will Radford three disappear?"

"The alternatives are he can lie low and leave on the normal return flight the real Radford would have taken, or more likely, he will be smuggled out as a queen's messenger assistant."

"How can you do that?"

"Quite simple really. Each week a QM and sometimes an assistant bring in and take out diplomatic mail. Our Radford three will go out as an assistant. All our Soviet Embassy has to do is inform the Soviet authorities who is flying out forty-eight hours in advance. Radford three will travel out under a different diplomatic passport."

There was a reflective silence before Graham asked, "What sort of data and intelligence will be passed to me?"

"At Oxford you'll have to memorize blueprints on computer plans for missile systems, rocket reentry and so on, so that you will recognize certain network blueprints when you make contact with our operative."

"How and where will contact be made?"

"We shall teach you simple codes." The commander paused to suck on his pipe. He watched smoke spiral to an invisible grate in a corner of the ceiling. "As to where, leave that to us. You will not know until it actually happens. That way we minimize the chance of a mistake. . . ."

George Revel arrived in London on Thursday, September 11, for an important part of his PICS assignment. He spent the best part of the first two days with Intelligence contacts in the British Foreign Office and the U.S. armed forces and embassy.

By late Friday he received a telephone call at the Connaught Hotel from Graham, for whom he had left a message at Ryder Publications. They planned to meet for dinner at an out-of-the-way Italian restaurant in Kensington. Although both men started cautiously, an easy rapport developed between them.

The Australian was surprised and delighted to make contact with the lawyer. He had often read about and admired his efforts to beat Lasercomp in the Justice Department court battle. He outlined his investigation without mentioning his cooperation with MI-6, and Revel told the Australian that the PICS assignment was considered important to high officials in the U.S. administration. They had a mutual interest in finding out how computers were being used inside the Soviet Union. The lawyer had contacts there, and by the end of their meeting he trusted Graham enough to share their names with him. Since they found that a few hours over dinner was not enough to exchange information, they planned to meet again the following day.

Normally Graham would have a workout on a Saturday morning and follow it with a three-mile run around Hyde Park. Now he could not risk any former routines. However, when he learned that Revel was a keen jogger, he invited him to join him for a run beside the river at Kew, a mile from his Strand-on-the-Green hideout.

By eleven the two tracksuited men had set themselves a steady pace in the drizzling rain. Early autumn yellow and green leaves were already falling in the almost deserted gardens.

"Those contacts may be able to speak to you," Revel said, puffing as they reached the first mile. "One is a Ukrainian-American. He will be in Kiev the same time as you. The other is Professor Boronovsky, a leading dissident scientist."

"I know of him. An expert in cybernetics."

"That's right. He has become quite vocal about human rights in the Soviet Union lately."

The drizzle had turned into rain, which became quite heavy as they jogged on.

Graham wondered how well the lawyer knew Dr. Donald

Gordon, the former computer scientist at Lasercomp . . . the man Jane Ryder had wanted to contact in Paris shortly before her death.

"I had met him several times," Revel said. "We worked in different areas, but his reputation in design made him one of the best-known names in the computer world."

"He was behind the early Cheetah development. But I believe he fell out with the Brogans about what they wanted to see built into the machine."

"Did you ever learn what that was?"

"No. I think only a handful at Lasercomp did. But it must have been damned important."

"Why?"

"Rumor said he had one of the biggest golden handshakes in American business history to shut up about the dispute, and not join an opposition corporation."

"Would he speak to you?"

"Possibly. But if I tried to arrange for us both to meet him, you would have to come to the States. He lives like a recluse near Washington."

"I may come over after I've been to the Soviet Union."

By September 15, another big problem for President Everett Rickard involving the Soviet Union had come to a head. Daily now he was being presented with evidence that it was breaking previous agreements and escalating its arms build-up in almost every weapons system area. The Cheetah put America ahead in "first strike capability." But with the knowledge that computers were being smuggled into the East, Rickard had to cover the risk that somehow these machines could be converted to military use. If that ever happened, with Cheetahs, the Soviet Union would be equal in the precision use of whatever weapons they had developed.

Until a few months ago he had been making steady progress in agreements with Soviet Premier Brechinov. Now the Soviet administration was ignoring them. Rickard suspected the Soviets could have been gambling on the fact that he might try to avoid confrontation just before an election.

The National Security Council assembled in a White House west wing conference room early on the morning of the fifteenth. Rickard had asked six representatives from Congress to join the meeting so that it could be briefed on the situation, which was potentially explosive.

Each person was given a copy of a note Rickard proposed to give the Soviet ambassador.

The note said that the U.S. would consider stringent trade sanctions against the Soviet Union if it did not agree quickly to maintain arms agreements.

Rickard asked if they had any comment.

Nicholas Stavelin, a burly, bespectacled Texan, drawled, "Mr. President, I am basically in agreement with the note. But I'm not sure about your threat to cut back trade. Is that absolutely necessary?"

"Yes," Rickard said firmly, "I think it is."

"But you've threatened trade sanctions before."

"And it has worked."

"Well, I want it on the record that I think you're overdoing it," the senator argued. "Mixing trade and politics is dangerous."

Rickard had expected this from the senator. He had long suspected him of being in the pocket of Lasercomp.

When he first became President, Rickard had caused an international stir by tearing up all previous agreements with the Soviet Union that called nations to stop interfering in the internal politics of other nations. He had demanded concessions for Soviet political prisoners when some big trade deals were made. Rickard knew he could not work miracles. But each time he had stood up to the Soviet administration, concessions had been granted. Occasionally political prisoners were released from mental hospitals, or allowed to leave the Soviet Union. And so far, trade between the two nations had not slackened.

Apart from the senator's objection, there were no other major criticisms of the note. Just at noon, Rickard closed the meeting.

"Well, gentlemen," he said, "Secretary Grove will hand it personally to the Soviet ambassador at three P.M. today."

Twelve hours after Rickard had made his decison to confront the Kremlin with its violations of agreements, Douglas Philpott met a contact with the State Department, who had direct access to the minutes of the President's special committee meeting. It was Gregor Haussermann, assistant Under Secretary of

State. He and Philpott had met once before. It was too much of a coincidence in the TV superstar's mind that this meeting had occurred only days after Huntsman of Lasercomp had brought pressure on him. He maintained the contact, and Haussermann was willing to supply exclusive information about the President's ultimatum to the Soviets.

Haussermann called Philpott at the FBS studio and arranged to meet him at a small Chinese restaurant. Quiet and relatively unknown, it was an ideal spot that Philpott often used for meetings. Once or twice over the years he had been recognized by a fan there, but never often enough to bother him. Even someone with his outsized ego needed a break from the admirers, backslappers and assorted sycophants.

This night, Philpott was more cautious than ever, because he was going to receive stolen documents. He arranged to meet Haussermann early. The two men made their way to an alcove cubicle, where they both ordered a light Chinese meal and a beer.

"It-it's all there," Haussermann stammered nervously at Philpott as he placed a thick manila folder in his lap. "Be-be care-care-ful how you-you use it. Don't refer to the documents. You-you must use your s-skill to cover the source. When you-you pass it on to the *Times*, have your own report made up and get rid of it."

The *New York Times* was the first to run the story of Rickard's ultimatum in the morning edition of September 17, with a front page headed: **"Exclusive: Rickard's Ultimatum to U.S.S.R."** It ran a fairly accurate story of about 2,500 words spilling onto an inside page. It covered the background to the three-month run-up to the decision to confront the Russians.

Three other big dailies then ran follow-up reports on the story of the controversial note, and Rickard was forced to confirm that the Kremlin had received it. A guarded White House press release refused to disclose its contents.

The controversy was kept going on television. Douglas Philpott claimed that he had been one of the first to receive the leak, and that he passed it on to the *New York Times*. With a fine balance of charm and self-righteousness, he told his huge audience: "I refrain from editorializing on the content of the note except to confirm its existence."

With his photogenic head filling the screen, he added in a halting tone meant to convey a great depth of sincerity, "I decided to pass on the note only after agonizing for several days . . . and being confronted with . . . an . . . an inescapable decision of . . . journalistic conscience. . . ."

It was an act worthy of an Emmy. The TV superstar was doing Lasercomp's bidding. The attempt to crush Rickard by every piece of sensation, scandal, innuendo and vilification had begun in earnest.

The Kremlin reacted with uncharacteristic speed to the report of Rickard's ultimatum. Within forty-eight hours, the Soviet news agency Tass denounced Rickard as a "danger to all mankind," and in vitriolic terms accused him of setting world peace back twenty-five years.

Rickard was told of the first Soviet reaction. Yet there had been no reply from the Soviet ambassador, which Rickard regarded as a better guide to gauging the Kremlin's reaction.

Lasercomp was quick to exploit Rickard's problem. Huntsman told Bilby that Brogan Senior was prepared to be interviewed on Philpott's evening program.

A feature was prepared for September 18. Filmed highlights of Brogan's career in dealing with the Soviets from Lenin's time were followed by the interview:

"You have been one of the biggest traders with the Soviet Union," Philpott began in his staged but convincing style. "Why do you say President Rickard's note to the Kremlin is a dangerous move?"

Brogan spat a reply. "Crass brinkmanship! One idiotic note has taken us all the way back to the 1950s and the Cold War."

"But if the Russians have broken arms limitation agreements . . ."

"Who says they have?" Brogan said in his rasping voice.

"President Rickard said he was acting on advice from his Intelligence and military advisers."

Brogan changed position in his chair indignantly and, leaning forward, said, "Look. I know the Russians like the back of my hand. They stick to agreements."

"Are you suggesting the President of the United States is

misleading the public?" Philpott had become the Great American Inquisitor.

"Of course he is," Brogan sneered. "It's been done before by Presidents, you know."

"That's a serious charge, Mr. Brogan."

"He is grandstanding. Playing politics. There's an election coming up." His tone was sarcastic. "He wants to show America how tough he is. Remember, the American people never elected Rickard. He got there by chance and I think he'll do almost anything to stay in power!"

Philpott paused and looked at the script board he was clutching. "Then why do you think the Kremlin has so far failed to reply?" he asked.

"Well, they're not fools. They're obviously considering it properly. Anyway, I disagree with your saying they have failed to reply. We've already had a reaction that is clear enough."

"You mean . . ."

"Their media, of course."

"And what have you heard, Mr. Brogan, with your strong contacts in the Kremlin?"

The Old Man remained silent for a few seconds, as if he was measuring what he was about to say very carefully. "I think you'll find they'll shut off their dealings with Rickard until they see which way the presidential election goes."

"What about trade?"

"Huh!" Brogan grunted with an appeal to the heavens. "Millions . . . billions of dollars' worth of contracts could go down the drain . . . the U.S. balance of trade will suffer. Rickard is saying do this and that or we will stop trading with you. Naturally, the Soviets don't like it. And I don't blame them!"

"One last question, Mr. Brogan. What do you think should be done if the official reply from the Soviet Union in response to Rickard's ultimatum is unfavorable?"

Brogan was acting like an old stager who had been there a thousand times before. He paused melodramatically and looked away as the camera moved in for a close-up. His wrinkled profile was a study of concentration as he said, "I think someone has to let the Soviet Union administration and its people know that Rickard's warmongering attitudes are not representative of the true American opinion."

"You?"

"I'm not a politician."

"Then who?"

Brogan paused again. "I would say it's a heaven-sent opportunity for Senator MacGregor to show he is a statesman," he said forcefully. "It's his real chance to let the Soviets know we are not about to wipe out years of growing ties because of one stupid and irresponsible act."

Present at a very special dinner two nights later in a discreet corner of Le Perigord, one of New York City's most fashionable restaurants, were Brogan Senior and Junior, Alan Huntsman, Senator Ronald MacGregor and his running mate, Governor Paul Mineva. They were being waited on in the opulent setting of crimson silk-covered walls and frosted glass mirrors, by European waiters who outnumbered the VIPs and the mandatory Secret Service agents at a nearby table by two to one.

Le Perigord's Swiss manager, an old acquaintance of Huntsman's, gushed over the distinguished guests and went to great lengths to explain each dish on the menu. Huntsman fussed with the manager in fluent French. As an appetizer, MacGregor and Mineva both liked the sound of *escargots de Bourgogne*, while Brogan Junior and Huntsman settled for *caviar aux blinis*. The Old Man indicated he would have just the main course later—a *sole au plat*. Huntsman managed to convince MacGregor that he should try the *canard aux pêches*, while Mineva and Brogan Junior went for *grenouilles Provençale*. Huntsman himself ordered a Chateaubriand for two without batting an eyelid, and then surveyed the wine list. With a pretentious flourish, he ordered a decade-old Nuits St. Georges and a white wine bottled especially for Le Perigord.

The conversation concerned MacGregor's campaign and general strategy.

"A lot of people have been urging me to go to Moscow," MacGregor said casually to the Old Man, as he fished for a last elusive snail. "I hear you think it would be opportune also."

"I most certainly do, Senator," Brogan Senior said with conviction. "A public meeting with Brechinov would gain you votes."

"Why?" MacGregor asked, as his steel claw utensil at last grasped the snail.

"Rickard's foreign policy is a failure. It's your chance to succeed where he has failed."

"I can't speak on behalf of the American administration. What do you see as the point of my meeting the Russians?"

Brogan Junior broke in. "Things aren't exactly harmonious between Rickard and the Soviets. A goodwill visit from you could be seen to warm relations between the two nations."

MacGregor looked skeptical. "What's in it for Lasercomp?" he asked with a wry smile.

"Plenty," the Old Man said. "The Soviets are already getting tough because of Rickard's stupid belligerence. As I said on Philpott's show the other night, millions' worth of contracts could be lost."

MacGregor looked far from convinced.

Brogan Junior tried to reassure him. "If you did make the trip," he said, indicating that a waiter should fill the senator's glass, "we would make sure whatever transpired would be conveyed to the right people."

MacGregor fell silent and examined the stem of his wineglass. On the one hand, he marveled at the enormous pull of the Brogans. They were able to command the attention of the head of any world government, with the exception of the Chinese. They were even guaranteeing the way a meeting would be conducted! On the other hand, he saw a caution light. It was public now that Lasercomp was advocating Rickard's ejection from office. If he went on the proposed trip, what would be the payoff? Pressure on the courts to lay off Lasercomp? An easing of restrictions of computer sales? So far there had been no mention of a quid pro quo.

His running mate, Mineva, spoke up. "I'd like to know how the media would react to such a trip."

Huntsman emerged from the gastronomical bliss of his caviar. "Favorably, I'm certain about that." He washed down the rest of his hors d'oeuvre with a mouthful of white wine, leaving a few black specks near the corner of his mouth.

Mineva seemed satisfied. "In that case, I don't think we have anything to lose," he said, smiling at everyone.

MacGregor shook his head. He had never been for Mineva

1 0 3

as running mate but had been left little choice. Mineva, with his support in the Midwest, the South and from big business, some minorities, and some of the bigger unions, had been the half-hearted compromise choice. And now MacGregor was having to live with it.

"You spoke of the extra votes we would get from a trip like this," he said, turning to Brogan Senior. "I'm not so sure it would be all that valuable. I'm beginning to think I'm spending a little too much time on foreign issues as it is. I've had more requests for interviews from foreign journalists, and film and television organizations than from our home media. Sure, they are all interested in any trip I take overseas. But American journalists want to know about taxes, federal welfare, urban planning, every day until November fourth. My campaign has to get its priorities right at this critical time. I'm not sure that backslapping with Brechinov right now will sway votes my way.

"In any case," he added deliberately, "I agree with Rickard when it comes to dealing with the Soviet administration. He's right in confronting them over arms *and* human rights."

An embarrassed silence was interrupted by the arrival of the main course.

Several waiters hovered around, serving from trolleys and opening more wine. When the diners were settled again, Brogan Senior turned to MacGregor.

"Senator, I guess one of your reservations about visiting the Kremlin is that you don't want it to look like a vote-gathering exercise."

MacGregor looked a little exasperated. "That's partly right. But the question, as I said, Mr. Brogan, is whether or not it *is* a vote-gathering exercise!"

"Well, if it would help, we could arrange for the Kremlin to invite you on an unofficial visit."

"I'll give it some thought," he said noncommittally, and in a manner that indicated the topic was closed.

Huntsman, buried in his Chateaubriand, was asked by the manager for the third time if everything was in order. The PR man wiped his mouth with a napkin. "Just perfect," he said with a satisfied smile.

Graham arrived back at his apartment from MI-6's crash

program at Oxford and immediately phoned Sir Alfred.

"How are you feeling?" the publisher asked.

"Not too bad considering we did about a year's work in four days. Why?"

"Some bad news, I'm afraid. Your flat was broken into yesterday."

The Australian gripped the receiver.

"What?"

"Your porter rang here in a panic. Apparently he disturbed them."

"Them?"

"Two men in blue overalls, masquerading as workmen."

"Was anything stolen?"

"Only you could tell that. But certainly the stereo, TV and so on are still there."

"Did you tell Gould?"

"A few minutes ago. Police have already been over the apartment for fingerprints."

"What did he say?"

"He will have a look at the police report. He wants you to speak to him later today."

"So the trip's off?"

"He didn't say that. It could have been an ordinary burglary. The police say hundreds of apartments are broken into each week in your area. On the other hand, nothing was taken. It could have been . . ."

After a few seconds' silence, Graham said thoughtfully, "Even if it was 'them' it should not stop the trip. Could just mean they're getting desperate to find me. . . ."

"On the subject of your trip, we collected your mail from the bank as instructed. There's something from Intourist."

"Could you open it?" Graham said nervously. There was a moment's pause.

"It's your visa and plane ticket."

Graham was determined to enjoy his last night in London after weeks of confinement. He took Françoise to a quiet romantic little Greek restaurant off the Bayswater Road. Toward the end of the meal, she said, "I don't want to spoil the evening, but hadn't we better discuss tactics?"

"I was saving it until last thing tomorrow," Graham said,

1 0 5

"but you're right." He leaned forward as a waiter hovered about filling their wineglasses. When he was out of earshot, Graham said, "Gould says you should leave at the first sniff of trouble. At the latest you must leave the company the day I'm scheduled to play Radford."

"I'm staying until then."

The Australian reached across the table and took both her hands.

"You have more courage than is good for you."

"If your cover is broken, I should ring Gould?"

"Right. His operatives in Russia will inform me if something goes wrong."

"Ed, I'm worried for you . . ."

He squeezed her hands.

"Don't be. At the slightest sign of trouble, I simply won't go through with the Radford impersonation bit. Promise. I don't plan to be a dead hero . . . besides . . ." he said, smiling cheerfully, "I've too much to look forward to back here."

"So much could go wrong. . . ."

"Not if I remember my lines. I told you, Gould and his mates have pumped everything into my thick skull. I know exactly what to look for . . . the blueprints to be memorized . . . I won't have to write anything. And I know all the do's and don'ts."

"The . . . ?"

"The rules. Do act like a tourist. Don't exchange money illegally. Don't talk to the Russian women . . ."

"The women?"

"Yes, I know it sounds like some cliché but the KGB are apparently likely to try to use a female contact. Gould says every prostitute either works for the KGB or ends up in jail. The smart ones learn to cooperate to stay out of trouble. They pass on to the KGB any little detail to keep them happy."

"Stay away from the smart ones, s'il vous plaît."

Graham smiled. "Jealous?"

"Bien sur!"

He leaned across the table and kissed her lightly on the lips. Looking for the waiter, he asked for the bill and took out his wallet. Taking a card from it, he wrote two telephone numbers on the back.

"Memorize those two numbers," he said, handing the card

to her. "The top one is Sir Alfred's private line. Ring him and he'll give you a job with his publishing house until you start with British Airways. The second one is vital. It will reach MI-6 at any time."

"I hope I don't have to . . ."

"You don't have a thing to worry about. You have police protection from now on anyway."

Graham signed the bill. The waiter scurried away. "Forget about the company. They will never harm you. Radford and the rest of his executives will be hit hard by the police within the next few weeks." He stood up to go. "No matter what happens to me . . ."

PART 2

THE SOVIET CONNECTION

"The computer is the common denominator of the worst excesses of Soviet Marxism and American Capitalism."

4

Soviet Ambassador Boris Ustinov was led into the Oval Office by a presidential aide at precisely 9:00 A.M. on Monday, September 22. Rickard moved forward to greet the Russian, a tall, bull-necked muscular man of sixty, dressed in a dark three-piece suit. Instead of offering his hand, he stood stiffly in front of the President's desk and unzipped his attaché case.

"President Rickard," he began with a jerk of his head.

"Please sit down, Ambassador," Rickard said, as he lowered himself into his own chair behind the desk. The ambassador remained standing.

"Mr. President, I have received a communiqué. I have been ordered to read it to you."

"Read it, please," Rickard said, his forthright instruction belying the apprehension and tension that bound his stomach.

Ambassador Ustinov put on reading spectacles, took out four yellow sheets from his attaché case, cleared his throat, and began to read the communiqué. It started with a flat denial of the breaking of any arms agreements, followed by accusations denouncing the President and saying that he had embarked on a dangerous course. In essence, Rickard thought, as the words rolled off Ustinov's tongue in clear, exact, uncolloquial English, the communiqué was simply an emasculated version of the attacks in the Soviet press. Only the last few paragraphs stiffened Rickard's insides.

The U.S.S.R. is forced to take the view that it cannot effectively negotiate with the United States under your administration and the present circumstances. The peoples of the Soviet Socialist Republics will await the coming judgment of the peoples of the United States before reconsidering relations between our two nations.

Until then, all major negotiations will cease, and all trade and diplomatic relations will be kept to a minimum.

The ambassador's final words hung in the room as he placed the note on the President's desk, took a pace back and closed his attaché case.

Rickard, who had been staring out beyond the French doors all through the reading, swiveled his chair around to face the ambassador. "Very well." He nodded vigorously, his voice steady. "Please inform your premier I have heard his note."

"I shall pass the message to him, Mr. President."

"Thank you, Ambassador," Rickard said.

He got up and saw Ustinov out through the French doors. He watched the aide escort him up the colonnaded walk and out of sight. Then he went back to his desk and sat down again. His eyes fell on the stark communiqué. Now the pressure would surely be on.

Rickard looked at the communiqué again and shook his head. It could not be Brechinov's hand, he was sure. Perhaps only a private letter to the Soviet premier could draw a clearer picture of the Kremlin's position.

Two days before the meeting in the White House, an Irishwoman crossed herself and an old couple gripped their armrests as Aeroflot Flight 884 headed off from Gatwick airport, bound for Kiev, at noon on Saturday, September 20.

Graham's tour was made up of ninety-eight people from different countries. There were also five Ukrainian and Russian émigrés on limited visas to see relatives.

By the time the plane had flown the three hours to Kiev, most of them had become familiar with Graham, as he wandered up and down the cabin, striking up conversations, especially with the younger women on board, and in particular with four laughing and friendly Spanish women—a deliberate effort to act out an amicable disposition.

They arrived in clear, cool weather at Kiev airport and Graham felt the pressure mount as the group was herded through customs. He was held up by a poker-faced young woman who insisted on giving his luggage a thorough search. She asked for all his literature and took some time examining *The Observer*, the *Guardian*, a small traveler's Russian dictionary, a novel by Patrick White, a book on anthropology, and the latest edition of *Playboy*.

Finally she decided to confiscate everything except the *Traveler's Russian*.

Graham packed his gear and moved to a lounge where the rest of the tour had gathered to listen to the chief tour guide, Victor, a handsome Russian with a shock of black hair which he brushed back in early Elvis Presley style.

The Australian could hardly believe he had made it. He half expected something dramatic to happen any moment.

During the first days in Kiev, Graham moved around as much as possible in the hope of giving contacts a chance of approaching him. He ran each morning around the nearby state park, attended organized tours and occasionally broke away from the group.

On Sunday afternoon he and the Spanish girls he had befriended on the flight from England went to an ancient monastery outside Kiev. In the evening he visited two art galleries alone in the city. But nothing happened.

Thanks to MI-6's briefing, the Australian was aware he would be watched. The tour guides had skillfully created an illusion of freedom by telling all the group that no organized tours were compulsory. They were not told that Intourist was essentially run by the KGB and that surveillance trebled on anyone who did not attend tours, or who went his own way.

The closeness of this surveillance was driven home to Graham when an American college student on the tour was apprehended by local police for illegally changing money at six times the official rate—with a local. The whole tour was abuzz with the news that the American had been quietly interrogated for four hours and given a warning that if it happened again he would be deported immediately. The American said the police had told him that the local would be charged and given a prison sentence of ten years' hard labor.

Graham discreetly elicited details from the American over

breakfast and was told that there must have been a twenty-four-hour surveillance on all the tour. All through the interrogation, one member of the police asked him several times if he had trouble with contact lenses. The American remembered having difficulty replacing his lenses on three occasions in Kiev. Each time it was when he had gone off on his own excursion in and outside the city.

The main contact promised Graham in Kiev was via George Revel. The Australian had been told that the contact would come to him, if it was safe.

After breakfast on Monday, Graham strolled down to the lobby of the Hotel Dnieper, where the tour group was staying.

Throngs of tourists were either buying souvenirs or exchanging money. Graham bought twenty postcards and decorative stamps and found an empty couch in the lounge. He had written a couple of cards when he was joined by a couple.

"Be careful what you write," the man said. He was a skeletal-thin American of about sixty.

Graham smiled politely. "I am," he said. The man could be one of Revel's contacts. But he could not be sure. The American squinted through his glasses.

"You English?" he asked.

"No, Australian."

"We're from Florida," the woman said. She was also about sixty with bottle-blond hair and fancy framed sunglasses. She wore a turquoise dress that accentuated her years and plumpness.

"On vacation?"

"Sort of," the man answered. "I'm a Ukrainian-American. My wife and I are visiting relatives, as best we can."

"Is it difficult?"

"We're always being tagged."

"Why?"

"I used to work with the New York police department as chief of security for visiting foreigners. I used to look after Khrushchev whenever he toured America."

It *was* one of the contacts that Revel had promised.

Graham said casually, "Can we talk here?"

"Yes. Just be careful. If anyone sits near us, change the subject." The glass wall of the lobby looked out over a square. "It's people you want to watch here. They'll tag you for sure." He pointed to several parked cars. "See that man smoking and the woman with him? That's our tail. They're hopeless. About the worst in the world. Last time I came here three years ago, I told the local chief of security—I've known him for fifteen years—that the tails they put on me were useless. I told him every move they'd made since I arrived. I told him always to tag with a couple because it was less obvious. Well, this time they have. And they're still useless!"

"Our friend told you what I was after?" Graham asked.

The American nodded. Keeping his voice at a normal level and smiling occasionally as he spoke, he said, "There is currently going on a massive computer network build-up in Kiev. I think it's the same in Leningrad and Moscow."

"For what?" Graham asked. Taking the cue from the American, the Australian smiled broadly. "The military? The police?"

"We don't know yet." The American looked casually around the lobby before he went on. "We do know the administration is gathering information for the system."

"What sort of information?"

"Everything from routine stuff about income, pensions and work to details on friends, where people have their vacations, whether they have relatives outside the republic they live in. . . . Not to mention every scrap of data possible on a person's politics. You think of it and it's apparently going into the network. . . ."

Graham stood up, stretched and moved over to a mailbox on the lobby counter and placed a card in it. When he returned to his seat he asked, again smiling broadly, "Where's the information coming from?"

"Everywhere. Sometimes police or government officials go directly to an apartment without warning. Things are collected at the office, in the factory, on the farm, in the universities. Even children at schools are asked to disclose information about their parents and their homes."

"How is this computer bank being built?" Graham had picked up another card and was writing on it.

"By three shifts of workers, twenty-four hours a day. . . ."

"Are they all Soviet scientists?"

"No, but most are. Each shift carries about eight hundred workers, all qualified computer people, programmers and so on. Nearly all are local. Each shift has about twenty 'supervisors.'

Some Russian, some German, some American. . . ."

Graham looked intently at the contact for the first time and then quickly resumed a casual air. "Where are the Americans from?"

The American shook his head and went on. "These workers go to the network center and sit down at desks or man computers at four-hour shifts, twice daily. The person is checked coming and going at each shift. He or she then goes on with the work of the previous shift.

"It is a continuous process, but randomly jumped. It means no one except possibly the supervisors knows the development of the total design."

The American paused. Suddenly the tenseness showed as his gnarled hands gripped the side of the couch.

"Nobody is allowed to enter or leave with any documents. This makes it difficult for my informants here to build a composite of what is actually being designed. . . ."

"Have you any idea . . .?"

Graham broke off as a sullen-faced young female Intourist guide in uniform sat down near them.

"Yeah, I used to work for Mr. K.," the American said.

"What was he like?"

"Rough as hell, and tough. Not all that bright, but he knew what he wanted and how to get it. I remember once in the United Nations when he was telling America off, he finished a tirade in Russian with, 'If America tries that, they'll get it in the ass!' He used the well-known middle-finger sweep to make his point. But the interpreter was discreet. His translation in English was, 'If America tries that, they'll get it in the end.'"

Graham laughed and the American woman showed some animation for the first time. The Intourist girl, who had not been looking at them, got up and went out of the hotel's front doors.

"We'll have to stop. It's a little hot. Don't look around, just act normally," the American said. Then he grinned, but just with his mouth.

"Yeah," he said, getting up and facing Graham squarely, "check out the Hotel Lenin bar for 'supervisors' and police HQ just up the road. . . ."

"I run past it every morning," Graham said, acting casually.

"Okay, take care," the American said, gripping Graham's

hand. He took his wife by the arm and escorted her to a staircase which led to the hotel dining room.

The Director arrived at Kennedy airport from Paris and had no trouble moving through customs. Officials did not even bother to look inside his case and only skimmed through his papers.

Within two hours he was in Washington knocking on the front door of a four-story old brownstone boardinghouse, Folgar Arms, 2127 South Street, S.W., about a half-mile from Capitol Hill. A short, plump Chilean woman unlocked two doors. She looked the stranger up and down with eyes which had an exophthalmic bulge, as he explained that he only wanted a room for about a week. She showed him in and led him up one flight of rickety stairs to a single room.

The Director surveyed the sparse furnishings—a single bed, a simple wooden table and three chairs, a shower recess and toilet, and a pint-sized refrigerator. He walked to the only window in the room and peered out through bars at a dilapidated building across the road.

Turning to the woman, the Director took out his wallet and paid her twice the tariff for the week. A minute later she helped him with the metallic case and a suitcase.

Rodriguez and his companion, the Director mused, had chosen well. The boardinghouse would be difficult to trace despite its central position, and the woman had neither asked him to sign a register nor taken his passport.

An hour later he answered a sharp knock at the door and let two men in. He stared in disbelief at one of the men before embracing him warmly. The Director had not seen Rodriguez for several weeks.

He knew the Argentinian had undergone plastic surgery, but was not prepared for the extent of the transformation. Gone were Rodriguez's chubby cheeks. They seemed to have been hollowed out to give him a gaunt appearance. The chin and nose were different. Rodriguez's own acquired skills of disguise had added to the change. The hair and eyebrows were fair rather than dark, the eyes green now instead of black.

Without a word, the Director unscrewed a bottle of Scotch he had picked up on the way, and poured a drink for Rodriguez and his companion, known as Martinez, also an Argentinian, of

1 1 7

twenty-eight. He was dark and swarthy, his physique slight. Not the frame of a killer with a victim for about every year he had lived.

Martinez had first met Rodriguez when they were both drifting around South America giving physical support to revolution. Unlike Rodriguez, he had no ideological bent. He was a killer in instinct rather than training and had joined forces with Rodriguez on several occasions, the last two with the Director in Europe and North Africa.

"You have completed the research?" the Director asked.

"Everything is ready," Rodriguez said, his newly shaped but still aquiline nose bending noticeably as he spoke. That bend was perhaps the one feature, the Director thought, that the surgeons would not be able to change short of shearing his nose right off.

"Then we are ready for a strike?"

Both the Argentinians nodded.

"When?"

"In two days," Rodriguez replied, as he spread a big map of Washington on the table.

For the next two hours he described in detail the strategy for a kill. The Director occasionally asked questions. Finally he shook his head. "It seems almost too simple to get into the building," he said. "Are you absolutely sure about it?"

"I have gone over the same route six times. The only difference when you go in, will be the extra security guards."

The Director frowned. "It's amazing," he said incredulously.

Rodriguez nodded. "I agree. Never have I been involved in such an easy hit with such a high person. I think one of the target's aides summed it up very well when I commented how easy it was to get up to the office, considering whose it was. She said indignantly, 'It is a democracy, you know. . . .'"

The Director smiled and said, "Where you are free to kill whom you choose. . . ."

Graham waited until Tuesday night before acting on the tip from the American about the computer network supervisors at the Hotel Lenin.

Just before midnight he slipped out of the Hotel Dnieper and began to walk in the opposite direction to the Hotel Lenin, ten

1 1 8

blocks away. He immediately noticed a tall, gaunt man following him through the crowds of strollers and workers making their way home. It was the same person the Australian had noticed tailing him during the day on three other excursions from the hotel. Finding steps to a subway, Graham moved down on the double and hurried through the bustling masses for about five minutes. When he was sure he had thrown off the tail, he made his way aboveground to the Lenin. As he went to enter the glass doors, he was blocked by a large, gruff attendant.

"Nyet! Pass!" he bellowed. It was patrons only at that hour, and he was having trouble turning away drunks who hovered around the doors in the hope of a last vodka for the night.

When the attendant was momentarily distracted, Graham brushed past. The man grabbed Graham by the arm, but soon let go when the Australian let go a barrage in English that made it quite clear he intended to go to the hotel's bar. Graham began to walk toward the winding flight of stairs to the bar, and the attendant gave up when a couple of drunks staggered through the front doors.

The room was dark, noisy and crowded. There was a long bar with a row of mirrors behind it. A great variety of Western liquor and cigarettes was displayed. Most of the signs behind the bar were in English. On the right were several tables, all occupied. As Graham moved a few paces into the room, the conversation near him stopped. The barman and several women examined the stranger. He walked to a couple of empty stools and swung himself onto one.

Three women soon appeared a few paces from him. The clothes—light blue cotton jacket, light trousers, open-neck shirt—and a large wad of American dollars protruding from his Gucci wallet, made it certain he was a Westerner. As Graham asked for a screwdriver, a hard-faced slant-eyed Tatar, with dress slit to the hip, sat at the only other bar stool near him. She took a long time lighting her cigarette, then smiled. He nodded back.

"You American?" she asked.

"No. Do I look it?" He smiled.

Several others close to them seemed interested in the conversation.

At that moment, a burly young Russian came and put his arm around the woman. He chatted and drank with her for a couple of minutes, with his back to Graham. But her attention was on the Australian, and when the Russian went back to his table, she resumed her conversation with him. After a few complimentary remarks about his clothes and looks, she stubbed out her cigarette and said matter-of-factly, "If you want me, fifty American dollars for the night."

Graham smiled. "Thank you for the offer. But I am on a tight budget."

"Thirty?"

"No, thank you," he said firmly, but not loud enough for others to hear.

She gave an as-you-wish toss of the head and left him to join the Russian. Within a minute, another woman, who had been standing nearby observing the Tatar's efforts, took her place.

She was tall, blond and elegant. Long hair fell across one side of her face, with classic high cheekbones, and big, wide-set eyes. Graham asked her if she would like a drink.

"Gin and tonic, thank you. Where do you stay in Kiev?"

"Dnieper."

"Are you here long?"

"Two more days. Then my tour goes to Leningrad."

The barman gave her a drink.

"Is this a tour hotel?" Graham asked as he took out a fifty-dollar bill to pay. The girl gestured with her hand to indicate "Sort of." She looked around the bar. "Most of them are on business," she said. "Some are scientists."

Graham lit a cigarette she had placed in a long holder. "Foreign?" he asked.

"As you can hear," the girl said, cocking her head to the tables, "there are many. They work together with Russians." She gave a disdainful look.

"You don't like them?"

"They are all very boring. All they do is work. No fun at all. Away at seven in the morning, back at seven at night."

Graham gave an understanding nod and sipped his drink. "What sort of work?" he asked quietly.

"Oh, it is so dull," she said, tossing her hair. "Computers and things."

Graham could see a head at the nearest table turn at the

mention of the word computer. "Yes, that is boring," he said, smiling at her. And then, "What is your name?"

"Tanya."

"Tanya, you are a most attractive woman. At home you would make an excellent model," he said.

She blushed and said, "Do you mean as in *Vogue*?"

"Yes."

"That is very nice," she said softly. She leaned forward so that her face was close to his, and lowering her voice said, "Would you like to stay with me tonight?" Her tone was appealing rather than seductive.

Graham held her gaze for several seconds, sighed and said softly, "I would like to. But I have someone tonight."

She looked disappointed. "Tomorrow night?" she asked, and scribbled a telephone number on a matchbox top. She gave it to him.

Graham squeezed her hand and said, "I shall ring you, if it is possible."

He got off the stool, finished his drink and went out, turning once to wave to the beautiful Tanya.

At 6:45 A.M. on the tour's last morning in Kiev, Graham hauled on his black tracksuit and running shoes for a run. He carried his camera with a telephoto lens strapped over his shoulder and held a little awkwardly to his hipbone as he moved. The tour had been allowed to take photographs most of the time, and Graham had been taking his fair share of pictures, often stopping on his runs to take in the sights. This time he hoped to photograph at police headquarters. If his thinking was right, the scientists at the Hotel Lenin would be arriving there soon after 7:00 A.M.

He slipped past the snoring female attendant curled up on a couch on the fourth-floor lobby, down the back stairs and out the front past two guards asleep against a wall.

The sight of the athletic figure loping away started the bizarre ritual of the last five mornings for two thugs. One, a wiry, black-mustachioed Georgian sitting in a battered Polski sedan car, turned to the back seat and vigorously shook the other, a huge mound of Mongolian muscle and flesh.

"Igor! Igor!" he growled at the man, who was fast asleep.

He awoke with a slobbery start, cursed furiously, and fumbled around for running shoes in the back of the car. His morning's work of chasing this crazy foreign mountain goat around Kiev's parks and hills had begun.

Graham ran lightly up the hill into green wooded parkland, bathed in a beautiful morning sun that filtered and flashed through the trees. He headed for the top, where there was a small former summer palace of the czars, and lookout areas. These gave the best views of the Dnieper River as it wound its way through the valleys on the outskirts of the city.

The only person in sight was a wizened old man sweeping up leaves, and he seemed oblivious of his early morning company. Near the top, Graham stopped and looked down the long steep path to see Igor on his way up, running off the path, through the plant beds and shrubbery. It was heavy going for the big man. Graham had not been worried too much about his tail. But today he had to lose him. He let him come within fifty yards, and then moved on, setting a hot pace across the top of the hill.

Igor could just catch glimpses of the Australian through the blinding sunlight. It appeared that the foreigner was heading for the steps leading back down the hill on the other side.

It would be much easier going downhill than this monstrous hike up, which was causing him to heave and sweat. He saw the Australian disappear down the steps.

Moments later he reached the top and looked down the 250 steps to the bottom. The foreigner was not in sight! Igor charged like a mad bull, too fast. He lost his balance. The big man tried to break the dangerous tumble by landing on his shoulder, judo style, but only succeeded in crashing over ten steps to a thumping halt against a tree.

Graham had hidden in the foliage to the right of the steps. He breathed a sigh of relief when he saw Igor sprawled on the ground and too badly injured to get up. That problem had solved itself.

He had no time to waste. It was 7:12 A.M. and Tanya had said the scientists were on their way to work by seven. He doubled back to the path he had come up. Halfway down, he ran off into the long grass near the edge of the hill where there was a thirty-yard drop to the road below. From that vantage point he had an excellent view of the police HQ. The building was a dull gray, functional example of Soviet stonework. Its only redeeming feature was a series of handsome fluted front columns. He lay on his back in the long grass and adjusted his telephoto lens.

It was 7:19. Graham decided he would wait an hour and pick up as many shots as he could. A few minutes later, the first of his possible subjects came into view. They were three men in Western-cut light gray suits. Graham waited until they were at the entrance and found there was enough time while guards examined their identification.

For the next thirty-five minutes, there was a steady trickle of men and women, some on foot and some in private vehicles or taxis. Some, such as people in overalls or young girls in miniskirts, he did not bother about. He concentrated on those given more VIP treatment, including a middle-aged couple who were driven up in a state Zil limousine. When he was satisfied with his coverage, Graham jogged down the path and stepped up the pace down the road to his hotel.

Across the square, in the Polski sedan, the Georgian was tending to the injured Igor. Two early morning workers had found the big man lying in agony and helped him down to the square.

The tall figure of the Director, in dark blue suit, white shirt, and smart dark blue and white check tie, marched into Washington's Delaware Avenue and up to the side of the Old Senate Building. In his left hand was a metallic briefcase. He was watched carefully by security police, some hidden, others sitting in cars along the avenue.

There were a few other people walking along the avenue, but none with the same purpose toward the side entrance.

As if to set an example rather than to carry out a thorough check, the assistant to the chief of security for Senator MacGregor, Mick Hallaway, stepped out of the evening shadows before the Director reached the side entrance, stopped him, and asked for his I.D. Satisfied with the man's papers after a close scrutiny, Hallaway, with an authoritative wave of the hand, escorted him the few paces to the double glass doors. There, the Director stood stiffly to attention and told a guard behind the desk, "I wish to see Senator MacGregor."

In the background could be heard the crackle of Hallaway's walkie-talkie in communication with Brad Nichols, MacGregor's security chief in room 452 on the fourth floor of the building.

"You have an appointment, sir?" another guard asked as he picked up a telephone.

"Yes, Heinrich Sneller. I'm from Krupper Films, Munich, West Germany," the Director said, unlocking his briefcase and producing a thick leather-bound diary. Flicking open a few pages and pointing, he said, "You see, I have an appointment."

The guard wanted to have a look at the contents of the briefcase, while another asked for identification.

When Senator MacGregor's office came on the line, the guard said, "One-thirty-two Miller here, sir. There is a Mr. Sneller from Krupper Films, Germany, to see the Senator, sir." He emphasized the uh in Krupper and was quickly corrected by the Director.

"Krooper!"

The guard ignored him as he said, "Yes, sir, right away," and put the receiver down. "The Senator will see you, sir. Take elevator two to the fourth floor."

"Thank you."

The guard checking the briefcase had taken out a Pentax camera, a Grundig tape recorder, and a small collapsible tripod. He was having a close look at the recorder.

"I'm here to interview Senator MacGregor," the Director said. "I'm also going to take some publicity shots of him."

The guard ran a metal detector over the Director and the equipment.

"Oh, please," the Director complained as he clutched his diary, "you will fog my film with that."

The guard replaced the equipment in the metallic briefcase and indicated elevator number two. The Director stepped into it as a guard relayed details of the security check on him to another guard on the fourth floor.

In room 452, Senator MacGregor, shirt sleeves rolled to the elbows and tie loosened, was putting the finishing touches to a speech he planned for the next day. It was 8:00 P.M. He had just said goodbye to his press secretary and was rushing his writing before the director from Krupper arrived. Scores of foreign film groups wanted to interview him. His office had agreed to most of them. A note on his desk from his press secretary reminded him of tonight's interview.

Stepping out of the elevator, the Director feigned distress.

"Please, where is there a toilet?" he asked. The guard who had met him pointed to the right. The Director found a cubicle and shut himself in. He placed the briefcase on the toilet seat and quickly took out the diary, tripod, camera and recorder. Deftly, he removed from them the parts of a small, modified Walther P.38 revolver. The camera held the magazine, and the legs of the tripod hid the barrel and silencer. He assembled the weapon, and snapped open the diary once more, to reveal a cut-out silhouette for the gun. The Director placed the gun in it and put it back in the briefcase. The whole operation had taken just two and a half minutes.

The Director flushed the toilet and left the washroom. As he came into the corridor, he thanked the guard and was escorted to room 452. The guard gabbled into his walkie-talkie in an indecipherable jargon as they followed the even numbers along the high-arched oak doors on their left.

The Director was ushered into an anteroom and greeted by security chief Nichols and another guard.

"I have come to see . . ."

"We know," Nichols said coldly, a holstered revolver discernible beneath his coat. "May I see your identification?"

The Director took out his papers with a sigh, and said, "You certainly are very thorough," as he handed them over.

Nichols sifted through them and handed them back. The security chief then knocked on MacGregor's office door and entered. Seconds later he came out and ushered the Director in. Nichols left them and closed the door behind him.

The senator got up from behind his desk, extended a hand to the Director and offered him a seat. "I'm afraid I haven't much time," he said.

"I shall be only a few minutes, Senator." The Director smiled as he placed the briefcase on the floor in front of him, the top facing the senator and concealing the contents. The Director took out the recorder and put it on a clear corner of MacGregor's cluttered desk. "Do you mind if I record?" he asked the senator politely. MacGregor shook his head as the Director reached into the case once more, flicked open the diary, and gripped the revolver. He raised it slowly and pointed it at MacGregor's head.

"Do not try to be brave or you will be killed," the Director said evenly. "Listen carefully. When I have finished instructing you, pick up the receiver and notify all security that I, Heinrich Sneller, will leave now and come back in an hour because the interview will take longer than you expected." He looked down at MacGregor's handwritten notes and asked curtly, "What's that?"

Confused and shaken, MacGregor blurted, "A speech for . . ."

"Good. Tell them you didn't expect this interview to take so long and that you want more time to complete your speech before we have the interview. Say also that Sneller will be leaving in a few minutes, and that you do not wish to be disturbed until he returns in an hour."

MacGregor nodded.

"Excellent. Do this and no harm will come to you. I need time to talk to you privately."

MacGregor felt a surge of hopeful relief flush over him as he picked up the phone. He swallowed several times to moisten a dry throat.

The senator managed to keep his voice steady throughout the instructions. He put the receiver down and watched the Director take a step back. The cold expressionless eyes of the assassin were the last thing he saw as two shots went straight into Mac-Gregor's forehead with a soft "plop" sound. The impact of the lead at that range bounced the senator straight back into his chair and he slumped head forward, arms dangling.

Making sure that no surgical miracle would save him, the Director took three steps around the desk and fired once more, this time from about four feet and directly into the cerebellum. What was left of the senator's head wrenched to one side.

The Director stepped around to the front of the desk and quickly placed his gun and recorder back in the briefcase. He walked to the door, opened it, and stepped into the outer office. Giving a theatrical little wave to the dead MacGregor, he closed the door.

Nichols and the guard were standing, ready to show the stranger out.

As the Director walked out into the corridor, he turned and said angrily, "I wish your politicians would keep appointments! I shall be back to see him in one hour exactly."

Nichols watched the stranger move toward the elevator. When he reached the side entrance, the Director resumed a leisurely pace past the four security men there. Assistant Security Chief Hallaway watched him go.

An hour later, Brad Nichols knocked on the senator's door. When there was no reply, he entered the office.

The department heads of the KGB sat in expectant silence in room 746 at their HQ, Dzerzhinsky Square, Moscow, as their chairman, Nicoli Andropolov, put the telephone receiver down hard in its cradle.

"That was the coordinator of Cheetah supplies calling from Stuttgart," he said to the ten people at the conference table, his moon face as vacuous as usual. "He assures me that the supplies of Cheetah will double next year. He is sending major suppliers here over the next few months to ensure they are aware of our requirements. If there are no unforeseen problems this is all very encouraging. Operation Ten is right on target."

There were murmurs of assent from the others.

"Now let us consider item fifteen," he said, adjusting his rimless spectacles and referring to an open folder. "Press reports on Operation Ten. The main problem seems to be this Australian journalist. Lasercomp is upset that we did not consult them about his liquidation." He pressed an intercom button in front of him. "Send Comrade Bromovitch in."

The deputy head of Department Four knocked and entered. Andropolov waved a hand at a seat at the other end of the table. All eyes turned to Bromovitch as he took his seat slightly self-consciously. Despite his apparent bungling of the attempt to eliminate the Australian journalist, everyone in the room held him in high regard. His reputation had been high ever since he had recently tracked down a top enemy agent from British Intelligence code-named Steven.

"Now, comrade, what is your report on Mr. Graham?"

"We have had some trouble locating him," the assassin said, shifting in his seat nervously. "He is not living in his apartment."

"Is he an agent?"

"It is highly likely. We are at present analyzing documents microfilmed in his apartment."

"How much does this man know?" asked General Gerovan, the sixty-seven-year-old KGB chief of Soviet military services.

"You have been briefed on what he learned in Vienna. We are still assessing his knowledge. Personally I think it is now more than enough to justify neutralizing him."

Andropolov took off his spectacles.

"We have agreed with Lasercomp not to do this until we see how he responds to their attempts to turn him off the investigation."

Bromovitch opened a file. There were several photographs of Graham taken in London.

"But, comrades, how long can this man roam free?" Bromovitch said. "Apart from his contacts, he has murdered one of our operatives in Austria. He is a deadly enemy of the state and our people!"

He looked around the table for support, but no eyes met his. They were all embarrassed by this quaint outburst of patriotic jargon.

While Bromovitch had been speaking, Andropolov was gazing at a portrait of Lenin staring down from the back of the room. Now the KGB focused on the assassin.

"We appreciate your enthusiasm in this case. But we all must appreciate the situation. Lasercomp is concerned that neutralizing this man may focus too much attention on Operation Ten, especially now he seems to be cooperating with the U.S. Government. I have just spoken to the main Western coordinator of supplies. We don't want anything to stop the flow of machines here."

Bromovitch stared at the KGB chief, who added, "Now, comrade, should this journalist fail to cooperate with Lasercomp, or should he give us any more trouble, then he will be liquidated."

Bromovitch nodded.

Andropolov looked at his watch and dismissed the assassin. "That covers item fifteen," the KGB chief said. "Could we now look at item sixteen, Professor Letovsky's report on progress at IOSWOP..."

Bromovitch left the meeting. To him item fifteen was still wide open.

President Rickard directed that the FBI should take charge

of the investigation into MacGregor's assassination. The local police and the rest of the nation's law enforcement agencies coordinated their efforts in the biggest manhunt in Washington's history. FBI chief James Dent first ordered that the city should be tipped upside down and shaken.

In the early hours of the morning of Friday, September 26, every Washington hotel from the smartest and most expensive to the sleaziest whorehouse was checked. Bars, nightclubs, restaurants, cabarets and cafés were haunted by every available cop and volunteer, who described the assassin to waiters, barmen and bouncers.

The home or hangout of every known political activist, from the most juvenile student Trotskyite to the local lobbyists for the Ku Klux Klan, was raided and turned over. There were arrests of people with everything from a German accent to a speech impediment, on the advice from one of the guards who described the assassin's accent as "not American and kinda funny." Those arrested were kept in custody for hours, and only released the next day, often without apology. Anyone in the street was picked up. Roadblocks appeared on all major access points to Washington and all transport out of the city was halted for twelve hours.

In the Washington underground, every Mafia mover and shaker and black leader was at work slipping through the haunts of pimps, prostitutes, hustlers, thieves, pickpockets, hoodlums and con men. The city was alive all night, because a man was dead.

The world watched a nation once more in agony and confusion, via the naked all-pervasive eye of satellite television. The cameras caught it all.

On the lawn outside the Old Senate Building, MacGregor's assistant chief of security, Mick Hallaway, told his version of events with thirty microphones pushed under his nose.

"I saw this film director go out of the building, and I thought to myself, 'He wasn't with . . . the . . . the . . . Senator long . . .'"

"But why didn't you check him properly in the first place?"

"Why didn't you stop him on the way out?"

"Why? Why? Why?"

On Delaware Avenue an ambulance arrived for MacGregor's wife, Judith. Bedraggled and hysterical, she had collapsed after seeing the crumpled body with two-thirds of the brain shattered.

Across the road at the Capitol, thousands of people gathered after hearing the assassination on late-night television.

Washington's ABC, NBC, CBS and FBS morning news programs told America two salient facts that had become highly embellished. Senator MacGregor had been assassinated. The assassin had not been caught. Most of the coverages included speculation and repetitive comment from leading politicians, and others, including the Vice-President, and several spokesmen for the dead candidate's party, including Paul Mineva. When asked who would now be the new nominee, he denied he would seek the nomination, telling interviewers indignantly that this was a "tragic" time. Not the moment to speculate on who would take Ronald MacGregor's place.

By midmorning the assassination squad was airborne from a field in southeast Florida. Each member of the squad had been met by a woman and driven to a place close to the field. The run had taken a leisurely eight hours and the couples had acted like holidaymakers fleeing the cold that was beginning to creep over the rest of the country. There were a few anxious moments with police patrols, and especially for Rodriguez's car, which had been stopped a hundred miles out of Florida. The police had found all they would expect from innocents heading to the Florida coast, including beach gear and golf clubs in the trunk.

Rodriguez had been supplied with a false driver's license and insurance details. His cool manner in the crisis covered for the woman driver, who had nearly panicked. Each woman had been told very little about her assignment except that each would earn $2,500 in cash on completion.

The nation had been alerted quickly to the assassin's act, but there were limits to the coordinated mobilization to round up the killers. One was the use of radar to track unspecified planes leaving the country. This allowed the two-engine private jet carrying the squad to avoid detection as it flew as low as possible to Cuba.

It wasn't until six days later that a group of hikers stumbled on three camouflaged cars in scrubland about a mile from the field. In each was the body of a woman with a neat bullet hole through the temple.

It did not take the FBI long to piece together the background to the assassination.

The most important evidence had come from MacGregor's own closest aides, especially Lionel Bannerman, his gangling six-foot, five-inch campaign chairman. Ever since MacGregor had won the nomination, his office had been inundated with requests from foreign media, not to mention myriad local requests, for interviews. Bannerman produced a list of ninety-nine approaches from foreign film companies, and 456 from foreign journalists. He had tried to group interviews every second Saturday afternoon, wherever MacGregor might be campaigning. Many, however, asked for exclusives.

One such group that intermittently kept in touch was Krupper Films of Munich, West Germany. A man calling himself Wolfgang Himmel, and purporting to be a Krupper representative, visited MacGregor's offices six times. He agreed to join ten other film crews one afternoon if Krupper was allowed an earlier ten-minute sound interview only with MacGregor. Himmel had explained that his Krupper film group planned to have many of their questions "voice-over" while film would show various Mac-Gregor shots on the campaign trail. The sound interview had been arranged for Thursday, September 25, at 8:00 P.M. and it was agreed that a Heinrich Sneller, who, it was claimed, was a leading producer/director with Krupper, would meet MacGregor at the Old Senate Building.

Bannerman had been able to produce the only two pieces of written communication between the MacGregor offices and Krupper Films sent on official Krupper letterhead paper. All other communications had been by personal contact, or telephone from inside America, and from France and West Germany. Bannerman had asked an aide to check out every organization that had contacted the office, a most tedious task assigned to a young girl undergraduate who was helping the MacGregor campaign for practically nothing. She confirmed that Krupper Films had a crew in the U.S. for three months from August. But she had not asked the reasons for the crew's visit. If the girl had taken that one little step, the bona fide Krupper would have told her that their crew was filming a special documentary: on sharks in the Pacific.

Identikit composites of the assassin and "Himmel" were flashed across the U.S. and around the world. President Rickard stepped in for the second time and directed that the FBI work in conjunction with the CIA, but FBI Director Dent would maintain overall control unless there were international developments in the hunt. It soon became rumored that a foreign-based squad could have been responsible.

This added fuel to speculation in the media. Some argued that the assassination had all the earmarks of a CIA operation. The President was castigated for bringing in the CIA at all, and so early. Other papers and magazines, such as *U.S. News & World Report*, postulated that only the KGB could be behind such a professional effort. But they were hard put to explain the motivation. If anything, the U.S.S.R. would be better off with MacGregor, who seemed to be promising a softer line on foreign policy than the incumbent. Others looked for still more obscure political groups with grievances against MacGregor.

His every word on foreign and domestic policy was put through an exhaustive sieve. Was he pro-Israel or pro-Arab? What were his views on Africa? And Southeast Asia? Himmel was described as looking Spanish, and could have been South American. Which way did MacGregor saddle up in that part of the world? Still others started by asking, "Who stood to lose most with Mac-Gregor as President?" or, "Who stood to gain most by having Rickard remain in power?"

Analysis led to innuendo. And it spared no one. Not even the President of the United States himself.

5

Graham's tour flew out of Kiev on Thursday afternoon, bound for the ancient Ukrainian city of Poltava for a twenty-four-hour stay, and then on to Leningrad. They arrived midafternoon, and Graham found that after checking in at the Soveyetsky Hotel he had a few hours to kill before a night at the Kirov Ballet.

He took a taxi to the Nevsky Prospect, Leningrad's main street. The autumn afternoon air was brisk, and despite the sun, many Russians were already wearing overcoats and fur-lined hats.

Graham sauntered toward the gilded steeple of the Russian Admiralty facing the Neva River, and stopped occasionally to photograph the blended styles of the prospect's austere classical façades alternated with baroque statuary. He found that every time he stopped, the young street merchants and illegal money-changers surrounded him. Just as in Kiev, they wanted to buy every item on him from sunglasses to shoes. He refused the offers of rubles for his clothes or his foreign currency and had to keep moving to avoid a crowd building up.

When he had almost reached the Hermitage, the former entrance to the Winter Palace of the czars, he crossed the prospect and walked back.

At the Griboyedov Canal running at right angles to and under the prospect, the silhouette of a multidomed structure caught his eye. He squinted into the sun and moved closer along the side of the canal to get a better view. It was the church of the Savior-on-the-Spilled-Blood, which was under repair. Scaffolding wound halfway around the front façade. Graham crossed a small footbridge which drew him up close to the church, and began to take snapshots. A woman came into view about fifty yards past the church, heading in his direction.

She was about thirty, tall and strikingly attractive. Dressed in a gray skirt, matching jacket and white silk blouse, she waltzed along swinging a handbag, her long legs pivoting with every step.

The woman stopped about ten yards from Graham. Shading her eyes, she looked up at the rococo structure, and diverted her attention to him momentarily. Graham's camera was pointed at her. She hurried on toward the prospect, twice looking back angrily.

Graham dined alone at the Hotel Europa on the Nevsky Prospect, and was in time for the start of the ballet at 8:30 in the opulent gold Kirov theater.

The powerful ballet, *A Legend of Love*, set in ancient Arabian times, had a quaint Marxist twist at the finish. (After winning the heart of the princess, the handsome worker decided to ditch her and stay with his fellow workers.)

The Australian was seated at the back of the first balcony. While the orchestra warmed up, he surveyed the glittering scene with opera glasses. The theater was packed with people well turned out in expensive attire. Some were foreign diplomats and their families, but Graham guessed the great majority were from Russia's elite, from the arts, sciences, the military and government. Just as he spotted people from his tour, a woman sitting alone near to them caught his attention. She was the one he had seen hours earlier at the church. At first he was not sure she was the same person, because her flaxen hair was now piled high to expose an elegant neck. But when she looked around there was no mistaking the fine straight nose and high cheekbones.

Graham watched her until the lights dimmed for the first act of the ballet.

After act one, he moved into a refreshment bar on the first floor. He ordered champagne and found a seat at a table occupied by a Frenchwoman and her young daughter, who had dropped a melting chocolate on her frilly white frock. The mother chastised her and dragged her off to the washroom. When Graham looked around again, one of the seats had been taken. It was the unwilling subject of his photography. She was looking the other way, sipping champagne.

"Good evening," he said softly.

She looked at him and feigned surprise.

"You with the camera."

The Australian smiled and nodded.

"Why did you photograph me?"

Graham looked directly into her wide blue eyes, which had more than a hint of fading youth at the corners. "I collect pictures of beautiful women."

Seemingly embarrassed, her eyes dropped momentarily. "Where are you from?"

"Australia."

"What is your work?"

"Anthropology. And yours?"

"I am an economist." She looked around the room each time she spoke. It seemed to be a nervous habit.

"Where do you stay?"

"Soveyetsky."

"You like Leningrad?"

"Yes. It is very beautiful."

Bells began ringing for the second act.

"Many parts of the Soviet Union are attractive." She smiled. "Do you go to Moscow?"

"Yes. Wednesday." He stood up to leave.

"Can we meet?"

Graham was slightly taken aback. "After the ballet?" he asked, thinking his luck was in.

"If you wish. In front at the finish?" She stood up and shook hands. "My name is Svetlana."

He nodded and smiled, and then moved off. The woman sipped her champagne, and allowed herself the faintest reflective smile.

A gusty wind drove rain through the streets of Miami as the power brokers of MacGregor's party reconvened at the Doral Hotel on Saturday, September 27, to choose a new nominee for the presidency. About thirty had quickly entrenched themselves in the hotel to organize the new contest, and to attempt to rekindle the fire of the traditional convention. There could not be the same revelry and style associated with normal selection. However, the media would be there in force to capture the one thing left to the party—its spirit.

The convention would be a close-fought, determined affair. Already fierce and intense lobbying had started across the country. On Saturday no potential candidate stood head and shoulders above the rest as MacGregor had done. Death had been a great leveler. Perhaps only Paul Mineva was a name that seemed to crop up more consistently than any other. Although no one seemed particularly inspired by the former Nevada governor, the media was widely predicting he would figure prominently. He had run second to MacGregor in well over half the state primaries. Despite the lukewarm popularity of the man within the party itself, he seemed to have a well-oiled team pushing him along.

As the telephones ran hot from the Doral across the nation, the organizers continued to canvass opinion, debate began about who should run, and who should be invited to run. By 10:00 A.M., in an attempt to assist delegates as they rolled into Miami, a list of possibles had been drawn up.

An hour later, the fight had been quickly whittled down to four contenders: Governor Mineva and Senators Seargent, Nelson and Kenneally—if he would run. Seargent, like Mineva, had fought hard but unsuccessfully right through the primaries but had never gained popular enough support to be a serious challenge to MacGregor. Nelson, a seasoned performer who had figured prominently at two past conventions, had shown up in the California primary in July as a last-minute possible and, predictably, had done poorly. Now, as an experienced, steadying influence, he had an outside chance. Out of the four, Kenneally would be the popular choice because of his name and good reputation throughout the party and the nation. However, by midmorning, he narrowed the choice to three, when he called from Washington to tell the party national committee chairman he would definitely not be a starter.

As the delegates showed up, the lobbying in the hotel rooms, in the bars and over brunch in the dining room reached a peak and continued until around 3:00 P.M. Then it became clear that Nelson had failed once more to get support. He had been vacationing on the Italian coast at Amalfi and had not heard about the assassination until late Friday. The committee was told he was trying to catch a plane from Rome's Leonardo da Vinci airport, back to Miami.

An airport strike had grounded Nelson and he could not possibly get to the Doral until late Sunday night. He was already being outlobbied to such an extent that the battle now was really down to two men: Paul Mineva and Daniel Seargent.

Graham was taken by Svetlana to the Hotel Astoria opposite St. Isaac's Cathedral for a drink after the Kirov Ballet. She introduced him to several friends, including a couple named Mars and Marina Gorsky, who said they planned to visit Moscow at the same time as the Australian.

Graham had been attracted by Svetlana's charm and beauty and was more than willing to enjoy himself with her until the early hours of the morning. With jacket and tie off, and shirt buttons undone to the waist, he danced with her to the Greek music of Theodorakis. As the hours slipped away, and the French champagne and atmosphere took hold of Graham, warnings from British Intelligence about Russian women faded with the prospect of bedding Svetlana. She seductively played up to him and eventually invited him to take a taxi back to her west Leningrad apartment.

Its lavish appointments—everything was Western-made, from the stereo to the marble coffee table—triggered a feeling of apprehension in Graham's stomach. Everything now smacked of a classic set-up by the Soviet secret police. He knew no ordinary Soviet citizen could obtain, let alone afford, such luxury. The Australian began to think through everything about their chance meeting as Svetlana made coffee, poured him a large cognac and put on some modern Western soul music. He decided there was little point in leaving her now and anyway it was 4:00 A.M. and probably difficult to get a taxi. As long as he didn't divulge anything that could incriminate him or make her suspicious . . .

After some passionate caressing on the couch, Svetlana pushed Graham away and asked, "Would you like to hear the news from London?" Bemused, the Australian gave an as-you-wish shrug. He leaned back on the couch and watched Svetlana move to her stereo unit and switch on the radio. She waved to him teasingly and disappeared into the bedroom.

Graham stood up, slid off his jacket and unbuttoned his

shirt. Suddenly he was aware of the words ringing out of the radio . . .

". . . in the assassination. Senator MacGregor was shot three times by an unknown man who visited his Washington office early on Friday morning, Moscow time . . ."

The Australian turned and moved toward the sound. The description of the assassin drained the color from his face.

". . . probably German, about fifty, with a faint scar, and a slight limp . . ."

It was brief but the same as that of the man last seen with Jane Ryder. Stunned, Graham sat on the couch again. He struggled to find a reason for the possible connection. What if . . .

He looked up to see Svetlana standing near him in a seductive see-through nightdress.

"Did you hear that?" he said incredulously. "Someone murdered MacGregor . . ."

"So?" Svetlana said sulkily. She was annoyed that the Australian's amorous advances seemed forgotten.

Graham restlessly got up and moved to a window that overlooked a bare stone courtyard three floors below. One bleak light flickered uncertainly.

"It couldn't be . . ." he said to himself. Svetlana looked slightly perplexed.

"What is the difference?" She shrugged. "He will be replaced by another. Politicians are all the same in the West. They are controlled by capitalists who grow fat exploiting the workers."

Her scoffing, unfeeling words stung the Australian. He swung around. "How the bloody hell would you know? You're not even allowed . . ." Graham checked himself. He walked over to the marble coffee table and reached for his cognac. Swirling it angrily for a few moments he looked around the room, but not at Svetlana. Then he downed the liquid quickly and made an effort to stop thinking about the assassination.

Taking off his shirt, he turned to look at her as she sat pensively on the couch smoking a thin Russian cigar. Svetlana looked up at his face. The eyes were intent and cold, a trace of a smile at the corner of her mouth. He took the cigar from her and stubbed it slowly, deliberately, in a tray. "Come on," he said, firmly pulling her up, "let's get more comfortable."

They walked into the bedroom. One side-lamp highlighted the pastel colors of the walls, ceiling and huge double bed, Svetlana slipped beneath the covers as Graham removed the rest of his clothes. All the time his gaze was fixed on her.

As the Australian moved in beside Svetlana, she reached to switch off the lamp above their heads. Graham grabbed her wrist and pulled it away from the light. She looked at him uncertainly and shook her head. Graham nodded mockingly and held her one free hand firmly. He then locked his knees on the inside of her legs just above the knees so that she could not close them. She resisted mildly as the Australian stared down at her with pleasurable anticipation.

As they moved together, it was with a violent urgency. When it was over, they were both calm and still. She felt his weight and his fingers releasing the grip from the hair at the back of her head. His heavy breathing subsided as the sweet-bitter smell of sex and sweat lingered. She turned her head to one side as the last involuntary twitches of pleasure pulsed unevenly. She looked at him and he smiled. It was a satisfied smile. Graham rolled easily away as Svetlana reached for the light again. This time there was no resistance.

Graham's suspicions about Svetlana were suspended at the back of his mind during most of Saturday when she showed him the sights.

In the morning it was a walk in Decembrists' Square; in the afternoon a taxi to the opulent Palace of Peter outside Leningrad, and at night a rock opera at the Gorky theater. Svetlana had been full of questions about his profession and background. But the Australian was not overly troubled. Her curiosity seemed normal and his cover was never tested by her inquisitiveness.

Only once were his doubts aroused and that was in the afternoon when he was taking snapshots at the Palace of Peter. Remembering their first encounter twenty-four hours ago, Graham again attempted to take photographs of Svetlana. But she reacted angrily when he pointed the camera at her as they sat on a garden bench. He wondered what her fear was.

What concerned him more was her occupation of his time. He had not had a chance to attempt a meeting with one of his most important contacts, Professor Boronovsky, the leading Soviet dissident scientist.

When George Revel had given Graham the contact, he had warned the Australian not to take any risks. The professor had been in trouble with the KGB over his activities as a political dissident. Surveillance on him was bound to be tight.

After the rock opera Graham made the excuse that he should get back to his hotel for the night and make an appearance with his tour group. He promised to see Svetlana the next day.

She protested mildly, but the Australian was insistent. No one from the tour had seen him for more than a day, he told her. A few friends in the group might be worried.

As they kissed and parted outside the Gorky theater, Svetlana said, "I shall call you in half an hour."

Graham thought the remark strange but did not dwell on it as he took a taxi back to his hotel.

On entering the lobby, he scribbled out notes for a couple of people in the tour group and then went to his room to wait for Svetlana's call. It came one slow cigarette later.

"I miss you," she said pleadingly.

"I miss you too," Graham replied affectionately. "We'll meet at three P.M. tomorrow, okay?"

"You don't want to see me tonight?"

"Of course I do, but we'll be together soon . . ."

There was a pause. Graham heard a click and some interference on the line. The call was being monitored.

"I think of you all night."

"Me too, Svetlana," Graham said softly. "Sleep well."

She hung up. The Australian kept the receiver to his ear. There was a definite double click sound once more. Then to Graham's alarm, Russian voices. Then nothing. He put the receiver down and stared at it for several seconds. That worm of fear was wriggling in his gut again. Perhaps it would be better to avoid the beautiful Svetlana. . . .

He walked down to the kiosk on his floor to buy some mineral water and found a few people buying things. It took five minutes to be served. On returning to his room he heard the telephone ringing. He ran down the corridor to answer it. It was Svetlana again.

"Where were you?" Her tone was strangely cold.

"I was just getting some water ..." The spying bitch! Graham thought.

"Why don't you want to be with me tonight?" she demanded.

"Look, Svetlana," Graham said aggressively, hiding his apprehension, "I'm tired. I'm going to bed. I'll see you tomorrow."

"You have someone else tonight?"

"Don't be absurd."

There was a long silence before she said curtly, "I see you tomorrow as planned," and hung up.

Graham put the receiver down. An eerie feeling crept over him and his instincts about avoiding her firmed. But then a more chilling thought hit him. If he ran from her, who would be spying on him next? Reluctantly he decided it would be better to keep the date.

"Mineva is the man." The message swept through the corridors of the Doral. By Sunday midafternoon, as far as the experienced party members, power brokers, ordinary delegates and the media were concerned, the story of the rushed, truncated and fiercely fought reconvention was over. Probably the one deciding factor that gave Mineva the nomination was the strong endorsement he received from the shattered MacGregor camp. There did not seem to be anyone with whom it could compromise after having faced the electorate with Mineva on the original ticket. Now the sharpened knives were being put away for another day. It had been, for most delegates, a most viciously fought convention. Attacks on candidates were merciless. Mineva's rivals claimed he had sabotaged their efforts with a spate of dirty tricks, such as the distribution of scandal about their private lives, and stories of mental illnesses, which seemed to be the favorite topics for reporters. East Coast Senator Daniel Seargent, a short, stocky and pugnosed man with a rather quiet and cultured disposition, seemed to be bearing the brunt of some wild accusations. Finally he was forced to prove he had a clean bill of mental health.

Mineva's camp also claimed to be under a lot of pressure and scrutiny from the media, especially in the area of tax returns and unproven accusations of secret sources of huge illegal campaign funds.

After these outbursts of accusation, public acrimony began

to subside as party members urged each other to close ranks behind the emerging new nominee. Seargent officially gave up the battle with a rushed little press conference.

"At this stage," he concluded, "I must concede that, after what has been a good fight, Governor Mineva will carry the convention. He has the numbers. I do not. There is nothing much else to say at this point. . . ."

Several reporters began to gabble at once. Most wanted to know why he had, only hours before, told a handful of journalists it had been a "rotten" rather than a "good" fight.

On Sunday night, in his hotel room, Mineva sat back in an open-neck shirt and slacks to watch the convention roll call, which was simply a formality to confirm what everyone knew. As the last important state came up in his favor to make the nomination mathematically and legally his, the press and media in the room moved forward to catch his reaction. He dream-walked around the room, as camera shutters clicked. There was much hugging of relatives and shaking of hands. The telephone was ringing in another room. An aide rushed to answer it. President Rickard on the line. Next, the Vice President. Then other calls from well-wishers. Everything Mineva said could be heard through an open door until one call came through from New York. For this, Mineva kicked the door shut as he exploded hoarsely down the receiver: "Christ! We've done it!"

There was a momentary pause as the nominees mounted the rostrum in the Hotel Doral ballroom. The national party chairman ordered up music from the band. About eight hundred in the audience and another ninety million or so in twenty-three million American homes watched at the prime viewing time of 9:30 Eastern time on Sunday night. Kenneally, Seargent and Nelson led the new nominee up as the band played, "Hail, hail, the gang's all here." Then to polite applause, other nominees, party prominents and celebrities, including some well-known film stars and sports heroes supporting the party, joined the others on the rostrum. Senator Kenneally spoke first to a hushed audience.

His words were authoritative and sensible. He promised his

1 4 2

full-hearted support for Mineva to overcome all obstacles. Next up to the microphone was the old warhorse and veteran campaigner, Nelson, who spoke briefly. His short, brilliant speech was full of emotion, and his words stirred the hearts of the party faithful. Despite his bitterness about being outflanked before he had a chance to get into the race fo the nomination, he spoke positively and praised Mineva. He set the stage for the nominee, the man of the moment, who stood up to make the most of it. Mineva motioned commandingly for quiet, his face now more a grimace than a smile. With silence, and after a characteristic sweep of his fair hair off the forehead, he was away.

"With an open heart and mixed feelings of intense gratitude and deep, deep sadness, I accept your nomination . . ." A nervous lull was followed by scattered applause which built to respectability with help from several on the rostrum.

"It is not the way I would like to have accepted your support. But if it must be this way, then I am ready. . . ." He emphasized the last words through clenched teeth and with a jabbing hand motion.

"My nomination is not the nomination of an individual. It is the continuation of a set of strong ideals which made, and will continue to make, this nation strong and great!" He did not wait for the applause. "It demonstrates that nothing, no person, no country, no organization can crush the spirit of our party and our nation." Applause caused him to stop a few seconds.

"Anyone can destroy an individual. We know only too well that we are but flesh and blood, and that is why we are here, reassembled today. . . ." He raised his voice. "But let us remind those that perpetrate such heinous crimes that you cannot destroy ideals. Not if they are strong and good!"

Mineva paused again for the less inhibited response. His words seemed to be striking the right chord. He decided to pluck a little harder. Continuing on the theme of ideals, he built emotion with references to MacGregor.

"My ambition as your nominee is to carry out the promises that Ronald MacGregor made to you after the July convention. And one of the first acts on my part will be to visit the Soviet Union, as he recently indicated to me he would!"

A wild supportive response caused Mineva to smile and

wave. His running mate, Pennsylvania Senator Samuel Dart, got up, and shook hands with the candidate and lingered on the rostrum for the clicking cameras. When Dart had returned to his seat and the whistles, clapping and stomping had subsided, Mineva continued.

"Our party, unlike the current administration, has always believed in peace more than anything else. So in the interests of this fundamental priority, I shall personally pledge peace, when I am elected President, through continued negotiation for the mutual benefit of ourselves and the Soviet Union, instead of foolish confrontation!" This led Mineva nicely into the ritual attack on the opposition.

"So nothing has changed. I hope Everett Rickard realizes what strength there is in our ranks even after such a great setback. We still have a mighty cause and a mighty purpose . . . ." His words were drowned in applause. Mineva waited again.

"In fact, I think Mr. Rickard should start writing his memoirs or looking for a new job right now. . . ." Applause. "Because we are going to win on November fourth!" There were cheers and sustained clapping. "And when I am in the White House, all of us together can exchange peace for confrontation, reasonableness for stubbornness and bigotry, love for hate and fear, so that we may go forward in the pursuit of our goals, our ideals, our dreams for a greater America and a safer world for us and our children and our grandchildren's grandchildren. . . ."

Instant polls taken after his acceptance speech said 36 percent would vote for the new man as against Rickard's 44 percent, with the rest undecided. A win for Mineva was not an impossible task, and many of the delegates to the convention were citing the improved performances of Truman and Ford in the last weeks before polling day. But there were only thirty-five days left to build a credible alternative to Rickard.

Graham took a taxi to Nevsky Prospect on Sunday morning after breakfast with the tour and found a telephone booth off a side street. He thought it was now too risky to make calls from his hotel if they were monitored. He dialed a number Revel had given to him, let it ring four times, and then dialed again. On the sixth ring a woman answered in Russian.

"Could I speak to the owner please?" the Australian said. Clearing his throat to overcome a slight tremble, he added, "I am a friend of the family." It was the code Revel had instructed Graham to use.

"Just a minute," the woman said, this time in English. After about forty-five seconds she returned to the phone. "He is not in. Could you call back?"

Graham hung up without saying another word. He left the telephone booth and had some difficulty lighting a cigarette. His hands were shaking. "Could you call back" meant a rendezvous would be planned.

Pulling his overcoat collar up over the back of his neck to shield against the brisk morning, he walked down by the Winter Palace, near the end of the prospect. Finding another telephone, he dialed the number again.

"Could I speak to the owner please? I am a friend of the family."

A man answered this time.

"Yes. He is at apartment eleven, number 457 Mechinov Street." The man repeated the address and hung up.

Graham left the booth, his brow knit in concentration. The number 457 indicated the time would be 7:00 A.M. for the meeting. He shut his eyes hard and saw the address up on an imaginary screen. It was his way of storing the information forever.

Seconds later he hailed a taxi. As he entered it, he had the uneasy feeling that he was being watched by unseen people in the crowd on the prospect and in the buildings.

Graham met Svetlana four hours later at the newsstand on the first floor of the Hermitage. She insisted on being his guide around its many treasure chambers, shrewdly made public for state propaganda against the czarist regimes that had originally acquired many of the works of art there.

Convinced now that she was spying on him, the Australian had the unsettling feeling that his every move and comment were being tabulated and recorded. It struck him most markedly when they had spent some time in the Impressionist and modern art section, where Graham had lingered enthusiastically to savor some works of the great masters. He thought of the break-in at his

London apartment. Didn't MI-6 say that the place could have been microfilmed? What if it had been by the KGB and they had photographed his library? In it were some eighty-odd books on all aspects of Impressionist and modern art. . . . What if someone somehow connected up the dossier on Edwin Graham and Svetlana's possible report on the interests of Dr. Ross Boulter? Hadn't they argued over the merits of the Russian composer Shostakovich? Graham had gathered nearly all his compositions in his music library. . . .

Suddenly his enthusiasm for the many fine Picassos around him faded and died.

Graham made a conscious effort to hide his feelings and concern, and to act as if his affections for Svetlana were growing. But he could not change the new perspective on his Russian companion. The habit of looking around nervously when she spoke to him now took on a distinctly furtive hue. The lines at the corner of the eyes now seemed to represent the result of probably a decade of KGB agent-prostitution rather than the first signs of fading youth and maturing beauty. . . . He began to wonder how many others before him she had literally bedded for information. . . .

And the eyes, on the occasion that they stayed long enough on his, gave more than a hint of suspicion and coldness rather than inquisitiveness and candor.

It was only later in bed that Graham felt he could cope better with the situation. There in the semidarkness he could feign his desire for Svetlana in the mechanical physicalness of mindless sex.

Just after six on Monday morning, Svetlana woke to find the Australian almost fully dressed. Looking at the luminous dial of the alarm clock on the dresser next to her bed she asked, "Why do you leave so early?"

Graham turned to her.

"I want to have breakfast with the tour."

"I can make . . ."

"Look. Some of my friends were worried about me last time. I'm joining them at the hotel and that's that."

She turned on the bedside lamp, rubbed her eyes, and stared at him as he swung his jacket on.

"When shall I see you?"

"I don't know, tonight maybe."

He leaned over to kiss her but she turned her head away. Graham gave a cynical grunt and walked out of the apartment. He took an elevator to the ground floor and hurried out of the building into the almost deserted street. One taxi was at the rank a hundred yards from Svetlana's place. Graham asked the driver to take him to the south bank of Vasilivsky Island. Once there, he waited for several minutes, looking out over the Neva Canal and the stone landscape silhouetted against the breaking dawn. Clearly in his head was a tortuous route of back streets he worked out from a map of Leningrad and a taxi tour he had taken after his telephone contact the previous morning. Looking around carefully for anyone who might be in pursuit, Graham began a brisk walk of two miles which took him behind Kazan Cathedral between Plehanova and Sadovaja streets, and a few minutes later to cobblestoned Mechinov Street. It was approaching 7:00 A.M. and workers were coming into the streets.

He turned down the third archway on the right into a small courtyard. He stopped and looked around. One kerosene lamp flickered. There was no one in sight. Graham found the entrance to back stairs and took the stone steps to the third floor. There was no light. He knocked gently on the thick oak door to number eleven. Two minutes later he knocked again and the door opened quickly. A figure ushered him in and the door was bolted behind him. The man stared at Graham for several seconds before moving over to a window facing Mechinov Street below.

Graham moved close to him. In the half-light of the dawn, he could see it was Dmitri Boronovsky. In his early forties, he looked fitter and taller than in press photos. His forehead was large, the size accentuated because of baldness. The nose was prominent and slightly twisted. The strong chin was marked with an ugly scar.

The scientist looked down to the street as he spoke in a deep, firm voice. "Sit down if you wish." He pointed to a tatty fold-out double-bed couch, the only piece of furniture in the musty-smelling room. The Australian remained standing. The atmosphere had put him on edge.

"I know little about why you are here," Boronovsky said,

"but the contact is absolutely reliable. I will help you if I can. I risk everything to speak to you like this. We must be brief." He glanced at Graham. "Were you followed?"

"I don't think so. I caught a taxi to the south bank and walked the rest of the way."

"The taxi may have been a trap."

"I was careful the driver didn't follow me." Graham lit a cigarette. "I'm mainly interested in what you can tell me about the administration's computer plans."

He offered Boronovsky a cigarette. The scientist moved a few paces from the window to accept it. Then he stepped back.

"How much do you know?"

"Only that some kind of sophisticated computer bank is being built."

"It's a master network based in Moscow, Leningrad and Kiev."

"For what?"

"The complete control of the Soviet military and society."

Graham's eyes narrowed on the scientist.

"Who controls it?"

"The KGB, although it did not initiate the network. The Twenty-fourth Communist Party Congress in 1971 set out a plan to improve the state's economic and social management. Top Soviet scientists suggested it was a job for advanced computers. They advocated a master network for the whole state economy."

Boronovsky suddenly leaned forward.

"Are you sure you were not followed?" he asked sharply without looking at the Australian.

"Why?"

"See that car. It has just turned around. . . ."

Graham stubbed out his cigarette on the bare stone floor and moved to the window. The car had stopped almost opposite them.

"What do you want to do?" he asked nervously.

"If someone comes we must go quickly. There is a way out."

Both men kept their eyes on the car.

"Let me continue," Boronovsky said, dragging on his cigarette but being careful not to hold it up in front of the window.

"The master network the administration planned needed

thousands of computers. We found we could not produce our own for many reasons. . . ."

"I think I know most of them. How did the KGB get involved?"

"Andropolov told the government chiefs and scientists he could get them by smuggling them from the West. He completely changed the purpose of the network and built his own power base in the process. The master network is his stepping-stone to total power within the Soviet Union."

Graham had not taken his eyes off the stationary car below. "What are the master network's priorities?" he asked, almost in a whisper.

"There are three. Build-up of the military part of the network has the highest priority. The biggest computers coming in are immediately converted to military machines controlling weapons systems."

"And the second?"

"The KGB wants watertight control over society. The network will allow mass repression. Andropolov and his technocrats are using it to crush anyone fighting for greater freedom or rights. . . ."

The car had crawled to the top of Mechinov Street and turned around.

"The third?"

"The third priority is a combination of the first and second: increased control over satellite and puppet nations. Wherever there is Soviet influence it will be greatly strengthened by military intimidation and computerized political control. . . ."

Graham had the overall picture. Time could be up any second. He had to have specifics. . . .

"Can you give examples of how the files are used for political control? Against dissidents, for instance?"

Boronovsky sighed. "They are innumerable. Perhaps the most vivid development is where a simple device is secretly added to a television set. It allows anyone, anywhere, to be spied on when their set is going. People can be observed and listened to. . . . I have forgotten the English technical term for this computer-controlled . . ."

"Interactive television. Is this operating?"

"Yes. We believe at least in all the homes of dissidents. . . ."

1 4 9

"You have some proof?"

"Yes. Our informants give us details about the KGB planting the device . . . and of course there is other proof. When people are arrested there is no doubt evidence gathered could only have come from this special form of electronic spying." Boronovsky's voice trembled more from rage than fear, Graham guessed. "It is the most disgusting form of surveillance. . . ."

"I want more examples like that," the Australian said urgently as they watched the car crawl down near their building once more.

"From personal experience we know the KGB has built computer identification checks. Soon anyone traveling any distance in the Soviet Union, or outside it, will have to carry a small computer card. The card of anyone seen as a threat to the state, such as myself, will activate computer scanner alarms for closer inspection. . . ."

He broke off for a few seconds as the car headlights went out. "Another form of surveillance by the network can analyze behavior patterns . . . an important MI-6 agent was recently uncovered by it . . ."

Boronovsky broke off suddenly. Four figures had quickly gotten out of the car.

"They have come!" The scientist grabbed Graham by the arm and pushed him toward a window at the back of the room.

"One more question," Graham whispered as Boronovsky struggled with a window latch leading to a balcony. "What computers are going into the network?"

"They're all Cheetah . . ." the scientist said urgently as he forced the latch. "When they come through the courtyard, go down there!" He pointed to a ladder of circular iron railings that ran down the wall about ten yards to the courtyard ground. Seconds later three men ran through the archway and headed for the back stairs. Graham edged into the balcony and descended the railings, Boronovsky following. Suddenly Graham stopped. He pointed down to one of the men who stood in the archway below. Boronovsky didn't see Graham's movement and accidentally kicked the fingers of his right hand which gripped the railing. Graham grabbed at the railing but lost his hold and fell. He landed awkwardly on top of the man, and they both sprawled on the ground.

The man seemed winded, but still managed to stun Graham with a kick in the back of the head and the stomach. They exchanged blows as they grappled. Boronovsky reached the ground and went to Graham's aid. They brought the man down with several blows, and then moved off fast, Boronovsky leading the way down several side streets. They brushed their way past workers for about four hundred yards until they reached an underground station.

Pale and out of breath, Boronovsky fumbled in his pocket. "I must leave you know," he gasped. "Quick, take these!" He shoved two train tokens into Graham's trembling hands. "I'll show you where to catch the train." The scientist hurriedly moved down more steps with Graham close behind. They stood at the top of the escalator. Boronovsky pointed to another about twenty yards away.

"You take a train down there for as long as you wish," he said, "then a taxi back to your hotel. You should be safe that way."

Both men looked urgently up to the entrance. Boronovsky mounted the escalator and Graham ran along the passage toward the other. He took one last look at the scientist as he shrank into the bowels of the very deep Leningrad subway. Echoing in Graham's mind, as if it were reverberating off the walls of the tunnels, was the vital answer to his last question—"Cheetah."

KGB agent 3342 Svetlana Moronova had put in an extra long report on Australian tourist Dr. Ross Boulter, which she hoped would gain the attention of her superiors.

She had been genuinely curious about her assignment. Yet, being truly honest with herself, her motivations were more for survival purposes than because of real suspicion.

Svetlana had been a state-agent prostitute for twelve years and she was becoming increasingly worried that her age could soon put her on the KGB scrapheap. Younger women were being persuaded to join the secret police all the time to do their sexual bit for the glory of the Great Leninist-Marxist State, and she had heard rumors that experienced women like herself had been imprisoned or even liquidated for knowing too much.

Svetlana had learned more than most. She had made her reputation on three major assignments, involving the compromising of a French ambassador, an American businessman in the rocket industry, and an Arab diplomat with foreign policy secrets.

But they had all been more than five years ago. Now she was being put on lesser assignments such as this touring anthropologist, a routine surveillance similar to thousands run each year on foreigners. Svetlana feared it was the slippery slope to nowhere. She was becoming desperate. She had tried hard to fill out reports on her last few assignments, but they had been boring nonevents. Dr. Ross Boulter offered more scope.

On Monday morning she received a telephone call at her apartment which appeared to offer new hope. It was her immediate superior who asked her to report to the KGB's Leningrad HQ an hour later.

Graham went straight back to his hotel after his underground escape. The back of his head throbbed and the pit of his stomach ached from the kicks. He was slightly concussed and fell into a deep sleep in his hotel room.

He awoke six hours later to the brain-vacillating ring of the telephone. Graham fumbled for the receiver.

"Hallo."

No one answered. Seconds later the telephone went dead.

Graham sat up on the bed and lit a cigarette. The mistiness in his head cleared enough for events to arrange themselves in time and space.

Meeting Boronovsky. The fight. The escape. He rolled over and the legacy from several blows shot to his brain.

The telephone rang again.

"Yes?"

"Hallo?"

"Svetlana. Did you call me a minute ago?"

"No," she said, a note of confusion in her tone. "Why aren't you with your tour group?"

"I'll explain later . . ." Graham struggled hard to sound alert. Tiredness strained his voice.

"Are you going to see me today?" Svetlana asked.

"No . . . let's have dinner tomorrow night." The Australian had to stall her to allow himself to recover completely. But he didn't want to leave the hotel. "Why don't you meet me in the lobby here at, say, eight-thirty?"

"If you wish," Svetlana said angrily and hung up. Again there was a ghostly click about fifteen seconds later.

Graham lay back on the bed and continued smoking. He wondered how much Svetlana knew. Had someone found out about the morning's incident? Suddenly he felt ill. He rolled off the bed and sat on the only chair in the room. His breath came quickly as people and events spun around in his head, thumping, colliding, deflecting.

Realizing he must be in a state of shock, the Australian went to the bathroom. Seconds later he was dry-retching over the toilet bowl, but without success. He shakily poured himself a glass of mineral water and walked unsteadily back into the other room. Sitting in the chair again, he drank the water. This seemed to cool him momentarily, but still not enough. . . . Would his cover be blown? Had he got Boronovsky into trouble? Could he end up in a mental hospital like MI-6's dead agent Steven?

Graham looked around the room at the light brackets, a stark, lonely flower painting, the telephone, the television set. He felt as if he were in a cell.

He thought of Boronovsky's information on surveillance by television, and the obvious telephone bugging. He wondered where the other bugs for sound were in the room. In the light brackets? Behind the picture?

Leaning his head back, Graham inwardly cursed himself for getting caught up in such a crazy nightmare. He felt there and then that he had cracked and could not go on with the investigation. Trying desperately to calm himself, he began to breathe deeply and slowly, concentrating on a void.

Minutes later the shock and panic subsided to a more rational, controllable fear. He wanted simply to get out of the Soviet Union as soon as possible. He picked up the telephone on the bedside table and asked reception to put him through to his tour guide, Victor.

"Yes, Dr. Boulter?"

"Victor, I want to catch the next possible flight out of the Soviet Union."

"That is not possible, Doctor," the tour guide said, sounding surprised. "Is there anything wrong? Are you ill?"

The last thing Graham wanted was to be examined by a

doctor. "No, I'm okay; I'm just sick of the place, that's all."

There was an embarrassed silence before Victor said, "I can only offer you an earlier flight out on the day you are scheduled to leave. But it is highly irregular and I cannot assure you of it. You will have to arrive at the airport about six A.M. and hope to leave on the seven A.M. flight to Gatwick, England."

"Thanks a billion," Graham said sarcastically, hiding his desperation. "Let me know if you can do better, please."

"We shall only know next Saturday morning. Officially your flight is still for two P.M."

Graham put the receiver down hard. The almost meaningless concession meant he still had nearly five days left in Russia. At that moment the Australian felt certain his nerves would not last the distance.

Anatoli Bromovitch had had a mixed day. He had spent most of it deeply engrossed in his favorite hobby, tending cymbidium orchids in the hothouse in the back of his dacha outside Moscow. This he enjoyed immensely because it allowed him to breed competition flowers, for which he was fast becoming famous throughout the Soviet Union. It was a patient yet rewarding pastime, made less frustrating by a computer terminal in his dacha which allowed the assassin to do his calculations by hooking up with a big computer in Moscow normally used for KGB activities. Everyone at Dzerhinsky Square HQ had for years turned a blind eye to this little office perk which had never meant anything until the KGB recently began its installation of Cheetah machines. Now he was breeding prizewinners.

What had upset the tranquillity of his otherwise perfect day was the news that Edwin Graham had completely disappeared. Operatives in London instructed to locate the Australian and await orders for eliminating him, had found no trace of him for more than a week. Callers to Ryder Publications were being told that he was "indisposed" until further notice. Bromovitch's first thought was that the Australian had secretly left London. But for where? Another part of the United Kingdom? Another country? The United States maybe? Or even Australia?

Almost idly, the assassin began to key in on his computer terminal other reports for the day that he had to check through for more than three hours.

About an hour into the reports an item appeared which held his attention for marginally longer than the others.

FROM: OPERATION 10 COMMITTEE SECRETARY
TO: ALL OPERATIVES ASSIGNED TO OP. 10
PERSONNEL ASSIGNED TO PROFESSOR BORONOVSKY INVOLVED IN VIOLENT INCIDENT, AT 0700 HRS, SEPTEMBER 29. 3147 RECEIVED FRACTURED CHEEKBONE IN INCIDENT FROM UNKNOWN ASSAILANT. ADDRESS AT INCIDENT, MECHINOV STREET, LENINGRAD. BORONOVSKY TO BE INTERROGATED.

Had the person been almost anyone else but Boronovsky, Bromovitch would have pressed the file button on his terminal without a second thought. The professor was a well-known dissident scientist. There was nothing new in such people being detained or scrutinized. The difference here that alerted the assassin was that the professor was a computer scientist who had on two occasions protested that not enough information was being made public about the administration's plan for central planning by computer. This immediately gave him the status of "potential threat" to Operation Ten.

Bromovitch punched up a request on the terminal for a full report on the incident. The normal turn-around time for such a request was about an hour. So the assassin continued viewing his "in" file. Half an hour later another report appeared that had him thinking. It was from a highly placed Soviet agent in the American Federal administration, Gregor Haussermann, which read:

PICS COMMITTEE MEMBER GEORGE REVEL INVESTIGATING COMPUTER FLOW IN THE SOVIET UNION EXPECTS SOON FRESH INFORMATION FROM UNKNOWN SOURCE INSIDE SOVIET UNION.

Again the assassin called for more detail. Just as he had done so an expanded report came in on the first incident. Only one comment added anything significant. There had been two assailants in the incident where a KGB man had been attacked. One naturally was thought to be Boronovsky and the other was definitely unknown. Perhaps it was the quick, visual juxtaposition of these seemingly unrelated pieces of information that riveted Bromovitch's attention. Or perhaps it was the fact that in each case an "unknown" person was involved. The report from Gregor Haussermann was unable to pinpoint the source of the expected new information and no one had any idea who had accompanied Boronovsky. . . .

Haussermann's report of "fresh" information indicated one of two things. An enemy agent in place in the Soviet Union would pass it on, or perhaps someone on a Soviet mission would try to get it.

Bromovitch left the terminal and sauntered out to the hothouse deep in thought. One other fact sent his agile mind racing. Graham was missing. Could it possibly be that the Australian was connected with one or other of the two incidents inside the Soviet Union? It was a slim chance, but one he had to check out thoroughly. There was only one way he could sift quickly through the thousands of foreigners visiting the country, and that was by the Cheetah network. Fondling one of the prize orchids he was currently nurturing for an all-republics competition, the assassin pondered on the father of modern genetics, Gregor Mendel. How much better off he would have been in his lifetime of experiments with peas if he had had access to a large Cheetah. . . .

Svetlana was annoyed and depressed by her superiors' action regarding her assignment. Just when she had hoped she would be allowed to follow the Australian to Moscow, the assignment had been snatched from her. No reason had been given.

The irony was that her exaggerated, highly imaginative report on "Dr. Boulter" apparently had been taken seriously. Svetlana's experience told her it may have been combined with other information on him. All indications were that the Australian was important to her superiors. The chillingly intriguing thought was that he could be a foreign spy. . . . Svetlana's final orders had been to stay with him on his last night in Leningrad. With this in mind, she had managed to persuade him to dine with her on board a floating restaurant called the Pirate.

Graham was at first reluctant to leave the hotel with Svetlana, but agreed when he learned the restaurant was within walking distance. He had ventured out with other members of the tour for lunch at the Europa Hotel and had felt gradually less tense as each hour since his meeting with Boronovsky slipped away. Yet he was far from completely relaxed and had been nervous about any unknown person near him in or outside the hotel. The nagging fear was that he would be arrested, yet reason told him that the police would most likely have swooped on him by now if he had been under suspicion of meeting Boronovsky, or if his cover had been blown.

They joined the Pirate just after 9:00 P.M. at University Quay, under the lights opposite the Anthropology and Ethnography Museum, and made their way below deck to the dining area. Strobe lights of red and blue flashed intermittently to introduce a floor show to the eighty or so diners seated in cubicles on either side of the dance floor.

Graham tried to ease the tension by complimenting Svetlana on her appearance. Her flaxen hair was piled high, as it had been when they first met at the ballet, and she was dressed in a tantalizing low-cut, full-length black chiffon dress.

He had detected a change in her attitude once he had agreed to dine out with her. She seemed edgy. That habit of looking around when she was talking seemed worse. The conversation was strained. It fell away completely as they sat sipping champagne, watching a contortionist go through her back-breaking routine.

Later, when they were ordering a seafood meal, they were joined at the table by three young couples. One young Russian struck up a conversation with Graham on hearing the Australian's voice. The man said he was a purser on board a Soviet liner that took the Pacific route to Australia.

When there was a lull in the conversation, Svetlana whispered indignantly, "You speak to him, why?"

"Is there anything wrong?" Graham asked, looking hard at her.

Svetlana wanted to tackle him about everything, from his photography to his reasons for coming to the Soviet Union. But she checked herself. Graham could sense she was holding back. He felt a great urge to find out why and verbally squeeze something out of her. But he couldn't risk an outburst that would put him under suspicion. He was already regretting that he had panicked by asking the tour guide to get him out of the Soviet Union earlier than planned.

Svetlana began to sulk, and Graham resumed his conversation with the others at the table. She excused herself. The Australian watched her leave the table and exchanged glances with one of the diners he had not noticed before—a casually dressed woman, in her late thirties, with chiseled, aquiline features, large mouth and huge emerald eyes. She was at a table a few yards away with a petite brunette of about the same age.

When Svetlana returned Graham seemed to be preoccupied with the people around him and especially the woman at the opposite table. When Svetlana noticed this she was crestfallen. The woman who had caught his eye was her replacement, special agent Irena Pavliovic, assigned to make contact with Graham in Moscow.

He and Svetlana left the boat just after midnight and took a taxi to her apartment. They rode along in silence until she asked, "You seemed to be in pain at the restaurant. What is wrong?"

"Yes, I was in a minor accident yesterday in the taxi coming back from your apartment."

"Oh, what happened?"

"There was a collision with another car."

"You were unlucky at that time in the morning."

Graham paused and looked out of the window.

"The other car came racing out of a side street. The taxi was swung sideways. I got a few bruises."

"You did not mention this before."

"No. It's nothing to worry about."

"Have you seen a doctor?"

"No. It's nothing."

"Was the accident reported?"

Graham looked hard at her. "I don't know. You're full of questions, aren't you?"

"It should have been reported. All accidents must be. Did the police come?"

"No," Graham said, restraining himself. "I told you it was a minor accident. The taxi drove away."

Svetlana gave him a skeptical look and said nothing more until they arrived at her apartment.

"Are you staying with me?" she whispered as the driver stopped.

Graham shook his head. "No. I'd like to, but the tour leaves early for the airport tomorrow and I'm tired."

She nuzzled close. "Please. This is our last night."

Graham responded halfheartedly. Her hand pressed his stomach. He flinched.

"You are hurt," she said, with a puzzled expression. "Let me help you . . ."

"No, Svetlana," Graham said, leaning across and opening her door. She climbed out, slammed the door and stormed off.

The taxi driver, a big gruff individual, looked around at the foreigner.

"Soveyetsky," Graham said. The driver grunted and drove him at high speed back to his hotel.

"Come in, Harry," President Rickard said to his press secretary, in his quick-fire, imperious tone, when he heard the knock at his bedroom door early on September 30.

Forty-year-old Harry Emmery, a dapper, diminutive fellow with a neat, black mustache, poked his head in the door and was slightly taken aback at what he saw. The President was sitting naked on his fourposter brass bed pulling on socks. It wasn't so much his unclad condition as the presidential paunch that widened Emmery's eyes. A noticeable spare tire had appeared since those summer conferences around the White House pool, and fat pectorals hung loosely as he leaned forward to straighten his socks to the knees.

"What the hell are you staring at? Come in," Rickard said, as he stood up and pulled on his shorts. "Oh, yes, I'm overweight. You'd better give me a game of squash soon. It must be months since I last played."

"Whenever you like, sir."

Rickard hauled on his suit trousers and fumbled in a closet for shoes, cursing his valet. "Harry, you've seen this morning's papers. Mineva plans to visit the Kremlin next Thursday. What do you think?"

"It's an obvious attempt to steal the limelight. Plenty of mileage in it. But with so little time, I'm frankly surprised they are going."

"So am I, Harry." Rickard sat on the bed and laced his shoes. "MacGregor got the invitation. But the day before he was murdered, he told me he would not go before the election. But this sonofabitch Mineva is playing it right for those in the Soviet administration who would like to see me out."

"Andropolov and his KGB cohorts?"

"Right. They'll do most anything to embarrass me politically."

"What about Brechinov?"

"I think he's in trouble." Rickard put on a white shirt and cursed as he struggled with a top button. "He may be on the way out. He's struggling to hold power from Andropolov."

"What makes you think that?"

"I sent Brechinov a letter, a personal appeal to the man's good senses. It stressed the need for the Soviet Union to cut back its arms build-up to within agreed limits. His reply was bellicose, rambling and illogical. Not at all like the man. I've known him for thirty years. He does not want confrontation with us. He must be under terrific pressure from the KGB. . . ." Rickard yanked a tie from a crowded rack.

"Harry, I want you to put pressure on Mineva. Let your best media contacts know I've written to him on the delicacy of Soviet relations. It tells him to watch his step over there. I've also mentioned invoking the Logan Act to put him off balance."

"The Logan Act?"

"It prohibits any American—and that's all Mineva is—trying to influence any foreign government without authority from the President." Rickard ran a brush through his short hair. "I want to impress upon him the irregularity of his visit. Especially when things are going to get nasty between us and the Soviets."

Emmery frowned. "What do you mean?"

Rickard turned to him. "Okay," he said, sighing deeply. "What I'm about to tell you is absolutely top secret." Rickard put on his jacket. His expression tightened. "The Russians and Chinese are at it again, but it looks very dangerous this time. The Chinese have asked us urgently for ten billion dollars' worth of conventional and nuclear arms. They're really desperate. There has been a dramatic build-up of Soviet troops and missile launchers on China's northern border. The Chinese think the Soviets might strike at any time."

"Is that possible?"

"Very," Rickard said, his steely blue eyes fiercely intent. "We want the Soviets to back down . . . we're giving the Chinese those arms. . . ."

On the night of September 30, Brogan Junior, Strasburg and Huntsman met in the HQ war room to discuss the PPP and Paul Mineva's forthcoming trip to Moscow. The corporation had volunteered to help Mineva get media coverage from selected journalists and TV people by offering to fly them to Moscow. Brogan Senior was already in Moscow on business and preparing Mineva's arrival.

"How many media guys have you gotten on board?" Brogan Junior asked Huntsman.

"Fourteen. About forty correspondents in all will be at the press conference in Moscow."

"Where'll that be held?" Strasburg asked.

"We're putting on a breakfast at the National on Gorky Street next Friday morning.

"Will it be manageable?" the lawyer asked.

"Soviet officials will cooperate in setting it up. Several Soviet writers will ask the right questions as well. We'll have to let a few questions from outsiders through. But it won't be a problem. We'll have control of who asks what."

"This Logan Act that Rickard has threatened Mineva with," Brogan Junior said to Strasburg, "is that bluff?"

"Mineva should let the Soviets answer the controversial questions on foreign policy. But if he gets a difficult one, I think he's experienced enough to get around it."

Brogan Junior nodded, satisfied that things would run smoothly in Moscow.

"Now I want to turn to the PPP," he said, punching a button on his control panel. "Rickard's popularity has dropped, but not enough according to the program's analysis. This is despite the fact that Alan has fed the media with all the skeletons we could find on Rickard."

"That sonofabitch is pretty clean," Huntsman said. "Makes Billy Graham look like a Mafia boss."

The latest PPP recommendations had appeared on the screen at the back of the room.

The program suggested fabricating tape-recorded conversations that would appear to involve Rickard in criminal activity.

"But he hardly tapes anything," Huntsman said, frowning. "Haussermann says he's extremely careful about what he records, even at innocuous staff briefings."

"So we have to put something together," Brogan Junior said. "According to the PPP, the right tape made public between now and November 4 could help sway the election."

"What does the program suggest?" Strasburg asked. Brogan

Junior punched another button and the screen flashed up a list of presidential crimes that could alter voting patterns. At the head of the list was:

INFERENCE OF POLITICAL ASSASSINATION, PRESIDENTIAL CANDIDATE.

"Political assassination," Huntsman said incredulously. "That's fine for the damned computer to throw up, but how the hell could we fabricate a tape implying Rickard's involvement in that?"

"We have the electronic expertise, don't we?" Brogan Junior said.

"Yes, but we need the right words."

Brogan punched a button that wiped the PPP off the screen. He turned to Huntsman and said, "Find them!"

Graham was extremely relieved to fly out of Leningrad.

He spent the seventy-minute flight thinking deeply about the three days ahead of him in Moscow.

The Australian felt certain the surveillance on him would continue and this influenced him to decide not to try to meet several contacts lined up in the capital. The risks were too high after the Leningrad incident.

Graham had some misgivings too about letting MI-6 down, because the last thing on his mind now was impersonating Radford. He was not at all confident, either, about the possibility of MI-6's Soviet agent trying to make contact with him. Would they be aware of how tight the surveillance on him was?

As the pilot banked the aircraft steeply for the descent into Sheremetyevo airport many in his tour group gasped at the beauty of sunbathed Moscow, which had been covered by a huge white crochet blanket of snow. Graham hardly noticed it. He was too busy thinking about the bed of professional spies that lay under that blanket, waiting for the callow amateur who was about to join them.

Forty minutes after touchdown, a bus took the new arrivals past farmhouses, villages and tenements, and along roads flanked by massive blocks of modern flats. Entering Moscow from the north, they drove past impressive Sverdlov Square, with its beautiful palms, and along busy Okhotny Street.

The bus rumbled down Mokhayava Street, briefly glimpsed the massive Lenin Library, and finally pulled into Marx Prospect and the National Hotel overlooking the Kremlin, where the tour was staying.

Just as Graham began to unpack in his room, the phone rang. It was Victor, the tour guide. His interest in the Australian had picked up since the request to leave the tour early.

"Are you coming on today's tours?"

"Probably."

"You have paid for all the tours but sometimes you do not come."

"Yeah, well, I like to find my own way around sometimes, Victor."

"As you wish. But we would like to know in advance so the rest of the tour is not held up."

No sooner had Graham replaced the receiver when it rang again.

"Room 508, Dr. Boulter?"

"Yes."

"There is a message for you," a Russian girl on the front desk said. "Mr. Mars Gorsky and his wife will meet you at the front entrance lobby at seven tonight."

Graham racked his brains for several seconds before it clicked. This was the couple Svetlana had introduced to him at the Hotel Astoria in Leningrad. He vaguely remembered their saying they would look him up when he arrived in Moscow. But he had not told them his arrival date or hotel.

The Moscow screws were being tightened already.

Graham left the hotel at seven and strolled along the streets and in Red Square, stopping for half an hour to watch the changing of the guard at Lenin's Mausoleum.

He wanted to avoid contact with the Gorskys. Anything to do with Svetlana spelled danger to him.

At nine he returned to the National's lobby and moved to the front desk to see if there had been any message. There was a note from the Gorskys to say they would call him later. As he turned from the counter, he recognized a woman standing next to him. It was the one who had been staring at him in the boat restaurant the previous night.

"Could you tell Mr. Sheppard Irena Pavliovic is here, please," she said in heavily accented English to the sullen female desk clerk.

"There's a note for you from Mr. Sheppard," the clerk said, handing over a piece of paper from a pigeonhole. The woman read it and pulled a face.

Graham turned away. He thought it must have been another Svetlana connection. But before he had reached the elevator, the woman was behind him, touching his arm.

"Excuse me, don't I know you from somewhere?" she said, studying him intently.

The Australian stared at her, stunned. It was the beginning of the MI-6 contact.

"I'm sure I know you," the woman continued with a thoughtful smile, "I never forget a face, especially a handsome one."

Graham forced a grin. "I'm sorry . . . or . . ." he faltered, "I don't believe . . ."

The woman kept looking at his eyes and she said pleasantly, "Forgive me," and then turned to walk out the front entrance.

The Australian continued on his way to the elevator. It had been too fast, too sudden. Why would they try that in a crowded lobby probably crawling with people just waiting for something suspicious? Then he thought ruefully, only *he* had acted in an uncertain way. The woman had been so poised, assured. He pressed the call button. The doors opened, three men got out. Graham looked back at the entrance. He could see the woman speaking to a taxi driver at the rank in front of the hotel.

He turned and walked quickly out of the entrance, into the street and over to her.

"I know now," he said brightly. "What a coincidence. Weren't you on the boat in Leningrad last night?"

The woman looked up with a blank expression at first, and then broke into an enormous grin. She thrust out her hand which Graham held lightly for a moment. "Of course. How marvelous!"

"Would you care for a drink?" Graham said, with as much cool as he could muster. He was aware that several taxi drivers nearby had been watching them.

"I have an appointment right now. Perhaps you would like to join me?" The woman slid into the back seat of the taxi.

"Fine," Graham said, getting in beside her.

"The Cloud," she ordered the driver. He started the sluggish black Volga sedan and drove them off on the short ride to Sretenka Street.

The woman introduced herself as Irena and then rapidly acquainted him with the people they were about to meet. One was Kerana Taram, the petite brunette Graham had seen Irena with the night before, and for whom she worked. The other was an American business client of theirs, the managing director of the 3C's company from Minnesota. Irena explained with much gesticulation that Kerana's business company, called Tork International, was in "communications." It introduced American business to contacts in the Soviet Union, and vice versa. Based in New York, and with branches in Moscow and Los Angeles, it had been started by Kerana. She had been born in Russia, but brought up and educated in the U.S. and was now capitalizing on her background, Irena explained carefully. Her own job, she said, was to act as a liaison between Kerana's company and the power circles of the Soviet government and bureaucracy.

The Cloud restaurant was in a quiet alley. The door was painted in shimmering black and white squares, and above it was a simple, white, mushroom-shaped nuclear cloud. Inside it was opulent and dimly lit for a romantic effect. Heavy black and crimson draperies, all velvet and brocaded and embroidered in gold, hung low in front of the dining area. The carpet was a deep red plush. A violinist dressed in a purple robe played superbly as Irena and Graham moved to the table where Kerana and the American, Bill Sheppard, were in the middle of a meal.

After introductions, and an effusive explanation by Irena of her chance meeting with Graham, Sheppard, a rangy bespectacled man in his early forties, ordered champagne.

A little taken aback when Graham didn't appear to know of the 3C company, he said proudly, "That stands for Computers, Communications and Cybernetics. We're the biggest supplier of peripheral equipment to those three areas that there is."

Sheppard poured champagne for Irena and Graham and insisted they have some chicken while he and Kerana Taram had dessert. Resuming his conversation with the Australian, he went on, "We supply everything from TV displays to cables and electrical equipment."

"I guess you must have trouble getting through the red tape here to make a sale," Graham said. It sounded like polite conversation. Sheppard was finding it hard to contain himself.

"It depends on what you're selling," he said, lowering his voice, "and what I've got they want. Very, very badly." He looked across at the two women, now engrossed in conversation in Russian. Sheppard drank his champagne and called for another bottle.

"Christ, man," he said, "you just have no idea. They're signing on the dotted line. They're desperate to get hold of anything to do with Lasercomp."

"Lasercomp? What are they doing here?"

"You mean what aren't they doing here!"

"I thought I read somewhere they were not allowed to sell their computers here."

Sheppard smirked. "That's true, but they're here, believe me, and I'm one of their biggest suppliers." He took off his coat, loosened his tie and filled all the glasses.

Graham looked skeptical. "NATO wouldn't allow it."

The American gave a knowing smile. "NATO-shmayto. Let's just say that where there's a will there's a way."

"How do you get around regulations?"

"We work out just where 3C's equipment would be seen as 'harmless' and for nonstrategic use, by the U.S. trade department and NATO, and we tell the Russians how to place orders." He paused to smile and salute the two women who had stopped to listen to the conversation. Kerana seemed perturbed but soon Irena was speaking to her again in Russian. Sheppard, leaning his arm on the back of Graham's chair and breathing alcohol into his ear, said, "You know, the Russians are pretty damned slow on the uptake when it comes to business. I have to say to them, 'Now, if you want such and such, you have to ask us for it, making sure you stipulate it's for cash registers in stores.' Then a little light goes on above their heads, and we get a request for equipment to go into a store cash register system."

"That's pretty shrewd, but surely there can't be that much business here. Lasercomp can't have too many computers in the Soviet Union."

Trying hard to look sober and serious, Sheppard, with his face almost touching Graham's, said, "Don't you believe it. I'm involved in some very big deals with the chairman of Lasercomp himself this week."

"Clifford Brogan?"

"Right. And he doesn't deal in peanuts. I'll be signing around fifty million dollars' worth alone this week."

"No wonder you're celebrating!"

At that point Kerana broke in. She had seemed slightly concerned about what Sheppard was telling the Australian. "Please. Can we go now? We have much business tomorrow . . ."

Sheppard leaned across the table and gave her a slobbery kiss. Graham smiled at Irena. Her intelligent eyes fleetingly locked on his as they all began to gather their things to leave.

He had waited apprehensively for the words he wanted to hear so much that would have signaled the Radford impersonation was off. But they never came. MI-6's Radford three would be on his way to Moscow tomorrow.

As they hailed taxis outside the restaurant, Irena turned to Graham. "It has been a pleasure to meet you. I would be pleased further if you would join me tomorrow night at the Bolshoi. . . ."

The Australian wondered for a second if she had perhaps slipped up. Maybe she had forgotten tomorrow was the day for the impersonation? Then he dismissed the thought as quickly as it had come. This woman was supposed to be MI-6's best agent in the Soviet Union. An error like that would be out of the question.

He shook hands with her and accepted the invitation.

"I shall phone you," she called, climbing into a taxi.

Graham returned to the National with Kerana and Sheppard, and politely refused his invitation to continue drinking at the bar. Once back in the hotel room, slowly, agonizingly, he turned his mind to the fact that the onus for the impersonation rested squarely on his shoulders.

He began to separate from the rest of his luggage the clothes and make-up he would require.

Commander Gould's warnings about abandoning the assignment if there were any doubts at all kept ringing in his ears. But the Australian could not sort out real from imagined fear. Everything in the end seemed to revert to one question. Did he have the nerve to go through with it?

He took out his camera, a replica of Radford's, and unconsciously played with the film shutter mechanism.

The spring had gone.

Graham tried it several times and then put it down as if it were contaminated. To him it was.

He had always been meticulously careful with any recording and film equipment and only six hours earlier the camera had worked perfectly when he had taken pictures in Red Square. Someone must have broken into his room. . . . He rummaged through his luggage. There was no indication that any of the Radford impersonation "kit" had been uncovered or isolated. Without foreknowledge, that would have been impossible. Yet the damaged camera was another excuse for aborting the impersonation.

He got into bed weak from the sense of relief that enveloped him. But it was to be a night of fitful sleep. His conscience was not going to let him forget that the coward in him had just won a round.

Resigned to seeing out the next two days as quietly as possible, Graham the next morning joined his tour group on a visit to the Lenin Museum.

As he walked the short distance across from the National he tried to satisfy himself that the trip to the Soviet Union would be successful enough without his actually getting into the computer operations center by impersonating Radford. He had gained valuable information from Boronovsky and the Ukrainian-American. There was a chance Irena would find a way to pass on the military and other details that MI-6 wanted. Apart from the personal dangers, he could foul up everything if he was caught now. On the other hand, Graham knew the only way to get a whole rather than piecemeal perspective of what the KGB was doing and planning was to go in, speak to scientists and see for himself. . . .

From London it had all looked easier. At close range events were *too* close. And conditions since his near slip-up in Leningrad had changed. The risks were now extremely high.

The Australian stopped in front of the museum as other members of his tour group moved inside to the warmth and away from the biting cold that howled across Red Square and swirled the light snow that was falling.

He stood staring at the long line of Soviet citizens waiting patiently across the square for a glimpse at Lenin in his mausoleum. A myth? A cult? A religion? Lenin and Leninism. Everything the KGB was attempting would be done in his name. Propaganda would tell the Soviet administration that the most advanced computers invented were the answer to all Marxist-Leninist dreams of central economic control and state planning. The fact that machines were being fed into the master network primarily to boost Soviet missile forces, and secondly for complete political control, would be kept secret.

Graham wondered what the Great Revolutionary Leader would make of events today. Would he have approved of police state tactics? He had himself introduced them even more efficiently than the czars. But would he consider them necessary in today's less turbulent political climate . . .?

The Australian drew his overcoat collar high over his neck and walked into the Lenin Museum. For the next ninety minutes he wandered around the museum with some of his tour party, trying to concentrate on what the guides were reverently saying about Lenin the god, and his achievements; trying to forget that time was slipping away, if he was going to do anything about Radford. . . . Many times his thoughts drifted to Radford three, who would right at that moment be halfway to Moscow. . . .

The end of the museum excursion was an hour-long show of old documentary films about Lenin and the Revolution. Somewhere in the course of those sixty minutes something in Graham's subconscious snapped. He got up just before the end and groped his way past the guides in the cinema and out into the cold, heading for the National.

Instead of going into the hotel he walked for about twenty minutes until he reached Gorkova Street. Finding a telephone booth he went in and lifted the receiver. Running through his mind was the role he had rehearsed awake and asleep, ad nauseam.

Grasping the phone firmly Graham dialed the number of Herr Fritz Muller, the Moscow director of Znorel Electronics. . . .

"Muller," a voice answered bluntly.

"Ah, Herr Muller, it's Harold Radford here," Graham said, affecting an upper-class English accent. "I am the managing director of Computer Increments, U.K. We have an appointment for this afternoon at three."

"Yes," the voice said with a trace more animation, "that is correct. Have you just arrived?"

The Australian was about to answer in the affirmative but stopped himself. "I'm about to check into my hotel."

"The Berlin?"

"Yes."

There was a few seconds' silence before Muller asked, "Do you know how to get here?"

"Oh, yes, I've been to the Lenin several times before on other visits here. Second floor, isn't it?"

"*Ja.* I see you at three then, Mr. Radford." Muller hung up and Graham shut his eyes and breathed deeply as he replaced the receiver. It was done now. He had to keep that appointment. Otherwise Moscow would be turned upside down looking for a Mr. Radford. . . .

The Australian hurried back to his hotel to disguise himself. He had just enough time to carefully prepare, take a taxi as Radford near to the Hotel Berlin and take another taxi to the appointment at the Lenin.

He began by washing his hair and brushing it forward with a distinct parting to the top of his skull on the left. Then he applied a skin cream to lighten the complexion. Next Graham tinged the edges of his hairline with gray paint, applying more above the ears and above the temples, and a little on the top of the scalp. To complete the transformation he changed into a three-piece Savile Row suit, white shirt and dark blue tie, and put on special thick-framed prescription spectacles.

Standing back from the mirror in the bathroom he compared himself with the head and shoulders portrait of Radford's forged passport. He had more hair than Radford and was not as heavy in the face. But to be exactly the same as the passport could invite suspicion.

Graham sauntered around the room attempting to ape Radford's bouncing gait. The movement relaxed him marginally. He was getting inside somebody else. He stepped up to the bathroom mirror and pulled a few faces, affecting Radford's pompous habit of looking down his nose. He laughed nervously and then said aloud to his reflection, "Time for a stiff drink, you bloody twit."

He unpacked some duty-free vodka, poured himself a liberal helping, and sat back on the bed. Half whispering to avoid being picked up by the bugging devices that were almost certain to be in the room, he ran through the key phrases in Radford's vernacular—"jolly good . . . frightfully kind of you . . . absolutely smashing . . ."

He looked at his watch. It was 2:30 P.M. Time to go. Making sure there was no one in the hallway, he walked quickly past the elevator and took the stairs to the second floor. He found the back fire escape. A back gate led to an alleyway which took him out to a side entrance of the National. Graham hailed a passing taxi and seven minutes later arrived a few hundred yards from the Hotel Berlin. He walked the short distance to the Berlin, waited near the front entrance and then caught a taxi to the Lenin, timing his arrival with a few minutes to spare.

Muller, short, stout and balding, greeted Graham at the entrance to his office, a converted hotel suite. Eying the Australian carefully through a pair of aluminum-framed spectacles perched on his beaklike nose, he ushered him in.

The office was comfortable and appeared underequipped. Only one ticking Teletype was in a corner of the room.

Graham took a seat opposite Muller, who sat down at a leather-topped desk.

"Now, Mr. Radford," he said, looking over the glasses, schoolmaster fashion, "first, I must ask you to show me your visa, passport and letter of introduction from Herr Znorel. A precaution we must take, you will understand."

The Australian nodded. "Typical German efficiency," he said, pulling the documents from an inside coat pocket.

Muller remained unsmiling at the remark and skimmed through Graham's forged note of introduction. He then picked up the visa and passport and eyed the photographs, then the Australian, and then the photographs again. Handing them back he said, "All right, Mr. Radford. Let us start at the beginning. How much do you know about what happens to the computers you send here?"

"Very little. That's why your managing director wanted me to visit you here."

Muller nodded, and coughed diffidently. "Of course. Herman told me you would soon be our second biggest supplier. He believes it is important that you are better informed."

"Naturally. It is to our mutual benefit."

Making a little play of fumbling for the right phrase, Muller said, "We, that is to say, our client, the Soviet government, is happy to inform you to a certain point. You must realize you are privileged to be here. Only one other of our suppliers has been here and actually visited the main computer center in Moscow.

"Herman tells me your company may be able to help a great deal in supplying communications systems," the little man said, eying his visitor carefully.

Graham's brain raced. He knew the real Radford had been studying communications systems in recent months. But he did not know if Radford had claimed he could supply them.

"Mr. Muller," he said arrogantly, "I know a great deal about communications. But I am not restricting my possible assistance to just this area."

"I see you are a businessman as well as a scientist," Muller said, with a sly look.

"I hope you will be able to show me the design for the whole network, so I may judge where I may be of greatest value."

"The master plan itself?"

"Yes."

"Absolutely out of the question. It is highly classified. However, you will be given general information." He looked at his watch, stood up and moved over to a coat rack. "If you are ready, Mr. Radford, I think we should visit the chief Soviet scientist on the project, Dr. Yuri Nolotov, at the network center. It's about one mile from here. Let us take the underground."

Five minutes later they entered the underground at V.I. Lenin Central station and caught a train for three stops—each one a glittering ballroom. Outside the underground they were soon on Kirov Street and heading for a modern twelve-story building surrounded by a high concrete wall. Graham noted the construction of an almost identical building going on behind it.

The entrance gate was well manned. Six guards could be seen in and around a guardhouse. Identification was checked and they were screened electronically.

Once inside, it quickly became obvious that the building was impenetrable. Every imaginable alarm and surveillance device, including closed-circuit cameras that could see into every corner, were operating.

Muller escorted Graham down one of five parallel glass

corridors which ran from a front administration section to the main body of the building behind. They took an elevator to five stories below ground level. There was more checking until they finally reached a guarded double doorway.

On the other side was the biggest single computer operations room the Australian had seen. A bank of perhaps twenty unmarked big computers surrounded the room against the four walls. In the center were about thirty smaller machines. Hundreds of television terminals were suspended from the ceiling. About a hundred people manned the equipment.

Muller stopped to speak briefly with two scientists in English and was directed to an office in a far corner of the floor. There Graham was introduced to Nolotov, a stout, middle-aged man with bushy, unruly black hair. Dressed in a drab sports coat and casual trousers, he remained seated at an aluminum desk almost completely covered with flow charts and computer print-out sheets. The walls of the small office were covered with shelf upon shelf of manuals, and thick looseleaf folders. Many carried the Lasercomp Cheetah logo.

All through Muller's quick pen-sketch of "Mr. Radford" from London, Nolotov kept his sad blue eyes on the Australian. The scientist welcomed Graham in halting English and asked him what he would like to know.

"I'd like to take notes," he said, turning to Muller.

The German shook his head. "I shall record any request you have. If it is possible we shall send you information." He took a notebook from his coat pocket and opened it. The Australian deliberately looked surprised. Turning to Nolotov again, he said, "The best start is for you to outline the master system. Then you can tell me your main requirements and problems, if any . . . and then we can take it from there . . ."

The scientist looked at Muller for approval. A lengthy discussion in Russian ensued. Muller did most of the talking. He was laying down firm guidelines about what could be said.

The scientist began haltingly. Occasionally he stopped to ask the German for the correct English word. It soon became clear that the discussion was heading away from the military use of computers and more toward the "master network to control the whole economy," which the Australian understood as the KGB's network for political control.

Graham was concentrating hard. He was picking up new, vital details with everything the scientist touched on. However, time was short. The Australian wanted most to learn about the military build-up. Picking each word carefully, he adroitly steered the scientist back into the areas concerning military computers. Sometimes it would be a question about a particular part of the computer hardware. Other times it would be about a program. There was never a direct reference to weapons as such. But each time Nolotov was telling him something important in his response. Gradually the scientist became more voluble as he gained confidence in speaking to this extremely knowledgeable Westerner. His technical knowledge was nothing like that of the others.

Muller became concerned. Intermittently he made terse comments to Nolotov. Even these gave the Australian new insights.

After the discussion had run on for nearly two hours, Muller interjected once more. Turning to Graham he said, "I did not realize you could be of assistance with military computers." Graham sensed a trace of suspicion. "Of course we can," he said confidently; "you would be surprised at what we can supply."

Muller frowned thoughtfully. "I'm sure Herman told me you could only help us with regular computers."

"As I said to you before, Herr Muller, my organization is expanding. We shall soon be the biggest supplier to the Soviet network, no matter what the requirement."

The German looked impatiently at his watch. "I'm afraid that's all we have time for," he said, standing up.

Nolotov seemed confused. Just when the discussion was warming up, it was ended. He shrugged and shook hands with Graham.

"Please. On another visit, come to us again ..." he said, managing a wan smile.

"Absolutely, Doctor. Thank you so much. ..." The Australian followed Muller out at the office. They made their way in silence to the front of the building. At the entrance checkpoint Muller stopped and said, "Will you be able to find your way?"

"Of course. I know Moscow ..."

They were both distracted by the approach of a chauffeur-driven Ford Customline. Graham got a nasty shock as he recognized the occupant. He turned his back on the car and pumped

Muller's hand vigorously. "This has been most helpful," he said. "I shall await your requests for equipment."

He waved goodbye and moved off briskly.

Muller was more concerned with the car than Graham's hurried farewell. He rushed forward when he saw it was Professor Letovsky, the Russian in charge of IOSWOP in Vienna.

Greeting him, Muller opened the car door.

"Tell me," Letovsky said, as they walked toward the main building, "who was that man?"

"Our main English supplier of Cheetah, Harold Radford." They both looked back. Graham was almost out of sight.

"Would you like to meet him?"

"No, no" Letovsky said testily. "I have more important matters at this moment. Brogan Senior is making a surprise visit here in about an hour to see the network before we go to Mineva's banquet."

Paul Mineva's flying visit to Moscow got under way on Thursday evening with a glittering state banquet in the St. George Hall at the Great Palace in the Kremlin. Soviet Premier Brechinov toasted his guest with a clinking of glasses and show of teeth for the press and TV cameras. There was little substance in the affair, with only a passing reference to Mineva's forthcoming election battle. Brechinov commented that "the Soviet people and government" saw Mineva as "a man of peace" and wished him every success in the fight for the presidency. Mineva replied to this with a short, veiled speech which attacked "warmongers in every part of the globe," and praised the Soviet administration for its peacekeeping efforts in several continents where "war machines had gotten out of hand." He ended by saying it would be wrong for him to comment on the foreign policy of his own country's administration, but promised "changes in America's attitude and direction," when he was elected President. This drew long applause from the banquet guests.

At 10:30 P.M. Mineva and his entourage left the Kremlin in three Ford limousines and headed south out of the city to a district of narrow roads and quaint old-fashioned houses dating back to the 1920s and 1930s. The streets were busy and it took them twenty-five minutes to reach their destination—a cul-de-sac,

Karolisakaya Street—which was sealed off by a barricade of cars and militia. At the end of the street was a three-story mansion in mock Italian baroque built in the early 1950s. Mineva, in overcoat and fur hat, left his aides and bodyguards and strode purposefully to the entrance, which was manned by four guards.

Graham took the subway back to the Hotel Berlin, his stomach bound in a nervous knot since the close call at the computer center.

He strutted into the lobby, feigned irritation at being kept waiting at the reception counter, and asked for his room key.

"What is your number?"

"I've forgotten. Please, I'm a busy man . . ." Graham said arrogantly.

"Your name?" the female desk clerk said tersely.

"Harold Radford."

The clerk reached across to 290 and handed him the key.

"Thank you," Graham said as he moved to the elevator. His heart was pounding hard. Radford three had arrived. Everything was going according to plan. He hurried to the room and found the luggage MI-6's man had left. There was a change of clothes for him and toilet items for washing away Radford. Graham went straight to the bathroom and took three or four minutes there. He then changed quickly into the clothes and hung the Radford suit in the closet, being careful to leave all the forged documents there.

Placing a prepared scribbled note on the bedside table requesting that the suit be pressed for Monday, Graham hurried to the elevator and down to the lobby. Realizing that he would be seen by several people, he strolled casually to the front entrance and into the street.

Once away from the hotel he took a devious route of back streets, every so often breaking into a jog, until he reached the Bolshoi Ballet on Sverdlov Square. There waiting for him was Irena, looking radiant under a smart fur hat.

Graham found it impossible to relax during the performance. Apart from the close call with Letovsky at the front entrance, he had a nagging fear about Muller's reaction to his discussion with Nolotov. The Australian was almost certain the German would check on Radford at the Hotel Berlin, and probably contact London. How long would it be before he confessed the blunder to the KGB?

For a moment or two he was able to think about his progress on the assignment. The meeting with Nolotov had been a tremendous breakthrough and had helped him piece together the broad picture of the Soviet master plan for military, and internal political control. But there were still two or three pieces missing. He did not have any hard information on exactly how the military was using the Cheetah machines smuggled in. Nor did he have the design specifications for the master plan itself. For that he needed the help of the woman sitting next to him, obviously enjoying the ballet. So far she had not made her move.

At ten, when the ballet had finished, Graham invited her back to the National for a drink. He hailed a taxi. The city traffic was heavy.

When they were near the city center they were held up for several minutes until a motorcade passed.

Irena gripped Graham's arm.

"Isn't that Mineva, the American candidate?"

Looking around sharply, Graham caught sight of him in the middle car of the motorcade flanked by two lines of motorcycle militia.

"Get the driver to follow him," Graham urged.

The driver, a fat fellow, whose flabby red neck fell over his collar, mumbled a protest at Irena's instruction.

The motorcade was slipping ahead and almost out of sight when the taxi was allowed to move on.

"Can't he go faster?" Graham asked impatiently.

Irena and the driver began to argue and he slowed down almost to a stop, gesticulating wildly.

"Tell him to forget it," Graham said as the motorcade disappeared ahead. Irena ordered the driver to continue to his original destination. She watched his beady, scowling eyes as they kept looking up into the rear mirror. Dropping her hands out of the driver's sight, she scribbled on a piece of paper and shoved it into Graham's hand. In the half-light that fell from the street light he managed to read it: *Mineva meets Brogans at Andropolov's home tonight.*

Graham wanted to look at her but resisted the temptation with the driver looking on. It was a fascinating bit of intelligence from MI-6's contact. He wanted to know more.

At the National, Irena got out with Graham and told the driver to wait. They walked out of earshot.

"Let us forget the drink tonight," she said quietly. "Tomorrow night. My place. It's important." She turned on her heel and got back into the taxi. Graham waved as it moved out of sight.

A light drizzle had begun to fall and the Australian pulled his coat collar up as he strolled toward the front doors of the National.

Graham moved into the lobby and was surprised to see several people unpacking pieces of luggage and film equipment. As he moved past them he recognized a tall ruggedly handsome middle-aged man. It was Charles Sullivan, a political reporter for the *Los Angeles Times*.

Sullivan looked across. Graham moved to the elevator.

"Ed!" came the cry across the lobby. Several heads turned. The Australian ignored him and walked toward the open staircase.

"Ed Graham!" Sullivan called, but Graham had already disappeared up the stairs.

An hour later, Graham rang the desk clerk and asked for Sullivan's room number. He had befriended the American earlier in the year when they were both covering the early primary campaigns.

The Australian knocked on his door at 1:30 A.M. Sullivan opened the door and Graham immediately motioned for silence. He entered the room and, looking around, picked up a large transistor radio. Beckoning to the bemused American, he led him into the bathroom and ran the shower hard. He turned on the radio.

"You sonofabitch." Sullivan laughed. "What gives?"

"Maybe bugs," Graham whispered. "I'm here on a false passport."

"Jesus Christ!" Sullivan breathed. "I'm sorry. No wonder you didn't answer me in the lobby. . . . I remember now. You wrote that article on Soviet computer smuggling."

"Why are you here?"

"Mineva's giving a press conference here tomorrow morning."

Graham looked thoughtful for a moment. "Have you some good questions for him?"

"Perhaps. But we hear it's going to be a tight, give nothing, cosmetic affair for television. The print media will probably take back seats."

"Would you like to nail Mineva?"

"You bet."

"Good. I've come across a few things that might just embarrass his little TV show. . . ."

Paul Mineva, wearing a conservative gray suit, white shirt and blue tie, looked supremely confident sitting at the official table facing a battery of television cameras, photographers and more than fifty journalists. They had gathered for breakfast, to be followed by a press conference in the cramped reception room at the National.

The conference began with a few introductory remarks from a Mineva aide and a Soviet official who spoke of the previous night's "highly useful and successful" reception at the Kremlin. Then Mineva stood up and gave one of his clockwork smiles which could be flashed twenty times a minute while he was glad-handing.

"Ladies and gentlemen. Welcome," he said. "I'd like to throw the conference open to you."

Notebooks and pens appeared as a Mineva aide, Leroy Hammond, an underweight chain-smoker, pointed to a journalist in the front row, who got to his feet. "Al Green, *Newsweek*. What do you think your discussions with Premier Brechinov have achieved?"

"The answer to that takes just one word: Understanding with a capital U. The Soviet premier understands my position on many world issues, and I understand his."

Several journalists were on their feet as Hammond picked another out.

"Georg Krause, *Frankfurter Allgemeine*. Governor Mineva, have you not contravened the American Logan Act by coming here for discussions?"

"At no stage have I contravened the act. Our discussions were about private views. About moves toward peace. Lasting, tangible peace on this planet."

For twenty minutes questions were fielded, or side-stepped with consummate ease, as Mineva's aide mainly picked those journalists who had flown to Moscow with the governor to ask questions.

Just as Mineva reached for a glass of water, an outside journalist was selected.

"Charlie Sullivan, *Los Angeles Times*. Governor Mineva, after your reception last night, you visited the home of KGB chief Andropolov. Could you explain the nature of this meeting and what discussions took place?"

All heads turned to see who had asked the question and then back to Mineva.

He forced a quick laugh. "I've heard of state surveillance, but this is ridiculous." It drew an odd chortle from the official table, but the press waited silently for a reply. "Let me say this," Mineva went on, "our Soviet hosts have been hospitable, as they always are, and I have had several conversations with leaders, ah, since we arrived last night at six P.M."

"Are you going to answer my question?" Sullivan asked pointedly.

Mineva's self-assured smile was replaced by an icy stare. "Let me repeat that we did not discuss American foreign policy. It was a private, social gathering . . ."

"Who was present?" Sullivan called out, as Mineva tried to ignore him.

Several reporters simultaneously rose to their feet and began shouting.

"Gentlemen, gentlemen!" Hammond implored above the uproar. "One at a time, please!" He took the chance to deflect the line of questioning to the back of the room and picked Philpott, dressed in a trendy off-white double-breasted Dacron suit and red open-necked shirt.

"Mr. Candidate," he said, as his television crew turned their camera on him, "how do you propose to use commodities such as food in dealing with the Soviet Union?"

Mineva's composure appeared to return. "Unlike the current administration, we would not resort to political blackmail. Nor would we interfere in internal Soviet affairs. We wouldn't say, do this or we won't send grain and you'll starve. No, we'd look at the whole range of commodities the Soviet Union wanted.

Everything from Pepsi-Cola to electronics and heavy machinery would be considered in any bargaining."

Six reporters were on their feet, speaking at the same time. Hammond pointed to a tall, smartly dressed young woman. "This lady was first!"

"Marianne Pelligry, *Paris Match*," came the delightful French lilt. "Could you please tell whom you spoke to last night?"

"There were several people in attendance. I suppose you mean from the Soviet administration?"

"Yes, who in authority?"

Mineva leaned over to speak to an adviser and then said, "From the Soviet administration, General Gerovan, and Mr. Andropolov."

Sullivan's voice boomed out in the lull that followed Mineva's answer.

"Do you consider they speak with authority within the Soviet administration?"

"Well, they are members of the Politburo," Mineva said. "Sorry to show up your scant knowledge of Soviet politics," he added sarcastically.

"Tell us what we both know, it won't take any longer!" Sullivan cracked back. There was a roar of applause. Hammond picked a red-faced reporter near the front row.

"Levine, *The Observer*, London. Governor, no doubt you are aware that these two men are the most senior officials of the Soviet secret police. . . ."

"What is your question, please?" Hammond snapped.

"My question, sir, is do you consider the KGB now speaks for the Soviet administration?"

Several on the official table and among the press howled protests. It was the hottest issue worrying Western nations about Soviet foreign and internal policies.

Mineva was flustered. "Gentlemen, I have spoken to almost every member of the entire Presidium since I've been on this visit, and on other occasions—when our Soviet friends have visited America and when I have visited the Soviet Union. So I really don't see the point of the question!"

Others lined up to ask questions as Mineva sat down. He leaned across the table to speak to a Soviet official. About twenty seconds later he stood up once more and opened his arms to the audience.

"There you are, gentlemen." He smiled. "I just spoke to a Russian, the assistant to the deputy premier, Mr. Kiruyan. Please have me arrested! He may know someone in the KGB!"

It drew a laugh from the press and the official table.

Hammond indicated another question from Philpott. "Do you, Mr. Candidate, endorse extending the most-favored-nation principle to the Soviet Union?"

Mineva nodded. "That, at last, is a good question, and one I am concentrating on. I think it can best be achieved through private negotiations."

From then on questions were restricted to those the candidate could handle. Many journalists were itching to put Mineva on the spot over human rights and political prisoners in the Soviet Union. But those who wanted to pin the candidate on tougher issues were ignored completely.

At ten, Mineva sat down and acknowledged the clapping during brief "thank-you" speeches. The journalists began to file out of the room and camera crews packed away their gear.

On balance, Mineva was confident the reports that would be hot on the wire to the U.S. and the world minutes after the conference would be favorable.

But the questions about the KGB had shaken him. He leaned across to Hammond, who was smoking furiously. "Do you think they'll bury that KGB bit?"

Hammond nodded. "Some won't even bother about it," he replied, flicking ash everywhere but in a tray provided. "Don't worry, Paul, you came through well. Real well."

Mineva smiled gratefully to a Russian waiter who placed coffee in front of him. He went to pick it up but found it difficult to hold. His hands were trembling. Perhaps he had won the conference on points, but now there was another score to settle. He turned to Hammond again. "How the hell did that sonofabitch Sullivan know about the meeting with Andropolov?"

The aide shrugged. "You forget about it. I'll let Huntsman know what happened."

Worried by "Mr. Radford" and his unusual line of questioning Herr Muller had tried to contact him again in the hope of learning more about his operations and motives. By noon Friday, the German became suspicious when he could not reach him at the Hotel Berlin. Staff there said the Englishman had not been seen since last evening. They had already alerted the police.

Muller immediately rang his boss, Herman Znorel in Stuttgart.

"They have not any deep knowledge of military hardware at Computer Increments," Znorel said adamantly. "Let me call London and find out what is going on."

Muller waited a half-hour for the return call from a near-hysterical Znorel.

"Radford never went to Moscow!"

"But I've . . ."

"You idiot . . . the man you met was an impostor . . . a fake . . ."

"He knew all about Computer Increments . . ."

Znorel swore loudly into the phone at the confused Muller.

"These are my orders . . . find that man. Find him today . . . otherwise our whole business is in danger. You must locate him and stop him from leaving Russia. I'm catching the next plane to you."

"What about the KGB?"

"Don't say anything yet. If we haven't found him by tomorrow morning we shall inform them. Now get to it! Everything is at stake. . . ."

Muller put down the receiver and wandered over to the window that gave a depressing view of the apartment block behind the Hotel Lenin. Locate an Englishman in his late thirties . . .

He grabbed his coat and headed for the door. The first stop would have to be the Hotel Berlin.

Half a mile away, Graham had joined his tour group for a visit to the Kremlin and the czarist treasures. As Victor the guide gathered some of them around the glass-covered gold-and-diamond-studded crown of Michael Federovitch, the Australian moved next to a forty-five-year-old American lawyer, Bob Halliday, who was with another tour party which often linked up with Graham's group.

"Bob, could you do me a favor tonight?" he whispered.

"Sure, Doc."

"I've met a really nice Russian lady I just might stay the night with."

"So what's new?"

"Seeing your tour's leaving early tomorrow for the airport, could I leave my case with you to make sure it gets to the airport okay?"

The American chuckled. The continuing nocturnal pursuits of this seemingly wild Australian stud had amused him throughout the tour.

"Sure, Doc. You know, you don't need a hotel room on a tour like this. You only need a goddamned locker!"

Anatoli Bromovitch gave a grunt of satisfaction. He was very close to a breakthrough in his efforts to track down Graham. It had taken him less than seventy-two hours.

In the last two days an exhaustive computer sifting had left him with the names of 1,737 male foreigners between the ages of twenty-five and fifty-five. They were possible suspects officially visiting the country at that time.

That morning Bromovitch had let the Cheetah network compare a huge file on Graham—mainly from data supplied by computer from Lasercomp files—with the limited files on the 1,737 which had mainly been obtained by agents watching and reporting on them at diminishing intervals of time. The Cheetah comparison eliminated exactly 1,700.

Now the assassin was patiently waiting at his dacha terminal outside Moscow to compare the Graham profile with the updated data on the remaining thirty-seven, which would come from agents inside the Soviet Union assigned to give an hourly report on the suspects.

Just after 2:00 P.M. the program was ready. He ran it. Thirty seconds later he had an answer:

SUSPECT ONE BOULTER, DR. ROSS, TOUR 87, CURRENTLY AT HOTEL NATIONAL, MOSCOW.

Bromovitch immediately called for a run-through of the computer's analysis. He found that Dr. Boulter had managed to evade surveillance on two occasions in Kiev and had found his way into the Hotel Lenin there, asking questions about the hotel's patrons. Most were scientists involved in the implementation of Operation Ten. In Leningrad agent Svetlana Moronova had reported Boulter's tastes in art, literature and music which coincided exactly with microfilmed evidence from Graham's London apartment. Most incriminating was the fact that Boulter had left her early the morning the agent tailing Professor Boronovsky was attacked.

The Australian anthropologist had shown an odd behavior pattern after that. Svetlana had noticed a change in attitude to her and that Boulter had occasionally winced with pain on their last evening together. This pointed to the possibility of a fight with the agent assigned to Boronovsky.

More and more evidence confirmed that Boulter and Graham were one and the same. The assassin called for photographic comparisons of Graham, Boulter's passport and of him in Moscow. This caused him to grunt again. Only two months earlier he had successfully used the behavior pattern method of computer detection to nail MI-6's Steven.

Strolling out to his orchids, he thought hard on the options left open to him. He could have Graham arrested immediately or take this golden opportunity to have him murdered.

Bromovitch had never agreed with his superiors in letting Lasercomp dictate KGB actions, even if the corporation was supplying Cheetahs. To the assassin, the liquidation of opposition was always the best choice. Their ideas died with them.

He reasoned that the elimination of Graham would mean less exposure for Operation Ten than arrest or detention. But he thought it unlikely KGB chief Andropolov would sanction the Australian's elimination inside the Soviet Union. Bromovitch would have to make it look accidental.

He quickly planned to establish an alibi and use fringe operatives to do the dirty work.

After an hour of calling around he managed to contact the two-man team of Igor the Mongolian and Menkelov the Georgian, both of whom, Bromovitch noted from the report on Dr. Boulter, had encountered his quarry in Kiev when they were doing a tail of foreign tourists.

Both were experienced at setting up accidents, and

Bromovitch knew they could be relied on to keep their mouths shut.

The assassin then took just five minutes more to establish that "Dr. Boulter" would be entertained by agent 8957, Irena Pavliovic, at her flat at midnight that night. She had been assigned to the foreigner since the Leningrad agent's long report on Graham had pushed surveillance on him into a higher category.

At 6:30 P.M. Bromovitch was with the two thugs at his dacha. Both men were pleased with the chance to break from their routine work and earn some good extra money.

"Comrades, we must be certain to make this foreigner's death 'accidental,'" Bromovitch said, as he poured them a shot of vodka each.

"We shall use the truck," the wiry Georgian said, turning to his huge companion, Igor. He gestured to a window at the front of the dacha. Sitting outside was a large vehicle with a wide front grille.

Bromovitch nodded approvingly. "You will report to me by nine A.M. tomorrow. Only contact me before then if there are any problems."

Irena answered Graham's knock at the hide-bound front door of her spacious villa apartment on the outskirts of west Moscow. It was just before midnight. She led him into an L-shaped living room. While she fixed him a drink, he wandered around the room examining the several priceless objets d'art and paintings adorning the room.

Irena, dressed in casual slacks and a loose sweater, handed him a vodka on the rocks, and then reclined on a red couch. She sank back against several multicolored cushions and studied Graham in the reflection of a large gold-framed eighteenth-century Italian mirror as he sauntered to a wall completely covered by shelves of leather-bound books in French and Russian. Irena's father, who had died in 1965, had been a famous Russian satirist and writer. A Moscow theater was named after him.

After looking at some of the books for a few minutes, Graham came over to Irena and casually sat down near her on a carved wooden chair. As she sipped her drink, Graham looked above her head at two excellent portraits, in which an artist had brilliantly captured her unusual, mobile features. In one she was smiling broadly. In the other, the artist had painted a serious profile study, which perfectly matched her expression now. She twirled the vodka around in her crystal-stemmed glass. Clinking ice cubes broke the silence.

"Have you a good memory?" she said.

"When it's important."

"Good. I have a lot to tell you." She tapped his forehead. "You must carry most of it in your head."

Three hours later, several diagrams and charts on scraps of paper covered a table in the living room. Graham closed a small notebook filled with his own shorthand, unintelligible to anyone but himself, as Irena gathered the paper. She threw it in an unused fireplace, lit it and smiled mysteriously as flames consumed the flimsy material.

"I would like to give you something for your memory of me," she said, pushing a round object into his hand as he got up from the table. It was an icon, no bigger than a coin. He looked closely at the colors that danced and leaped from it. On the front was the Madonna and child. On the back was a two-bar cross with a crescent shape under the bottom bar.

"The cross represents Christ in heaven," Irena said softly, as she took the icon and carefully pressed a fingernail into the minute groove made by the first bar of the cross. She repeated the action with the second bar. "This represents Christ's feet, resting. And this—she ran her fingernail around the crescent's groove— means Christianity will triumph over Islam."

The icon flipped open in her hand like an oyster shell. Just discernible was a tiny spool of microfilm. She closed it, and placed it back in his hand. "You must not lose this," she whispered, and kissed him warmly on both cheeks. Irena took him by the hand and led him to the front door. She gathered his overcoat and scarf. "I hope we meet again, when we have more time." She opened the door.

Graham moved to the bottom of the stairs that led to a doorway out of the building and waved goodbye.

Outside, where the cold wind had subsided and light snow was falling, Igor and Menkelov waited. The Mongolian was asleep in the back of the truck while Menkelov sat vigilantly in the front cabin. Both men wore thick overcoats and turtleneck sweaters to meet this early patch of Moscow winter.

The apartment block was surrounded by trees. There was only one way back to the road leading to Moscow city center. From the cabin of the truck, Menkelov had a good view of anyone entering or leaving the area. He had parked the truck about fifty yards from a taxi stand.

After a long stretch and a yawn, Menkelov turned the heaters in the truck down a little. He was beginning to feel drowsy. He tapped his feet to keep the blood circulating, and looked at the clock on the cabin dashboard. The foreigner had been in there three hours.

"Is he screwing her or something?" Menkelov asked himself. He was becoming impatient for the kill.

Snow was falling lightly outside as Graham walked between two tall apartment blocks. Only one street light shone weakly about fifty yards away near the small taxi stand. He walked quietly up to the only taxi. The driver was curled up in the front fast asleep. Graham looked around, opened the driver's door and shook him by the shoulder. It took several seconds to stir him awake. Graham leaned into the car, and turned the key in the ignition. The driver sat up as the car coughed to a start.

A second later, the sound of a truck lumbering out of the darkness caused the Australian to back away from the taxi. It stopped five yards from him and Menkelov began to climb from the cabin. Graham turned and ran toward the taxi. The driver had staggered out with the commotion around him. Graham pushed him to the ground, scrambled into the car and pulled the door closed. The car engine was running. He slammed it into first gear and planted his foot on the accelerator. The Mongolian reached the car and drove a fist hard down on the roof as it jerked away. Igor chased it for a few yards and gave up, cursing wildly. He ran back to the truck and hauled Menkelov back into the cabin, leaving the confused taxi driver remonstrating in the middle of the road.

Graham had grated the car through its four gears and put his foot evenly on the accelerator to build up to top speed. Snow on the windshield obscured his vision. He tried the windshield wipers. They worked very slowly so that he couldn't remove the permanent build-up of snow.

The rearview mirror flashed the truck's headlights on high beam. It started to gain ground on a flat, almost straight, run of about five miles. Graham put his foot flat to the boards. The truck was gaining fast. When the taxi reached a winding section of the road, the truck was right on its tail and Graham was having to swerve to avoid being hit. But he couldn't. There was a bone-jarring thud which sent the taxi's back wheels off the ground. The car skidded to the right. Graham fought the steering wheel. He managed to straighten up and was bashed again, so hard this time, that the bumper bar was loosened. It unhinged and trailed along, leaving sparks, as Graham overcorrected to the left. The Mongolian eased the truck left in the third effort to crash the taxi. Both vehicles were almost on the wrong side of the road. There was a long turn ahead. Graham edged right when he saw the headlights of oncoming traffic. A large transport hauler, like a brightly lit monster, rounded the bend. Graham swung the car right and just squeezed away. The Mongolian's reactions were much slower. He seemed to panic and applied the brakes as he spun right, but it was too late and too much. There was a tremendous screech of brakes as the transport caught the side of the truck with a tearing sound of metal on metal. The truck was deflected into a skid for about 130 yards before it did a slow-motion tumble to end up on its roof.

Graham's taxi had gone into an uncontrollable skid on the slippery road surface, to end up harmlessly facing the wrong direction but on the correct side of the road about forty yards from the upturned truck. He could see the transport hauler driver pull his damaged vehicle to a halt, jump from his cabin and run toward the truck.

Graham was hesitant for a moment and then made a quick decision. He jumped out of the taxi, wrenched off the trailing bumper bar and got back in. Slamming the taxi into gear, he drove in an arc and sped off. Through the rearview mirror he saw a flash as the upturned truck burst into flames. The hauler driver was driven back by the heat as he made a vain attempt to extricate the two KGB thugs trapped inside. Within seconds they were roasted alive.

Graham drove straight back to the center of Moscow, but not directly to the National. Instead, he parked in Gorky Street about four hundred yards from the hotel. Finding a telephone booth, he rang Irena.

After about fifteen rings, she answered.

"Yes?" she said drowsily.

"Someone tried to kill me when I left your apartment."

"Kill you?"

"Yes. Two bastards in a truck. They tried to run me off the road."

"You are not hurt?"

"I'm still shaking, that's about all, but it was a near thing."

"I do not understand," Irena said incredulously.

"Neither do I. All I want to do is get out of this damn country in one piece. Could you find out what's going on? If there is a plan to get me?"

"I'm sure there can't be."

"Should I go back to the hotel? Or hide? Perhaps I should head for the airport now and wait for the tour?"

"Let me make a call. Call me back in five minutes."

The telephone clicked dead at the other end while Graham was putting the receiver down. He lit a cigarette. The snow was drifting down lightly and had covered the whole street. About forty yards away, a fire flickered from a camp where workmen were repairing the road.

After seven minutes, he phoned her again.

"It's safe to go back to the hotel." Irena had checked by telephone with her contact at KGB HQ who had managed to get her assigned to Graham.

"You're sure?"

"Yes. The official surveillance on you is tight. But that's all, unless you're wanted for something I don't know about."

"Okay," Graham said, sighing deeply. "Thank you, Irena. 'Bye."

He left the telephone and hurried down the street, but instead of going directly to the front of the hotel, he waited on the corner and watched the entrance for about ten minutes. No one came near it. There wasn't an occupied car within sight. He walked cautiously to the entrance and had to knock on the glass doors to arouse a guard, not at all pleased at being awakened at such an ungodly hour.

Graham took the elevator to his floor and moved quickly to his room. He unlocked the door cautiously, switched on the light and then locked the door securely behind him. It was 5:10 A.M. The tour group going early to the airport would be having breakfast at 5:30. He turned off the light, sat in a chair and waited.

After breakfast, Graham collected his luggage from Bob Halliday and joined the bus that was to take them to the airport.

They arrived at the airport at 6:15 and went through currency and customs checks. Graham looked around for Victor and found him preoccupied with some of the tourists, who had discovered the airport officials would not change their surplus rubles back into their own currencies.

When Victor saw the Australian he broke away and went over to him.

"You've managed to come early, Doctor," Victor said with a trace of cynicism. "I'm afraid you will have to be patient and wait to see if there is a seat on the seven A.M. flight."

Graham's hopes sank. Uppermost in his mind now was the strong possibility that someone had learned of his cover or his impersonation of Radford. There seemed no other explanation for the attempt on his life. If he had to wait another six hours for a flight it might be too late.

"Just see what you can do, Victor," the Australian said, forcing a smile.

At 6:40 the departure call for the 7:00 A.M. flight to London—810—caused the tour group to make their way to the plane.

Graham was about to speak to Victor again, when he approached him. "You are in luck, Doctor," the tour guide said with a sly smile. "Here is your boarding pass and seat number."

Graham refused to allow himself to relax as he sauntered out to the airplane at the rear of the tour group. He braced himself when he saw there were four armed militiamen at the foot of the gangway. Two were collecting visa cards. The others eyed the passengers.

The Australian was last to reach the gangway. A guard collected his visa, looked at him for a second and then pointed to the door of the plane. Graham didn't need a second invitation as he moved briskly up the steps and into the cabin.

Even during takeoff he didn't allow himself the luxury of a thankful cheer along with the other passengers. Until he was out of the aircraft and on English soil he would still be officially inside Soviet territory.

Bromovitch arrived at KGB HQ before 9:00 A.M. on Saturday and waited patiently for the call that never came. He tried several times to contact Menkelov and Igor and learned that two men answering their description had been burned to death in a road accident. He moved quickly to have Graham hauled in.

Twenty militia and KGB personnel were ordered to the National Hotel. Bromovitch found a tour guide who informed him that Dr. Boulter had gone to the airport with a tour leaving earlier in the hope of catching the 7:00 A.M. flight to England.

The assassin was furious. He grabbed a telephone in the hotel lobby and got through to Victor, who was at the airport preparing for Graham's original tour group's departure at 2:00 P.M.

The distressed tour guide confirmed that Dr. Boulter had been cleared by the Intourist central computer and allowed to go on an earlier flight.

"Put me through to the traffic controller," Bromovitch ordered angrily as he looked at his watch. It was 10:10 A.M. Seconds later a voice came on the line: "Sheremetyevo traffic control here."

"Comrade, this is the deputy chief of Department Four, state security. I want you to order Flight 810 to return to Moscow immediately. There is a foreign criminal on board."

Bromovitch heard the crackle of a radio transmission as the controller contacted the 810 Flight captain. Seconds later the assassin was told, "Comrade, 810's passengers have just disembarked. . . ."

Once down the steps of the gangway from the Aeroflot jet Graham hurried across the tarmac ahead of members of the tour group.

Near the entrance to the hallway which would take him through to Immigration, he stole a glance over his shoulder at the airplane and noticed two, three, then four men in overcoats close behind him, none recognizable as members of the tour.

"Keep moving!" one of them ordered as the Australian slipped through the doors and headed toward Immigration. Within yards of the desks one of the men moved next to him.

"Follow me, Mr. Graham, please," he said with a quick glance.

The Australian looked back. The other three had fallen behind at different intervals along the hallway. Each was facing the jet, hands in pockets.

Graham was led past Immigration and through to the luggage area. He waited patiently for his suitcase while the man who had spoken to him stood nearby. When the suitcase arrived Graham grabbed it from the conveyor belt and turning to the man said, "I take it you're with Commander Gould."

The man nodded, smiled again and led Graham to an office where the commander was waiting. He was beaming and Graham reflected it was the first time he had seen the Intelligence man smile.

"Have a great holiday?" he said, shaking the Australian's hand.

"Terrific." Graham grimaced. "Can't wait to get back."

"Anything to declare?"

"Yes. One shattered human being."

The Australian felt in his coat pocket and handed Gould the icon containing the microfilm.

"When you feel ready for the debriefing, call me." He handed Graham a card. "That's a hotel in Hampstead. All your belongings at Strand-on-the-Green have been transferred there. Hope you don't mind."

Graham shook his head. "No," he said wearily. "I suppose you'll have someone watching the new place?"

Gould nodded.

"I'm going away tomorrow for about five days. I must have a break. A friend of mine has a flat at Brighton. . . ."

"I would appreciate knowing where we could contact you. . . ."

Graham nodded and picked up his case. "I'll let you know." He left the office.

Rounding the customs barrier, he was suddenly conscious of the hundreds of people waiting to greet arrivals. He thought of Françoise.

"Ed, darling," he heard an excited voice say, and then felt those familiar long arms around his neck as she embraced him.

PART 3

THE
PUPPET
CONNECTION

*"What the mind can perceive,
the mind controlling the computer can achieve."*

7

President Rickard was furious about the leak of a top-secret decision to supply the Chinese with ten billion dollars' worth of arms for its potentially dangerous confrontation with the Soviet Union. Less than a week after he and his National Security Council made the decision, the story was plastered over the front pages of America's daily papers.

After the earlier leak of the confrontation note to the Soviet administration, Rickard had called in the FBI to investigate the holes in information security in Washington. Then his orders had been, "I don't care how the hell you do it, but find out the leak."

FBI Director James Dent had dutifully carried out his President's rather frustrated orders, deducing that the leak must have come from either the President's staff or the Secretary of State's offices. In the early afternoon of October 2, Rickard received a telephone call from him.

"We have a breakthrough, Mr. President."

"You've traced the source?"

"Yes. We were right. It was the Secretary of State's department."

"Who?"

"Assistant Under Secretary Gregor Haussermann, sir."

"Haussermann," the President breathed. "Are you absolutely positive?"

"No doubt about it. We have conclusive taped information."

"Tape? How?"

"We tapped his phone, and recorded conversations."

"Where?"

"At his office and his home."

"You have other evidence? You know we couldn't use bugging."

"Yes. We know how he gets classified data in and out, who he passes it to and where he does it. The tapes verify everything."

"Okay. Get all the evidence including the tapes to me. I want to be positive myself before I make another move. You know how delicate this one is."

By late Thursday afternoon Washington time, Rickard had played the tapes of Haussermann's conversations in the presence of the Secretary of State and FBI Director Dent. Rickard decided to fire Haussermann as soon as possible. The second assistant Under Secretary of State was summoned to the Oval Office. At 6:30 P.M. he eased his slight frame into a chair facing Rickard, who was talking on the telephone. Haussermann shifted uncomfortably as the President made obvious reference to him.

"He's right here now sitting in front of me . . . we'll find out from him . . . we'll see what he says . . ."

After three nerve-racking minutes, President Rickard put the receiver down and then scribbled on a notepad, not looking up at Haussermann for nearly another minute. Taking off his glasses, he rubbed his eyes and said, "Now, Mr. Haussermann, you know why you are here?"

Haussermann looked perplexed and blinked nervously. "N-no I don't, Mr. P-President."

Rickard's gaze pierced into the other man's skull. "Well I'll get straight to the point. I know without a shadow of doubt you have been leaking important confidential administration minutes."

Haussermann reacted visibly. The irises dilated. His nostrils and lips quivered. His mouth opened and closed twice before he managed to blurt out, "You're . . . you're . . . you're wro-wro-wrong!"

The President snapped, "No, I'm not!" He then read off in detail the classified information Haussermann had relayed, the times when he had done it and the people to whom he had passed it.

Haussermann was shocked. The confrontation had not

helped his speech impediment. "You-you can't pro-pro-prove any-any-any of it."

"I have!" Rickard thundered. "I want your resignation by tomorrow and I'm going to ask you to submit to questioning by the FBI and CIA, just in case you've passed on any more secrets we should know about."

"Oh, no . . . oh, no . . . you can't do that!" Haussermann breathed, his words coming very fast. "You must have bugged me. You should be impeached for that!"

"Look. I don't want any arguments, Haussermann," Rickard shouted angrily. "You're finished!"

"Ju-just like Ro-Ro-Ronald MacGregor."

"What did you say?" Rickard glared. "Just like MacGregor. What do you mean by that?"

"We-well, he's dead, isn't he? And so am I, if you-you persecute me like this."

"Is there anything else you want to tell me? Anything else you want to say?"

"All right . . . all right . . . I'll resign right here! Right now!" Haussermann pulled a pen and a piece of paper from the front pocket of his suit coat, leaned forward on the President's desk and began to scribble.

"Get hold of yourself, man. I said by tomorrow. Now if you have nothing more to say . . ."

Haussermann's pen rested in a shaky right hand. "I see," he said, nodding quickly. "You-you are going to interrogate me with your Gestapo tactics! Well, I will not go as easily as MacGregor! Why don't you-you admit you-you had MacGregor assassinated?"

"I had MacGregor assassinated? Are you insane?"

Perhaps, the President thought, with a sudden flash of compassion, the rush of guilt may have unbalanced the poor devil.

Haussermann carried on regardless. "He would have beaten you. So you had an assassin strike him down!"

Rickard had had enough. "I'd like you to leave now, Mr. Haussermann," he said firmly, as he placed his spectacles back on.

"I ha-have evidence on MacGregor's death."

"If you do have evidence, you had better give it to me, or the director of the FBI."

Haussermann laughed cynically. "Oh, yes . . . so you-you could be smar-smart and destroy incriminating evidence. You-you must be joking!"

"I'm not joking, Mr. Haussermann. You are talking about a very serious situation. I have personally ordered the direction of the investigation into MacGregor's death. It's my responsibility to hand over any relevant information!"

Haussermann got up, his pen and paper still in his hand. He seemed in two minds whether to start writing again or obey the President's wishes. "I have evidence you killed MacGregor," he hissed.

"Fine," Rickard said calmly but firmly, thinking it best to humor the man. "If you have evidence that I killed MacGregor, then hand it in." He leaned across his desk and flicked an intercom switch. "Rachel. Send in a security guard."

"Is everything all right?" his secretary's voice squeaked.

"Absolutely. Just send one in."

Seconds later, a burly guard knocked and entered.

"Show him out, will you?"

Haussermann backed away from Rickard. As he reached the door he yelled, "You're a murderer!"

The guard took him under the arm and began to escort him forcibly.

"Okay," the President said, with a sigh and shake of the head, "I'm a murderer."

As the guard departed with Haussermann, Rickard's secretary poked her head in at the door. "What on earth was that all about?"

"Don't worry, Rachel," Rickard said, as he sat down at his desk again. "It was one of those moments when all of a man's sins return to haunt him. He was guilty as hell, I guess. He went off his rocker for a minute there."

"You've had a difficult day, Mr. President. Would you like coffee or something?"

"Yes. Good idea, Rachel . . . just another tribulation in the trial of this great office," he said sardonically.

Inside he had to agree with her. First there was the leak, then the wire taps and now the dismissal of a senior official. Yes, he thought, taking a deep breath, it has been an extraordinarily tough day. But he was certain things were going to get tougher before the election.

He proved himself right the next day, when he went to New York.

The firing of Haussermann made the headlines in the morning papers, but that didn't bother him. What put his blood pressure well over his doctor's recommended level, was a feature in a weekly women's magazine, which had been picked up by the daily press and television. A young blonde in California calling herself Valeri Hudson claimed in an interview with the magazine that she was pregnant by Rickard. The woman, who was a former National Security Council employee, said she had visited the White House more than forty times to make love to him, and that they had formed a "very close" relationship over an eighteen-month period. She promised to make her true identity known in about six weeks' time, when "their" child was expected.

Rickard was furious. His first thoughts were for his wife, Lillian, and he rang her at noon from his party's New York campaign headquarters. But she was at a Washington charity fashion show and could not be contacted immediately. He ordered his press secretary to put out a statement saying that both the woman and the magazine would be sued for substantial damages. He categorically denied the suggestions in the feature story and added that it was "most definitely part of a major smear campaign" as election day drew nearer. Despite this, he could do nothing to stop the media turning the story into a full-scale "possible" scandal. And with "Valeri" in hiding somewhere in Europe, it soon became the gossip point for matrons' hairdressing salons and men's bars right across the nation. Photographs in the press accompanying the story showed that the woman was extremely attractive, and this made her story even more juicy and credible.

Rickard finally got through to the First Lady.

"Just answer me one question, darling," Lillian Rickard, an intelligent and demure forty-five-year-old, said. "Have you ever made love to this woman?"

"Oh, my God! No, I have not!"

"Everett. There's no need for you to get excited. The most important thing is that you don't get worried."

"You're right, darling."

"Remember, even if it were true," she added huskily, "I wouldn't run out on you."

Rickard was glad he was sitting alone in a campaign office. His stomach suddenly had butterflies and his throat had gone dry. Rushing into his mind came the memory of his only "affair," if it could have been called that, when he was Ohio's state attorney general ten years ago. For some reason he was never really able to explain even to himself, he had got entangled with his private secretary, a prim and ordinary-looking woman. It lasted only half a year. Then, as now, he thought, the incredible woman at the other end of the line had supported him.

"Darling," he said softly, "can I tell you for the one billionth time how much I love you. . . . I told you after the last time I wouldn't play around ever again. And I haven't."

"I believe you, honey."

"I love you so much I want to cry. Really . . ."

"Everett, darling, please don't let it upset you. Just get on with running this country. . . ."

Brogan Senior cupped one hand to his forehead and watched the tiny white ball as it glided off and veered left of the green at the fifth hold of Lasercomp's private Black Flats Country Club. The Wednesday afternoon nine-hole game was a must for the sprightly octogenarian, who on this sunny October 8 was accompanied by Strasburg.

"How's our old friend Judge Shaw?" the Old Man asked, marching off down a slope to a buggy as Strasburg swung hard.

The lawyer followed Brogan Senior as his ball lobbed into trees right of the fairway. "He's fine," he said, as he hopped into the driver's side and drove on. "I saw him last night at the theater. We couldn't say much. Too many people around."

"What about the case?"

A decision in the Lasercomp versus U.S. Government legal battle was due shortly. The Old Man was beginning to get anxious about its outcome.

"We're doing all we can," Strasburg said, as he guided the buggy over a rough patch. "We've hit him from every angle with our version of which way his decision should go. It must be embedded in his skull by now."

Over the six years the case had been running, Lasercomp had used their knowledge of Shaw's reading habits as one way of trying to influence his decision. Every magazine and paper he read had favorable comment about the corporation and the consequence for the nation if he dared decide that Lasercomp should be broken up into smaller independent units. Every circular from banks, and even his own stockbroker, told him the same story. Occasionally they carried articles, written by supposedly "independent" people, which spelled out what Lasercomp would like the content of his decision to be.

As they approached the spot where Brogan's ball had landed, the Old Man said, "What about the carrot of a Supreme Court appointment?"

Strasburg stopped the buggy and pulled on the handbrake. "We have to convince Shaw that if Mineva is elected, he would appoint him once Judge Rathbone dies." He jumped out and opened the passenger side door for Brogan. "Incidentally, I hear Rathbone's cancer is so bad that he may resign soon anyway. Shaw's life ambition is to make the big bench. That empty seat will be looming larger every dream he has."

The Old Man strode to his ball just left of center of the fairway and lined up his shot to the green. "How are you going to let Shaw know Mineva would appoint him?"

"Before the decision, he'll just happen to meet the future President of the United States."

"I had MacGregor assassinated," Everett Rickard's voice on the tape said as an electronics expert in a basement apartment in Alexandria, Virginia, switched it off in annoyance.

He sat on a stool at a bench surrounded by innumerable pieces of electronic equipment and looked up, deep in concentration, at the track lighting that crisscrossed the ceiling and lit the sealed room brilliantly. Then he reached for the recorder again.

"Why don't you admit you had MacGregor assassinated . . ." the voice of Haussermann said.

"I had MacGregor assassinated," Rickard's voice said again.

The expert stopped it and rewound it a fraction.

On. " . . . assass . . ." Off. Rewind.

On. ". . . assassin." Off. Rewind.

On. ". . . assassina." Off. Rewind.

The man worked fast and methodically, his deft control of the levers on the mixing panel an art in itself. Intermittently, the sound of the two voices would come off the tape.

The man stretched and yawned. It was time for more coffee. He switched on an electronically controlled and timed percolator which produced a brew to his own satisfaction. Sitting on a comfortable couch opposite the bench, he sipped his coffee, and contemplated his efforts. A minute later he switched on the three-and-a-half-minute tape. The modulation of certain words taken from several pieces of tape was marginally different.

As he was about to play the tape again, the face of Haussermann filled a television screen which monitored the front entrance of the man's apartment. He let the former State Department official in and offered him coffee.

"Would you like to hear it so far?"

"Haussermann nodded. When it was through, he said, "That sounds excellent to me."

"Oh, no, it's not! Your voice is okay. We can record changes now. But it's the pitch of certain words from Rickard that is giving me hell." He pinpointed a section of the tape. "Listen to this again."

Haussermann's voice was heard. "Why don't you admit you had MacGregor assassinated?"

Rickard's voice said, "I had MacGregor assassinated."

The expert played it once more. "We have you okay. And Rickard says the actual words 'I had MacGregor assassinated.' But it comes out as a question rather than a statement. The word 'assassinated' is the tough one. It has such a strong upward inflection. I think I can modulate it down. But if I can't, I'll have to pull the word out of one of Rickard's speeches."

"Can you get it right?"

"It'll be difficult. But I think so."

"I'll need it before the end of the week. I'm off to Europe then."

"It should be ready by Friday. Who has to hear it from the corporation?"

"Huntsman. If he likes it, we use it."

• • •

"That's the reason I have to get to the States pretty soon . . ." Graham said, as he tossed Françoise some newspaper clippings collected for him by Ryder Publications while he was in the Soviet Union. "See the small Reuters piece dated October sixth?"

Françoise picked up the clippings and read the six-paragraph article. It quoted Dr. Donald Gordon as saying in a lecture on computer technology and marketing at Georgetown University, Washington, that the unchecked flow of sophisticated computer technology into the Soviet Union was a major military threat to the West.

"That guy is the one Jane Ryder tried to see just before . . ." Graham got up from the couch in the Brighton flat and wandered over to a window that gave a view of the beach about one hundred yards up the road. The wind was up and the sea was pounding the deserted beach. "Gordon is a key to my investigation, I'm sure of it. He's trying to say something. I have to speak to him."

There was a short silence.

"You've been back from Russia four days . . ." Françoise began in an exasperated tone; "you've only just begun to look a little healthy again and you want to go charging off to the States. Haven't you gathered enough material already?"

Graham shook his head. Françoise moved to him.

"I don't understand you," she said with a confused, slightly hurt expression. "Do you want to go through life with one of them following you everywhere?" She pointed contemptuously at a car in the street five floors below. It was one of Commander Gould's men.

"He's only going to be with us while I put together all the information for MI-6. I have facts they want. They'll protect their investment until it pays off in a few days' time. . . ."

"And then who will it be down there? The KGB? Someone from Lasercomp contracted to kill you?"

"I don't know," he said softly.

She lit a cigarette and studied him for a moment. He was staring at the sea. It seemed to have him mesmerized.

"Why are you pushing yourself?" she asked gently. "Is it because of Jane Ryder?"

"She is a factor. But it's more. Something . . . something very deep in my gut is pushing me to finish this damned business . . . to get the whole truth. I can't explain it more than that."

He looked at her. "No one wants it to end more than me. I'm scared. I've had it up to here . . ."

"Can't you leave it to . . . to them?"

"No. I couldn't just walk away from it now and wonder about it for the rest of my life. It would haunt me. I must see it through." He laughed mirthlessly. "Besides, what you said before is probably right. If it's not MI-6 down there, it'll be someone else. . . . I'm in too far anyway. . . ."

Dr. Donald Gordon was desperate. Somehow he was going to have to make the effort to extricate himself from his self-imposed predicament, or go under. When he had left Lasercomp six years earlier, after big disagreements with the Brogans, they had warned him to keep quiet about his knowledge of the Cheetah series, which he had helped develop, and Lasercomp's secret plans. He knew about the dynastic master plan and the PPP, but had discreetly kept his mouth shut after Lasercomp had paid him off handsomely. But now all the things for which he had privately condemned the Brogans had begun to surface over the last year, and he could stand it no longer. He felt like the scientists who had split the atom. They had helped create something that was both of great benefit to mankind and its potential destroyer, if allowed to fall into the wrong hands. Cheetah, if misused, could be equally destructive. It could more precisely propel the weapons of total annihilation than any previous computer. Coupled with this was the potentially insidious use of the machine by totalitarian regimes.

Gordon had chosen invitation lectures to universities in Europe and the U.S. as the medium for his indirect protests, which were couched in generalities, and never mentioned the corporation.

In recent weeks, he had received warnings from Lasercomp that if he continued his lectures he could be in "trouble." And Gordon knew what that meant. It was the same kind of "trouble" that Jane Ryder had found herself in.

His dilemma was whether to continue his lectures or keep quiet.

Gordon had been living alone at his home in Virginia, and since Jane's death had decided to cover himself by gathering all the data he knew about Lasercomp's plans, especially information he thought would be damaging to the corporation and the Brogans. First he left a copy with his lawyer, and then, summoning up considerable intestinal fortitude, he decided to confront Brogan Senior.

Gordon had no trouble arranging an appointment. He was shown to the executive suite area of Lasercomp's HQ at Black Flats at 8:30 P.M. by one of the score of security guards. Brogan was still working in his office when Gordon entered the suite. He was told the Old Man would only be a minute or two.

The scientist had become extremely nervous. In an effort to calm himself he wandered around the room looking at pictures and portraits. Yet this only made him more anxious. It sharpened Gordon's sensitivity to the power of the Brogans and the runaway monster corporation they had created, nurtured and let loose on the world.

On one wall there was a tribute to Brogan Senior, the creator, and the early selling days starting in the Midwest and spreading across America. There were shots of him on the podium at sales conferences preaching to his devoted corporate followers, and shaking hands with important heads of state and presidents of six generations. These particularly affected the scientist as they accentuated some of his fears. The Brogans, he realized more fully, were not content with strongly influencing these people and their successors. They wanted complete control. And they were prepared to do anything to get it.

On another wall were colorful photographs of the great laboratories and research centers, theatrically lit to appear like eerie shrines. On a third wall, pictures were dedicated to the focal point of what the years and the billions of dollars had created: the outside and inside of the Cheetah computer. These showed the circuits, the laser technology, the components magnified ten million times. They were artistically displayed in a tribute to everything clinically engineered, aseptic and profitable, and they had created the new unemotional environment to allow Lasercomp to expand into tomorrow and eternity.

Every picture increased Gordon's fears. He had been a misfit at Lasercomp, a scientist with a conscience. His kind, he reflected with a shiver, had to be expendable in the eyes of such an organization. Suddenly the total awesome reality of just what he

2 0 9

was confronting hit him. He panicked. Gordon turned to leave. Brogan Senior was standing in the doorway to his office. The scientist was shocked. He wondered how long the Old Man had been watching him as he was greeted with all the effusiveness of an old and dear friend. Gordon was stunned but not initially fooled because he had seen the Old Man with "outsiders" a thousand times before in the past and he remembered the orders he would give when their backs had turned. "Finish him," or "Buy her," or "I want a dossier on that one . . ."

The scientist was given a drink and taken into an adjoining lounge area, usually reserved for heads of state and other VIPs who would sooner or later become Lasercomp customers.

There, seated on comfortable chairs, Brogan Senior's reminiscences began with such apparent respect for an old comrade-in-arms that Gordon was confused and found his initial determination crumbling. The Old Man spoke of the good times, the big breakthrough in computer memory development that Gordon had pioneered, the big government contracts and the winning of new markets. No, he told Gordon ruefully, scientific brains like his were becoming harder and harder to find. His manner, the scientist knew, was an intimidation in itself. Dare Gordon upset it? He got his opportunity when Brogan finally asked, "To what do I owe the honor of your visit?"

Gordon braced himself. "Some of your people have been threatening me."

The Old Man arched his eyebrows. "Threatening?"

"Yes, because of my lectures." Gordon silently cursed the Old Man's thick-lensed glasses which hideously distorted his eyes and made it more difficult to gauge a reaction.

"Some of my people have interpreted them as breaking our agreement." The Old Man's words were cool, measured. A storm would surely follow.

"I have not named you or made any specific ref—"

"You alluded to it," Brogan snapped. "That's all my enemies in the government, the press, business . . . that's all they need."

"Look, Clifford," Gordon said, hearing his own voice quivering, "I don't want anything to happen to me."

"What do you mean?"

"Oh, Christ! You know what I mean. That English girl investigating Soviet computer smuggling, you can't tell me her death was an accident!"

"I don't know what you are talking about," Brogan sneered angrily.

"No? I think you were worried she may have been on to your little secrets. Secrets that could destroy your empire."

"Secrets? Come on, don't be so melodramatic!"

Gordon was amazed. His words had held back the storm. He sensed the complex dials in the Old Man's head turning, feverishly trying to check himself and calculate the impact of what was being said.

"You forget, Clifford. I was in on the early planning of Cheetah and its markets."

"Things have changed since you left."

"Look. I can read. I can hear. I see the odd report about the computer build-up in Russia. I hear Lasercomp is going all-out for all major government contracts over the next few years. Not just the military, but the FBI, the CIA, everything."

"And why not? We still live in a free enterprise system."

"Yes, but the master plan is the same for Russia and here, isn't it Clifford? With you sitting astride the two nations manipulating everything. . . ."

"That's enough!" he yelled. "Why are you here?"

"To tell you I have everything documented. The plans, the ways, the means. Everything, the machine itself."

"The machine?"

"Yes. The inbuilt devices to allow you to tap the data in any Cheetah, anywhere in the world."

"That was drawing board stuff. It was abandoned just after you left."

"Those devices were the reason I left, and you know it. How many employees do you have? Half a million? Well, some of them break the code, and they talk. You went right through with the original Cheetah design."

Brogan stood up, walked over to a mantelpiece and seemed to be examining a steel management toy of eight balls suspended from wires. He pulled two of the balls to the left and let them swing into the others. It started a symmetrical motion. He stood mesmerized by the steady "click, clack" for a few seconds, before he said menacingly, "I don't know why you are so paranoid." He turned to face Gordon again. "You have nothing to worry about unless you continue your unfortunate public lectures. . . ."

"I have"—the scientist faltered—"taken out my own insurance by collating everything I know . . . it's all with a lawyer. . . ."

"That sounds like blackmail!"

"Not at all . . . but call it what you will. If anything happens to me . . ." The scientist trailed off. He couldn't bring himself to sound threatening.

Brogan turned away and started the toy game again. "If such information was released, nothing could be proved about Lasercomp activities inside the Soviet Union for a start." He smiled cynically at Gordon. "And we would take our chances that such ridiculous allegations would not damage us, or our business, in this country."

The scoffing confidence of the last statement sent a chill through Gordon. Most of the major government contracts Lasercomp was chasing would probably be decided finally by the American President early in the new year. They would at least need his countersignature because of their size and importance, especially in the military field. He knew Rickard would do his best to stop Lasercomp getting the big ones. But what, he wondered, would happen if Rickard lost the election?"

"And what about Paul Mineva?" he blurted.

Brogan stared back at him, face muscles tensed, for several seconds, before he said evenly, "What do you mean?"

"I have a lot . . ." He stood up and finished his drink. "I have nothing more to say. . . ."

"Well, I have one more thing to say," said Brogan, moving close to Gordon as he headed for the door. "I'm glad you mentioned that girl journalist. I just want to remind you of it now, again." He opened the door and a guard appeared. With a sick smile the Old Man said quietly, "Show him out. . . ."

Kendall Gould seemed to be in an expectant mood when Graham rang him to arrange a debriefing session. The commander ordered a viewing auditorium at the Department of Defence and the contents of Irena's microfilm were set up.

Graham referred to the copious notes he had assembled in the five days he had been back from the Soviet Union, using a reading lamp on his chair in the darkened auditorium.

"These first ten frames compare the KGB structure before and after computerization. It is now a more manageable ten departments. Hence the code name for the whole operation of smuggling and installing computer systems—Operation Ten."

The next five frames gave diagrammatic details on each new section of the KGB.

"General Gerovan of the Politburo controls all armed forces, military communications and weaponry. He heads the new KGB department where there has been a big build-up of converted Cheetah computers."

Gould switched the auditorium lights on. "Converted Cheetahs?"

"Yes."

"My understanding was," Gould said, pausing to fill his pipe, "that only a very few American scientists knew how to convert Cheetahs for military use. They need to be programmed a special way. It is highly classified."

"That may still be true."

"But it would mean Lasercomp scientists were cooperating in improving Soviet strike power!"

"A market is a market to Lasercomp." Graham shrugged. "You buy a machine from them and they'll help you install it."

"Have you any more details on this?"

"I can give you the broad picture I've put together with Irena's help."

"Which is?"

"Lasercomp scientists at IOSWOP in the palace in Vienna and elsewhere are designing the master systems—Operation Ten. They instruct Soviet scientists on the overall design and how to convert ordinary Cheetahs into those for military use."

"Do these Lasercomp scientists visit the Soviet Union?"

"I'm going to check that out in the U.S. It's likely that they make periodic visits to installation sites in the Soviet Union."

"To supervise the installation of the master system?"

"Yes."

They looked at the next frame. It held details on a new KGB set-up—the control of communications and satellites.

"There's a plan for direct communication links with other Eastern-bloc countries, Cuba and some African states. It's already partially operating."

"Where these satellites are to be used to bounce information from a computer in one country to a computer in another?"

"Yes. The master plan's top political priority is to build a system of stronger control inside the Soviet Union. The second priority is to use computers to give the Kremlin greater control over other communist countries, and eventually help pull other nations into its orbit of influence."

"Eventually?"

"Irena says that will not be working completely for ten years. But control inside the Soviet Union is working right now."

"Lasercomp is involved in this satellite set-up too?"

"Yes."

"There must be a huge number of computers needed for the whole of Operation Ten."

"About fifteen thousand are in the blueprint."

"The cost must be stupendous!"

"That figure includes everything from small mini-Cheetahs right through to supersized machines. If you averaged each computer at five million dollars, it's an extraordinary bill of roughly seventy-five billion American dollars, written off over the next decade, and probably the one after."

"How can the Soviet administration afford it? They don't have that much foreign exchange."

"The KGB is desperate to set up the master plan. They see it as the main way of keeping a Stalin-like grip on society. They are using every means possible—their own money, funds from special loans in the West, money from other nations involved. They've even set up a primitive international barter system where the computers are exchanged for other goods—cars and so on."

Gould puffed on his pipe for a few moments. "By the way," he said, "would you tell your friend Françoise not to worry about her boss Radford? He and three other executives of Computer Increments are being arrested today. They'll be charged under several sections of the U.K. Crimes Act concerning espionage, illegal foreign trade and dealing in contraband."

"She'll be relieved to hear it. But what about the Russians they were dealing with in London?"

"Unfortunately they've all got diplomatic immunity. But we have enough on ten in the Soviet trade mission to expel them straight away. . . ."

"That's great news, Commander," Graham said, as he punched up the next frame on the screen. "Now let's have a look at the blueprints for the specific military networks in the Soviet military arsenal. . . ."

"I agree that Mr. Graham should be accommodated," the Director said to Herman Znorel, who was calling from Stuttgart, "but the price I have in mind is twice yours."

"That is ridiculous! You are already paid a—"

"Don't waste my time," the Director snapped. "This would be a major piece of planning and coordination to be added to our current assignment. The risks are high."

"We can't go any higher."

"Then find another contractor."

The Director was gambling on the fact that Znorel would not like to engage another hit team.

"That is your final answer?"

"Yes. You must weigh up the importance of this man to you."

After a pause, Znorel replied, "I shall relay your message."

"Good. I must insist that we fulfill the contract in Paris. We would need Mr. Graham here."

"That may prove difficult."

"I think your employer will understand if you explain the difficulty of carrying on the special assignment for it, and doing extra contract work, which takes time and careful planning. It must pay for this and cooperate with us."

Znorel sighed. "I shall explain the situation. Goodbye, Herr Director."

In New York City, Brogan Senior was making one of his regular visits to Lasercomp's biggest office block, on Second Avenue.

The Old Man would often visit corporation offices and factories in many parts of the world, but he was especially interested in his employees on the top five floors of this block. Here, programmers and systems design people worked on continually updating the secret master program and its subprogram. These workers were each assigned different parts of the program which never allowed them to grasp the overall design. There was no permanent staff. Employees from a Lasercomp office around the world would be assigned to New York for a two-year period.

Managers in dark suits, stiffly starched white shirts and polished shoes, tripped over each other opening doors and introducing employees.

Brogan Senior stopped a few yards from a group of programmers working with a Cheetah mini, and frowned. His elephantine memory had failed him.

"Who is that young man nearest the window?" he said to a manager in the entourage.

"Ken Jungwirth, sir."

The Old Man was impressed by his neat appearance. He shuffled across to him.

"Mr. Jungwirth, you're on assignment from our L.A. branch, aren't you?"

"Yes, sir, research and development."

"How are you enjoying it here in New York?"

"It's a nice change, sir."

"Keep up the good work."

The Old Man turned to the manager. "Triple Mr. Jungwirth's salary."

The manager blinked and nodded as Brogan Senior smiled to the appreciative employee and moved on.

"Uh, Mr. Brogan, did you mean for the year?" the manager asked when the workers were out of earshot.

"No, just this month."

As he was about to engage another programmer in conversation, the Old Man was tapped on the arm.

"Henry Strasburg on the line," a female secretary said.

Brogan Senior broke away from the entourage and picked up a telephone on the nearest empty desk.

"Henry?"

"C.B.?"

"Henry, I had a visit from Donald Gordon last night."

"Gordon! What did he want?"

"Huntsman will explain later. I want you to find out who his lawyer is and exactly what he has documented on Lasercomp. We want it, Henry, and I don't care how you get it."

• • •

Douglas Philpott stepped forward to loud organized applause from the live audience of his nightly television show and a plump, awkward woman handed him an inscribed silver plaque.

"On behalf of the twenty million members of our association, The Television Watchers of America, I have great pleasure in giving you this plaque which designates you The Most Trusted Man in America. . . ."

Philpott held the trophy up modestly in one hand and shook hands with the woman. He mouthed a sincere-looking "thank you" twice to the woman as she continued. "Several million Americans voted you this honor ahead of politicians, businessmen, church leaders, academics and other members of the media. Might I say that over the years the integrity of your reporting and commentary, and that of the great team around you, has justly earned you this finest of awards."

She moved forward to kiss Philpott on both cheeks as he turned to the audience.

"This is indeed a truly great honor," Philpott said reverently, "and I am deeply moved by it and the tribute on the plaque here which reads, 'Greater faith has no man than to completely trust another.' . . . I thank you one and all very, very much. . . ."

There was near-hysterical applause as Philpott raised both hands to calm them. "Let me say that I have always sought truth and honesty in the news and information behind it . . . and tonight's show will be no exception."

There was a commercial break as Philpott moved back to behind the anchorman's desk. When he reappeared he seemed confused by his crew and team of reporters who had begun to talk to him from off-camera. As he was about to read the news, he said, "My team here apparently wants to show a short, unscheduled film clip. So let's see it . . ."

On the screen were strung together several pieces of film collected over the years of Philpott winning several other awards, ranging from the recent "Best Known Face in America" to those of a decade ago, "The Most Popular Face," and "The Most Sexy Newsperson."

When the clip was finished the cameras turned to Philpott who appeared dismayed and embarrassed. "Well, viewers, that's the last time I let a clip go on unscheduled. . . ."

As he spoke the screens were filled with a montage of supposedly off-camera "unrehearsed" facial shots of Philpott and a final shot of his head on a poster with the caption: "Would you buy a used television from this man?" It cut to Philpott throwing his hands in the air in mock horror to a background of sniggers and guffaws from his crew and reporting team. There was another commercial break and Philpott came back looking decidedly poker-faced.

"Now that the guys have had their fun—heaven knows where they got those shots of me!—let's look at today's main stories. . . ."

In the last five minutes he announced an exclusive for his show regarding rumors of a tape recording containing information that, he claimed, "could affect the fast-looming presidential election."

In the last week, several newspapers had speculated that this mysterious tape might contain information about the death of Ronald MacGregor. Philpott went one better in his attempt to keep pushing to his huge audience veiled innuendos directed at vilifying Rickard. His exclusive began: "This tape is now rumored to be a conversation between President Rickard and the recently dismissed assistant Under Secretary of State, Gregor Haussermann. We have been in contact with the White House. It denies categorically the existence of any such tape or that Rickard has had a secret bugging system reinstalled at the White House.

"Nevertheless," Philpott went on, "interest around Washington is mounting. News-hungry reporters have begun to work their telephones and see contacts in the hope of being first to crack a sensation that some are saying may even rival Watergate. If these unproven rumors do amount to anything, FBS will be right in there. . . . Today we tried to contact Haussermann. But when our reporter Bob Grisewald went to find the former State Department official, he had disappeared. . . . Bob?"

The camera turned to the reporter. "That's what we found, Doug. No Haussermann and no tape. We spoke to his wife at their Chevy Chase Friendship Boulevard apartment. Mrs. Haussermann said she had not seen her husband for several days. She refused to go on camera, but did say her husband had been in contact with her by phone . . . from Europe. . . ."

"I won't be here when you return," Françoise said quietly as she drove Graham to Heathrow airport on his way to New York.

"Why?" the Australian frowned at her.

"Oh." She shrugged. "Because you are impossible. You have a death wish. I don't want to come to your funeral. . . ."

"So that's why you've been so moody these last few days." Graham leaned across to kiss her cheek.

"Please, not while I'm driving." Françoise moved her head away.

Graham sighed heavily and looked out of his window at the endless line of cars they were overtaking.

"Look. The presidential election is only twelve days away. I'll be back the day after it at the latest. . . ."

"I tell you I won't be here. . . ."

"But the assignment will be over. We can go for a vacation somewhere. Perhaps to the south of France. Your hometown Montpellier . . . you told me you would like me to come there. . . ."

"You are impossible . . . very stupid! Commander Gould warns you not to continue the investigation, Sir Alfred Ryder pleads with you. But you take no notice. You are going to get killed. I feel it. I can't stand it any more."

There was a long silence until they hit the flat stretch of motorway to Heathrow. Graham leaned across and looked at the speedometer. It showed a hundred miles an hour and the Citröen was swaying as it approached top speed.

"Who's got a death wish?" Graham said, trying to break the ice. She ignored him and pressed her foot down harder.

They didn't speak again until the car pulled up outside the terminal. Graham went to kiss her again and she pulled away, wiping the tears away.

"Oh, God! Don't start that, you'll have me going in a second . . ." He got out of the car and pulled his suitcase from the trunk. He moved around to the driver's side and tapped on the window. She wound it down.

"Where are you going to go?" he asked.

"Probably home."

"Montpellier?"

"Perhaps."

"I'll join you."

"No . . ."

"As soon as this is over."

"No."

"Yes." He held the hair at the back of her head and, leaning through the window, kissed her. She responded warmly.

He pulled away and strode into the terminal. Without looking back.

8

Graham's first contact in New York was with Revel, now back in the U.S. awaiting the decision in the Justice Department's Lasercomp case. The Australian called him on arrival and arranged a meeting with the lawyer at Chicago, a bar on Park Avenue South, for 6:00 P.M. This gave him just enough time to take a bus to Grand Central station and from there a taxi to an apartment on East Thirty-sixth Street where he had stayed in New York earlier in the year.

Both men arrived at the bar on time and found themselves an isolated booth. Revel spoke first about a few points of interest concerning Lasercomp in Europe and then listened carefully to Graham's findings in the Soviet Union. All of it was vital information for the lawyer's part of the special PICS report to Rickard.

"You say this company called Znorel based in Stuttgart coordinates all the smuggling on Lasercomp's behalf," Revel said, when Graham had finished speaking of his key discoveries. "How does the smuggling operate?"

"It's a huge operation, rather like arms smuggling to South Africa. Lasercomp, the supplier, and the KGB, its client, make a deal. Lasercomp agrees to supply it with a certain number of computers a year. The corporation, of course, cannot be seen dealing directly with communists."

"So it uses Znorel to do its dirty work?"

"Right. Lasercomp 'legitimately' sells Cheetah to about forty companies in about thirty Western countries. These organizations are usually private—some of them bogus. It is up to these companies, under Znorel's direction, to get those machines into the Soviet Union."

"That's how Lasercomp's books always look okay to auditors. Revenue always comes from Western companies. This doesn't contravene any laws."

Graham nodded. "Lasercomp comes into the act again when its scientists design the network. They supervise its installation in the Soviet Union."

"How do these companies make their profit?"

"They buy a computer from Lasercomp for, say, four million dollars, and then up the price to the Russians to, say, five million."

"Then Znorel is a sort of computer broker between West and East?"

"Exactly. It takes a fee for organizing the smuggling from both the companies and the KGB."

"Then there is now way of proving a direct link between Lasercomp and Znorel?"

"It's not easy to break into Swiss bank accounts. But if you could, I'd bet you would find that Lasercomp owns Znorel, or a substantial chunk of it."

Graham pulled an envelope from his inside coat pocket and handed it to Revel.

"What's in this?"

"Some important shots for your family album. Vienna is the central smuggling point for the Cheetahs. The men in those shots, I think you'll find, are all in some way connected with Lasercomp. They design the master plan for the Soviet system. They work with Soviet scientists at Vienna's Stölenburg Palace."

"So Vienna is the central clearing house for the smuggling, and also the focal point for designing the master plan. It's beginning to fit." Revel paused to sip his drink. "Where did you take these photos?"

"At the KGB's center in Kiev."

"They could even be incriminating evidence."

"I know two at least for sure are on Lasercomp's payroll. They're on two-year assignment to IOSWOP."

A young couple had just settled into the booth next to theirs. The two men sat silently for a minute until they heard the couple engaged in conversation.

Revel leaned forward. Lowering his voice, he said, "I'll get our authorities onto this right away."

"As soon as there is some action, I want to write an article for the press here and in London."

"Isn't that dangerous?"

"Maybe. But I want to draw those bastards at Lasercomp into the open. We could make it a very hot week for the giant. Especially if you win your court battle."

Revel winced.

"You're confident, aren't you?"

"Absolutely. We presented a winning case. But I'm still nervous about it." Revel had tried to put the coming decision out of his mind. Since learning more about the corporation's clandestine and ruthless activities in recent weeks, he was desperately wanting the decision to go his way. He changed the subject.

"What are your plans?"

"I'd like to see Dr. Donald Gordon. He may be able to help on a few things that are puzzling me."

"That may be difficult. I called him yesterday for you. He was ultracautious about a meeting. He said it would be dangerous for him to see anyone from the press."

"Well, what's he afraid of? That's all the more reason for seeing him."

Gordon had been under terrific tension since his confrontation with Clifford Brogan, Sr., almost a week ago. He had hardly ventured out of his home, a two-story wooden building called the Captain's Mansion, in Maryland, Virginia. It was once owned by a seafaring gentleman from the Maryland region, and stood at the end of a dirt road about a hundred yards from the next house. It backed onto a lonely grassland swamp area, and overlooked the Pioneer Point conjunction of the Corsica and Chester rivers. Not a quarter of a mile away, the Soviet Union had a forty-five-acre prime waterfront retreat for their embassy and espionage staffs and their families.

Gordon took some comfort from the fact that he had built the home into an electronic fortress over the last twenty years. It was surrounded by a ten-foot-high wood-plank fence, which had sensory devices ingrained in its top. If any person or beast tried to get over the fence they would activate a warning system. This had a high-pitched buzzer sound like a dentist's drill, a lighting arrangement that floodlit the grounds, and an elaborate electronic eye monitoring device which, Gordon boasted, could look into every corner of the house and grounds. The scientist had also built an excellent bomb shelter beneath his basement library.

On the night of October 23 Gordon was reading in the library when the buzzer sounded. At first he thought it was a stray cat which had often activated the system. He went to switch it off. As his hand moved over the deactivation switch he looked up at the four television monitor screens in each corner of the ceiling. Four figures dressed in hooded masks were running toward the house. Gordon ran for the steel trap door leading to the bomb shelter. He pulled it shut just as he heard glass shattering. He slid down a ladder, turned on the light in the shelter and immediately switched on another television monitor screen. The scientist watched in horror as the four men broke in and began to scour the house. They were all armed with handguns. His monitoring system was also geared for sound and he could hear and see the men stumbling around occasionally smashing something. They went through every room before he heard them.

"He's not here!"

"He has to be damn well here!"

"Then where the hell is he?"

Gordon dialed the police.

The gunmen noticed the scanners and began to shoot at them.

"Jesus! This place is creepy!" one of them said. "Let's get out of here."

The four men clambered out of the house, ran across the grounds, and hurled themselves over the wall.

Gordon watched their escape. His worst fears about tackling Lasercomp had been terrifyingly verified.

Graham arrived in Washington by Metroliner from New York late on Friday the twenty-fourth and immediately took a taxi to a small hotel on Sixteenth Street opposite Lafayette Park and the White House.

Checking in under a false name, the Australian went straight to his room, unpacked and went to bed.

Just as he was drifting off to sleep the telephone rang. It was Revel, who had flown into Washington that morning.

"This is important. Can you meet me immediately?"

Graham looked at his watch. It was just after midnight. "Can't it wait until morning?" he asked wearily. "I really am tired, George. . . ."

"Ed, it's urgent. A limousine will pick you up in five minutes. Come as you are."

He rang off before Graham could object. The Australian cursed.

"Come as you are?" he muttered to himself as he looked at his naked state in a bureau mirror.

Four minutes later, he was waiting in front of the hotel. A government car cruised up and stopped near him.

"Mr. Graham," a marine said, as he bounced from the car and opened a back door. The Australian nodded and hopped in. He began to wonder what Revel was up to.

The car swung around the park, and much to Graham's surprise, was ushered through a heavily guarded back entrance to the White House. It pulled up abruptly near the west wing. The marine opened the door and led Graham to a side entrance, where a plainclothes man mumbled a greeting to the Australian and took him to a large room where Revel was waiting.

"You could have dressed a little more formally," he said, smiling nervously and eying Graham's turtleneck sweater.

"You didn't tell me it was a White House ball . . ."

Revel laughed, and paced the room.

"George, what the hell's going on?"

The lawyer walked up close to Graham. "You are about to meet the President of the United States," he said melodramatically.

"What?" Graham asked in disbelief. "You're putting me on!"

Revel shook his head. "Nope."

"But haven't you already let the attorney general know . . .?"

"Yes, this afternoon. But Rickard expressly wanted his meeting with you. He's like that. He has a lot of journalistic contacts. Feels easy among them."

"At this time of night?"

"This guy's a workaholic. And you've given him something to get his teeth into. I was with him this afternoon when he set in motion a delicate line of action with the West German government and police, NATO, Interpol and the CIA . . ."

He cut off as an aide entered the room.

"The President will see you now," he said to both of them. Revel arched his eyebrows at Graham and motioned for him to go first. They were led out of the room and down a hallway which swung right of the Oval Office. The aide knocked at the President's study and ushered Graham and Revel in. Rickard was sitting at a small desk leaning forward with one hand rubbing his brow as he spoke rapidly on the telephone.

"Hold them right there . . . what did they have on them? . . . oh, my God! . . . traitorous assholes!" He looked up, saw the two men and began to get up from behind the desk. "Okay, Dick, you get back to me first thing tomorrow our time. Good night . . . I mean morning. . . ." He put down the receiver and moved around the desk to shake hands with the Australian.

"Mr. Graham, please sit down."

The telephone rang as both Graham and Revel took the only two seats in front of the desk.

"Yeah . . . hold everything. That'll wrap it up for the night. . . ." Rickard slammed down the receiver.

"Well, gentlemen, we've just arrested eight people—five men and three women—in Stuttgart en route from Vienna to Moscow. They'll be charged with illegal passing of restricted and classified military documents. There'll be a closer inspection tomorrow but it looks as if all the documents are part of important computer design specifications for NATO, American nuclear missile systems and the latest in our laser weaponry. Quite a haul. But we've got them!" He paused to take off his glasses. "Thanks to you, Mr. Graham." His craggy face flashed the briefest of smiles as he focused hard on the Australian.

Graham, embarrassed and a little nervous, nodded as Rickard picked up photos that the Australian had taken in Kiev. "I had the FBI check these today. Eight, those arrested, were identified as either employed by Lasercomp in Europe, or on assignment from the corporation at IOSWOP in Vienna. I want to see how Lasercomp tries to wriggle out of this one. . . ." He smiled victoriously at both of them.

"Now Mr. Revel has briefed me on your little trip, and I have the CIA version via MI-6, you'll be interested to know, of what you were up to. . . . Now first, I want to apologize for getting you over here now, and second, I would like to ask you just one or two questions about your Soviet mission. Only if you're willing, you understand. . . ."

"I'll answer them if I can, Mr. President. . . ."

"Okay. This is off the record completely. You've never met me. . . ."

Graham nodded vigorously to that condition.

"Now you were there when Mineva was in Moscow. Did you get any inkling from your contacts of just why the Russians want Mineva as President?"

"I don't think the whole administration does. Only the KGB clique led by Andropolov. It seems to be wielding the power right now . . . but if I may say so, you've made yourself unpopular with the KGB clique. . . ."

Graham paused. Rickard nodded for him to continue.

"You're a definite threat to their plans for internal control and expansion outside Soviet territory. Halting the flow of Cheetahs halts their arms build-up. They don't like you confronting them. The arms deal with China has meant there can be no love lost between you and the KGB. . . ."

"Hmmmm . . . why do you think Lasercomp helped Mineva in Moscow?"

"I can only guess at that. . . ."

"Go ahead, go ahead . . ."

"Well, Brogan Senior may well have convinced the KGB that Mineva would be a better bet for their aims than, with respect, 'bogeyman' Rickard. Lasercomp cooperated with the KGB in trying to make Mineva look like a statesman, and you a warmonger. You're a common enemy to both. . . ."

Rickard leaned back and rubbed his eyes again. "I think you're right . . . they have formed the unholiest of alliances." He sighed deeply. "The worst excesses of Soviet Marxism and American capitalism gone haywire. . . ."

"They have a lot in common, if I may say so, Mr. President," Revel chipped in. "They both want absolute power in their respective domains. The computer is the common denominator for both."

Rickard looked hard at Revel and nodded slowly. Then turning to Graham he said, "That's all I wanted to know and thank you for your replies." He stood up and moved around to them. Graham and Revel got up and shook hands. "When I'm under a little less pressure early next year, I want to have a longer chat with you," he said to Graham.

"I look forward to that. . . ."

"On one condition."

"It's off the record. . . ."

Rickard nodded and smiled as a marine came in to escort them out.

Graham and Revel followed him in silence to a waiting limousine. They were driven back to Graham's hotel.

"Damn it!" Graham exclaimed as he got out. "I forgot to ask him if I could write anything . . ."

"Don't worry, I've already spoken to him about that. He says you have the exclusive as long as—"

"—the source is a high government official."

"You got it . . . oh, I almost forgot . . ." Revel said, winding down the window to speak more softly, "Gordon phoned me last night in a real sweat. Someone tried to kill him. He wants to talk now. . . ."

"When can we meet him?"

"I've said we'll drive out to his home Monday."

"Good. That gives me the weekend to write a piece on the arrests for the press in London and here. . . ."

"See you Monday night, better make it about nine."

Graham nodded and Revel signaled the driver. The Australian watched the limousine slip away and then turned for the hotel entrance. There was one week until the election and he had a story to write.

MONDAY, OCTOBER 27

The normally cool, clinical efficiency of Lasercomp's HQ executive offices looked like a hospital casualty ward on October 27. Young emissaries were sent scurrying from floor to floor with scribbled memos, while small groups of grim-faced executives met briefly along the plush-carpeted corridors.

The problem, which caused more than the usual flurry at photocopying machines, was a New York Times article written by "a special correspondent." It was Graham's article but not attributed to him. At the weekend he had used contacts at the paper to get the exclusive published. The report was headed: **"Lasercomp Link in Scientists' Arrests."** It ran on page one and on to page three.

By midmorning, the corporation's management committee had convened hurriedly in the war room. Brogan Junior, in the chair, got quickly to the heart of the problem. "We have to cover two points as quickly as possible," he said, putting on spectacles to look at the article. "One is obviously where it says that all those arrested had a direct link with us." He looked up at Huntsman, whose chubby fingers were working overtime taking notes. "You'll have to get something into a release dissociating us or any of our subsidiaries in Europe, from the scientists', shall we say, 'regrettable' actions." He added vehemently, "Sacrifice the bastards! Express our shock that any of our middle managers on assignment could ever get involved in breaking NATO regulations." He looked at the article again.

"The second priority is where the report says, 'The men arrested might be involved in a wider effort to illegally feed the KGB with vital computers.' All we have to do there is restate our policy on selling to the communist countries."

"What about action against those arrested?" Huntsman asked.

Brogan nodded. "I suppose you'd better mention something. Keep it fairly low-key. 'Action will be taken internally if necessary, following our own inquiry.' Say something about a plan to tighten up our internal security, and the movement of Lasercomp personnel into communist countries." He took off his spectacles. "We must find out who wrote this. Any ideas?"

Huntsman sighed and nodded. "It could only have been Graham."

Brogan Junior grimaced. "Has Znorel been in contact with the Director?"

"Yes, but he wants double—"

"I don't care what he wants," Brogan Junior interjected in a rare show of emotion more in keeping with the Old Man, "pay him. Just get rid of that problem!"

Graham and Revel drove in the lawyer's early model brown Ford Mustang coupé along Route 50 out of Washington and joined

301 coming from Richmond on the road to Annapolis. Route 301 took them to the little town of Canterville and Gordon's home. They arrived just after 11:00 P.M.

When Revel announced himself over an intercom at the front, a huge iron gate automatically swung in. He drove to the front door, where the now skeletal-thin Gordon greeted them. He was dressed in a red turtleneck sweater and baggy trousers, and looked dour and nervous as Revel introduced Graham to him. He ushered the two visitors down to the basement. Gordon left them in his library and went up to a kitchen on the first floor to fix drinks. Two walls of books, ranging from the highly technical on computer design to the political works of Hegel and Marx, gave a hint of the scientist's considerable intellect. A small log fire crackled in one corner. On a mantelpiece above it was a framed picture of the word *Cogitate*—Lasercomp's motto.

Gordon returned after a minute and handed Graham and Revel drinks. He sat down with them in easy chairs, and began to speak of his brief past working association with Revel at Lasercomp. The two had on a few occasions worked together on special computer designs.

Graham began by quizzing the scientist about his contact with Jane Ryder. He explained that she had telephoned him twice in Paris.

"Did you see her?" Graham asked.

Gordon hesitated. "Yes. I lied to French Intelligence."

"Why did you see her?"

"She was very persistent and I was scared Lasercomp was going to do something to me after my Paris lectures. I told her some incriminating facts about the corporation. I thought it might stop them."

"So they murdered her."

Gordon nodded. "They apparently bugged my hotel room in Paris and found out what I had told her."

"And now you think they're after you?" Revel asked.

"Yes."

"What did you tell Jane?" Graham asked.

"Why I split with the corporation. I objected strongly to the Brogan marketing plans."

"What were they?"

"Huge sales to the KGB for a start. Cheetahs in their hands

were, in my opinion, a definite blow to human rights inside the Soviet Union and potentially dangerous to the West."

"Was it just marketing plans that upset you?"

"No. There were also my own secret designs for Cheetah. Or perhaps I should say my technical refinement of a Brogan design idea. You see, the Brogans had this all-pervasive motto— 'What the mind can perceive, the mind controlling the computer can achieve.' I had to make or program their ideas in practice."

"What was it he forced you to design, that you objected to?"

"The main one was a tapping device. This could extract information electronically from any Cheetah installed anywhere in the world. The Old Man wanted to be able to sit in his war room and call up any data, at any time, from anywhere. So Lasercomp scientists spent years perfecting it. Finally, all he would have to do would be to activate a code, get into a computer and steal any information he wanted. If it was on the other side of the world, he could still do it via a satellite."

The implication hit Revel. "That would certainly give him colossal power!"

"When you think of it—ultimate power. Most information is stored on Cheetah equipment, and he can get his hands on it."

"How many people know about this secret device?" Graham asked.

"Perhaps ten or twelve. About one hundred and fifty scientists helped in parts of the design. Another five hundred workers put the programs together."

"If the attempt on your life was ordered by the Old Man, he must believe he has the means of neutralizing the information you have about Cheetah."

"That's why I've decided to speak to you. They may just call off the dogs if I fight back. . . . I don't see any other possible way out."

"Is there anything else you told Jane?"

"Yes. I told her about Lasercomp's secret programs."

"What do you mean?"

"Ten years ago, some of my Lasercomp colleagues and I were asked by the Brogans to prepare a PPP, or Program for a Potential President. The aim was to design a computerized path to show how to get someone into the White House."

Gordon paused to sip his drink.

"It seemed like a management plaything at first. Using computers to work out a presidential candidate's campaign strategy was not new. But soon we found ourselves building far more complex programs than had ever been thought of before. Every imaginable factor was to be incorporated. We became intrigued as we were all soon ordered full-time on to the assignment. Within weeks it had become very sophisticated. About three hundred programmers were working on it. Within eight months, we had a model covering every contingency for a ten-year run at the presidency."

The scientist got up slowly from his chair and moved to the fire.

Graham asked, "What kind of things did you feed into the model?"

"Well, the simple, early programs were based on those for past campaigns, and covered a wide range—people for a candidate to see, people to be seen with, analysis of all previous winning and losing campaigns. We even threw in analysis of what made some Presidents appear strong and popular. There were also the mundane things, like being seen in a particular state a certain number of times in the actual presidential election year. It wasn't until new concepts became important that I wanted to cut out of the whole damned assignment."

"What were they?" Revel asked.

"Brogan Junior added a guy to the PPP team I'd never met before. He was a psychiatrist. He wanted us to build emotional factors into the program. They were to be quantified like everything else."

"Such as?" Graham asked.

"We were supposed to do extensive surveys to see how people reacted to certain words in a candidate's speech. Statements like 'Trust me' or 'I would never lie to you' were measured in every state. This allowed the PPP to instruct speech writers how many times these words should be used, depending on where the candidate was to say them."

Gordon laughed joylessly. "We even measured how different people reacted to knowing a candidate was religious, or sexually permissive. They were known as the 'God factor,' and the 'sex factor.'" The scientist swallowed the rest of his drink. "Anyway, that was it for me. I wanted out."

"You kept in touch with it?" Revel asked.

"Yes. Colleagues would often brief me. I guess it was morbid curiosity on my part."

"How would the PPP account for the unexpected over those eight years?" Revel asked. "Say, for instance, a President was impeached. Wouldn't that throw the PPP out of kilter?"

"Not at all. In fact, this was its strength. The programs were ongoing, and automatically changeable. New information was continually fed into the PPP at one end and instructions and calculations kept coming out the other. One new factor like that would immediately change the calculations for millions of others."

"What about the emergence of rivals to a candidate?" Graham asked.

"They were also catered for. I want to come back to that later. But first, let me tell you how the PPP was initially used." He moved across to a cabinet and poured himself another bourbon. "When the model was finished, several 'guests' were individually invited to meet Lasercomp's senior executives—the Brogans, Huntsman and Strasburg. These guests were mainly bright young senators and budding governors. The meetings were to see if one of them might fit the PPP. Only one was told that the corporation would be willing to help, if he wanted to be President of the United States. Lasercomp offered to help plan his long-term strategy and campaigns."

Gordon took a hefty swig of his drink. "He really took on the PPP idea wholeheartedly."

"Who was it?" Revel asked.

But Gordon was taking his time. "He had worked on the Apollo program at NASA before going into politics. He was very experienced in computers."

"Mineva was a computer engineer at NASA at one time, wasn't he?" Graham asked.

Gordon hesitated, but finally nodded his head. "You're right, Mineva."

"You believe Mineva has followed the PPP for ten years?" Revel asked disbelievingly.

"Yes, perfectly. Right down the line. And I can show you

the most important aspects of the original PPP. You can check the step-by-step Mineva campaign, right from when he ran for Nevada governorship to chalk up a record in government."

"But how do you account for MacGregor?" Revel asked.

"That was virtually Mr. Graham's question about rivals before, and this is what I hope will worry Lasercomp."

"You mean assassination was in the PPP if an unbeatable rival appeared?" Graham asked.

"Exactly."

"But it would not have specified Ronald MacGregor ten years ago as the target."

"Not then, of course, but elimination by assassination was a built-in contingency. MacGregor's name would have come up fast in the instructions and calculations when he started winning the primaries."

"You said you had a copy of the original PPP?" Revel asked.

"Yes."

"That should be strong proof of a Lasercomp-Mineva connection, and a link to MacGregor's assassination!"

"Not necessarily. The corporation would deny it and say the PPP was similar to just another macabre Rand-type study."

"Then how do you prove a Mineva-Lasercomp connection?" Graham asked.

"Perhaps the only way is to get conclusive evidence that the PPP is in operation on Lasercomp computers at HQ."

"Did Mineva know about the secret devices in Cheetah?" Graham asked.

"I'm not sure. Cheetah was not completely developed when he took on the PPP."

"But the secret devices had been designed then?"

"Oh, yes. It was just a matter of a firm management decision when the new machines would be mass produced and marketed."

"It could have been demonstrated to Mineva?"

"Definitely."

"It would have been a great incentive to become President," Revel said. "Using those secret devices, he would know what everyone using a Cheetah was doing. Including the Soviet Union."

"Is there anything significant in the PPP that Lasercomp may have yet to exploit fully to win the election for Mineva?" Graham asked.

"Yes: television. That doesn't mean simply how much exposure a candidate gets. More important was the actual manipulation of television." Gordon was slurring his words. The drink and general fatigue had taken its toll. "I feel it was the main factor in getting the whole damned PPP to work. Alan Huntsman interfered a lot here and insisted that his former protégé at FBS, Philpott, the then rising star of the networks, would soon be the most important commentator on television. Huntsman said we could count on Philpott supporting whoever was chosen as the Lasercomp puppet. He insisted we allow for it in the PPP."

"Do you think there is a connection with the PPP and the Haussermann tape rumors?"

"I'm sure of it."

"Why?"

"Because exhaustive analysis was done for the PPP on how false information used in the press and other media could be used against Mineva's rivals for the presidency."

"Including information on tape?"

Gordon nodded. "Tape is very evocative. It's one of Lasercomp's and FBS's main ways of pushing rumor and vicious innuendo against Rickard. Vilification is one of the oldest tricks in American politics. Only goddamn difference is, Lasercomp has quantified and computerized it!"

The word swept through Washington that Haussermann was hiding out in Paris. By evening, every television and radio newscast was carrying the story about how the former State Department official had left the country before being questioned by the FBI and the CIA about his leaks of important government documents. Only Philpott had managed to track him down. He was using all his professional skills to fool the public into believing this was a spontaneous piece of "scoop" reporting. In reality, Lasercomp had set it up with his connivance. Halfway through his show's news report a commentator announced: "Now our exclusive. Our anchorman Douglas Philpott has done it again. He has just been on the line from Paris to tell us he has an interview there ready with Gregor Haussermann, the controversial former leading State Department official. We're ready. He's ready, so here it is by satellite."

Haussermann's hunched figure filled the screen. He was wearing dark glasses and his normally trim beard had overgrown into a splotchy mess. He smoked incessantly as the camera pulled back to show reporter Philpott shoving a microphone near his face.

"Why are you hiding out here in Paris?"

"Because my life is in danger."

"Why? Does someone want to kill you?"

"Yes."

"Who?"

"The-the-Pres-President of the United-ted States and the CIA."

"President Rickard and the CIA? Why?"

"Be-because I have a tape."

"Of what?"

Haussermann dragged nervously on his cigarette and adjusted his glasses. "A con-conversation between the Pres-President and me, which . . ." He looked up at the camera.

"Which what, Mr. Haussermann?"

"It will prove who-who kill-kill-kill . . ." Haussermann stopped, and waved his hand at the camera. He seemed under tremendous stress.

Philpott was not going to let this exclusive disappear so easily. "It will prove who killed whom?"

Haussermann nodded several times as if to force out the name. "Ronald MacGregor."

"Prove? What do you mean by prove? Are you suggesting President Rickard knows who killed MacGregor?" Once again it was Philpott the Inquisitor.

"Yes-yes! On the tape! He admits it! He admits he wa-wa-wa-was responsible!"

"I don't believe the President of the United States would be involved in such a thing," Philpott said skeptically. "Can we hear this tape?"

"I-I-I-I'll be releasing it soon. I haven't spoken to my-my-my lawyers yet." He stood up and moved side-on to the camera.

Philpott followed him.

"Why not now?"

"Look, I've said enough. Sh-shut that thing off!" He waved a menacing fist at the camera. "They'll find me!" He walked hurriedly out of view with Philpott gabbling excitedly, "That was Gregor Haussermann who has just made an astonishing statement. He claimed that President Rickard admitted on a tape in a conversation with him that he, the President, was responsible for the death of Ronald MacGregor. I'll be back with further developments as they happen. This is Douglas Philpott reporting directly to you via satellite from Paris, France. . . ."

TUESDAY, OCTOBER 28

President Rickard appeared in the living quarters of the White House clutching a satchel full of files and newspaper reports. The turmoil resulting from the Haussermann accusations had upset his work schedule and he had taken them home to catch up.

He was still in a rage hours after the first flying off the handle at the news report from Paris. His wife gamely tried to calm him, but didn't get much chance because the telephone was running hot in Rickard's study. The only way to take some of the pressure off, she thought, was to have some food prepared. This she did, and brought him a medium steak and vegetables, which he wolfed between calls.

He got into bed at about 2:00 A.M. with reports scattered around him and on the floor. Still he wouldn't leave the telephone alone. His wife was now beginning to lose patience. She kept going in and out of the room to persuade him to rest, only to hear snippets of wild conversation.

". . . Wait until I get my hands on that bastard . . .! I'm definitely going to sue . . .! To hell with public opinion . . .! I've got a good mind to have that sonofabitch arrested . . .!"

Crash! Down went the receiver. Then he dialed his press secretary. "I want you to go along personally to FBS President what's-his-name—Bilby—and ask him what the hell is going on! Let all the members of his board know I'm going to sue! Even with a retraction and apology! I want a few explanations out of that goddamn network . . .!"

2 3 7

Finally, Lillian Rickard could not stand it any more. "Why don't you relax?" she said. "Honestly, honey, it can't be doing your health any good."

The tension in Rickard's face eased slightly, and he said, smiling, "You're right, Lillian." He embraced her warmly, accidentally knocking some of the reports off the bed. "Can't let those bastards get on top."

She lay on the bed next to him and he kissed her.

"You're only going to torture yourself with all these reports at this hour. You won't take them in. Especially with this other silly thing on your mind."

He nodded his reluctant agreement. "Why don't you sleep here tonight, honey?"

Lately the First Lady had been sleeping alone in the yellow bedroom on the second floor because Rickard had been working from his bed well into the early hours.

"Okay. Down here tonight, if you promise lights out in no more than twenty minutes. I'll get my things from upstairs." She padded off to her room to gather her night attire and decided to undress there. Just as she was unzipping her dress and gazing out of the window at the spectacular floodlit view of the Jefferson Memorial, she heard a muffled cry from the floor below.

The buzzer alarm system throughout the White House began to ring. Lillian rushed downstairs, calling out, "What's wrong, Everett? What's wrong?" and nearly collided with two security guards at the bottom of the stairs. Agonizing groans were coming from the President's bedroom. Half out of bed, face red, and with both hands clutching his chest, Rickard struggled for breath. He slumped on the floor. One guard tried to revive him and another fumbled with the scrambler which would bring the President's physician. Lillian Rickard momentarily lost control and screamed, "Is he dead? . . . Oh, God . . . is he dead?"

The first bulletin on Rickard's condition came at 9:30 A.M., seven hours after he had suffered what the White House described as a "mild heart attack." His doctor confined him to bed in Walter Reed Hospital for at least two weeks. All his duties were to be turned over to Vice President Cosgrove, who had assumed most of the chief executive's role within twenty minutes of Rickard's collapse.

A stunned nation, which had hardly had time to recover from the shock of the assassination of MacGregor, was sent reeling once more. Despite the medical report's assurance that Rickard would probably be able to resume all normal duties inside five weeks, speculation was rife about his political future. Would he recover enough to carry on?

Philpott went live on his evening newscast to expound on the dramatic interview with Haussermann. He told his public he would do everything he could to interview him again and even perhaps get the tape before the election. The main items in the news were Rickard's condition and its possible effect on the coming election, and the significance of a nationwide Gallup Poll.

Philpott wound up the night's program by saying, "This latest poll shows that if the election were held today, forty-two percent of you would vote for Rickard, and thirty-eight percent for Mineva with the rest undecided.

"Only three weeks earlier, immediately after the death of MacGregor, the figures with the same poll stood at forty-five for Rickard and thirty percent for whoever took MacGregor's place.

"The people of America are asking themselves tonight if they should vote for such a sick man . . . accused by a former high public official of being involved in a murder. . . ."

Brogan Junior switched off the television set in his father's executive office at Black Flats and flopped in a chair. Next to him, seated on a comfortable couch and surrounded by reports, was the Old Man, engrossed in a weighty computer print-out.

"Did you hear those figures?" Brogan Junior asked. "Mineva must win now. What manna from heaven Rickard's heart attack is!"

"I'm not so sure about that," the Old Man said gruffly, peering over his half-moon reading spectacles. "We've already programmed it into PPP and it says here it means only a point three percent swing to Mineva. It even cautions that Rickard will get a sympathy vote."

"But he can't be doing any campaigning, and the PPP says there will be as much as a three percent swing against Rickard if the Haussermann tape factor goes according to plan. Assuming other PPP predictions are right, Mineva will be only point three behind Rickard by the weekend. We're practically home."

"No we are not!" the Old Man said, slamming a clenched fist into an open hand. "We've got about two and a half billion dollars' worth of contracts that will be waiting on the President's desk for a countersignature by February. If Rickard's in, we'll never get them. If Mineva's in, they're ours. There is so much riding on this for our plans we can't afford to be complacent."

"Look, I don't see what you're worried about. The PPP says Mineva will win. I believe it's right."

"You honestly believe that goddamn thing is infallible, don't you?"

"Yes."

"Nothing constructed by man is infallible!"

"This can be. You've never really had the faith in computers I have, have you?"

"Computers didn't make me in the twenties and thirties! Hard man-made sweat, and selling, and selling and more selling, did!"

"But they've made this corporation. And you damn well know it."

Instead of launching into the chicken-and-egg argument the two of them had been through many times before, the Old Man changed the subject.

"I spoke to Strasburg this afternoon," he said coolly. "After all the assurances, the promises, the predictions, he still couldn't tell me categorically if Judge Shaw was going to come down on our side. After six years' litigation, we've still got to wait until he enters that courtroom tomorrow to see if the government has managed to ruin us."

"As far as I'm concerned, the case is ours. It's all sewn up."

"But we haven't actually heard it from Shaw himself."

"I think we near as damn well have."

"You mean the way he acted at the country club the other night when he met Mineva?"

"Yes. According to one of Mineva's aides, the candidate gave a virtuoso performance, as if he were already President. Over dinner he spoke of the nation 'moving forward with a powerful enforcement of the law and the Constitution.' Somehow he got around to speaking about how he planned to work with Congress, the unions and the 'mighty' forces of big business."

The Old Man liked what he was hearing.

"Apparently the conversation got around to the Supreme Court, and Judge Rathbone's imminent death. Shaw's old tongue was really hanging out. Then Mineva skipped the conversation away again and began to compliment the judge on his long career. Late in the dinner he actually dropped a few words of praise for Lasercomp! He said he hoped our profits would soar in his first year in office!"

"I'd still be happier with a categorical thumbs-up from Shaw now. . . ."

"Don't worry. We will get that tomorrow."

WEDNESDAY, OCTOBER 29

"All rise and remain silent," a bailiff cried clearly from the rear of the New York Southern District courtroom as Judge Shaw shuffled his way down a corridor to a side entrance. The press, lawyers, students, housewives, businessmen and politicians who had gathered midmorning, waited. Shaw entered, face solemn. All eyes were fixed on him as he paused before the bench for a continuation of the bailiff's chant: "Hear ye, hear ye, hear ye, the United States Court for the Southern District of New York is now in session. Draw near that you may be heard. God save the United Stats and this honorable court. Please take your seats."

"God save the United States" . . . the words echoed in Revel's brain as he resumed his seat at the head of the prosecution table, never taking his eyes off the judge's face.

Shaw flopped in his chair behind the bench. He cleared his throat to indicate he was about to commence his judgment.

"Have you got the courage?" Revel felt like yelling, as Shaw said: "In 99 Civ. 500, the United States of America versus the Lasercomp Corporation . . ."

". . . Lasercomp, the world's biggest computer manufacturer, today won its historic court battle with the U.S. Government

2 4 1

when Judge Peter K. Shaw brought down a decision overwhelmingly in the corporation's favor. . . ."

Graham switched off the 6:oo P.M. news report in disgust and paced his Washington hotel room.

He could feel the pressure of Lasercomp's power. It had proved invicible in the courts. It had moved relentlessly forward, as Graham had witnessed in the Philpott-Haussermann television interview, in its efforts to denigrate Rickard. Now the arrests of the eight scientists suddenly seemed such a small, even hollow victory. The great weight of information supplied by Gordon showed the strength of Lasercomp's all-encompassing plans for absolute power. It had taken the Australian three days to wade through the details on the Cheetah design, plans to sell a computer network first to the Soviet Union and, piece by piece, a similar system to government agencies, and also the original PPP program for Mineva's run to the White House.

Graham now had a great base of information and felt the urgency of getting back to the relative sanctity of London, locking himself away and writing the whole story, before the corporation caught up with him. . . .

He put a call through to Sir Alfred in London.

"I'm catching the night flight back. I've got everything I want from here."

"See me as soon as you've slept off your jet lag," Sir Alfred said. "I have something urgent to tell you . . . also you've had several calls from Huntsman of Lasercomp. . . ."

"What did he want?" Graham asked edgily.

"He wants you to ring him in New York. . . ."

"Christ! That's all I need. Sir Alfred, I'll see you tomorrow. . . ."

Graham put down the receiver and sat for a minute pondering Huntsman's attempt to speak to him. The Australian was tempted to confront the corporation and see if he could learn something that would connect Lasercomp to the deaths of Jane Ryder and Ronald MacGregor. Yet confrontation was dangerous. Gordon had done this and there had been an attempt on his life.

Graham decided to return Huntsman's call to at least gauge some reaction. He knew that if he kept the call to less than three minutes it would be difficult to trace.

Packing quickly, he reserved a taxi for the airport and then phoned the PR man at Lasercomp's Black Flats HQ.

"Yes, Mr. Graham, there are a couple of things . . . are you in New York?"

"No."

"Oh, uh . . . we wondered why you had not been in contact."

"I changed my mind about writing for you."

"Uh, if it's money we can go higher . . ."

"It wouldn't matter what you offered."

"Isn't that being a little unreas—"

"What else did you ring me about?" Graham said curtly, as he looked at his watch. Forty-five seconds.

Graham heard Huntsman's hand go over the receiver as he spoke in a muffled tone to someone.

The Australian was about to hang up when Huntsman said, "Sorry, I was distracted for a moment . . . uh, our management wants to make a statement about its marketing inside the Soviet Union." The temperature of his voice had dropped considerably. "We want you to have an exclusive."

"Why me?"

"We know that you're behind the attacks on our Soviet marketing. We want you to have a better perspective . . . the full story behind our operations there."

Graham looked at his watch again. One minute thirty-five seconds.

"How?"

"It depends on where you are. Are you planning to stay in the U.S.?"

"No."

"Then if you're going to be in England we could arrange that you meet with Jean Marie Cheznoir . . ."

"Cheznoir?" Graham sounded interested. But all the danger signals were flashing.

"Yes, as you know he is the brain behind our day-to-day dealing with the Soviet Union. It would be a world exclusive for you. . . ." Huntsman could see the chance to set Graham up for the Director.

"I don't want to waste my time with your usual PR crap."

"I assure you this will be big news. Very big. Uh, he is of course Paris-based, could you make it there? I'll be there myself tomorrow for a week. . . ."

"I'll phone you in Paris . . ."

Graham replaced the receiver abruptly. The call had lasted two minutes fifty-five seconds. He heard the taxi outside and decided to call Revel in New York from the airport.

Revel got himself drunk with his prosecution team in the Hotel Intercontinental in New York City after Judge Shaw's decision, which allowed Lasercomp to continue expanding unhindered.

There were a few minor directives from the judge, such as Lasercomp having to sell off all its noncomputer lines like typewriters and copying machines. There were also a few sober admonishments for its "ruthless treatment of some competition." But in essence the judgment was one of overwhelming support for the corporation and its activities at home and abroad in computer marketing.

Revel could not remember hearing the uproar in the courtroom when the main thrust of the judgment became clear. Nor had he felt the wringing hands of consolation or seen the triumphant and relieved faces of Lasercomp's defense, led by Strasburg and Cartwright. He had just wanted to sink into a hole in the courtroom floor.

Following a sad three-hour lunch, a boozed and bewildered Revel staggered to his room and slept it off. He was awakened by the telephone. It was Graham calling from Washington, minutes before his flight to London.

After a few words of consolation, he said, "I've spent the best part of the last three days going through Gordon's information and the PPP. If it's accurate, Lasercomp is probably going to use Philpott's last show before the election to crush Rickard."

"How?"

"It could have something to do with the Haussermann tape. The original PPP of ten years ago allows for the 'Philpott factor.' It even measures the impact of his TV programs, and their influence on an audience before an election."

"But he only has two shows left."

"Right. Consider how much more important those two

shows are now compared to when the original PPP was made—particularly when he claims to have a tape where the President of the United States is supposed to be admitting responsibility for assassinating a rival."

"I'm seeing the attorney general on Saturday to present my part of PICS. Maybe I could persuade him to look into it."

"If you could only see Philpott's script for his last program before the election. That's the one I think could do the most damage to Rickard."

A weak, gaunt and disgruntled Everett Rickard propped himself up in his hospital bed among the myriad red roses and get-well cards and began his first piece of presidential business since his heart attack three days earlier.

This consisted of a one-hour conference call to the Vice-President, attorney general, Secretary of State and his campaign managers, who informed him of his wife's brave thirty-hour vote-catching foray to the Southern states and New York on his behalf.

Rickard's doctor warned him that even these conversations could cause a relapse. But he informed the Vice-President that vital national and international decisions were still to be made by Rickard himself.

Rickard insisted that his press secretary brief him fully on media matters. Rickard was particularly concerned with clearing up the continued attacks on him by FBS, and some sections of the press.

The President munched gently on a salad dinner as Emmery explained what steps he had taken since Rickard had ordered him to take action on the FBS bias. "I've been in touch with every member of the FBS board . . ."

"And?"

"There was a general consensus that you seemed to be coming in for an unnecessary attack. But they didn't know why."

"Surely they have editorial control!"

"They do. However, they said they tried to keep from meddling in day-to-day programming trends."

"Passing the buck," the President mumbled.

"Maybe, but several of them, including FBS Vice-President Jack Carruthers, appear to be sympathetic to your position."

"Why aren't we seeing it on television?"

"Carruthers said he intended to call a special board meeting to look at the coverage of the election and your complaint."

FBS's board attended a meeting in the conference room of the network's Fifth Avenue New York offices. It had spent the last six hours watching reruns of excerpts from Philpott's recent program. Jack Carruthers, a granite-faced nuggety little man of forty-five, who was not known for mincing his words, opened the meeting.

"Everyone wants to know what we are going to do about this anti-Rickard bias."

"Look, Jack, we all know we get this sort of criticism every goddamn election," Cary Bilby said, looking around at the other six board members. "It's no different. I can't see what all the fuss is about."

"I don't agree. We've just seen Philpott's performance."

"He's the best goddamn asset this network has!" Bilby said defensively.

"No one is disputing that, but if he continues to slant his programs, FBS will lose credibility."

Phil Roberts, a quiet-spoken retired stockbrocker, said, "That's what we want to discuss. That's the issue."

"It seems that you're the only one who doesn't think he is out to break Rickard," Carruthers said to Bilby.

"So what am I supposed to do? Tell Philpott how to run his show? His ratings are higher than anyone ever before. Advertising revenue is rocketing because of his shows. We've never had to interfere in editorial programming."

"Let's not get our priorities mixed," Helen Masters, a forty-five-year-old former newspaper owner, said, patting her swept-back, blue-rinsed hair. "This network has had a reputation for integrity. We don't want to sacrifice that for advertising revenue. Newscasters and advertisers come and go."

"It's things like the Haussermann 'tape affair,' as Philpott calls it," Carruthers said. "I don't like it. There are too many unsubstantiated inferences for my liking!" There were mumbles of agreement around the table. "Rickard is quite entitled to sue us for libel."

"I think you are showing your political bias!" Bilby said to Carruthers. "You want Rickard to win."

"I want this network to present the truth! That's what's at stake here!" Carruthers said angrily.

"I agree!" Helen Masters said.

"Now hold on," Bilby said. "Just who do you want to win, Jack, who?"

"I've made no secret of my feelings. Rickard's record is good. He deserves to carry on. And I think he is personally a far better bet than Mineva to run this country! But that has nothing at all to do with this meeting!"

"I think it has a big goddamn bearing on our attitudes!" Bilby said.

"I think Jack is right," Helen Masters said. "Rickard is the better man. He's a tough, but good and intelligent President. Mineva's too plastic."

"Now we're getting personal!" Bill Cookson, the oldest member of the board, said. "But Philpott is persecuting Rickard and helping Mineva. It stand out a mile in those reruns."

There was a sudden nervous lull in the conversation as Bilby realized he was outnumbered. "All right! I'll have a word with Philpott, if you all think it's that bad!" He picked up a folder and stormed out of the meeting.

THURSDAY, OCTOBER 30

Mineva and his entourage made a triumphant drive down Fifth Avenue in crisp autumn sunshine to a welcome by around two hundred throusand people. As their route took them down Fifth Avenue, along Forty-second Street past the porn movie houses and down Seventh Avenue to the heart of the garment district, many people broke through the police barriers and ran alongside Mineva's open car. Bands played and there was something of a carnival atmosphere in spite of the cold as the candidate's campaign reached its peak and took the media limelight almost completely.

By contrast, everything seemed to be going wrong for Rickard's support team. While the President languished helplessly in his hospital bed, Vice President Cosgrove had made a speech the night before in Chicago but found his flight delayed for two hours because of snow at the city's airport the next morning. He had been doing his best. But there was little doubt that Rickard's sudden illness had caused his campaign to falter badly. On top of this, he seemed to be coming under terrific attack for his handling of the Sino-Soviet flare-up, which had reached a dangerous point. Both Peking and the Kremlin were threatening each other with all-out attack. There was also a continual barrage about the Haussermann tape affair and accusations about his President's income tax returns, and alleged sexual misadventures. All his staff could do was issue bland denials. Without the tough-minded Rickard to easily field and turn aside the criticisms of his presidency and himself, his campaign had gone very much on the defensive.

A distinct feeling of loneliness crept over Graham as he entered the stark suite at hotel hideout in Hampstead after his rough flight from Washington. Françoise had left him.

There was a note on the bedside table: "I love you. Regret au revoir. Françoise."

The Australian slumped on the bed and stared at the note. The cold emptiness without her made him realize how much through the hell of the last two months he had grown dependent on her nearness, the anticipation of her touch . . . her warmth. . . . He looked at the telephone and was in two minds whether or not to call her and plead with her to come back. Then he shook his head in disgust.

To drag her back to the dangers would be cowardly and selfish. Instead he vowed to keep his promise to see her when the investigation was over. . . .

He slept soundly for six hours and awoke fresh. His first thought was to call Sir Alfred. His private secretary told him the publisher would be waiting at his Pall Mall club at 6:00 P.M. Graham had just enough time to shower and dress.

He took twenty minutes to brief Sir Alfred on his latest findings and then asked, "What's the information you have for me?"

"Gould says the KGB has a contract out on you after your Soviet escapade."

"How did he learn that?"

"The Intelligence grapevine can transcend all boundaries. Your little coup in getting into the computer center there and managing to get out of Russia alive is being seen as a big points score for our Intelligence people."

"Now they want my balls for a necklace," Graham said ruefully. "I'm not surprised, but hearing it directly is not very palatable." He lit a cigarette. "They're coming at me from both sides now. Lasercomp wants to meet me in Paris."

"You're not going?"

Graham frowned but said nothing.

"You're mad, Ed! Stay in the U.K. where Gould can guarantee you protection."

"But it may be the only way ..." Graham said, deep in thought.

"Of what? In God's name!"

"Of proving that Jane and Ronald MacGregor were murdered by the same person."

"If what you've already uncovered is correct that is a logical possibility ... but ..."

Graham was far away again. "There may be a direct link between the corporation and an assassination squad. Proving that solves everything ... who killed Jane ... MacGregor ... the only way to know is for me to act as a bait."

Sir Alfred took a long, thoughtful sip from a double Scotch. He looked hard at the Australian. He knew that tight-set jaw and deep concentration only too well. Graham would find a way to Paris and nothing would stop the crazy fool! This time, however, Sir Alfred was sure the Australian would trip himself up. So far by luck and brilliant planning he had stayed alive. But now with the very real possibility of two contracts out on him there would be no hope. Sir Alfred felt a deep obligation.

"If you are hell-bent on this madness, I insist you have French police protection."

"You mean Colonel Guichard?"

"Yes. As you know, I've kept him informed on everything, including your idea that the assassin who killed MacGregor may be linked to Rodriguez, and also Jane's death. He has been genuinely interested."

"I would feel happier with protection. Would Guichard want to help?"

"There's only one way to find out." Sir Alfred eased himself from the armchair. "I shall ring him immediately."

Sir Alfred made the call from the club lobby and returned to Graham twenty minutes later.

"Well, it seems he's going to help. The prospect of drawing Rodriguez into the open had the man jumping."

"What's he want to do?"

"He was meeting with several of his men when I rang. They are trying to close the net now because they think he's still in Paris. Guichard said he would ring me back at my apartment after midnight . . ."

"That quick?"

"Yes. And he will. Guichard has always been more action than talk." Sir Alfred stood up. "Let's have something to eat."

Five hours later, at 1:00 A.M., a third game of chess between the two was interrupted by Guichard's call to the publisher's flat.

"I have a plan to trap Rodriguez. But I must have complete control over the operation," he told Sir Alfred firmly.

"You had better speak to Edwin about that. He is the one taking the biggest risk." Sir Alfred handed the receiver to the Australian.

"Yes, Colonel, what have you in mind?" Graham said, fumbling for a cigarette.

"Mr. Graham, we have a plan here that may work if our mutual friend Rodriguez is here in Paris. But I must insist that you follow my orders. . . ."

Graham paused before answering and looked at Sir Alfred. "I agree."

"Bon. Now the corporation has no idea where you will be in Paris, or how you will get there?"

"They don't even know I'm coming for sure."

"Bon. Then my plan makes two assumptions. One, that you are definitely being set up by Lasercomp; and two, that the assassins will try to find out how you plan to get to Paris, and where you will stay. Therefore, we will arrange for a plane to fly you to Aerospace Spatial tomorrow afternoon at one P.M. You will arrive at about two P.M. at a private airfield outside Lyon. There will be a car waiting for you there. You will drive directly to Paris—and stay at the Hotel Étoile Maillot. The moment you know what your arrangements are with the Lasercomp people, let me know. Make a rendezvous with them somewhere at night. Arrange dinner so that it will finish at midnight."

"How will I contact you?"

"There will be a radio phone in the car you pick up at Lyon. Whenever you pick up the receiver it will connect with me or one of my men."

Graham repeated the instructions and Guichard said, "You will have complete protection from when you arrive in France. You will be safe, I assure you, Mr. Graham."

"I hope so."

"I thank you for your cooperation in this matter. If we catch this maniac Rodriguez, you will be doing many nations a great service."

Graham's throat was a little dry. "I hope I'm around to get the applause."

Haussermann was worried. In the last few days the "protection" for him in the Paris Pigalle hideout had changed into a guard. His movements had been restricted ever since he arrived in Paris a few weeks ago. There had been the odd night or lunch at a secluded restaurant, and even a break for a weekend in the Normandy countryside. Now he was being told to remain indoors and out of sight. One of his "protectors," Martinez, was with him around the clock. The flat seemed, to the fretting fugitive, to be more like a prison.

Haussermann had tried to occupy himself reading papers, books and magazines, or watching television. His only consoling thought was the promise of freedom once he had made another short television film clip with Philpott within the next few days.

Safely in his wallet was a false passport under an assumed name and a one-way ticket to São Paulo, while securely locked in his memory was the number of his untraceable Zurich account—the key to a fortune earned from Lasercomp in the last few months. All he needed to do now was wait for the leader of his "protectors," a man he heard referred to as the Director, to tell him when and where to meet Philpott.

At 11:00 P.M., after the French news, he switched off the television and looked across at Martinez asleep on the couch. The sudden withdrawal of the television's steady gabble woke him.

Haussermann tried to smile but it came over as a nervous twitch. "Er . . . Marty," he said, "I woo-woo-wouldn't mind a cigarette."

Martinez fumbled in the back pocket of his trousers and threw him a crumpled packet of Camels and a lighter.

Haussermann lit up. "You've got a gun. I have seen it under your coat. Woo-why?" he asked.

Martinez was standing at a drink cabinet pouring himself a large cognac. "We told you, we have to protect you."

"Woo-who is it exactly you-you people are protecting me from?"

"As you told the American people, it's the CIA. That is who would like to silence you. . . ."

9

Paris was sunny and cool on Friday afternoon when the Australian headed the supercharged Peugeot he had found waiting for him at Lyon, off the ring road at Port Maillot. His destination—Étoile Maillot—was a small, quaint bed-and-breakfast hotel near the Arc de Triomphe between two spokes running off it: the Avenue de la Grande Armée and fashionable, tree-lined Avenue Foch. •

Just after 5:00 P.M. Graham made a call from his room to Lasercomp's Paris HQ and asked for Huntsman.

"Good to hear from you, Ed. How long do you intend to stay in Paris?"

"Only a couple of days."

"Great. I've kept the weekend open. Cheznoir says he will meet you any time."

"Tomorrow perhaps?"

"Fine. We'll take you to dinner."

Graham could hardly believe his ears. Just what Guichard wanted. Then a chill of second thought hit him. They could be setting him up.

"Thank you," Graham said, scrambling for pen and paper on a dresser.

"There's a real nice restaurant called Perouse on Boulevard St. Germain in the Latin Quarter . . ."

"I know it. It's not that hot. May I suggest one?"

"Sure," Huntsman said, trying to hide his lack of enthusiasm.

"There's a little place in the street first left off rue Marbeuf which runs off the Champs Élysées. It's called Les Innocents. My favorite place to eat here. Can we meet there at, say, nine-thirty?"

"Whatever suits you, Ed. Where are you, uh, staying in Paris in case there is a problem with Cheznoir?"

"I'll be out and about. Maybe it would be better if I phoned you to confirm. Where are you staying?"

"The Intercontinental."

"I'll ring you at noon, okay?"

"Fine, Ed, look forward to meeting you."

"Same here. And it will be interesting to meet Cheznoir. You don't often get exclusives like that. Goodbye, Mr. Huntsman."

Graham went down to his car in rue des Bois du Boulogne fronting the hotel and got quickly through to Guichard on the radio-telephone. The Intelligence chief was pleased. He related the rest of his plan.

"Park your car in rue Marbeuf. My men will be in position. When you come out after the dinner, go straight back to your car. Then I want you to drive toward the outskirts of Paris. There is no sense in getting innocent members of the public into danger." Guichard gave the Australian a detailed route. "Just drive there at normal speed. If anyone follows they will be caught. The important thing is that you keep your head. I am sure you will. Two of my men will be on guard at your hotel around the clock. You are safe, Mr. Graham!"

By 6:00 P.M. Friday afternoon, the Director, Rodriguez and Martinez had been working several hours on a new plan to murder the Australian based on fresh information from Huntsman. They had spent part of the afternoon surveying the area around Les Innocents.

The three men were sitting at a card table in the living room of their Pigalle hideout with about a hundred Polaroid photographs, half a dozen maps, and several pencil diagrams scattered all over the table. They were debating the best place to make the hit.

"I don't know if we can risk it outside the restaurant," Rodriguez said. "We can't be one hundred percent certain it isn't a police trap. You know the whole French police force is after me."

"Okay. It is your neck this time," the Director said. "But remember, it is a quiet cul-de-sac. There are two opportunities. When he arrives and when he leaves."

Early in the evening of the same day, two small boys searching for muskrats on the edge of Chesapeake Bay, sixty-one miles from Washington, came across a 1950 Aston-Martin car, partly submerged in mud and undergrowth. Slumped across the front seat was a dead man. A police patrol was on the scene twenty minutes later when alerted by the two young, excited voices from a callbox. The police assumed the car had been driven at high speed off the slipway approach to the bridge, judging from the distance it had fallen from the edge of the slipway twenty yards above.

"Hell, Sarge, this guy musta been really plastered. Look at that!" the patrolman said to his police companion, knee-deep in mud, as they hauled the body from the car. He was pointing to a half-empty bottle of bourbon on the back seat. There was a strong stench of alcohol in the car.

With some difficulty they laid the body across the Aston-Martin's battered and twisted hood. The sergeant searched through the man's pockets and found his wallet. Several documents identified the man as Dr. Donald Gordon.

After a quiet evening meal alone Graham went up to his room and put a call through to Revel in New York.

He had not spoken to him since leaving the States two days ago and the Australian wanted to know how the lawyer was progressing in getting some action on Philpott's last show.

"I'm pleased you got in touch, Ed. I have some mixed news for you. Number one, brace yourself, Gordon is dead."

"What?" Graham breathed. "But how?"

"Washington police say a car accident near his home. They suspect he was drunk. I'm trying to get the details."

"I can't believe it. It's all too coincidental."

"You can bet Lasercomp's behind it! Proving it is another thing."

"Have you managed to find out anything about Philpott's last show before the election?"

"I mentioned it to Attorney General Cardinal when I gave

him my part of the PICS assignment this morning. He said that pressuring anyone to review a script would smack of political interference and censorship. Cardinal was sure Bilby and Philpott would use this to cause a backlash against Rickard. However, Philpott's movements are being monitored."

"What if a fake tape exists and Philpott intends to use it?"

"If we could prove that, we'd have something to go on. I think Rickard would ask Carruthers to look at Philpott's script."

"How is Rickard?"

"Improved slightly. He's going on TV tomorrow night in a speech to the nation which he'll tape earlier. His campaign team want to prop him up in front of a camera and let him speak to the people—to reassure them he is fit to run the country."

"Let's hope he stands up to it." There was a slight pause before Graham added, "I'll be on trial tomorrow night too. I'm meeting Huntsman and Cheznoir."

"Isn't that dangerous?"

"Don't worry, I'm not taking any chances."

"Let me know how it goes."

"I'll phone you after it's finished."

"You must take care, Ed. Think of poor Gordon . . . you know how vulnerable you are . . ."

SATURDAY, NOVEMBER 1

Graham had a night of fitful sleep. He awoke several times and wandered around the room, often looking from the balcony of his room on the fifth floor down to the silent streets below.

A full breakfast in his room hardly lifted the Australian from his drowsy and depressed condition. He dressed casually and at ten o'clock walked slowly down to a newsstand on the Grand Armée and bought French and English newspapers. The weather was cool but sunny, so Graham stopped to have a cup of coffee at a nearby open-air café. He had been there five minutes when a quiet voice from close behind him said, "Mr. Graham, the Colonel says not to stay away from the hotel too long."

The Australian was slightly startled. He looked around at a smartly dressed young Frenchman sitting facing the opposite direction. Without acknowledging him, Graham folded the papers and walked briskly back to his hotel.

There he continued to read but found it difficult to concentrate as his mind wandered to the coming meeting. He began to think of all the things that could go wrong. What if "they" stormed the hotel and gunned him down? What if the colonel, with the best intentions and planning in the world, made a mistake? And what if French Intelligence had made a secret decision to catch Rodriguez at any price?

He took the elevator up to his room and, in an effort to take his mind off his fears, wrote a strenuous exercise routine which he went through rigorously for an hour.

At noon he rang Huntsman at the Intercontinental. He was not in, but had left a message to confirm the night's dinner engagement.

"At one, instead of taking lunch, Graham felt fatigued enough to try to sleep again. He managed three solid hours, which made up for the restless periods during the night. He had a couple of cups of black coffee with the manager, a balding, bespectacled old man, in the dining room downstairs, and talked to him for an hour about French politics and the American election. The manager told him that he was welcome to watch the French news on television at five. It touched briefly on the American election build-up and announced that President Rickard had made a last-minute decision to go on television.

Graham had hope that Colonel Guichard would ring and call off the plan. But the clock ticked relentlessly toward his appointment.

Everett Rickard was a little shaky as he made his way into the Oval Office for the first time since his heart attack. Technicians were waiting to test his voice and the lighting in preparation for his taped speech to the nation, which would be shown later.

Rickard sat down gingerly and nervously stacked the loose pages of his speech. He had lost weight since the heart attack, and his face was ghostly pale.

A camera crew asked him to try out the microphone.

"Right. You want a voice lead," Rickard said in a confident tone. He picked up the first page of the speech and began: "Good evening, America. I am speaking to you tonight . . ." The voice was as imperious as ever.

"Fine, Mr. President," a technician said. "Good luck, sir!"

Rickard beamed a thank-you and said to a cameraman, "Hey, Joe, sure you can see me? I've lost a lot of weight, you know."

"No trouble, Mr. President, just as long as you don't turn side-on . . ."

There were smiles all round and it seemed to ease the tension. Rickard looked over at the people peeping around the Oval Office door.

"I need you in here," he said, waving at them. In filed his wife, two teenage sons and twenty-year-old daughter. They joined four Secret Service agents and two doctors at the back of the room. Seconds later a technician called out, "One minute to go, Mr. President."

Rickard cleared his throat. Silently he urged himself to make a strong and confident performance.

At 9:00 P.M. Graham, nervous, but alert and ready, stepped out of Étoile Maillot. Paris was cold but alive with people strolling the streets, or on their way by car to a Saturday night's entertainment.

Graham drove slowly in the heavy traffic along the Avenue de la Grande Armée toward the Arc de Triomphe. When he had rounded the arch and was heading down the Champs Élysées, he picked up the radio-telephone. Colonel Guichard came on the line.

"I'm on my way. I'll be in rue Marbeuf in about three minutes."

"Bon. We are ready. Stay calm, Mr. Graham. You will be safe."

Once in rue Marbeuf, the Australian found a place to park the Peugeot very close to Les Innocents restaurant. The pressure of the moment took hold as he turned off the ignition. Suddenly, Colonel Guichard's repeated assurances of safety meant nothing. He sat rigidly in the car and stared into the rearview mirror. Then he watched the faces of people going past. Some were walking into shops. Others were looking in windows. He focused on faces sitting in restaurants. Which of them, he wondered, could be waiting to put a bullet in his head?

Before terror could take a grip, he gritted his teeth and got out of the car. He locked it, and then marched off along the sidewalk, turning left into rue Robert Estienne. He felt a prickly sensation in his back and head. It gave him a tremendous urge to run as he briskly covered the forty yards to the end of the cul-de-sac, and the restaurant.

The petite brunette manageress, Brigette, ushered him in with a welcome smile. A feeling of relief surged over him as the door was closed and the restaurant's safety and warmth enveloped him.

"Have my friends arrived?" he asked, looking at his watch.

"No, monsieur. Would you like a drink?" Brigette asked, taking his coat, scarf and gloves.

Graham shook his head. Settling at the bar, he looked around at his favorite French restaurant. It was an intimate and romantic setting under low lights and cross-beamed ceiling. Soft velvet couches and fine wooden tables were tucked away from each other to ensure privacy. A mastiff hound lay quietly in one corner.

It was not the setting Graham would normally have liked with his company this night. But it was territory he knew. He felt it would give him a psychological advantage over the two Lasercomp executives.

As soon as Huntsman and Cheznoir arrived at 9:35, Graham asked Brigette for a table.

For most of the dinner, conversation was strained and trite. Cheznoir, with Huntsman's occasional support, explained Lasercomp's official policy in dealing with the Soviet Union. It was the same old corporate stuff, and it firmed the Australian's conviction that it was a set-up. Just as coffee and cognac were served, he lost patience.

"Look, gentlemen, I really don't understand the point of this meeting. All you've said so far, I could have lifted from the old Lasercomp songbook."

Cheznoir forced a laugh. Huntsman, who until now had slobbered happily over the cuisine, was angry. "We tried to set you straight. Your information could get you into trouble."

"Trouble?"

"Well, uh," Huntsman began squeamishly, "you're touching nerves in the Soviet Union . . ."

The Australian's expression tightened. "You'd better explain what you mean."

"I think you should realize that there are, well . . ." Cheznoir said, pausing to gesture, "many in the Soviet Union who would not like their trade with the U.S. upset. . . ."

Graham turned sharply to the chubby PR man. "You said nerves. Whose nerves?"

Huntsman swallowed and just managed to keep down a belch. "I meant . . ."

"The KGB, perhaps? They're worried you might be stopped smuggling them computers. Is that it?"

"That's ridiculous!" Cheznoir hissed.

Graham decided to put the knife right in. "Like the murders of Jane Ryder, Donald Gordon and Ronald MacGregor!"

Huntsman and Cheznoir looked edgily at people at other tables.

The Australian twisted the knife. "I've got information that will screw you and your beloved Lasercomp."

"Such as?" Huntsman asked as he wiped his mouth. He was perspiring freely.

Graham leaned back in his couch and lit a cigarette. "Such as your whole smuggling chain right into the Soviet Union's network. Such as the KGB master plan. Such as a direct link from Lasercomp to the assassination of Ronald MacGregor."

"I've never heard so much rubbish!" Huntsman sneered. "You seem to have an obsession with attacking Lasercomp. Maybe you need psychiatric help. . . ."

Graham laughed. "You've tried that tactic before with other people who have questioned your clinically clean and faultless corporation. Probing Lasercomp equals mental instability—right? You bastards have more in common with the KGB than just computers, haven't you?"

Huntsman was boiling over. "We could easily screw you in court!"

"Go ahead and try. But remember, I spoke to Donald Gordon last week. He spilled everything. The PPP and every single detail of your power-crazy games!"

A waiter approached the table. There was a long silence as he cleared it and left the bill.

"How do you propose to use these lies?" Cheznoir asked, as he picked up the bill.

"It'll be published very shortly."

"Fiction!" Cheznoir said fiercely, as he pulled his wallet from an inside coat pocket.

"Oh, no, Mr. Cheznoir, it'll be fact, checked and checked again. What you might call an exposé."

The Australian stubbed his cigarette and stood up to leave as Cheznoir placed a credit card on the bill.

"Thank you for the dinner," Graham said coldly. "That, at least, was pleasant." He moved away from the table and asked for his coat. He didn't bother to look back as the manageress opened the door and wished him good night.

Graham moved quickly to his car, got in and drove straight up rue Marbeuf, watched by twenty of Colonel Guichard's disguised and armed men in cars, and strolling the street. The Peugeot was followed by two unmarked cars which had been sitting behind "road repair" signs in rue Françoise. The colonel, in a command vehicle, and a squad of six more cars followed soon afterward.

Rodriguez took a call in a small restaurant-bar off the Champs Élysées thirty seconds after Graham had left. It was Huntsman at Les Innocents.

"Now!" he said firmly and hung up.

Rodriguez moved quickly to where Martinez was waiting in a black late model Maserati with the engine running. They watched Graham's car swing into the Champs Élysées. As the Peugeot cruised past them, Rodriguez felt he could have done the job there and then with the submachine gun wrapped in brown paper resting on his knees. But he restrained himself. There were too many cars about. They waited until a few other cars passed, and then began to tail Graham.

They followed him to the lights at Pont de la Concorde over the Seine. The Peugeot crossed the bridge and then headed south along floodlit Quai Branly with the Eiffel Tower on the left.

The midnight traffic was heavy.

"Get closer," Rodriguez ordered as the Peugeot moved faster. It began to zigzag through the traffic at increased speed. Several motorists honked their horns in anger at the seemingly careless driving.

Rodriguez's first thought was that Huntsman had succeeded in getting Graham drunk. "Don't lose him," he said to Martinez. He began to thread his way through the traffic once more, to the chagrin of other drivers—all except for nine cars scattered in the four lines of traffic heading one way. In them were eighteen heavily armed members of Guichard's Intelligence squad.

Graham's erratic driving was under orders that squeaked over the radio-telephone resting on the Peugeot's front seat.

The idea was to cause any tail to show itself. And it did.

I think we may have something," Guichard said calmly as he noticed the Maserati. "Keep up speed."

Graham checked his rear vision. He could see nothing but a blaze of headlights through the thin frost on his back windows. Guichard, now on a direct line of traffic fifty yards behind Graham, gave a flurry of orders. "Two and three move in. Four and six ease ahead. Straight ahead. Five and seven stay wide in position. Eight and nine steady. Everyone steady."

Graham reached the lights at Port d'Issay where the traffic had thinned.

At exactly that moment, thirty-year-old Sergeant Hubert de Roqueforte turned his police car into Quai André, the very place at which Graham, the assassins, and their pursuers had just arrived. He was returning across to home base in the sixteenth *arrondissement*, to repair his radio which was out. The young sergeant spotted the sleek black Maserati slipping through the traffic making a nuisance of itself. Like every policeman in the city that night, he had been alerted to a plan to apprehend some important terrorists. He was also aware the plan was under way somewhere near where he was now. But at that precise second, he had no idea what was going on around him. De Roqueforte made hot pursuit after the Maserati, light flashing and siren on.

Guichard saw the maverick police car and tried desperately to make radio contact.

"Get out of there . . .! Leave the Maserati . . . repeat . . . leave that Maserati! Get out of there! *Merde!* Who is that idiot!"

"What the hell are you doing?" Graham yelled at the telephone. He could see the police flasher.

"Mr. Graham, keep going as planned. Just drive," Guichard said.

There was no chance to draw the Maserati to the outskirts of the city now. The colonel rattled off orders to the other cars. They closed on the Maserati, which sat at the lights to Pont d'Issay, thirty yards behind the Peugeot.

Rodriguez could see the police car pushing toward him.

"Go right!" he ordered and pointed across the bridge. Martinez skidded the Maserati away fast. Once over Pont d'Issay, Martinez made two illegal right turns which took them down a slip road to Quai Louis Blériot, running north beside the river. He then accelerated with Guichard's fleet and the maverick police car in pursuit a hundred yards behind and slipping away. Rodriguez kept looking back as the Maserati hit a hundred miles an hour at Avenue de President Kennedy. He knew they would have to get off the main one-way road, or risk being trapped.

"Take the next slip road," he said as they hit Avenue New York.

The Maserati slowed as they approached the stretch of the avenue which ran under Pond d'Ienna. Martinez adroitly swung left off the avenue, up the slip road, and straight into trouble. A police car following Guichard's orders to block off the avenue ahead of the Maserati, was coming the wrong way down the same slip road. Both drivers did well to avoid a head-on crash as the police car smacked the rear side of the Maserati. It hit a railing on the side of the road and spun side-on. Martinez frantically turned the ignition. It coughed to a start at the third try. He spun the wheel to turn the car. But a back fender had been wedged against a tire. Another police car appeared at the top of the slip road and blocked the Maserati's path. Rodriguez, armed with his machine gun, was out of the car first.

Guichard's fleet had reached the bottom of the slip road. Martinez fell out, holding a machine gun that had been on the back seat. Rodriguez ran toward the car at the top of the slip road and opened fire. He brought down two policemen.

Martinez ran down the slip road toward Avenue New York. Two distinct orders told him to surrender. He ignored them and wielded his gun in a wide arc, firing at everything that moved. It was the signal for fifteen weapons to open up on him. The bullet that stopped him slithered through his neck. Within five seconds, a tremendous onslaught of lead lifted his feet off the ground and dumped him in the middle of the slip road.

At the top, Rodriguez made a bid to escape on foot. But his way was blocked by police cars on the approach to Pont d'Ienna. He ran straight across the approach and down another slip road leading back onto Avenue New York. Orders were being shouted from every direction. Several people had spotted him. When Guichard's car screeched to a half at the foot of the road, Rodriguez opened fire wildly and ran back up the road to the bridge. He blasted his way past several of Guichard's men, who scattered behind cars. He ran for the other side of the bridge. Lights from a line of four cars were turned on high beam in front of him. Seconds later, the whole bridge was floodlit. Rodriguez was caught in the spotlight.

"Surrender. You cannot escape!" Guichard called, using a bullhorn. The terrorist fired blindly in both directions along the bridge. Guichard signaled for him to be brought down.

Marksmen at each end aimed. There was a sharp crack. One bullet shattered Rodriguez's forearm. A second hit him in the left side and spun him to the ground. A third bullet cannoned into his chest, and the chase was over.

Twenty minutes later, Graham, who had driven straight on toward the original destination, answered Colonel Guichard's radio call to Avenue New York. He arrived in time to see the bullet-ridden bodies of the two terrorists. An ambulance team was attending four of Guichard's men hit in the shoot-out, three of them seriously. Guichard thanked Graham sincerely for his help and apologized profusely for the bungle.

"Today we start a big manhunt for the Director," Guichard said wearily. "If your theory that he has worked with Rodriguez is correct, and he is in Paris, he will be in hiding. But you can have round-the-clock protection while you are—"

"Thank you. But it won't be necessary any more."

"What are your plans?"

"I'll fly back to London soon. There are a few things I still have to do here."

"Bon. If I could ask you to come to HQ before you go so that we can complete our official report?"

"Of course."

"Please, have the car until you leave, and use the radio phone if you want to contact me."

"Thank you."

They shook hands and Graham drove up the slip road past police hoisting the battered Maserati onto a breakdown truck.

Back at his hotel, Graham decided to ring Revel.

"Are you sure it was Rodriguez?" the lawyer asked.

"Guichard is pretty certain. They're going to run fingerprint, dental and other tests on him to check."

"What are you going to do now?"

"Get some shut-eye."

"Ed, I know you've had a rough night, but could you check something out? It could be important. You know we've been monitoring Philpott's movements. Well, we've found out that he will try to make a secret rendezvous with Haussermann. Apparently Lasercomp is going to fly him in and out of Paris tomorrow."

"When and where?"

"The plane's expected to arrive at Orly around noon at the private flights section, runway five."

"You want me to tail him?"

"If you could. It would be interesting to know if he makes contact with Haussermann. But don't take any risks."

"I'll do what I can."

"Thanks. It could just lead to the tape."

"How did Rickard's speech go?"

"Very well. Though, Christ, he looked fragile!"

"What do the polls say?"

"He's about half a percent ahead of Mineva."

In his Pigalle hideout, the Director listened grim-faced to the Paris 8:00 P.M. radio news as it told him the reason his assassination crew had not been in contact. . . .

"Though police would not confirm that one of the men killed in the shoot-out was the notorious assassin-terrorist known as Rodriguez, they did not deny it. He was responsible for the deaths of three French Intelligence men five years ago."

He switched it off and immediately phoned Znorel in Stuttgart.

"This is the Director."

"I told you never to call unless there was an emergency!"

"This is an emergency. The others had an accident early this morning on the way to see Mr. Graham. You'll hear it on the news."

"This should not alter the main assignment. Get Haussermann to meet Philpott and give him the tape this afternoon. Clear?"

"Yes."

"Good. You have no need to call this number again—under any circumstances. Understood?"

"Yes." The Director hung up. He went into the living room of the apartment where Haussermann was already up reading the Sunday papers. The shoot-out had occurred too late for them to run the story.

The Director sat down on a couch and, without looking at Haussermann, began to wipe his glasses.

"There has been a change of plans," he said.

"Wh-why?"

"You don't ask why," the Director said curtly. "Just listen to instructions! You will call Philpott at the Intercontinental Hotel at one P.M. You will make a rendezvous with him for two P.M. I shall tell you where later this morning. At this meeting you will hand over the tape. After that, you will not return here until eleven P.M. on Monday night. I shall work out a route for you to return by, and which hotel you should stay at tonight." He finished polishing his glasses, tried them on, and looked at Haussermann. "Just in case you have any ideas about disobeying orders and trying to run away," he added icily, "I shall keep your passport and plane ticket here."

SUNDAY, NOVEMBER 2

Light rain was falling in the afternoon as Graham watched the private Lasercomp jet arrive at Orly.

He waited in the Peugeot and spotted Philpott and a film crew moving out of the airport lounge half an hour later. They piled into a waiting station wagon with their equipment. Graham followed it to 40 Avenue Mahon off the Arc de Triomphe in the center of Paris.

The Australian pulled his Peugeot into the curb about thirty yards from where Philpott and the crew disappeared into a doorway.

Despite the bad weather, the avenue was alive with Parisians buying from stall merchants selling their flowers, food and wine. Graham decided to get out of the car to make sure he saw whoever came and went from number forty. As he swung the door open on the pavement side, he grazed a man scurrying past.

"Excusez moi," Graham said.

The man looked at him with frightened, darting eyes, and moved on. It was Haussermann. He moved past number forty and stopped to look back.

Graham crossed the road to a flower stall and immediately started up a conversation with a bristly-chinned little man.

"Some flowers for a special lady, monsieur," Graham said in French.

The flower-seller chuckled. "You are in love, monsieur?"

"Oui."

"Then of course it must be roses." He reached for a bunch. Graham pretended to be watching the curves of an attractive woman across the road. He nudged the flower-seller, who croaked a laugh and nodded his approval. The woman had moved close to the direct line with number forty and Graham caught a glimpse of Haussermann. He had walked past the door and close to Graham's car again.

"How much?" Graham asked.

"Twenty francs."

Haussermann moved past number forty again.

"You are generous, monsieur," Graham said, doffing his brown velvet beret to the Frenchman with a sweeping gesture. The flower-seller eyed the beret and complimented the Australian on it.

Out of the corner of his eye he could see Haussermann, who had stopped and was looking around.

"It's yours," Graham said, placing it on the flower-seller's head.

"Oh, no! No, no, no, no, no!" he protested as Graham stood back to admire him in it, just far enough to see Haussermann move inside the doorway to number forty. Graham waved goodbye to the flower-seller, who pleaded, "Ah, monsieur! It is so expensive! Please . . .!" The Australian walked briskly back to his car and got in.

Two hours later Philpott and the crew emerged from number forty in a hurry and got into the station wagon. Graham was in two minds now. Should he follow Philpott, or wait for Haussermann? Philpott's car veered right of Avenue Mahon toward the air terminal, indicating that the American might be heading for the airport and the U.S. Graham pulled the car away from the curb. The furtive figure of Haussermann jumping into the back seat of another taxi made Graham's mind up. He would follow the fugitive.

Five minutes later Haussermann was dropped off at the Hotel Roosevelt close to the Champs Élysées, where he checked in for two nights. When he had moved to the elevator Graham also checked in and immediately put a call through to airline reservations. Then he rang Revel.

"I'm pretty certain Haussermann has given Philpott the tape and there has been a filmed interview. They met for a couple of hours. Philpott's probably on his way back to the U.S."

"Thanks, Ed. I can get things moving at this end."

"Good. I'm still on Haussermann's tail. We're both checked in at the Hotel Roosevelt."

On the flight from Paris back to Washington, Philpott was feeling particularly satisfied. Everything seemed to have gone according to plan. He had the Haussermann tape tucked away in his combination-lock briefcase, and the film of the interview was safely in the can. Philpott was set to produce the most important show of his career. He expected it to clinch a presidential election for Mineva. These gratifying thoughts swept him happily from Dulles airport to FBS's Washington studio and Bilby's office. But the ashen face of the network president blacked them out.

"Christ! Have you got it?" he asked.

Philpott nodded and began to unlock the case. "What's wrong?"

"There is a big doubt about the tape's authenticity." Bilby grabbed the small metal canister from Philpott. "Apparently someone in Paris tipped off the White House that you had managed to get the tape from Haussermann. Now my board has called a meeting." He opened the door. "I've got to play it to them right now. They also want to view the rushes of your TV interview with Haussermann as soon as they're in. . . ."

Haussermann stayed in his room in the Roosevelt the rest of Sunday. Graham relieved the boredom by having a light snack and coffee, and taking an occasional stroll without venturing too far from the hotel. At 1:00 A.M. he paid the concierge two hundred francs to alert his room should Haussermann check out suddenly in the night, and then went to bed.

"At 4:00 A.M. he was startled awake by a steady buzz from the telephone. His first thought was that Haussermann must be on the move again. But it was Revel.

"Cary Bilby has been fired by his own board. Carruthers is now acting president of FBS."

"Is it over the tape?"

"Yes. Bilby insisted it should be played along with the Haussermann interview as an exclusive on Philpott's show tomorrow night. Not one member of the board supported him. They took a vote on suspending his position as president. And he was out!"

"What about Philpott and the show?"

"He has to confront the FBS board himself tomorrow morning."

Rickard was last to enter the White House conference room just after 9:00 A.M. He still looked very ill as he waved the others to be seated. Present were Attorney General Roger Cardinal, Secretary of State Grove, Vice President Cosgrove, FBI Director James Dent, his secretary, Rachel Dyer, and a doctor. Rickard greeted them all cheerfully and seemed to be hiding a nervousness as he looked at a portable tape recorder in the middle of the long table opposite James Dent.

"So what are we waiting for?" Rickard said, looking at the FBI director. "Let's hear the damn thing."

There was a frigid silence as Dent reached across and pressed the starter button. The tape reel began to move. The first sound was the voice of Haussermann apparently in mid-sentence:

"... admit that you ordered the death of Ronald MacGregor. You could be impeached for that."

Rickard's voice was then heard: "Look. I don't want any argument, Haussermann. You're finished."

H: Just like Ronald MacGregor.

R: Just like Ronald MacGregor.

R: Is there anything else you want to tell me? Anything else you want to say?

H: You're wrong.

R: I want your resignation by tomorrow ... [unintelligible] ... you ... [garbled] ... submit ... FBI and CIA ...

H: I see [unintelligible] ... Gestapo tactics. Well, I will not go as easily as MacGregor.

H: Why don't you admit you had MacGregor assassinated?

R: [slowly] I had MacGregor assassinated.

H: He would have beaten you. So you had an assassin strike him down.

R: I'd like you to leave now, Mr. Haussermann.

H: I have evidence on MacGregor's death.

R: If you do have evidence, you had better give it to me.

H: Oh, yes. So you could be smart and destroy incriminating evidence. You must be joking.

R: You are talking about a very serious situation. I [unintelligible] personally ordered MacGregor's death. It's my responsibility ... hand any relevant information to me.

H: I have evidence you killed MacGregor.

R: I killed MacGregor ... If you have evidence then hand it in. Rachel, send in a security guard.

Rachel Dyer (over intercom): Is everything all right?

R: Absolutely. Just send one in.... Show him out, will you?

H: You're a murderer.

R: I'm a murderer.

The tape ran out. All eyes flashed to Rickard. He met each look in turn.

"Well, as you heard, it could never have worked. Fortunately, we were tipped off about the tape." He leaned back in his chair and pointed to the recorder. "That is what Philpott had gone to so much trouble to get for his television program tonight. Luckily FBS had their doubts about it. Electronics experts have already found anomalies." He paused and added thoughtfully, "It makes you wonder what they may have up their sleeves."

"But what could they possibly hope to gain from it?" Cardinal asked. It's so crude . . ."

"I don't think they ever intended to play it. My hunch is that it was part of a wider campaign against me."

"Are you going to take action against the network?" Cardinal asked.

"I could sue them. But I'm going to sit tight for the moment. James figures that whoever is responsible for this quaint little fabrication may be linked to MacGregor's assassination."

"You want Haussermann arrested and extradited?"

"Yes, that's our first action on this. Get him back here as soon as possible."

"Mr. President, if I may . . ." Rachel Dyer chipped in.

"Yes, Rachel?"

"I'm intrigued by the way Haussermann managed to tape the conversation."

Rickard smiled. "I wondered about that too."

He took a pen from his coat pocket. "He apparently used a pen-sized recorder, which he held in front of him like this for a lot of the conversation. I always wondered why he used that god-damn thing whenever I was in his presence."

"Did you notice the big compliment whoever edited the tape paid Haussermann?" Grove asked the President.

"Yes. He didn't stutter once!"

The President held his hands up to indicate that the meeting was over. "Roger, Ted," he said to the attorney general and the Secretary of State, "could I have a quick word."

As the others left the room Cardinal and Grove moved close to the President. "I spent four hours yesterday reading the PICS report," he said, opening a thick folder in front of him. "There is a strong case for a criminal investigation into Lasercomp. I want action on this before January. No matter what happens tomorrow we are going to give them hell well into the new year!"

Philpott emerged from a fierce half-hour confrontation with the FBS board at noon. It had been a shattering ordeal. His hands were trembling and he felt weak at the knees.

Philpott had tried to reason with the board. That had been useless. Any further reference to the tape, or the Paris interview, the FBS board had told him, could ruin the network. He was under orders to change the entire script for his last program, or the show would not air, and he would be fired immediately. Philpott now had to meet Carruthers at 5:00 P.M. with a completely new script.

His first instinct was to let Huntsman know. Minutes after the confrontation, he was speeding with his script in his dark green Lamborghini toward Lasercomp's offices.

When Philpott reached Huntsman's suite, the PR man and Brogan Junior were there waiting for him. He threw the script on a desk.

"I can't help you any more."

"Oh, yes you can!" Huntsman said fiercely.

"But Mineva may lose now we can't use the tape! I'm not going to stick my neck out and ruin everything I've built up . . ."

"He will win!" Brogan Junior thundered. "Our calculations say there's practically nothing between him and Rickard now!"

"But without the tape and the interview there's no show!"

"Look, forget about the tape," Brogan Junior said. "We never wanted to use it anyway. It was just part of our program to defeat Rickard."

Philpott was stunned and confused. For the first time he realized fully how the Brogans and Huntsman had used him as a pawn in the election battle.

"I don't know if I can . . . go on . . ."

"You're in this up to your neck," Brogan Junior said vehemently; "you're going through with it!"

"Doug, you can help tip the balance. We're going to show you how," Huntsman added. "Think of that one and a half million in your Swiss account. I authorize it on election day. . . ."

"And don't forget your new job once this has all cooled down next year," Brogan Junior said persuasively but with less hostility as he saw Philpott wavering. "Mineva will appoint you director of government communications. You'll earn more money and you'll have more power than you ever dreamed of. . . ."

Graham had bribed the Hotel Roosevelt concierge to alert

him should Haussermann attempt to leave the hotel. Late on Monday night it paid off. Haussermann emerged from the hotel for the first time in thirty hours, and Graham made it downstairs just in time to see him get into a taxi at the front entrance. Graham ran for his Peugeot and followed Haussermann across the city to Pigalle. Haussermann got out at 4 rue Brunel, and let himself in through the large wooden door of the five-floor block of flats.

Graham waited at the top of the avenue. When the taxi drove off, he eased about forty yards past number four at the end of the street and then turned the car around. Now what? he wondered, as he switched off the engine. Should he try to speak to him? At that moment it seemed futile. Haussermann could simply refuse to see him.

It had begun to rain. He switched on the Peugeot's windshield wipers. As their whirring sound accompanied the rain in a harmonious, repetitive symphony, fear struck Graham. Going over and over in his mind was the possibility of the Lasercomp-Haussermann link, and the connection between the corporation and an assassination squad. Was the triangle complete? Were Haussermann and the Director in there together?

Inside the fourth-floor flat, Haussermann was having a double brandy. He had just told the Director of his last thirty hours.

"Christ! I've been so worried that my bowels have not worked for three days!" he said, and then laughed as he let go a loud fart.

"Ah," he sighed, sinking back into his chair, "that's better."

Seconds later he said, "Excuse me," got up from his chair, and headed for the toilet off the hallway, taking his brandy with him.

When he was out of sight, the Director walked over to a bureau and quietly slid open a drawer. He took out his Walther and deftly screwed on a silencer. Moving down the hall he could hear Haussermann shuffling around and humming. The moment he sat down, the Director swung the door open and took a step forward into the toilet. The assassin fired twice and the top half of the victim's head was blown off in every direction. Little bits of hot brain, blood and bone hung from every part of the closet as Haussermann, with a sickening stench, finally relieved his constipation. Involuntarily.

"Thank you, Mr. President. Could you just pretend to be signing that again," the White House press photographer said as he took Rickard from another angle. He was sitting at his desk in the Oval Office with Cardinal and Cosgrove. It was Monday evening, and press secretary Emmery had arranged a "business as usual" scene for release to the morning papers in his efforts to feed the media with evidence of Rickard's recovery.

The President, in fact, was feeling ill. The excitement and activity since the weekend had drained his limited energy. His doctor had repeatedly urged him to rest, telling Rickard not to read or watch anything to do with the election.

Strictly contrary to this advice, the President invited Cardinal and Cosgrove to stay at the White House to watch Philpott's program to be broadcast live from Washington. They joined him in the yellow room, the formal living room in the family quarters.

Sitting back in a rocker, the President asked for the television set in front of him to be switched on.

"Relax, gentlemen," he said with a wan smile, "let's see what our friend Mr. Philpott has done to his program."

Three miles away in the exclusive suburb of McLean, Brogan Junior, Huntsman and Strasburg were gathered at the chief legal counsel's home. They sat quietly in the living room as Strasburg ordered his Chinese manservant to switch on the television.

At Black Flats, New York, Brogan Senior sat alone in the war room, exhausted after one of the most hectic days his long memory could recall. In the morning he had taken a trip to Wall Street to meet his stockbroker for a discussion about the strong rise of Lasercomp stock since its victory in the court over the government. The corporation had risen to more than 450 points for the first time in its history and was still moving up when he took a brief visit to the Exchange itself to watch the stampede to buy the stock. That exhilarating experience put extra spring into the Old Man's step for the rest of the morning.

He was feeling on top of the world by midafternoon when

the latest Gallup Poll had Rickard's lead down to 0.3 percent and closing. By 5:00 P.M. Brogan Senior was back to the thing he loved best—wheeling and dealing in millions of dollars, this time with a series of coded telexes from Moscow. Precisely at seven he turned up his hearing aid and began to watch the last Philpott show. . . .

In FBS's studio, dressed in an unobtrusive light gray suit and floral tie, Philpott sat with legs crossed and script in hand in the middle of the brilliantly lit set. He waited, ready for the cue that would bring him into twenty million American homes.

Behind him was a huge backdrop with two big photos of Mineva and Rickard. Around him at the ready were twenty technicians and four cameras. An assortment of cables and wires crisscrossed the studio floor in an ungainly pattern. High in the booth in front of Philpott sat frizzy-haired program director Bob Maloney, and his bespectacled young female script assistant. Above their heads were ten screen monitors.

The countdown for the show began. Maloney had been instructed to keep a tight rein on the revised script of the program which had been scrutinized and approved by Carruthers. There was no reference to the tape, the Haussermann interview or any other controversial issue concerning the President and Mineva. At the first sign of any attempt by Philpott to divert from the script, Maloney was ready to take action. He was in ear-microphone touch with everyone on the studio floor, including Philpott.

"Ready to go," he said softly.

The floor manager called quietly, "Okay, studio, thirty seconds to air."

Philpott looked up at the autocue, and was away: "Good evening, America . . ."

By midnight Paris time, Graham had been sitting in the Peugeot for nearly an hour. He decided to try to get into the flat and see if he could find some clue to who was in there. But he had nothing with which to protect himself. He looked around the car, and took a jack handle from a tire-change kit in the trunk.

Seconds later, he stood outside number four and looked at the five intercom buttons for the flats. The first three had French names. Four and five had no names. If he rang the wrong one and the Director was in there . . .

He would pick one of the named flats—number three, Lefroy—and press button number two. He pressed and pressed again. A disgruntled voice said, *"Oui?"*

"Lefroy," Graham mumbled.

The front door buzzer sounded. He pushed the door, and was in. He moved into a darkened hallway. There was a light at the elevator ten yards away and a circular stair running around it. He crept up the stairs to the floors—each one eerily lit with false Roman candles.

Reaching the fifth floor, he stood staring at the wood-paneled door to the flat. He decided he couldn't take the risk of the assassin's being in there. Best, he thought, to alert Revel to Haussermann's whereabouts and perhaps wait outside to see who eventually came out.

Just as he turned to go downstairs, he heard the whirr of the elevator. Someone had called it. But from which floor? Graham got halfway down the stairs to the fourth floor and then froze. Below him and through the wire mesh of the shaft, he could see a man standing at the gate. He was pulling on gloves. Graham crouched down to see the man's face. It resembled a description and Identikit photograph embedded in his memory forever. It had to be the Director! His first thought was to rush down and bash him with the jack handle. But Graham knew he would be spotted easily if he moved just two more paces down. The elevator reached the fourth floor. The Director placed a suitcase in it and got in. Graham could see him push the ground-floor button. The elevator began its descent. Graham leaped down and struggled with the gate. It wouldn't budge. He wedged the jack handle into it and pushed with all his strength. The locking device broke. The gate opened, and the elevator halted with a hideous grating sound that reverberated up and down the shaft. It was stuck between the second and third floors.

The Director ran his fingers across the buttons for each floor and the one marked *Emergency*. He shook the elevator gently at first, then hard.

Graham's fear turned into exhilaration. He had him! He had to get the police!

"Get me out!" the Director yelled in French. He yelled again, and then cursed in German. Seconds later a woman on the second floor opened the door to her apartment.

"What's wrong?" she called.

"I'm stuck," the Director said.

Graham made a sound on the shaft cage and yelled in French: "What's going on?"

"I am stuck in this thing!" the Director called, as he looked up to where the voice had come from. 'Can't you see?' Please get me out!"

"Ah! Mon Dieu! Another failure," Graham said, as he moved down the spiral staircase. "Do not worry, monsieur, we shall get you out in no time!" As he scurried past the Director he waved two reassuring hands at him so his face was partially hidden. He reached the woman on the second floor. She was standing in a doorway clutching her dressing gown.

"I'll need help," he said, and beckoned her to follow. When they reached the first floor, Graham said urgently in a half whisper, "Do not go near that man! Do not help him! He is a murderer!" The woman started with horror.

"I am going to get the police. If anyone tries to help him, stop them. Scream your lungs out! But don't go near him!"

She nodded, wide-eyed and mouth open.

Graham raced to the front entrance and sprinted down rue Brunel to the Peugeot. He fumbled the driver door open and grabbed the radio-telephone.

"Help! Please help!"

"Who is this?" the radio control officer at Paris police HQ said. He was surprised at not getting the normal signal on a top priority frequency used by French Intelligence.

Graham had to say something sensational to get somebody there. "There has been a murder! Get somebody to four rue Brunel, Pigalle, fast . . . please! Four rue Brunel. I have the murderer trapped in the elevator."

"Monsieur, please, your name?"

"Graham. For Chrissakes get someone here!"

"Gray-Am?"

"Yes!"

"How did you get on this frequency?"

"I helped Colonel Guichard get Rodriguez. He gave me this car and the radio link . . ."

"Colonel Guichard?"

"Yes! Are you getting help here?"

"As fast as we can, monsieur."

Graham swung around to face the building as he heard a gun report.

Inside, the Director, still trapped, was desperate. He had fired up the shaft to get attention again. Those two people who went to get the elevator going; where were they? He shook the elevator violently. A half-dressed man poked his head out of a door on the first floor. The woman Graham had left shivering there screamed at him, "Don't help him! He is a murderer! He has a gun!"

"I'll get the police!"

"Yes! Yes! Call the police!"

"Come in! He may shoot you!" the man said.

The woman obeyed. The man looked in a directory and phoned the local police.

Outside, Graham was still trying to get help. "The man is armed! I heard a shot!" he yelled.

"Who, monsieur? Who is armed?"

"The man trapped in the elevator . . . God! If he gets out . . . can you get Guichard?"

"There is help on the way."

A police car, siren blaring, hurtled around the corner into rue Brunel. Graham jumped from the Peugeot and ran around to the driver's side. Urgently but precisely, he explained that an armed man was trapped in the elevator. Then they heard another shot. The two policemen in the car groped for their holstered guns, clambered out and ran toward the doorway of the building. Graham scuttled back into his car as another police car appeared. The first two policemen on the scene shouted to the other car which radioed for more help.

Graham grabbed the radio-telephone again. "Hallo. This is Graham again. The police are here. But I think you should try to get Colonel Guichard."

"Mr. Graham, I'm on the way," a voice said. It was the colonel. "Who is it you have trapped?"

"The Director! It's him! I'm sure!"

Seven minutes later, Guichard arrived with several of his men to take control. Two police were at ground-floor level with guns trained up the shaft. The elevator was still perched between the second and third floors. There had not been a sound from it since the second shot. The Director inside was waiting and listening, his Walther at the ready.

Graham briefed Guichard at the entrance to the building and the colonel went quickly into action. He turned to one of his men. "Get in through the fifth floor. Take five with you."

It took them ten minutes to scale the outside façade of the building with the help of people on each floor who had stayed in their rooms when they heard gunfire and the arrival of police cars. Weapons were passed up. A few minutes later the six men were crouched, guns at the ready, in the hallway and on the stairs at the third- and fourth-floor levels, waiting for Guichard's orders.

He edged toward the elevator at ground level.

"The building is surrounded," Guichard called. "We are above you and below you. You cannot escape. Are you going to surrender?"

The Director, crouched low in the elevator, didn't reply.

"You have a choice," Guichard said. "You can either surrender, or we'll come and get you. What's it to be?"

There was no response. Beckoning to one of his men, the colonel whispered, "Go up the stairs, but don't take any risks. Be careful."

The man, gun at the ready, edged his way up step by step. He reached the second-floor hallway. The Director spotted his shadow on the wall. The split second the man appeared, the Director fired and hit him in the shoulder. He staggered back to the ground floor and was helped outside to a waiting ambulance.

The colonel decided to move in. He sent word for the gate to be closed on the fourth floor. All guns trained on the shaft as the gate was slid across. The elevator recommenced its descent. But only a foot, as the Director pushed the stop button. A police officer rushed up to the second floor and fired up the shaft at the Director, and missed. The Director returned fire and hit him in the stomach. He tumbled back down the stairs. Guichard pushed the call button again. The Director scrambled to stop the descent once more, and the elevator shuddered to a halt after going another two feet.

Guichard saw the second injured man carried out on a stretcher. He gave a silent hand signal, waited thirty seconds, and then pushed the call button.

The Director had his left hand over the stop button. He turned and fired up as he heard a shuffling sound on the stairs above him. The distraction gave five others just enough time to get a bead on him. The Director, quick as a cat, pivoted around to see figures coming at him up and down the stairs. He fired blindly as shots were angled into the elevator from every direction. Seconds later there was silence.

"We got him!" one of Guichard's men yelled.

The colonel pushed the call button for the last time, and the elevator made a painfully slow descent to ground level.

At Guichard's request, an officer hurried out of the building and called Graham in. Without a word, the colonel led him over to the elevator. The first thing Graham saw was the Director's right hand which still gripped the Walther. He looked at the bullet-ridden body, then the bloodied face, and quickly jerked his head away to avoid vomiting. A stray bullet had snapped open the suitcase the Director had with him. Photographs were scattered on the floor of the lift. Graham slowly picked one up, looked at it for several seconds, and then handed it to Guichard. It was a hazy Polaroid shot of Les Innocents restaurant.

Across the Atlantic, Philpott's makeshift show was running smoothly to a finish. Program director Maloney considered it had been as fair and balanced as the FBS board had wanted.

"Three, move in now," he ordered the camera to Philpott's right so that the commentator's face filled the screen. Despite the heavy make-up, he appeared drawn and blanched. The mouth was taut and a little line of sweat beads had appeared on his top lip. After an uncomfortably long pause in which Maloney was nearly compelled to switch to a longer shot with another camera, Philpott looked up.

"Tomorrow ninety million Americans go to the polls . . ." he said hesitantly.

Maloney was alerted to an improvization, and the strain in Philpott's voice. He grabbed the script from his assistant as the commentator stared down the lens.

"Are you okay?" Maloney yelled into the microphone.

Philpott didn't register a flicker as Maloney punched a button. The commentator leaned forward speaking quickly and precisely.

"I have proof that Rickard had MacGregor assassinated. The tape I brou—"

Philpott's head disappeared. A sign appeared: *Due to a technical fault we are temporarily off the air.* Seconds later there was a commercial. The sound track began: "Fighting for tomorrow today, and your future: The Lasercomp Corporation."

Philpott's accusation shocked America. Television, radio and newspaper switchboards were jammed as people tried frantically to find out more.

FBS's Carruthers was quick to make a statement refuting Philpott's comments. But Lasercomp's PR network quickly counteracted this. Bilby released a press statement saying that he fully defended Philpott's editorial freedom to present important issues "in the public interest." He said they had both been the victims of a "conspiracy" by the White House to interfere in FBS's independence, and that was why he had been forced to resign his job.

All Lasercomp's influential media connections kept the speculation about the veracity of Philpott's accusation going well into election day. This forced other media outlets to carry the sensational story and continue to investigate it. The corporation was using all its media muscle to exploit the situation it had created.

The nation's leading newscaster had forsaken his neutral position and made real political news himself. Everyone wanted to speak to him, but he had gone into hiding. Every few hours a statement was released by a Philpott "connection" supporting his comments, which added that he would break the details of the story within a few days. He was in hiding, the report said, because he feared for his life. Reports of Haussermann's brains being blown out in a Paris apartment appeared to back up Philpott.

Rickard had been confined to bed at the White House following a slight relapse. Fortunately for the President, his doctor had been close at hand when Philpott's show was over. He had managed to quickly calm Rickard and drug him to sleep. He was not allowed to receive any more information about Philpott's comments or the progress of the election. The White House went into a panic trying to cover up the President's illness, saying he was resting completely until the result of the vote was known.

How much the whole Philpott affair had affected the vote as 136,700,000 Americans went to the polls became the number-one news point concerning the election. By 10:00 P.M. Eastern time on election day, television newscasters were predicting that their network's computers would soon be telling them the result as the electoral college votes for the states rolled in.

In the war room at Black Flats, the Brogans, Huntsman and Strasburg were watching the four networks on sets beneath the large screen which showed the PPP's prediction that Mineva would win. As each state's final score came up it was checked against the Cheetah PPP prediction.

"That's most of the states in and the PPP right every time," Brogan Senior said, intently leaning forward in his seat at the semicircular table facing the screen.

"It hinges on New York, Texas, and Illinois now," Huntsman said nervously. "Mineva has to win two of them. And he is home."

"We say he takes Illinois and Texas," Brogan Junior said calmly.

The lights went up for Rickard in New York and Mineva in Texas. The tension mounted. Minutes later, all the television network's computers gave Illinois to Mineva. He had won.

The Program for a Potential President was over.

WEDNESDAY, NOVEMBER 5

Graham switched on the radio in the Peugeot as he sped along the Autoroute du Sud on the five-hundred-mile journey to Montpellier, and Françoise.

A 6:00 A.M. news report told him of Mineva's victory, now official in the U.S. Lasercomp had won.

All Graham's feelings of relief after the liquidation of the assassins evaporated. He flicked off the radio in disgust. The Australian began to worry about the consequences of the result, but quickly tried to put them out of his mind for the moment. Colonel Guichard had given him the car for a couple of weeks in gratitude for his help in finding and eliminating Rodriguez and the Director. He had got away to an early morning start in search of some real relaxation in the south of France. As the dawn of a clear day broke and the first signposts for Montpellier came up, Graham was brightened and excited by the anticipation of seeing the loving and warm Françoise. After his vacation he would turn his mind to the daunting task of writing the story of the whole investigation. Perhaps the story was not yet over.

About the same time, the wheels of an Aeroflot jet from Moscow screeched to a halt at Charles de Gaulle airport, and the smoke from the tires wafted along the runway. Minutes later the passengers, mainly Russians and French, were filing down the steps. Almost indistinguishable in the long line of innocent-looking businessmen was the stocky, baggy-suited figure of KGB assassin Anatoli Bromovitch.